GALAXY

GALAXY

Thirty Years of Innovative Science Fiction

Edited by

Frederik Pohl,
Martin H. Greenberg, and
Joseph D. Olander

℘

A Playboy Press Book

CONTENTS

Contents

Contents

INTRODUCTION

In 1950 a new science-fiction magazine hit the stands.

This was an uncommon event in those days. New science-fiction magazines were rarer than quintuplets—there had been only one significant other in the better part of a decade—so the first appearance of *Galaxy* prompted both hope and doubt. Would the magazine find enough new talent to fill its virgin pages creditably? Or would it rip off the readers with sloppy pulp hype and regurgitated space opera?

Aficionados like me hoped history—however short, in the case of science fiction—would repeat itself. *Amazing*, after a slow start in 1926, had found new—and big—writers like Doc Smith and John Campbell. *Wonder Stories* had repeated the feat in the early 1930s. Even with the severe handicap of low and slow pay, the magazine had turned up the likes of Stanley G. Weinbaum. And when Campbell turned from writing to editing later in the decade, he had exploded a host of new writers on the field—A. E. Van Vogt and Robert A. Heinlein, L. Sprague de Camp and Lester del Rey, Theodore Sturgeon, and a dozen more.

But there were plenty of failures, too. The boomlet around 1940 had flooded the market with shoddy material; so history gave no guarantees. The new magazine could go either way. It all depended, of course, on the editor.

Well, what did we know about this new kid on the block named H. L. Gold? Did he know anything about science fiction, to begin with? He had written some for John Campbell, had even been an editor in the *Thrilling Wonder* magazine mill. But that turned out to be only a minor part of his writing and publishing background. Comics. Radio scripts. Fact detective stories. As editor, which way would he lean? It was worrisome . . .

. . . but not for long. Before *Galaxy* was a year old it was clearly the place where the action was.

It didn't rule undisputed. The Boucher-McComas *Magazine of Fantasy and Science Fiction* had an edge, perhaps, in terms of graceful prose. Campbell's *Astounding/Analog* probably had a larger overall audience, plus a reader loyalty going back to 1930. But it was in *Galaxy* that the stunning new kinds of science fiction—like Bester's *The Demolished Man* and Leiber's *The Big Time* and Sheckley's and Tenn's and Kornbluth's and Knight's mordant wit—flowered, and changed everything in science fiction.

It may not seem like a change now, because we have got used to it. Let me try to offer an explanation, and an example.

Before *Galaxy*, most magazine science fiction was brash and naive. Problems were meant to be solved. There were always solutions, once you found the right scientist to look for them, and when a problem was solved it *stayed* solved. Its solution did not generate new problems. When Richard Ballinger Seaton liberated atomic energy in *The Skylark of Space*, he didn't have to worry about nuclear fallout or radiation damage. Atomic energy did what he wanted it to do, and nothing else.

Of course, the world was like that then—brash and confident. We had not quite perceived that the price you pay for technology isn't just measured in the monthly car installments or the air-conditioner repair man's bill, but is also exacted in unforeseen and more damaging ways, as California smog and power blackouts. By 1950 we were beginning to realize that things were more complicated. Came *Galaxy*, and its writers began translating some of those new realizations into science fiction. If Horace Gold had a single imperative for his writers, it was to encourage them to look at what came *after* the event, the invention, the surprise. What *Galaxy* brought to magazine science fiction was a kind of sophisticated intellectual subtlety, previously quite rare and found mostly in books like *Brave New World* and *1984*. After *Galaxy* it was impossible to go on being naive.

I speak from personal experience, since C. M. Kornbluth and I wrote *Gravy Planet*, one of the early *Galaxy* serials. After it had run its three installments Cyril and I offered it to every trade book publisher in the United States who published science fiction. Unanimously they rejected it.

By and by a new publisher came along, Ian Ballantine, who retitled our story *The Space Merchants* and published it as a book. I think it's fair to say that *Space Merchants* has done rather better than most books do over the years, with sales of some millions of copies worldwide, in forty-odd languages. So why did eight or ten competent publishers, all of them hungry to fill their insatiable new science-fiction lists, turn it down so peremptorily? I think I know. They hadn't caught up yet with the changes *Galaxy* was making in the field of science fiction. *The Space Merchants* did not contain any titanic space battles or dazzling inventions; it didn't even have a single eight-armed or green-skinned monster in it. They didn't think it was science fiction.

I should concede, if it isn't apparent already, that anything I say in praise of *Galaxy* is self-serving. Doesn't mean it's untrue; it just means that you should bear in mind that I am not unbiased.

Galaxy has been a part of my life for all its three decades. While Horace Gold edited the magazine, I was his most prolific contributor. When he had to step down as editor, I replaced him for nearly ten years. When I left as editor, I went back to writing for it again; so, man and boy, I have felt and still feel a deep personal attachment to *Galaxy*—as have thousands of readers over the years.

A magazine is not just a grab bag of stories. A magazine is a living thing that grows and changes and has a personality of its own. If it is to be successful, its personality must be so engaging that it becomes your friend.

You welcome your true friends into your home because you expect their company to be rewarding to you—as it's been in the past. You don't demand a guarantee that they will amuse and delight you on every specific occasion. Instead, you are interested in *them*, not just in the performance they give at any particular moment, and you invite them back primarily just because you want to know what they've been up to.

A magazine is a more commercial proposition than a neighbor, to be sure. A certain amount of calculated cunning goes into building that kind of friendship called "reader loyalty." But that doesn't make the relationship any less real or powerful. The stories are most certainly the major element in the mix, but reader loyalty is concocted from a dozen other ingredients as well. Columns. Features. A certain style of blurb writing. A certain style of artwork. These are the hidden persuaders, the recognition signals that add up to the personality of the magazine. *Galaxy* had some very special ones.

Willy Ley's name leads all the rest. His column, "For Your Information," began almost as soon as *Galaxy* did and lasted until Willy's death.

I first met Willy Ley around 1940, a decade before *Galaxy* was born. He was not long from Germany where, with Wernher von Braun and a handful of other spacestruck German kids, he had helped form the German Rocket Society. Willy knew something about *everything*. In his column, he touched all the bases. This month the Tunguska meteorite; next month, the story of statistical sampling techniques; the month after, the curious biological traits of small mammals. As a *Galaxy* reader, I always turned first to Willy's column, as did thousands of others. When I became *Galaxy*'s editor, I found that column to be a major treasure—not just because it helped keep readers happy but also because it kept me informed. If I came across something in science that I didn't understand, or wanted to hear more about, all I did was drop Willy a note and he wrote a column about it. Noble Roman families used to buy Greek household slaves for that. I had Willy.

Nearly every science-fiction magazine has a book-review column now—it's a way to get book publishers to buy advertising space—but such columns were a great deal rarer in 1950. (So were the advertisements.) *Galaxy* devoted a column to books from the very beginning. Groff Conklin, pioneer editor of science-fiction anthologies, took a turn as a reviewer, then Floyd C. Gold—brother to Horace, and therefore pseudonymously "Floyd C. Gale." While I was editor, the principal reviewer was Algis Budrys. The readers of *Galaxy* were well served, in three quite different ways, by these quite different critics.

In addition to the outside columnists, Horace Gold's airy editorials tickled readers, as did the "nonfact" articles expounding deadpan the anthropology of nonexistent extraterrestrial races and the geology of future Earth. And everything was embellished and brightened by what is now called "graphics." (In the 1950s and 1960s we just called it "art.") During the first dozen years of its existence, *Galaxy* was expensively printed by offset on high-quality paper. The combination made much possible: Soft shades of gray. Halftones. Type laid over the art, art integrated with the text. *Galaxy*'s two principal art directors, W. I. Van der Poel and Sam Ruvidich, understood the possibilities and exploited them well—beautifully, in fact. I still treasure Sam Ruvidich's meticulous translations of Jack Vance's characters from *The Dragon Masters* into Jack Gaughan's lovely drawings. Indeed, the art for that single story was nominated for a Hugo, perhaps the only time that a single story's art drew that honor. Financial considerations later led to a switch to letterpress. The artists did their professional best, and the profit-and-loss statement began to look a good deal better. But the look of *Galaxy*, I'm afraid, was not the same any more.

Editors, assistants, artists, columnists, writers, publishers, art directors, production people, distribution people—several hundred persons, at least—were involved in the creation of *Galaxy* from first to last. They are what gave the magazine its personality and its success.

But when all is said and done, it is the science-fiction stories themselves that finally determine the merit of a science-fiction magazine. And that's what this book is—the stories. Here they are—a couple dozen of them, selected from nearly thirty years of *Galaxy*, from 1950 to 1979.

On behalf of my colleagues, Joe Olander and Martin Harry Greenberg; on behalf of my predecessor, Horace Gold, and those who came after us; and especially on behalf of myself, to whom almost every one of these stories has a personal significance, I hope you'll enjoy them.

FREDERIK POHL

Red Bank, N.J.
June 1979

GALAXY

HORACE L. GOLD

When Horace Gold wrote about himself in *Gold on Gold* (included in the volume *Gold on Science Fiction*, published by IDHHB Inc.), he said:

> I was born the year World War I started, graduated the year Roosevelt and Hitler came to power, got married the day World War II began, had a son 20 days after Pearl Harbor, founded *Galaxy* magazine just minutes ahead of the Korean war, got divorced the year of Sputnik, remarried the year of the Gulf of Tonkin Resolution. In other words, I'm a historical Typhoid Mary.

Nobody else would call Horace Gold that. Not any more, although when he was editing *Galaxy* a lot of his hard-driven contributors called him a lot worse.

I was one of those contributors—in fact, for the first ten years of *Galaxy*'s life, its most prolific contributor—and as an agent (until 1953) I represented a lot of others. Horace Gold was not your pussycat editor. He was acerbic, demanding, exasperating, and relentless . . . and charming, loyal, insightful, and just plain damn brilliant as well. There's a character in *The Space Merchants* modeled after Horace. For Cyril and me it was a way of working off the maddening frustrations of completing the novel, at Horace's high-speed tempo, to Horace's ever-changing and always unreasonable satisfaction. I'm not sure we ever did satisfy him, but he did publish it at last, and then other people began to. A substantial reason for the book's success was the nagging, nagging, nagging presence of Horace Gold over our shoulders the whole time we were writing it. We might even owe him the book's very existence. If he hadn't demanded it for publication *at once* when I tentatively showed him the first few chapters, we surely would not have written it at that time, and maybe not ever.

Horace lives now in Los Angeles with his marvelous wife, Nicky, and is preparing his great fantasy novel, *None But Lucifer*, for book publication. I visited him there not long ago and I asked him to talk about editing *Galaxy*. Here's what the tape recorded.

FP

Gold on Galaxy

The first issue of *Galaxy* came out in 1950, but it really got started along about 1944. When I went into the army I was a partner in a publishing company with Ken Crossen, and one of our employees was a girl named Vera Cerutti. Time passed. The publishing partnership blew up. I served my World War II hitch in the Pacific; and then, late in 1949, Vera called me on the phone. She told me that she had a new job.

Vera had become editor-in-chief of the New York branch of a French-Italian publishing company called Edizioni Mondiale, which translates into World Editions. They had prospered immensely with a magazine called the Italian equivalent of *Fascination*, half beautifully drawn and reproduced illustrations, the other half the sappiest kind of immature love stories. Since they were selling three million copies a week of it in Europe, they figured it would be easy to come to America with it and murder the American market. Vera, who was trilingual, had been hired to translate the French and Italian into English.

What she wanted from me was a course in the mechanics of putting out a magazine. She had some idea of what went on from her job with Crossen and me—comics and a detective-fiction reprint magazine—but World Editions was something different. Besides *Fascination*, they were planning a knitting magazine and had a fashion magazine on the drawing boards.

The fashion magazine never came to pass. The knitting magazine did—worse luck. Proofreading things like K1P2 and so on was a horror, and I had to show them how to do it, line by line, letter by letter, and number by number.

Fascination was launched with an initial press run of something like a million copies and a huge advertising and promotion campaign, with car cards in the subways and all over the place. They put out something like five issues, and the fifth issue sold something like five percent. They were badly wounded. They didn't want to leave the American market with their tails between their legs, so they asked Vera to submit a publishing program on a more modest scale. And in turn Vera asked me what they should publish.

I surveyed the market very thoroughly. Everybody was putting out fashion magazines and Western magazines and detective magazines, but there were only two science-fiction magazines of quality: *Astounding* and *The Magazine of Fantasy and Science Fiction*. Both of them seemed flawed to me. *Astounding* was deeply involved with things like dianetics. *F&SF* was more fantasy than science fiction. Except for them, there was nothing in the science-fiction field but *Amazing*, the Lowndes magazines, *Thrilling Wonder*, and the rest of the Standard group, all trailing way behind.

On the basis of my own experience, I should have recommended anything *but* science fiction. I had written it, sure—for Desmond Hall when he edited *Astounding* for F. Orlin Tremaine, for John Campbell (*A Matter of Form*), and a couple for other magazines. But my science-fiction writing career had just about ended in 1939, and here it was 1950. When Campbell started *Unknown* he didn't want science fiction from me any more, he wanted fantasy—*Trouble with Water, Warm, Dark Places*, and *None But Lucifer*—and after the war, when I returned to writing, I was producing very copiously and successfully in true detectives, comics, and radio. And I was becoming housebound.

Nevertheless, I recommended a science-fiction magazine. Then, because I had the background with *Unknown* and knew those readers and saw that there was nothing being published for them, I recommended what turned out to be *Beyond*. I also figured that a paperback science-fiction novel program was a good idea, because at that time publishers were just beginning to do science-fiction novels: a little later, that became the *Galaxy Novels* series.

Vera turned my prospectus over to a man named Lombi, who was the representative of the Italian office of World Editions. Lombi was a great guy. He had been in the Italian Army in World War II, was captured by the British, and spent the war in a POW camp. When he was let out he became housebound. He was very sympathetic and understanding. At the same time, he respected my judgment. I asked for (and he agreed to) really good-quality paper and printing, CromeKote covers, a minimum of three cents a word for the writers, and world first serial rights only, because we had the intention of having foreign editions. As we ultimately did, and I got copies of *Galaxy* in French and Finnish and heaven knows what all. World Editions was in a beautiful position to capitalize on foreign editions because they dealt in soft currencies to begin with. They didn't have to be paid in dollars.

Lombi wired his boss in Europe, a strange figure who lived on the Riviera and had shot up out of nowhere with millions of dollars. They accepted the proposal. They hired a former music publisher as corporation president, got a circulation director, and made Vera editor-in-chief and me editor. We signed a contract with American News Company for distribution and hired Washington Irving van der Poel, Jr., as art director. Van der Poel had been doing the art for industry trade papers like *Iron Age* and had just the right touch; he came to us through Groff Conklin, our book reviewer. I needed help to deal with manuscripts, proofreading, and so on, and had a series of assistant editors: Jerome Bixby (later he wrote stories like "The Good Life" and the script for *Fantastic Voyage* under a pen name), A. J. Budrys (very inexperienced, but very good; reliable; as talented as he could be—and now famous for novels like *Michaelmas* and *Rogue Moon*), and Sam Merwin, once of the Thrilling Group and a highly skilled editor. I couldn't pay any of them what they deserved, which was a lot.

We were all set to go. But we didn't have a title for the magazine.

I came up with two that had never been used—*Galaxy* and *If*. I liked either one. But which?

So Van designed cover layouts. My present wife Nicky's first husband, Frank Conley, lettered logos. We borrowed Harry and Evelyn Harrison's apartment, spread all these layouts over the walls, invited a bunch of editors, artists, writers, and fans, and had a secret ballot of which title, layout, and lettering they liked best. We must have invited a couple of hundred people who trudged through the apartment before they voted. They all agreed that *Galaxy* and the inverted-L layout were their own personal favorites, but they didn't think anyone else would like them.

So we dropped *If* and went ahead with *Galaxy*, Van's layout, and Frank Conley's lettering. (A little later, after we had vacated the title *If*, James Quinn came out with it. It appeared for a number of years under Quinn, and then he sold it to us.)

Writers began flocking in. The whole field came to life. The very first contents page had Clifford D. Simak, Fritz Leiber, Katherine

Maclean, Theodore Sturgeon, Richard Matheson, Fredric Brown, Isaac Asimov, and, of course, Willy Ley. Willy had not yet begun his regular column for *Galaxy* that was one of our most popular features right up to the time of his death. In that first issue, he was fielding a contest that had been imposed on me—something like "Are Flying Saucers Real?" He wrote a noncommittal article. I cut it down drastically before I printed it. He couldn't understand why I had done that after paying him for all of it, but I wanted as little as possible to do with flying saucers.

In that first issue I invited the readers to tell me what they wanted, saying, "What you want goes." The results were a surprise, and made me change direction in several instances. Among other things, I had thought I wanted a letter column. The readers didn't. We drew six thousand letters, and something like eighty-five percent of them said no letter column. A lot of people simply wouldn't believe that this was so; I was accused of doctoring the figures. Actually, I missed the column. I *like* letters from readers. They are the first thing I read in other magazines. What the readers wanted was editorials. I didn't want to write them, but the readers insisted, so I did. And they wanted a science department, and that was how Willy's "For Your Information" came to be. It turned out the readers also wanted book reviews, but not the incisive, in-depth sort of essays that critics like to write. What they wanted was a shopping list: what's worth buying and what isn't. Groff Conklin found that a strain, but he went along with it.

We were in business. In five issues we were in the black. That was incredible. All around us were the corpses of other magazines, and there we were, blooming.

I worked hard with writers, and they didn't always enjoy it. One thing I never had trouble with was appraising a story at any point in its creation, no matter at what point I intervened—idea, outline, rough draft, whatever. In some specialized areas I was less sure of myself. I turned down Walter Miller's *A Canticle for Leibowitz* because I didn't know whether it was blasphemous or not. Tony Boucher, being a good Catholic, did know. When my tenure was near an end Cliff Simak told me that he had learned more about writing from working with me than from any other editor—and he wasn't a damn bit grateful for it.

I had known Alfie Bester for some time, through his wife, Rollie, a radio actress who had appeared in several of my scripts. Alfie didn't consider himself a science-fiction writer, although he had sold some stuff to the magazines years before. I kept after him; he gave me the outlines of two short stories, and I suggested combining them into a novel. He called it *Demolition*. I published it as *The Demolished Man*. And for a year and a half Alfie and I spent four hours a week on the telephone, talking about *The Demolished Man*. Then he finally sat down and wrote it in less than three months. I worked in the same way with other writers—Pohl, Sturgeon, Kornbluth, Knight.

One manuscript that came my way was *Prelude to Space*, by Arthur C. Clarke. I read it and wanted to use it, but I could see that it wouldn't break up into a serial. So I asked Clarke's agent, Scott Meredith, if we could run it as a *Galaxy Novel*, warning that all we could pay was five hundred bucks. He said sure. I said, "Why do you say sure so quickly? It's a good story and you should think it over." He said, "It's been kicking around for three years. A publisher's a publisher." So I got it for five hundred, and as soon as it came out everybody realized they'd passed up a hell of a bet.

I had some basic editorial requirements for material. One was, if you've got a premise, start with it. Don't end with it. Don't end with, "My God, it's a time machine!" Or, "My God, it's Adam and Eve"—or whatever. If you've got a time machine, well, fine. Now what?

The second thing was, if it's an old, trite idea, then take it literally. Turn it inside out. Carry it as far as it will go, even beyond the snapping point. If you're writing about overpopulation, then why isn't overpopulation not only good but necessary to maintain your society? If there's a depression, perhaps it is caused by underconsumption—that one turned out to be Pohl's *The Midas Plague*. Third, seek paradoxes. In Alfie Bester's *The Stars My Destination*, I suggested that since everybody could go anywhere instantaneously, by teleportation, the very rich would be carried in sedan chairs.

I found I was being handicapped very badly by having too high a standard. Every mail brought something good; but either you made *Galaxy* or you didn't. I didn't have a way to bring new writers along. A few years later Jim Quinn sold *If* to us, and I used it for that. I kept it at the one-cent rate Quinn had been paying, and that gave me a place to put writers who couldn't quite make *Galaxy* and develop them at a penny a word, until they could hit *Galaxy* at three or four times as much.

It was much easier for me to deal with writers through an agent than personally, unless there was something specific I wanted to work out with the writer. I didn't have to compose pained and apologetic reasons for turning down a story. All I had to do was send it back.

On a personal level, I spent a lot of time with writers and others in informal ways—especially the regular Friday night poker game.

I don't know how it got started. All of a sudden it was an institution. A. J. Budrys was a regular. So was Jerry Bixby, and Jerry brought along a bunch of composers—Morton Feldman, John Cage, Louis and Bebe Barron (who later composed the electronic music for *Forbidden Planet*). We also had editors like Bob Stein of *Argosy*, later of *Redbook* and still later the publisher of *McCall's*, and Bob brought some of his writer friends. Plus Sturgeon, Pohl, William Tenn (a.k.a. Phil Klass), Lester del Rey, and a bunch of other science-fiction writers. It became a problem, because only seven people can really play, and even with allowance for kibitzers we were running out of space. It got to be a lot for me to handle. I could function on a kind of psychic level as a poker player, because I was wide open to every thought and feeling that everyone else had, being so high on anxiety and Seconal—and having agonizing back pains that weren't diagnosed until twenty-one years after the incident as a broken spine. My mind was in a constant fog. I was asked at a lecture the other day whether *Galaxy* would have been better or worse if my mind had been clearer. I don't know which, but it would have been different.

In every issue I always had at least one "bridge" story to appeal to newcomers, and I always made sure that I had at least one story that appealed to women, and one that was a real breakthrough. In every issue there were always at least one or two stories that I wished I had written. (Some of them I did!)

Galaxy was me. I was it, and it was me. Anything that threatened it threatened me. Anything that threatened me threatened the magazine. Complete identification. Total.

If I were to edit a magazine now (which I wouldn't!), I don't think I would have that sort of damn near fatal identification. It almost killed me. If I hadn't been forcibly hospitalized a year after my accident, when I weighed not much more than a hundred pounds, I wouldn't have survived.

COMING ATTRACTION

November 1950

Fritz Leiber

(b. 1910)

The son of the noted American actor of the same name, Fritz Leiber is one of the most versatile writers in the sf field. He has written "hard" science fiction ("A Pail of Air," Galaxy, December 1951), developed some of the most famous series characters in sf and fantasy (the Gray Mouser), written one of the all-time great novels on witchcraft (Conjure Wife, 1953), won several Hugo and Nebula awards (for books like The Wanderer, 1964, and The Big Time, 1958 serialized in Galaxy) as well as the World Fantasy Award.

Leiber has published dozens of stories in Galaxy over the years, including "Nice Girl with Five Husbands" (April 1951), "A Bad Day for Sales" (July 1953), and "Time in the Round" (May 1957).

The following story, "Coming Attraction," is aptly titled, for it is a watershed story in the development of modern science fiction. It heralded an era of sf with social—and often satirical—themes, later to be enthroned in the pages of Galaxy.

COMING ATTRACTION

The coupe with the fishhooks welded to the fender shouldered up over the curb like the nose of a nightmare. The girl in its path stood frozen, her face probably stiff with fright under her mask. For once my reflexes weren't shy. I took a fast step toward her, grabbed her elbow, yanked her back. Her black skirt swirled out.

The big coupe shot by, its turbine humming. I glimpsed three faces. Something ripped. I felt the hot exhaust on my ankles as the big coupe swerved back into the street. A thick cloud like a black flower blossomed from its jouncing rear end, while from the fishhooks flew a black shimmering rag.

"Did they get you?" I asked the girl.

She had twisted around to look where the side of her skirt was torn away. She was wearing nylon tights.

"The hooks didn't touch me," she said shakily. "I guess I'm lucky."

I heard voices around us:

"Those kids! What'll they think up next?"

"They're a menace. They ought to be arrested."

Sirens screamed at a rising pitch as two motor-police, their rocket-assist jets full on, came whizzing toward us after the coupe. But the black flower had become an inky fog obscuring the whole street. The motor-police switched from rocket assists to rocket brakes and swerved to a stop near the smoke cloud.

"Are you English?" the girl asked me. "You have an English accent."

Her voice came shudderingly from behind the sleek black satin mask. I fancied her teeth must be chattering. Eyes that were perhaps blue searched my face from behind the black gauze covering the eyeholes of the mask. I told her she'd guessed right. She stood close to me. "Will you come to my place tonight?" she asked rapidly. "I can't thank you now. And there's something else you can help me about."

My arm, still lightly circling her waist, felt her body trembling. I was answering the plea in that as much as in her voice when I said, "Certainly." She gave me an address south of Inferno, an apartment number, and a time. She asked me my name and I told her.

"Hey, you!"

I turned obediently to the policeman's shout. He shooed away the small clucking crowd of masked women and barefaced men. Coughing from the smoke that the black coupe had thrown out, he asked for my papers. I handed him the essential ones.

He looked at them and then at me. "British Barter? How long will you be in New York?"

Suppressing the urge to say, "For as short a time as possible," I told him I'd be here for a week or so.

"May need you as a witness," he explained. "Those kids can't use smoke on us. When they do that, we pull them in."

He seemed to think the smoke was the bad thing. "They tried to kill the lady," I pointed out.

He shook his head wisely. "They always pretend they're going to, but actually they just want to snag skirts. I've picked up rippers with as many as fifty skirt-snags tacked up in their rooms. Of course, sometimes they come a little too close."

I explained that if I hadn't yanked her out of the way, she'd have been hit by more than hooks. But he interrupted, "If she'd thought it was a real murder attempt, she'd have stayed here."

I looked around. It was true. She was gone.

"She was fearfully frightened," I told him.

"Who wouldn't be? Those kids would have scared old Stalin himself."

"I mean frightened of more than 'kids.' They didn't look like 'kids.'"

"What did they look like?"

I tried without much success to describe the three faces. A vague impression of viciousness and effeminacy doesn't mean much.

"Well, I could be wrong," he said finally. "Do you know the girl? Where she lives?"

"No," I half lied.

The other policeman hung up his radiophone and ambled toward us, kicking at the tendrils of dissipating smoke. The black cloud no longer hid the dingy facades with their five-year-old radiation flash burns, and I could begin to make out the distant stump of the Empire State Building, thrusting up out of Inferno like a mangled finger.

"They haven't been picked up so far," the approaching policeman grumbled. "Left smoke for five blocks, from what Ryan says."

The first policeman shook his head. "That's bad," he observed solemnly.

I was feeling a bit uneasy and ashamed. An Englishman shouldn't lie, at least not on impulse.

"They sound like nasty customers," the first policeman continued in the same grim tone. "We'll need witnesses. Looks as if you may have to stay in New York longer than you expect."

I got the point. I said, "I forgot to show you all my papers," and handed him a few others, making sure there was a five-dollar bill in among them.

When he handed them back a bit later, his voice was no longer ominous. My feelings of guilt vanished. To cement our relationship, I chatted with the two of them about their job.

"I suppose the masks give you some trouble," I observed. "Over in England we've been reading about your new crop of masked female bandits."

"Those things get exaggerated," the first policeman assured me. "It's the men masking as women that really mix us up. But, brother, when we nab them, we jump on them with both feet."

"And you get so you can spot women almost as well as if they had naked faces," the second policeman volunteered. "You know, hands and all that."

"Especially all that," the first agreed with a chuckle. "Say, is it true that some girls don't mask over in England?"

"A number of them have picked up the fashion," I told him. "Only a few, though—the ones who always adopt the latest style, however extreme."

"They're usually masked in the British newscasts."

"I imagine it's arranged that way out of deference to American taste," I confessed. "Actually, not very many do mask."

The second policeman considered that. "Girls going down the street bare from the neck up." It was not clear whether he viewed the prospect with relish or moral distaste. Likely both.

"A few members keep trying to persuade Parliament to enact a law forbidding all masking," I continued, talking perhaps a bit too much.

The second policeman shook his head. "What an idea. You know, masks are a pretty good thing, brother. Couple of years more and I'm going to make my wife wear hers around the house."

The first policeman shrugged. "If women were to stop wearing masks, in six weeks you wouldn't know the difference. You get used to anything, if enough people do or don't do it."

I agreed, rather regretfully, and left them. I turned north on Broadway (old Tenth Avenue, I believe) and walked rapidly until I was beyond Inferno. Passing such an area of undercontaminated radioactivity always makes a person queasy. I thanked God there weren't any such in England, as yet.

The street was almost empty, though I was accosted by a couple of beggars with faces tunneled by H-bomb scars, whether real or of makeup putty, I couldn't tell. A fat woman held out a baby with webbed fingers and toes. I told myself it would have been deformed anyway and that she was only capitalizing on our fear of bomb-induced mutations. Still, I gave her a seven-and-a-half-cent piece. Her mask made me feel I was paying tribute to an African fetish.

"May all your children be blessed with one head and two eyes, sir."

"Thanks," I said, shuddering, and hurried past her.

". . . There's only trash behind the mask, so turn your head, stick to your task: Stay away, stay away—from—the—girls!"

This last was the end of an antisex song being sung by some religionists half a block from the circle-and-cross insignia of a femalist temple. They reminded me only faintly of our small tribe of British monastics. Above their heads was a jumble of billboards advertising predigested foods, wrestling instruction, radio handies, and the like.

I stared at the hysterical slogans with disagreeable fascination. Since the female face and form have been banned on American signs, the very letters of the advertiser's alphabet have begun to crawl with sex—the fat-bellied, big-breasted capital B, the lascivious double O. However, I reminded myself, it is chiefly the mask that so strangely accents sex in America.

A British anthropologist has pointed out that, while it took more than 5,000 years to shift the chief point of sexual interest from the hips to the breasts, the next transition to the face has taken less than 50 years. Comparing the American style with Moslem tradition is not valid; Moslem women are compelled to wear veils, the purpose of which is to make a husband's property private, while American women have only the compulsion of fashion and use masks to create mystery.

Theory aside, the actual origins of the trend are to be found in the antiradiation clothing of World War III, which led to masked wrestling, now a fantastically popular sport, and that in turn led to the current female fashion. Only a wild style at first, masks quickly became as necessary as brassieres and lipsticks had been earlier in the century.

I finally realized that I was not speculating about masks in general, but about what lay behind one in particular. That's the devil of the things; you're never sure whether a girl is heightening loveliness or hiding ugliness. I pictured a cool, pretty face in which fear showed only in widened eyes. Then I remembered her blonde hair, rich against the blackness of the satin mask. She'd told me to come at the twenty-second hour—10:00 P.M.

I climbed to my apartment near the British consulate; the elevator shaft had been shoved out of plumb by an old blast, a nuisance in these tall New York buildings. Before it occurred to me that I would be going out again, I automatically tore a tab from the film strip under my shirt. I developed it just to be sure. It showed that the total radiation I'd taken that day was still within the safety limit. I'm not phobic about it, as so many people are these days, but there's no point in taking chances.

I flopped down on the daybed and stared at the silent speaker and the dark screen of the video set. As always, they made me think, somewhat bitterly, of the two great nations of the world. Mutilated by each other, yet still strong, they were crippled giants poisoning the planet with their respective dreams of an impossible equality and as impossible success.

I fretfully switched on the speaker. By luck, the newscaster was talking excitedly of the prospects of a bumper wheat crop, sown by planes across a dust bowl moistened by seeded rains. I listened carefully to the rest of the program (it was remarkably clear of Russian telejamming) but there was no further news of interest to me. And, of course, no mention of the moon, though everyone knows that America and Russia are racing to develop their primary bases into fortresses capable of mutual assault and the launching of alphabet-bombs toward Earth. I myself knew perfectly well that the British electronic equipment I was helping trade for American wheat was destined for use in spaceships.

I switched off the newscast. It was growing dark and once again I pictured a tender, frightened face behind a mask. I hadn't had a date since England. It's exceedingly difficult to become acquainted with a girl in America, where as little as a smile, often, can set one of them yelping for the police—to say nothing of the increasingly puritanical morality and the roving gangs that keep most women indoors after dark. And naturally, the masks, which are definitely not, as the Soviets claim, a last invention of capitalist degeneracy, but a sign of great psychological insecurity. The Russians have no masks, but they have their own signs of stress.

I went to the window and impatiently watched the darkness gather. I was getting very restless. After a while a ghostly violet cloud appeared to the south. My hair rose. Then I laughed. I had momentarily fancied it a radiation from the crater of the Hell-bomb, though I instantly should have known it was only the radio-induced glow in the sky over the amusement and residential area south of Inferno.

Promptly at twenty-two hours I stood before the door of my unknown girl friend's apartment. The electronic say-who-please said just that. I answered clearly, "Wysten Turner," wondering if she'd given my name to the mechanism. She evidently had, for the door opened. I walked into a small empty living room, my heart pounding a bit.

The room was expensively furnished with the latest pneumatic hassocks and sprawlers. There were some midgie books on the table. The one I picked up was the standard hard-boiled detective story in which two female murderers go gunning for each other.

The television was on. A masked girl in green was crooning a love song. Her right hand held something that blurred off into the foreground. I saw the set had a handie, which we haven't in England as yet, and curiously thrust my hand into the handie orifice beside the screen. Contrary to my expectations, it was not like slipping into a pulsing rubber glove, but rather as if the girl on the screen actually held my hand.

A door opened behind me. I jerked out my hand with as guilty a reaction as if I'd been caught peering through a keyhole.

She stood in the bedroom doorway. I think she was trembling. She was wearing a gray fur coat, white-speckled, and a gray velvet evening mask with shirred gray lace around the eyes and mouth. Her fingernails twinkled like silver.

It hadn't occurred to me that she'd expect us to go out.

"I should have told you," she said softly. Her mask veered nervously toward the books and the screen and the room's dark corners. "But I can't possibly talk to you here."

I said doubtfully, "There's a place near the consulate . . ."

"I know where we can be together and talk," she said rapidly. "If you don't mind."

As we entered the elevator I said, "I'm afraid I dismissed the cab."

But the cab driver hadn't gone for some reason of his own. He jumped out and smirkingly held the front door open for us. I told him we preferred to sit in back. He sulkily opened the rear door, slammed it after us, jumped in front, and slammed the door behind him.

My companion leaned forward. "Heaven," she said.

The driver switched on the turbine and televisor.

"Why did you ask if I were a British subject?" I said, to start the conversation.

She leaned away from me, tilting her mask close to the window. "See the moon," she said in a quick, dreamy voice.

"But why, really?" I pressed, conscious of an irritation that had nothing to do with her.

"It's edging up into the purple of the sky."

"And what's your name?"

"The purple makes it look yellower."

Just then I became aware of the source of my irritation. It lay on the square of writhing light in the front of the cab beside the driver.

I don't object to ordinary wrestling machines, though they bore me, but I simply detest watching a man wrestle a woman. The fact that the bouts are generally "on the level," with the man greatly outclassed in weight and reach and the masked females young and personable, only makes them seem worse to me.

"Please turn off the screen," I requested the driver.

He shook his head without looking around. "Uh-uh, man," he said. "They've been grooming this babe for weeks for this bout with Little Zirk."

Infuriated, I reached forward, but my companion caught my arm. "Please," she whispered frightenedly, shaking her head.

I settled back, frustrated. She was closer to me now, but silent and for a few moments I watched the heaves and contortions of the powerful masked girl and her wiry masked opponent on the screen. His frantic scrambling at her reminded me of a male spider.

I jerked around, facing my companion. "Why did those three men want to kill you?" I asked sharply.

The eyeholes of her mask faced the screen. "Because they're jealous of me," she whispered.

"Why are they jealous?"

She still didn't look at me. "Because of him."

"Who?"

She didn't answer.

I put my arm around her shoulders. "Are you afraid to tell me?" I asked. "What *is* the matter?"

She still didn't look my way. She smelled nice.

"See here," I said laughingly, changing my tactics, "you really should tell me something about yourself. I don't even know what you look like."

I half playfully lifted my hand to the band of her neck. She gave it an astonishingly swift slap. I pulled it away in sudden pain. There were four tiny indentations on the back. From one of them a tiny bead of blood welled out as I watched. I looked at her silver fingernails and saw they were actually delicate and pointed metal caps.

"I'm dreadfully sorry," I heard her say, "but you frightened me. I thought for a moment you were going to . . ."

At last she turned to me. Her coat had fallen open. Her evening dress was Cretan Revival, a bodice of lace beneath and supporting the breasts without covering them.

"Don't be angry," she said, putting her arms around my neck. "You were wonderful this afternoon."

The soft gray velvet of her mask, molding itself to her cheek, pressed mine. Through the mask's lace the wet warm tip of her tongue touched my chin.

"I'm not angry," I said. "Just puzzled and anxious to help."

The cab stopped. To either side were black windows bordered by spears of broken glass. The sickly purple light showed a few ragged figures slowly moving toward us.

The driver muttered, "It's the turbine, man. We're grounded." He sat there hunched and motionless. "Wish it had happened somewhere else."

My companion whispered, "Five dollars is the usual amount."

She looked out so shudderingly at the congregating figures that I suppressed my indignation and did as she suggested. The driver took the bill without a word. As he started up, he put his hand out the window and I heard a few coins clink on the pavement.

My companion came back into my arms, but her mask faced the television screen, where the tall girl had just pinned the convulsively kicking Little Zirk.

"I'm so frightened," she breathed.

Heaven turned out to be an equally ruinous neighborhood, but it had a club with an awning and a huge doorman uniformed like a spaceman, but in gaudy colors. In my sensuous daze I rather liked it. We stepped out of the cab just as a drunken old woman came down the sidewalk, her mask awry. A couple ahead of us turned their heads from the half-revealed face, as if from an ugly body at the beach. As we followed them in I heard the doorman say, "Get along, grandma, and cover yourself."

Inside, everything was dimness and blue glows. She had said we could talk here, but I didn't see how. Besides the inevitable chorus of sneezes and coughs (they say America is fifty percent allergic these days), there was a band going full blast in the latest robop style, in which an electronic composing machine selects an arbitrary sequence of tones into which the musicians weave their raucous little individualities.

Most of the people were in booths. The band was behind the bar. On a small platform beside them a girl was dancing, stripped to her mask. The little cluster of men at the shadowy far end of the bar weren't looking at her.

We inspected the menu in gold script on the wall and pushed the buttons for breast of chicken, fried shrimps, and two scotches. Moments later, the serving bell tinkled. I opened the gleaming panel and took out our drinks.

The cluster of men at the bar filed off toward the door, but first they stared around the room. My companion had just thrown back her coat. Their look lingered on our booth. I noticed that there were three of them.

The band chased off the dancing girl with growls. I handed my companion a straw and we sipped our drinks.

"You wanted me to help you about something," I said. "Incidentally, I think you're lovely."

She nodded quick thanks, looked around, leaned forward. "Would it be hard for me to get to England?"

"No," I replied, a bit taken aback. "Provided you have an American passport."

"Are they difficult to get?"

"Rather," I said, surprised at her lack of information. "Your country doesn't like its nationals to travel, though it isn't quite as stringent as Russia."

"Could the British consulate help me get a passport?"

"It's hardly their . . ."

"Could you?"

I realized we were being inspected. A man and two girls had paused opposite our table. The girls were tall and wolfish looking, with spangled masks. The man stood jauntily between them like a fox on its hind legs.

My companion didn't glance at them, but she sat back. I noticed that one of the girls had a big yellow bruise on her forearm. After a moment they walked to a booth in the deep shadows.

"Know them?" I asked. She didn't reply. I finished my drink. "I'm not sure you'd like England," I said. "The austerity's altogether different from your American brand of misery."

She leaned forward again. "But I must get away," she whispered.

"Why?" I was getting impatient.

"Because I'm so frightened."

There were chimes. I opened the panel and handed her the fried shrimps. The sauce on my breast of chicken was a delicious steaming compound of almonds, soy, and ginger. But something must have been wrong with the radionic oven that had thawed and heated it, for at the first bite I crunched a kernel of ice in the meat. These delicate mechanisms need constant repair and there aren't enough mechanics.

I put down my fork. "What are you really scared of?" I asked her.

For once her mask didn't waver away from my face. As I waited I could feel the fears gathering without her naming them, tiny dark shapes swarming through the curved night outside, converging on the radioactive pest spot of New York, dipping into the margins of the purple. I felt a sudden rush of sympathy, a desire to protect the girl opposite me. The warm feeling added itself to the infatuation engendered in the cab.

"Everything," she said finally.

I nodded and touched her hand.

"I'm afraid of the moon," she began, her voice going dreamy and brittle as it had in the cab. "You can't look at it and not think of guided bombs."

"It's the same moon over England," I reminded her.

"But it's not England's moon any more. It's ours and Russia's. You're not responsible.

"Oh, and then," she said with a tilt of her mask, "I'm afraid of the cars and the gangs and the loneliness and Inferno. I'm afraid of the lust that undresses your face. And—" her voice hushed— "I'm afraid of the wrestlers."

"Yes?" I prompted softly after a moment.

Her mask came forward. "Do you know something about the wrestlers?" she asked rapidly. "The ones that wrestle women, I mean. They often lose, you know. And then they have to have a girl to take their frustration out on. A girl who's soft and weak and terribly frightened. They need that, to keep them men. Other men don't want them to have a girl. Other men want them just to fight women and be heroes. But they must have a girl. It's horrible for her."

I squeezed her fingers tighter, as if courage could be transmitted— granting I had any. "I think I can get you to England," I said.

Shadows crawled onto the table and stayed there. I looked up at the three men who had been at the end of the bar. They were the men I had seen in the big coupe. They wore black sweaters and close-fitting black trousers. Their faces were as expressionless as dopers. Two of them stood about me. The other loomed over the girl.

"Drift off, man," I was told. I heard the other inform the girl: "We'll wrestle a fall, sister. What shall it be? Judo, slapsie, or kill-who-can?"

I stood up. There are times when an Englishman simply must be maltreated. But just then the foxlike man came gliding in like the star of a ballet. The reaction of the other three startled me. They were acutely embarrassed.

He smiled at them thinly. "You won't win my favor by tricks like this," he said.

"Don't get the wrong idea, Zirk," one of them pleaded.

"I will if it's right," he said. "She told me what you tried to do this afternoon. That won't endear you to me, either. Drift."

They backed off awkwardly. "Let's get out of here," one of them said loudly, as they turned. "I know a place where they fight naked with knives."

Little Zirk laughed musically and slipped into the seat beside my companion. She shrank from him, just a little. I pushed my feet back, leaned forward.

"Who's your friend, baby?" he asked, not looking at her.

She passed the question to me with a little gesture. I told him.

"British," he observed. "She's been asking you about getting out of the country? About passports?" He smiled pleasantly. "She likes to start running away. Don't you, baby?" His small hand began to stroke her waist, the fingers bent a little, the tendons ridged, as if he were about to grab and twist.

"Look here," I said sharply. "I have to be grateful to you for ordering off those bullies, but—"

"Think nothing of it," he told me. "They're no harm except when they're behind steering wheels. A well-trained fourteen-year-old girl could cripple any one of them. Why, even Theda here, if she went in for that sort of thing . . ." He turned to her, shifting his hand from her waist to her hair. He stroked it, letting the strands slip slowly through his fingers. "You know I lost tonight, baby, don't you?" he said softly.

I stood up. "Come along," I said to her. "Let's leave."

She just sat there, I couldn't even tell if she was trembling. I tried to read a message in her eyes through the mask.

"I'll take you away," I said to her. "I can do it. I really will."

He smiled at me. "She'd like to go with you," he said. "Wouldn't you, baby?"

"Will you or won't you?" I said to her. She still just sat there.

He slowly knotted his fingers in her hair.

"Listen, you little vermin," I snapped at him. "Take your hands off her."

He came up from the seat like a snake. I'm no fighter. I just know that the more scared I am, the harder and straighter I hit. This time I was lucky. But as he crumpled back, I felt a slap and four stabs of pain in my cheek. I clapped my hand to it. I could feel the four gashes made by her dagger finger caps, and the warm blood oozing out from them.

She didn't look at me. She was bending over Little Zirk and cuddling her mask to his cheek and crooning: "There, there, don't feel bad, you'll be able to hurt me afterward."

There were sounds around us, but they didn't come close. I leaned forward and ripped the mask from her face.

I really don't know why I should have expected her face to be anything else. It was very pale, of course, and there weren't any cosmetics. I suppose there's no point in wearing any under a mask. But as for the general expression, as for the feelings crawling and wriggling across it—

Have you ever lifted a rock from damp soil? Have you ever watched the slimy white grubs?

I looked down at her, she up at me. "Yes, you're so frightened, aren't you?" I said sarcastically. "You dread this little nightly drama, don't you? You're scared to death."

And I walked right out into the purple night, still holding my hand to my bleeding cheek. No one stopped me, not even the girl wrestlers. I wished I could tear a tab from under my shirt, and test it then and there, and find I'd taken too much radiation, and so be able to ask to cross the Hudson and go down New Jersey, past the lingering radiance of the Narrows Bomb, and so on to Sandy Hook to wait for the rusty ship that would take me back over the seas to England.

TO SERVE MAN

November 1950

Damon Knight
(b. 1922)

Damon Knight has achieved success in the science-fiction field as an editor (the excellent Orbit series of original stories and many notable reprint anthologies), critic (his 1967 collection of book reviews, In Search of Wonder, *won him the Pilgrim Award of the Science Fiction Research Association), and author.*

His fiction appeared regularly in Galaxy, especially during the 1950s, and includes "Ticket to Anywhere" (April 1952), "Man in a Jar" (April 1957), "Cabin Boy" (September 1951), the novella "Natural State" (January 1954), and the classic "To Serve Man."

Memoir by Damon Knight

It is unnervingly easy to recapture the summer afternoon in Greenwich Village in 1950 when I wrote this story. I was twenty-eight; I was living in a studio apartment with a piano I couldn't play, a blond wife I wasn't getting along with, and a small black dog that crapped on the stairs. In some ways life was simpler then; there were two rooms in that place, and when my wife was out with the dog, as she was that afternoon, I had it all to myself. (Now I live in a house with five bedrooms and two offices, and it is not big enough.)

My agent, Fred Pohl, handed the story over to Horace Gold, and Horace bought it. I don't think any of us believed it was anything special, but it made me famous in Milford, Pennsylvania, where I was living a few years later, when it was dramatized on "The Twilight Zone" and it has since been reprinted in all kinds of unlikely places. I got the name of the French criminologist from a high-school classmate of mine, Philip Leveque, who, by a neat coincidence, is now a forensic pathologist in Oregon, but his folks had dropped the diacritical marks, and it took me years to get them right: Lévêque.

TO SERVE MAN

The Kanamit were not very pretty, it's true. They looked something like pigs and something like people, and that is not an attractive combination. Seeing them for the first time shocked you; that was their handicap. When a thing with the countenance of a fiend comes from the stars and offers a gift, you are disinclined to accept.

I don't know what we expected interstellar visitors to look like—those who thought about it at all, that is. Angels, perhaps, or something too alien to be really awful. Maybe that's why we were all so horrified and repelled when they landed in their great ships and we saw what they really were like.

The Kanamit were short and very hairy—thick, bristly, brown-gray hair all over their abominably plump bodies. Their noses were snoutlike and their eyes small, and they had thick hands of three fingers each. They wore green leather harness and green shorts, but I think the shorts were a concession to our notions of public decency. The garments were quite modishly cut, with slash pockets and half-belts in the back. The Kanamit had a sense of humor, anyhow.

There were three of them at this session of the U.N., and, lord, I can't tell you how queer it looked to see them there in the middle of a solemn plenary session—three fat piglike creatures in green harness and shorts, sitting at the long table below the podium, surrounded by the packed arcs of delegates from every nation. They sat correctly upright, politely watching each speaker. Their flat ears drooped over the earphones. Later on, I believe, they learned every human language, but at this time they knew only French and English.

They seemed perfectly at ease—and that, along with their humor, was a thing that tended to make me like them. I was in the minority; I didn't think they were trying to put anything over.

The delegate from Argentina got up and said that his government was interested in the demonstration of a new cheap power source, which the Kanamit had made at the previous session, but that the

Argentine government could not commit itself as to its future policy without a much more thorough examination.

It was what all the delegates were saying, but I had to pay particular attention to Señor Valdes, because he tended to sputter and his diction was bad. I got through the translation all right, with only one or two momentary hesitations, and then switched to the Polish-English line to hear how Grigori was doing with Janciewicz. Janciewicz was the cross Grigori had to bear, just as Valdes was mine.

Janciewicz repeated the previous remarks with a few ideological variations, and then the secretary-general recognized the delegate from France, who introduced Dr. Denis Lévêque, the criminologist, and a great deal of complicated equipment was wheeled in.

Dr. Lévêque remarked that the question in many people's minds had been aptly expressed by the delegate from the U.S.S.R. at the preceding session, when he demanded, "What is the motive of the Kanamit? What is their purpose in offering us these unprecedented gifts, while asking nothing in return?"

The doctor then said, "At the request of several delegates and with the full consent of our guests, the Kanamit, my associates and I have made a series of tests upon the Kanamit with the equipment which you see before you. These tests will now be repeated."

A murmur ran through the chamber. There was a fusillade of flashbulbs, and one of the TV cameras moved up to focus on the instrument board of the doctor's equipment. At the same time, the huge television screen behind the podium lighted up, and we saw the blank faces of two dials, each with its pointer resting at zero, and a strip of paper tape with a stylus point resting against it.

The doctor's assistants were fastening wires to the temples of one of the Kanamit, wrapping a canvas-covered rubber tube around his forearm, and taping something to the palm of his right hand.

In the screen, we saw the paper tape begin to move while the stylus traced a slow zigzag pattern along it. One of the needles began to jump rhythmically; the other flipped halfway over and stayed there, wavering slightly.

"These are the standard instruments for testing the truth of a statement," said Dr. Lévêque. "Our first object, since the physiology of the Kanamit is unknown to us, was to determine whether or not they react to these tests as human beings do. We will now repeat one of the many experiments which were made in the endeavor to discover this."

He pointed to the first dial. "This instrument registers the subject's heartbeat. This shows the electrical conductivity of the skin in the palm of his hand, a measure of perspiration, which increases under stress. And this"—pointing to the tape-and-stylus device—"shows the pattern and intensity of the electrical waves emanating from his brain. It has been shown, with human subjects, that all these readings vary markedly depending upon whether the subject is speaking the truth."

He picked up two large pieces of cardboard, one red and one black. The red one was a square about three feet on a side; the black was a rectangle three and a half feet long. He addressed himself to the Kanama.

"Which of these is longer than the other?"

"The red," said the Kanama.

Both needles leaped wildly, and so did the line of the unrolling tape.

"I shall repeat the question," said the doctor. "Which of these is longer than the other?"

"The black," said the creature.

This time the instruments continued in their normal rhythm.

"How did you come to this planet?" asked the doctor.

"Walked," replied the Kanama.

Again the instruments responded, and there was a subdued ripple of laughter in the chamber.

"Once more," said the doctor. "How did you come to this planet?"

"In a spaceship," said the Kanama, and the instruments did not jump.

The doctor again faced the delegates. "Many such experiments were made," he said, "and my colleagues and myself are satisfied that the mechanisms are effective. Now"—he turned to the Kanama —"I shall ask our distinguished guest to reply to the question put at the last session by the delegate of the U.S.S.R.—namely, what is the motive of the Kanamit people in offering these great gifts to the people of Earth?"

The Kanama rose. Speaking this time in English, he said, "On my planet there is a saying, 'There are more riddles in a stone than in a philosopher's head.' The motives of intelligent beings, though they may at times appear obscure, are simple things compared to the complex workings of the natural universe. Therefore I hope that the people of Earth will understand, and believe, when I tell you that our mission upon your planet is simply this—to bring to you the peace and plenty which we ourselves enjoy, and which we have in the past brought to other races throughout the galaxy. When your world has no more hunger, no more war, no more needless suffering, that will be our reward."

And the needles had not jumped once.

The delegate from the Ukraine jumped to his feet, asking to be recognized, but the time was up and the secretary-general closed the session.

I met Grigori as we were leaving the chamber. His face was red with excitement. "Who promoted that circus?" he demanded.

"The tests looked genuine to me," I told him.

"A circus!" he said vehemently. "A second-rate farce! If they were genuine, Peter, why was debate stifled?"

"There'll be time for debate tomorrow, surely."

"Tomorrow the doctor and his instruments will be back in Paris. Plenty of things can happen before tomorrow. In the name of sanity, man, how can anybody trust a thing that looks as if it ate the baby?"

I was a little annoyed. I said, "Are you sure you're not more worried about their politics than their appearance?"

He said, "Bah," and went away.

The next day reports began to come in from government laboratories all over the world where the Kanamit's power source was being tested. They were wildly enthusiastic. I don't understand such things myself, but it seemed that those little metal boxes would give more electrical power than an atomic pile, for next to nothing and nearly forever. And it was said that they were so cheap to manufacture that everybody in the world could have one of his own. In the early afternoon there were reports that seventeen countries had already begun to set up factories to turn them out.

The next day the Kanamit turned up with plans and specimens of a gadget that would increase the fertility of any arable land by 60 to 100 percent. It speeded the formation of nitrates in the soil, or something. There was nothing in the newscasts any more but stories about the Kanamit. The day after that, they dropped their bombshell.

"You now have potentially unlimited power and increased food supply," said one of them. He pointed with his three-fingered hand to an instrument that stood on the table before him. It was a box on a tripod, with a parabolic reflector on the front of it. "We offer you today a third gift which is at least as important as the first two."

He beckoned to the TV men to roll their cameras into closeup position. Then he picked up a large sheet of cardboard covered with drawings and English lettering. We saw it on the large screen above the podium; it was all clearly legible.

"We are informed that this broadcast is being relayed throughout your world," said the Kanama. "I wish that everyone who has equipment for taking photographs from television screens would use it now."

The secretary-general leaned forward and asked a question sharply, but the Kanama ignored him.

"This device," he said, "generates a field in which no explosive, of whatever nature, can detonate."

There was an uncomprehending silence.

The Kanama said, "It cannot now be suppressed. If one nation has it, all must have it." When nobody seemed to understand, he explained bluntly, "There will be no more war."

That was the biggest news of the millennium, and it was perfectly true. It turned out that the explosions the Kanama was talking about included gasoline and diesel explosions. They had simply made it impossible for anybody to mount or equip a modern army.

We could have gone back to bows and arrows, of course, but that wouldn't have satisfied the military. Besides, there wouldn't be any reason to make war. Every nation would soon have everything.

Nobody ever gave another thought to those lie-detector experiments, or asked the Kanamit what their politics were. Grigori was put out; he had nothing to prove his suspicions.

I quit my job with the U.N. a few months later, because I foresaw that it was going to die under me anyhow. U.N. business was booming at the time, but after a year or so there was going to be nothing for it to do. Every nation on Earth was well on the way to being completely self-supporting; they weren't going to need much arbitration.

I accepted a position as translator with the Kanamit Embassy, and it was there that I ran into Grigori again. I was glad to see him, but I couldn't imagine what he was doing there.

"I thought you were on the opposition," I said. "Don't tell me you're convinced the Kanamit are all right."

He looked rather shamefaced. "They're not what they look, any-how," he said.

It was as much of a concession as he could decently make, and I invited him down to the embassy lounge for a drink. It was an inti-mate kind of place, and he grew confidential over the second daiquiri.

"They fascinate me," he said. "I hate them instinctively still—that hasn't changed—but I can evaluate it. You were right, obvi-ously; they mean us nothing but good. But do you know"—he leaned across the table—"the question of the Soviet delegate was never answered."

I am afraid I snorted.

"No, really," he said. "They told us what they wanted to do—'to bring to you peace and plenty which we ourselves enjoy.' But they didn't say *why*."

"Why do missionaries—"

"Missionaries be damned!" he said angrily. "Missionaries have a religious motive. If these creatures have a religion, they haven't once mentioned it. What's more, they didn't send a missionary group; they sent a diplomatic delegation—a group representing the will and policy of their whole people. Now just what have the Kanamit, as a people or a nation, got to gain from our welfare?"

I said, "Cultural—"

"Cultural cabbage soup! No, it's something less obvious than that, something obscure that belongs to their psychology and not to ours. But trust me, Peter, there is no such thing as a completely disin-terested altruism. In one way or another, they have something to gain."

"And that's why you're here," I said. "To try to find out what it is."

"Correct. I wanted to get on one of the ten-year exchange groups to their home planet, but I couldn't; the quota was filled a week after they made the announcement. This is the next best thing. I'm studying their language, and you know that language reflects the basic assumptions of the people who use it. I've got a fair command of the spoken lingo already. It's not hard, really, and there are hints in it. Some of the idioms are quite similar to English. I'm sure I'll get the answer eventually."

"More power," I said, and we went back to work.

I saw Grigori frequently from then on, and he kept me posted about his progress. He was highly excited about a month after that first meeting; said he'd got hold of a book of the Kanamits' and was trying to puzzle it out. They wrote in ideographs, worse than Chinese, but he was determined to fathom it if it took him years. He wanted my help.

Well, I was interested in spite of myself, for I knew it would be a long job. We spent some evenings together, working with material from Kanamit bulletin boards and so forth, and with the extremely limited English-Kanamit dictionary they issued to the staff. My conscience bothered me about the stolen book, but gradually I became absorbed by the problem. Languages are my field, after all. I couldn't help being fascinated.

We got the title worked out in a few weeks. It was *How to Serve Man*, evidently a handbook they were giving out to new Kanamit members of the embassy staff. They had new ones in, all the time now, a shipload about once a month; they were opening all kinds of research laboratories, clinics, and so on. If there was anybody on Earth besides Grigori who still distrusted those people, he must have been somewhere in the middle of Tibet.

It was astonishing to see the changes that had been wrought in less than a year. There were no more standing armies, no more shortages, no unemployment. When you picked up a newspaper you didn't see H-BOMB or SATELLITE leaping out at you; the news was always good. It was a hard thing to get used to. The Kanamit were working on human biochemistry, and it was known around the embassy that they were nearly ready to announce methods of making our race taller and stronger and healthier—practically a race of supermen—and they had a potential cure for heart disease and cancer.

I didn't see Grigori for a fortnight after we finished working out the title of the book; I was on a long-overdue vacation in Canada. When I got back, I was shocked by the change in his appearance.

"What on earth is wrong, Grigori?" I asked. "You look like the very devil."

"Come on down to the lounge."

I went with him, and he gulped a stiff scotch as if he needed it.

"Come on, man, what's the matter?" I urged.

"The Kanamit have put me on the passenger list for the next exchange ship," he said. "You, too, otherwise I wouldn't be talking to you."

"Well," I said, "but—"

"They're not altruists."

I tried to reason with him. I pointed out they'd made Earth a paradise compared to what it was before. He only shook his head.

Then I said, "Well, what about those lie-detector tests?"

"A farce," he replied, without heat. "I said so at the time, you fool. They told the truth, though, as far as it went."

"And the book?" I demanded, annoyed. "What about that—*How to Serve Man?* That wasn't put there for you to read. They *mean* it. How do you explain that?"

"I've read the first paragraph of that book," he said. "Why do you suppose I haven't slept for a week?"

I said, "Well?" and he smiled a curious, twisted smile.

"It's a cookbook," he said.

BETELGEUSE BRIDGE

April 1951

William Tenn

(b. 1920)

William Tenn (the pen name for Philip Klass) was one of the great joys of Galaxy *in the 1950s. His typewriter always dripped with wit and satire, and he never let you down. His relative absence from science fiction for the last fifteen years is one of the tragedies of the field, one that we hope will soon be corrected. Fortunately, almost all of his work has been reprinted in his single-author collections, including* The Human Angle *(1956),* Of Men and Monsters *(1968),* The Wooden Star *(1968),* The Square Root of Man *(1968),* The Seven Sexes *(1968), and* Of All Possible Worlds *(1955).*

Choosing one story from among his appearances in Galaxy *was a nightmare. "Venus Is a Man's World" (July 1951), "The Servant Problem" (April 1955), "Project Hush" (February 1954), "Party of the Two Parts" (August 1954), and a dozen others all deserve inclusion, but we could find space only for "Betelgeuse Bridge."*

From a Cave Deep in Stuyvesant Town—
A Memoir of Galaxy's Most Creative Years
by Philip Klass

The complex of buildings had been put up just north of Manhattan's Fourteenth Street by a big insurance company after World War II. You went into the street entrance that looked like all the other street entrances in the huge complex, you rode up in a bright, plastic-looking elevator, you walked out into a bright, plastic-looking corridor, and you came to a bright, plastic-looking door. All around you were apartment doors behind which people lived and cooked and slept, behind which they yelled at each other and murmured at television, but this one door was different. Behind this door was a cave, and in the cave Horace L. Gold lay hidden from the day while he went about his business of sending writers to the outermost edges of time and the universe.

I mean it. Horace suffered from agoraphobia, the fear of open spaces, and there were many weeks when he couldn't leave his apartment or even his bedroom. And from that apartment—or even bedroom—Horace edited *Galaxy*, a magazine he founded on the premise that space was there to be explored, *all* space, physical space, mental space, social space, space inchoate, space unending.

You discussed a new idea with Horace in a corner of his entrance hallway or you argued a revision with him in the tiny kitchen area— because Horace couldn't take you out to lunch as other editors did. You debated Vaihinger's philosophy or Sapir's linguistics around Horace's dining-room table where you were playing fifteen-cent-limit poker with the likes of John Cage and Daniel Stern and Robert Sheckley and Fred Pohl—because, after all, Horace couldn't go out to other people's poker games, nor could he go to clubs and conventions where writers and artists met. You worked out deadlines and word rates and similar business problems near the coffee table in his living room during an evening party for the Cyril Kornbluths or the Fritz Leibers just in from Chicago—because Evelyn, Horace's wife, was determined that Horace would have a full social as well as a full professional life, agoraphobia or no agoraphobia.

At one of these parties, Horace paused on his way to refill drinks and began rolling his pants legs up to his knees (which he always did as the evening got late: he claimed his knees felt stuffy and needed more air). He noticed he was standing near Asimov. "Oh, Ike," he said. "I have to tell you. I'm bouncing your latest story."

"*Why?*" Asimov yelped in utter outrage. "What's wrong with it?" The rest of the room fell silent. All the writers present—Sturgeon, Budrys, Simak, Merril—waited for the oral rejection slip.

"Only one thing," Horace said. "It's meretricious." Then he continued on his way to the kitchen with the empty glasses.

Ike stared after him. "And a happy New Year," he said bitterly to the backs of Horace's knees.

Horace rejected what I still believe to be three of my best stories: "The Tenants" ("Maybe it's supposed to be funny? Is that it, Phil, a *humorous* story?"), "The Custodian" ("You simply cannot make me believe that there's anyone to whom art is that much more important than life"), and "The Liberation of Earth," a story attacking both American and Russian involvement in the Korean war and which many people believe to have been written much later, about the war in Viet Nam. Horace said that, considering his youthful radical background (and mine, and mine!), the very idea of publishing "The Liberation of Earth" spang in the middle of the McCarthy period made him sweat green.

Like Campbell, he was always pushing ideas at me—and watching them curl back at him. He is directly responsible for only two of my stories: "Down Among the Dead Men" and "The Flat-Eyed Monster." Relative to the first, he challenged me to write a space opera that really said something—"but it has to be honest, slam-bang, parsec-ricocheting stuff." When I gave him the story, he paid me one of his strongest compliments: "Phil, a tour de force. Real space opera, real bangety-bang, but all the action takes place *offstage*. It's a pleasure to read such deviousness." I wrote "The Flat-Eyed Monster" flat on my back in a hospital bed: I was broke and needed a sum of money to pay for a good surgeon. Horace offered to advance the price of a novella if I would write it then and there and guarantee that it would be very funny. *Very* funny? I munched on sedatives and tried to imagine what would make him laugh.

He ruined many more stories for me than he made. From his cave in Stuyvesant Town, he called me two or three times a week, each and every week (I knew that I was on some sort of roster, that I had my appointed place on his wheel). He would ask me what I was writing and how I was handling the idea; then he'd tell me where I'd gone wrong and the only way to save the story. "But that's *your* story, Horace," I'd say despairingly, watching what had been an exciting idea fall apart into separate bits and pieces all over my typewriter table. He'd apologize and I'd have my phone pulled out for a while and later—a week, a month—it would start all over again.

I knew that for a man limited most of the time to his apartment, the telephone was a vital connection to the outside world. But at my end it was much less than vital; at my end it felt like a noose.

The moment I picked up the phone and heard his voice I would begin babbling about all kinds of troubles—anything but writing troubles. I would tell him about the orgasm problems of the girl I was currently seeing, about my landlord's attempt to raise the rent, about the possible identity of the person who was sending me strange, unsigned postcards. And Horace would listen warmly and help warmly—he'd really help. He'd give me some therapy over the phone and he'd hang up. I'd flex my mental sickness and be able to go on writing.

Later, when Bob Sheckley and I met and became good friends, I discovered that Bob had worked out exactly the same relationship with Horace, out of exactly the same kind of desperate self-protection. Later still, when I got married, Fruma would always answer the telephone. Horace would call and ask to speak to me, and Fruma would say, "No, you can't." And Horace would ask her what I was writing, and Fruma would say, "I won't tell you." Horace got to hate her. But then he'd swallow his rage and call up and ask her what she was cooking for supper that night.

Ultimately, the thing wrong with Horace was what he had found most unbearable in John Campbell back in the *Astounding/Unknown* 1930s and 1940s. It was also what made both men cause, at different times and in totally different ways, a science-fiction efflorescence, conceptually and stylistically. Both men were intricate thinkers about a thousand things, and both men were great editors with a single, magnificent flaw: They had so completely become editors that they saw their writers as mere pencils or typewriters (I can hear the anxious rustle of Horace's breath: "Oh, Phil, *you* were never mere."), mere instruments to record their thousands of intricate thoughts.

It was awful to be treated like an instrument when you were a distinctive person and a writer of some stature; it was so awful to find a paragraph of Horace's private musing in the middle of one of my stories that I swore (falsely) never to send him a manuscript again; it was so awful for Ted Sturgeon to find his sentences in "Baby Is Three" changed about and their rhythm destroyed that he began writing "STET" in the margin of every single page in indelible pencil; it was awful, humiliating, aesthetically painful beyond belief, *but:*

Horace created a unique milieu in that cave in Stuyvesant Town over on Fourteenth Street, just as Campbell had earlier created one in his Street & Smith office. If you lived in that milieu, if you moved in it at all, if you did nothing more than correspond with it from time to time, you were enlarged in special ways and began to move in directions that were novel to you and remarkably exciting. These special ways, these novel directions, had substantially more to do with the personalities of the individual writers.

In *Galaxy*, as well as in *Astounding*, a literature of ideas, science fiction, was brought into focus by a powerful editorial mind. Whether writers like it or not (*I* don't), providing focus has been the great duty of editors in this field since the time of Hugo Gernsback.

The difference between John W. Campbell and Horace L. Gold? You might say that after Campbell had taken a telescope to concept, Gold took a microscope to social insight. Both instruments were necessary in their time.

I doubt that *The Demolished Man* or *The Space Merchants* or *More Than Human* would quite have come to pass without *Galaxy*. I know that I might never have written "Betelgeuse Bridge" if it had not been for the magazine and the milieu that Horace Gold created. It's my kind of story and my kind of idea—it was the first conscious effort in what I call my "Here Comes Civilization" series —but it needed a context where it could fit comfortably. Horace gave me that. How, I still don't quite know, with all of his damaging phone calls, compulsive overediting, quixotic rejections, and prying and puttering into my work.

Before *Galaxy* I wrote science fiction. After *Galaxy* I wrote only *my* kind of science fiction. And for that, I must admit, the responsibility lies with one of the most irritating and aggravating men I've ever known. From deep within his editorial cave, Horace Gold somehow changed me. I believe he changed us all.

BETELGEUSE BRIDGE

You tell them, Alvarez, old boy; you know how to talk to them. This isn't my kind of public relations. All I care about is that they get the pitch exactly right, with all the implications and complications and everything just the way they really were.

If it hurts, well, let them yell. Just use your words and get it right. Get it all.

You can start with the day the alien spaceship landed outside Baltimore. Makes you sick to think how we never tumbled, doesn't it, Alvarez? No more than a hop, skip, and a jet from the Capitol dome, and we thought it was just a lucky accident.

Explain why we thought it was so lucky. Explain about the secrecy it made possible, the farmer who telephoned the news was placed in special and luxurious custody, how a handpicked cordon of

M.P.s paced five square miles off into an emergency military reservation a few hours later, how Congress was called into secret session, and the way it was all kept out of the newspapers.

How and why Trowson, my old sociology prof, was consulted once the problem became clear. How he blinked at the brass hats and striped pants and came up with the answer.

Me. I was the answer.

How my entire staff and I were plucked out of our New York offices, where we were quietly earning a million bucks, by a flying squad of the F.B.I. and air mailed to Baltimore. Honestly, Alvarez, even after Trowson explained the situation to me, I was still irritated. Government hush-hush always makes me uncomfortable. Though I don't have to tell you how grateful I was for it later.

The spaceship itself was such a big surprise that I didn't even wet my lips when the first of the aliens *slooshed* out. After all those years of streamlined cigar shapes the Sunday-supplement artists had dreamed up, that colorful and rococo spheroid rearing out of a barley field in Maryland looked less like an interplanetary vessel than an oversized ornament for a whatnot table. Nothing that seemed like a rocket jet anywhere.

"And there's your job." The prof pointed. "Those two visitors."

They were standing on a flat metal plate surrounded by the highest the republic had elected or appointed. Nine feet of slimy green trunk tapering up from a rather wide base to a pointed top, and dressed in a tiny pink-and-white shell. Two stalks with eyes on them that swung this way and that, and seemed muscular enough to throttle a man. And a huge wet slash of a mouth that showed whenever an edge of the squirming base lifted from the metal plate.

"Snails," I said. "*Snails!*"

"Or slugs," Trowson amended. "Gastropodal mollusks in any case." He gestured at the roiling white bush of hair that sprouted from his head. "But, Dick, that vestigial bit of coiled shell is even less an evolutionary memento than this. They're an older—and smarter—race."

"Smarter?"

He nodded. "When our engineers got curious, they were very courteously invited inside to inspect the ship. They came out with their mouths hanging."

I began to get uncomfortable. I ripped a small piece off my manicure. "Well, naturally, Prof, if they're so alien, so different—"

"Not only that. Superior. Get that, Dick, because it'll be very important in what you have to do. The best engineering minds that this country can assemble in a hurry are like a crowd of South Sea Islanders trying to analyze the rifle and compass from what they know of spears and windstorms. These creatures belong to a galaxy-wide civilization composed of races *at least* as advanced as they; we're a bunch of backward hicks in an unfrequented hinterland of space that's about to be opened to exploration. Exploitation, perhaps, if we can't measure up. We have to give a very good impression and we have to learn fast."

A dignified official with a briefcase detached himself from the nodding, smiling group around the aliens and started for us.

"*Whew!*" I commented brilliantly. "Fourteen ninety-two, repeat performance." I thought for a moment, not too clearly. "But why send the army and navy after *me*? I'm not going to be able to read blueprints from—from—"

"Betelgeuse. Ninth planet of the star Betelgeuse. No, Dick, we've already had Dr. Warbury out here. They learned English from him in two hours, although he hasn't identified a word of theirs in three days! And people like Lopez, like Mainzer, are going quietly psychotic trying to locate their power source. We have the best minds we can get to do the learning. Your job is different. We want you as a topnotch advertising man, a public-relations executive. You're the good-impression part of the program."

The official plucked at my sleeve and I shrugged him away. "Isn't that the function of government glad-handers?" I asked Trowson.

"No. Don't you remember what you said when you first saw them? *Snails!* How do you think this country is going to take to the idea of snails—giant snails—who sneer condescendingly at our sky-scraper cities, our atomic bombs, our most advanced mathematics? We're a conceited kind of monkey. Also, we're afraid of the dark."

There was a gentle official tap on my shoulder. I said "*Please!*" impatiently. I watched the warm little breeze ruffle Professor Trowson's slept-in clothes and noticed the tiny red streaks in his weary eyes.

"'MIGHTY MONSTERS FROM OUTER SPACE.' Headlines like that, Prof?"

"Slugs with superiority complexes. *Dirty* slugs, more likely. We're lucky they landed in this country, and so close to the Capitol too. In a few days we'll have to call in the heads of other nations. Then,

sometime soon after, the news will be out. We don't want our visitors attacked by mobs drunk on superstition, planetary isolation, or
any other form of tabloid hysteria. We don't want them carrying
stories back to their civilization of being shot at by a suspendered fanatic who screamed, 'Go back where you come from, you furrin sea-
food!' We want to give them the impression that we are a fairly intelligent race, that we can be dealt with reasonably well."

I nodded. "Yeah. So they'll set up trading posts on this planet instead of garrisons. But what do I do in all this?"

He punched my chest gently. "You, Dick—you do a job of public
relations. You sell these aliens to the American people!"

The official had maneuvered around in front of me. I recognized
him. He was the undersecretary of state.

"Would you step this way, please?" he said. "I'd like to introduce
you to our distinguished guests."

So he stepped, and I stepped, and we scrunched across the field
and clanked across the steel plate and stood next to our gastropodic
guests.

"Ahem," said the undersecretary politely.

The nearer snail bent an eye toward us. The other eye drew a
bead on the companion snail, and then the great slimy head arched
and came down to our level. The creature raised, as it were, one
cheek of its foot and said, with all the mellowness of air being
pumped through a torn inner tube, "Can it be that you wish to
communicate with my unworthy self, respected sir?"

I was introduced. The thing brought two eyes to bear on me. The
place where its chin should have been dropped to my feet and
snaked around there for a second. Then it said, "You, honored sir,
are our touchstone, the link with all that is great in your noble race.
Your condescension is truly a tribute."

All this tumbled out while I was muttering "How," and extending
a diffident hand. The snail put one eyeball in my palm and the
other on the back of my wrist. It didn't shake; it just put the things
there and took them away again. I had the wit not to wipe my
hands on my pants, which was my immediate impulse. The eyeball
wasn't exactly dry, either.

I said, "I'll do my best. Tell me, are you—uh—ambassadors, sort
of? Or maybe just explorers?"

"Our small worth justifies no titles," said the creature, "yet we are both; for all communication is ambassadorship of a kind, and any seeker after knowledge is an explorer."

I was suddenly reminded of an old story with the punchline, "Ask a foolish question and you get a foolish answer." I also wondered suddenly what snails eat.

The second alien glided over and eyed me. "You may depend upon our utmost obedience," it said humbly. "We understand your awesome function and we wish to be liked to whatever extent it is possible for your admirable race to like such miserable creatures as ourselves."

"Stick to that attitude and we'll get along," I said.

By and large, they were a pleasure to work with. I mean there was no temperament, no upstaging, no insistence on this camera angle or that mention of a previously published book or the other wishful biographical apocrypha about being raised in a convent, as with most of my other clients.

On the other hand, they weren't easy to talk to. They'd take orders, sure. But ask them a question. Any question:

"How long did the trip take you?"

"'How long' in your eloquent tongue indicates a frame of reference dealing with duration. I hesitate to discuss so complex a problem with one as learned as yourself. The velocities involved make it necessary to answer in relative terms. Our lowly and undesirable planet recedes from this beauteous system during part of its orbital period, advances toward it during part. Also, we must take into consideration the direction and velocity of our star in reference to the cosmic expansion of this portion of the continuum. Had we come from Cygnus, say, or Bootes, the question could be answered somewhat more directly; for those bodies travel in a contiguous arc skewed from the ecliptic plane in such a way that—"

Or a question like, "Is your government a democracy?"

"A democracy is a rule of the people, according to your rich etymology. We could not, in our lowly tongue, have expressed it so succinctly and movingly. One must govern oneself, of course. The degree of governmental control on the individual must vary from individual to individual and in the individual from time to time . This is so evident to as comprehensive a mind as yours that I trust you forgive me my inanities. The same control applies, naturally, to individuals considered in the mass. When faced with a universal necessity, the tendency exists among civilized species to unite to fill the need. Therefore, when no such necessity exists, there is less reason for concerted effort. Since this applies to all species, it applies even to such as us. On the other hand—"

See what I mean? A little of that got old quickly with me. I was happy to keep my nose to my own grindstone.

The government gave me a month for the preparatory propaganda. Originally, the story was to break in two weeks, but I got down on my hands and knees and bawled that a publicity deadline required at least five times that. So they gave me a month.

Explain that carefully, Alvarez. I want them to understand exactly what a job I faced. All those years of lurid magazine covers showing extremely nubile females being menaced in three distinct colors by assorted monstrosities; those horror movies, those invasion-from-outer-space novels, those Sunday-supplement fright splashes—all those sturdy psychological ruts I had to retrack. Not to mention the shudders elicited by mention of "worms," the regulation distrust of even human "furriners," the superstitious dread of creatures who had no visible place to park a soul.

Trowson helped me round up the men to write the scientific articles, and I dug up the boys who could pseudo them satisfactorily. Magazine mats were ripped apart to make way for yarns speculating gently on how far extraterrestrial races might have evolved beyond us, how much more ethical they might have become, how imaginary seven-headed creatures could still apply the Sermon on the Mount. Syndicated features popped up describing "Humble Creatures Who Create Our Gardens," "Snail Racing, the Spectacular New Spectator Sport," and so much stuff on "The Basic Unity of All Living Things" that I began to get uncomfortable at even a vegetarian dinner. I remember hearing there was a perceptible boom in mineral waters and vitamin pills. . . .

And all this, mind you, without a word of the real story breaking. A columnist did run a cute and cryptic item about someone having finally found meat on the flying saucers, but half an hour of earnest discussion in an abandoned fingerprint-file room prejudiced him against further comment along this line.

The video show was the biggest problem. I don't think I could have done it on time with anything less than the resources and influence on the United States government behind me. But a week before the official announcement, I had both the video show and the comic strip in production.

I think fourteen—though maybe it was more—of the country's best comedy writers collaborated on the project, not to mention the horde of illustrators and university psychologists who combined to sweat out the delightful little drawings. We used the drawings as the basis for the puppets on the TV show and I don't think anything was ever so gimmicked up with Popular Appeal—and I do mean *Popular*—as "Andy and Dandy."

Those two fictional snails crept into the heart of America like a virus infection: overnight, everybody was talking about their anthropomorphic antics, repeating their quotable running gags, and adjuring each other not to miss the next show. ("You *can't* miss it, Steve; it's on every channel anyway. Right after supper.") I had the tie-ins, too: Andy and Dandy dolls for the girls, snail scooters for the boys, everything from pictures on cocktail glasses to kitchen decalcomanias. Of course, a lot of the tie-ins didn't come off the production line till after the Big Announcement.

When we gave the handouts to the newspapers, we "suggested" what headlines to use. They had a choice of ten. Even the New York *Times* was forced to shriek "REAL ANDY AND DANDY BLOW IN FROM BETELGEUSE," and under that a four-column cut of blond Baby Ann Joyce with the snails.

Baby Ann had been flown out from Hollywood for the photograph. The cut showed her standing between the two aliens and clutching an eye stalk of each in her trusting, chubby hands.

The nicknames stuck. Those two slimy intellectuals from another star became even more important than the youthful evangelist who was currently being sued for bigamy.

Andy and Dandy had a ticker-tape reception in New York. They obligingly laid a cornerstone for the University of Chicago's new library. They posed for the newsreels everywhere, surrounded by Florida oranges, Idaho potatoes, Milwaukee beer. They were magnificently cooperative.

From time to time I wondered what they thought of us. They had no facial expressions, which was scarcely odd, since they had no faces. Their long eye stalks swung this way and that as they rode down shrieking Broadway in the back seat of the mayor's car; their gelatinous body-foot would heave periodically and the mouth under it make a smacking noise, but when the photographers suggested that they curl around the barely clad beauties, the time video rigged up a Malibu Beach show, Andy and Dandy wriggled over and complied without a word. Which is more than I can say for the barely clad beauties.

And when the winning pitcher presented them with an autographed baseball at that year's World Series, they bowed gravely, their pink shell tops glistening in the sunlight, and said throatily into the battery of microphones: "We're the happiest fans in the universe!"

The country went wild over them.

"But we can't keep them here," Trowson predicted. "Did you read about the debate in the U.N. General Assembly yesterday? We are accused of making secret alliances with nonhuman aggressors against the best interests of our own species."

I shrugged. "Well, let them go overseas. I don't think anyone else will be more successful extracting information from them than we were."

Professor Trowson wriggled his short body up on a corner of his desk. He lifted a folderful of typewritten notes and grimaced as if his tongue were wrapped in wool.

"Four months of careful questioning," he grumbled. "Four months of painstaking interrogation by trained sociologists using every free moment the aliens had, which admittedly wasn't much. Four months of organized investigation, of careful data sifting." He dropped the folder disgustedly to the desk and some of the pages splashed out. "And we know more about the social structure of Atlantis than Betelgeuse IX."

We were in the wing of the Pentagon assigned to what the brass hats, in their own cute way, had christened Project Encyclopedia. I strolled across the large, sunny office and glanced at the very latest organizational wall chart. I pointed to a small rectangle labeled "Power Source Subsection" depending via a straight line from a larger rectangle marked "Alien Physical Science Inquiry Section." In the small rectangle, very finely printed, were the names of an army major, a WAC corporal, and Doctors Lopez, Vinthe, and Mainzer.

"How're they doing?" I asked.

"Not much better, I'm afraid." Trowson turned away with a sigh from peering over my shoulder. "At least I deduce that from the unhappy way Mainzer bubbles into his soup spoon at lunch. Conversation between subsections originating in different offices on the departmental level is officially discouraged, you know. But I remember Mainzer from the university cafeteria. He bubbled into his soup the very same way when he was stuck on his solar refraction engine."

"Think Andy and Dandy are afraid we're too young to play with matches? Or maybe apelike creatures are too unpleasant looking to be allowed to circulate in their refined and aesthetic civilization?"

"I don't *know*, Dick." The prof ambled back to his desk and leafed irritably through his sociological notes. "If anything like that is true, why should they give us free run of their ship? Why would they reply so gravely and courteously to every question? If only their answers weren't so vague in our terms! But they are such complex and artistically minded creatures, so chockful of poetic sentiment and good manners, that it's impossible to make mathematical or even verbal sense out of their vast and circumlocutory explanations. Sometimes, when I think of their highly polished manners and their seeming lack of interest in the structure of their society, when I put that together with their spaceship, which looks like one of those tiny jade carvings that took a lifetime to accomplish—"

He trailed off and began riffling the pages like a Mississippi steamboat gambler going over somebody else's deck of cards.

"Isn't it possible we just don't have enough stuff as yet to understand them?"

"Yes. In fact, that's what we always come back to. Warbury points to the tremendous development in our language since the advent of technical vocabularies. He says that this process, just beginning with us, already affects our conceptual approach as well as our words. And, naturally, in a race so much further along— But if we could only find a science of theirs which bears a faint resemblance to one of ours!"

I felt sorry for him, standing there blinking futilely out of gentle, academic eyes.

"Cheer up, Prof. Maybe by the time old Suckfoot and his pal come back from the Grand Tour, you'll have unsnarled a sophistry and we'll be off this 'Me, friend; you come from across sea in great bird with many wings' basis that we seem to have wandered into."

And there you are, Alvarez: a cheap advertising small-brain like me, and I was that close. I should have said something then. Bet you wouldn't have nodded at me heavily and said, "I hope so, Dick. I desperately hope so." But, come to think of it, not only Trowson was trotting up that path. So was Warbury. So were Lopez, Vinthe, and Mainzer. So was I, among others.

I had a chance to relax when Andy and Dandy went abroad. My job wasn't exactly over, but the public-relations end was meshing right along, with me needed only once in a while to give a supervisory spin. Chiefly, I maintained close contact with my opposite number in various other sovereign states, giving out with experienced advice on how to sell the Boys from Betelgeuse. They had to adjust it to their own mass phobias and popular myths; but they were a little happier about it than I had been without any clear idea of what public behavior to expect of our visitors.

Remember, when I'd started, I hadn't even been sure those snails were housebroken.

I followed them in the newspapers. I pasted the pictures of the mikado receiving them next to their nice comments on the Taj Mahal. They weren't nearly so nice to the akhund of Swat, but then when you think of what the akhund said about them . . .

They tended to do that everywhere, giving just a little better than they got. For example, when they were presented with those newly created decorations in Red Square (Dandy got the Order of Extraterrestrial Friends of Soviet Labor while, for some abstruse reason, the Order of Heroic Interstellar Champion of the Soviet People was conferred upon Andy), they came out with a long, ringing speech about the scientific validity of communist government. It made for cheering, flower-tossing crowds in the Ukraine and Poland but a certain amount of restiveness in these United States.

But before I had to run my staff into overtime hours, whipping up press releases which recapitulated the aliens' statement before the joint houses of Congress and their lovely, sentimental comments at Valley Forge, the aliens were in Berne, telling the Swiss that only free enterprise could have produced the yodel, the Incabloc escapement in watches, and such a superb example of liberty; hadn't they had democracy long enough to have had it first, and wasn't it wonderful?

By the time they reached Paris I had the national affection pretty much under control again, although here and there a tabloid still muttered peevishly in its late city final. But, as always, Andy and Dandy put the clincher on. Even then I wondered whether they really liked DeRoges's latest abstraction for itself alone.

But they bought the twister sculpture, paying for it, since they had no cash of their own, with a thumb-sized gadget which actually melted marble to any degree of pattern delicacy the artist desired, merely by being touched to the appropriate surface. DeRoges threw away his chisels blissfully, but six of the finest minds in France retired to intensive nervous breakdowns after a week of trying to solve the tool's working principles.

It went over big here:

ANDY AND DANDY
PASS AS THEY GO

Betelgeuse Businessmen
Show Appreciation
for Value Received

This newspaper notes with pleasure the sound shopper's ethics behind the latest transaction of our distinguished guests from the elemental void. Understanding the inexorable law of supply and demand, these representatives of an advanced economic system refuse to succumb to the "gimmies." If certain other members of the human race were to examine carefully the true implications of . . .

So when they returned to the United States after being presented at the British court, they got juicy spreads in all the newspapers, a tug-whistle reception in New York harbor and the mayor's very chiefest deputy there on City Hall steps to receive them.

And even though people were more or less accustomed to them right now, they were somehow never shoved off page one. There was the time a certain furniture polish got a testimonial out of them in which the aliens announced that they'd had particularly happy and glossy results on their tiny shell toppers with the goo; and they used the large financial rewards of the testimonial to buy ten extremely rare orchids and have them sunk in plastic. And there was the time . . .

I missed the television on which it broke. I had gone to a side-street movie theater that night to see a revival of one of my favorite Chaplin pictures; and I'd never enjoyed the ostentatious greet-the-great hysterics of "Celebrity Salon" anyway. I hadn't had any idea of how long the M.C., Bill Bancroft, had waited to get Andy and Dandy on his program, and how much he was determined to make it count when the big night arrived.

Reconstructed and stripped of meaningless effusion, it went something like this:

Bancroft asked them if they weren't anxious to get home to the wife and kiddies. Andy explained patiently, for perhaps the thirty-fourth time, that, since they were hermaphrodites, they had no family in any humanly acceptable sense. Bancroft cut into the explanation to ask them what ties they *did* have. Chiefly the revitalizer, says Andy politely.

Revitalizer? What's a revitalizer? Oh, a machine they have to expose themselves to every decade or so, says Dandy. There's at least one revitalizer in every large city on their home planet.

Bancroft makes a bad pun, waits for the uproarious audience to regain control, then asks: And this revitalizer—just what does it do? Andy goes into a long-winded explanation, the gist of which is that the revitalizers stir up cytoplasm in animal cells and refresh them.

I see, cracks Bancroft; the pause every decade that refreshes. And then, after being refreshed, you have what as a result? "Oh," muses Dandy, "you might say we have no fear of cancer or any degenerative disease. Besides that, by exposing ourselves to revitalizers at regular intervals throughout our lifetime and refreshing our body cells, we quintuple our life expectancy. We live five times longer than we should. That's about what the revitalizer does, you might say," says Dandy. Andy, after thinking a bit, agrees. "That's about it."

Pandemonium, and not mild. Newspaper extras in all languages, including the Scandinavian. Lights burning late at night in the U.N. Headquarters with guards twenty deep around the site.

When President of the Assembly Sadhu asked them why they'd never mentioned revitalizers before, they did the snail equivalent of shrugging and said the Betelgeuse IX equivalent of nobody ever asked them.

President Sadhu cleared his throat, waved all complications aside with his long brown fingers, and announced, "That is not important. Not now. We must have revitalizers."

It seemed to take the aliens awhile to understand that. When they finally became convinced that we, as a species, were utterly entranced with the prospect of two to four centuries of life instead of fifty or sixty years, they went into a huddle.

But their race didn't make these machines for export, they explained regretfully. Just enough to service their population. And while they *could* see as how we might like and must obviously deserve to have these gadgets, there was none to ferry back from Betelgeuse.

Sadhu didn't even look around for advice. "What would your people want?" he asked. "What would they like in exchange for manufacturing these machines for us? We will pay almost any price within the power of this entire planet." A rumbling, eager "yes" in several languages rolled across the floor of the assembly.

Andy and Dandy couldn't think of a thing. Sadhu begged them to try. He personally escorted them to their spaceship, which was now parked in a restricted area in Central Park. "Good night, gentlemen," said President of the Assembly Sadhu. "Try—please try hard to think of an exchange."

They stayed inside their ship for almost six days while the world almost went insane with impatience. When I think of all the fingernails bitten that week by two billion people . . .

"Imagine!" Trowson whispered to me. He was pacing the floor as if he fully intended to walk all the way to Betelgeuse. "We'd just be children on a quintupled life scale, Dick. All my achievement and education, all yours, would be just the beginning! A man could learn five professions in such a life—and think what he could accomplish in one!"

I nodded, a little numb. I was thinking of the books I could read, the books I might write, if the bulk of my life stretched ahead of me and the advertising profession was just a passing phase at the beginning of it. Then again, somehow I'd never married, never had had a family. Not enough free time, I had felt. And now, at forty, I was too set in my ways. But a man can unset a lot in a century . . .

In six days the aliens came out. With a statement of price.

They believed they could persuade their people to manufacture a supply of revitalizers for us if— An IF writ very large indeed.

Their planet was woefully short of radioactive minerals, they explained apologetically. Barren worlds containing radium, uranium, and thorium had been discovered and claimed by other races, but the folk of Betelgeuse IX were forbidden by the ethics to wage aggressive war for territorial purposes. We had plenty of radioactive ore, which we used chiefly for war and biological research. The former was patently undesirable and the latter would be rendered largely unnecessary by the revitalizers.

So, in exchange, they wanted our radioactive elements. All of them, they stated humbly.

All right, we were a little surprised, even stunned. But the protests never *started* to materialize. There was an overwhelming chorus of "Sold!" from every quadrant of the globe. A couple of generals here, a few militaristic statesmen there managed to raise direly pointing forefingers before they were whisked out of position. A nuclear physicist or two howled about the future of subatomic research, but the peoples of the earth howled louder.

"Research? How much research can you do in a lifetime of three hundred years?"

Overnight, the United Nations became the central office of a planet-wide mining concession. National boundaries were superseded by pitchblende deposits and swords were beaten into pickaxes. Practically anyone with a good, usable arm enlisted in the shovel brigades for two or more months out of the year. Camaraderie flew on the winds of the world.

Andy and Dandy politely offered to help. They marked out on detailed contour maps the spots to be mined, and that included areas never suspected of radioactivity. They supplied us with fantastic but clear line drawings of devices for extracting the stuff from the ores in which it assayed poorly, and taught us the exact use of these devices, if not their basic principle.

They hadn't been joking. They wanted it all.

Then, when everything was running smoothly, they buzzed off for Betelgeuse to handle their part of the bargain.

Those two years were the most exhilarating of my life. And I'd say everyone feels the same, don't they, Alvarez? The knowledge that the world was working together, cheerfully, happily, for life itself. I put *my* year in at the Great Slave Lake, and I don't think anyone of my age and weight lifted more pitchblende.

Andy and Dandy came back in two huge ships, manned by weird snaillike robots. The robots did everything, while Andy and Dandy went on being lionized. From the two ships, almost covering the sky, the robots ferried back and forth in strange, spiral aircraft, bringing revitalizers down, carrying refined radioactive elements aloft. No one paid the slightest attention to their methods of instantaneous extraction from large quantities of ore: We were interested in just one throbbing thought—the revitalizers.

They worked. And that, so far as most of us were concerned, was that.

The revitalizers *worked*. Cancer disappeared; heart disease and kidney disease became immediately arrested. Insects which were introduced into the square one-story lab structures lived for a year instead of a few months. And humans—doctors shook their heads in wonder over people who had gone through.

All over the planet, near every major city, the long, patient, slowly moving lines stood outside the revitalizers, which were rapidly becoming something else.

"Temples!" shouted Mainzer. "They look on them as temples. A scientist investigating their operation is treated by the attendants like a dangerous lunatic in a nursery. Not that a man can find a clue in those ridiculously small motors. I no longer ask what their power source can be. Instead, I ask if they have a power at *all!*"

"The revitalizers are very precious now, in the beginning," Trowson soothed him. "After a while the novelty will wear off and you'll be able to investigate at your leisure. Could it be solar power?"

"No!" Mainzer shook his huge head positively. "Not solar power. Solar power I am sure I could recognize. As I am sure that the power supply of their ships and whatever runs these—these revitalizers are two entirely separate things. On the ships I have given up. But the revitalizers I believe I could solve. If only they would let me examine them. Fools! So terribly afraid I might damage one, and they would have to travel to another city for their elixir!"

We patted his shoulder, but we weren't really interested. Andy and Dandy left that week, after wishing us well in their own courteous and complex fashion. Whole population groups blew kisses at their mineral-laden ships.

Six months after they left, the revitalizers stopped.

"Am I certain?" Trowson snorted at my dismayed face. "One set of statistics proves it: Look at your death rate. It's back to pre-Betelgeuse normal. Or ask any doctor. Any doctor who can forget his

U.N. security oath, that is. There'll be really wild riots when the news breaks, Dick."

"But *why?*" I asked him. "Did we do something wrong?"

He started a laugh that ended with his teeth clicking frightenedly together. He rose and walked to the window, staring out into the star-diseased sky. "We did something wrong, all right. We trusted. We made the same mistake all natives have made when they met a superior civilization. Mainzer and Lopez have taken one of the revitalizer engine units apart. There was just a trace of it left, but this time they found the power source. Dick, my boy, the revitalizers were run on the fuel of completely pure radioactive elements!"

I needed a few moments to file that properly. Then I sat down in the easy chair very, very carefully. I made some hoarse, improbable sounds before croaking: "Prof, do you mean they wanted that stuff for themselves, for their *own* revitalizers? That everything they did on this planet was carefully planned so that they could con us with a maximum of friendliness all around? It doesn't seem—it just can't— Why, with their superior science, they could have conquered us if they'd cared to. They could have—"

"No, they couldn't have," Trowson whipped out. He turned to face me and flung his arms across each other. "They're a decadent, dying race; they wouldn't have attempted to conquer us. Not because of their ethics—this huge, horrible swindle serves to illustrate *that* aspect of them—but because they haven't the energy, the concentration, the interest. Andy and Dandy are probably representative of the few remaining who have barely enough git-up-and-go to *trick* backward peoples out of the all-important, life-sustaining revitalizer fuel."

The implications were just beginning to soak into my cortex. Me, the guy who did the most complete and colossal public-relations job of all time—I could just see what my relations with the public would be like if I was ever connected with this shambles.

"And without atomic power, Prof, we won't have space travel!"

He gestured bitterly. "Oh, we've been taken, Dick; the whole human race has been had. I know what you're going through, but think of me! I'm the failure, the man responsible. I'm supposed to be a sociologist! How could I have missed? *How?* It was all there: the lack of interest in their own culture, the overintellectualization of aesthetics, the involved methods of thought and expression, the exaggerated etiquette, even the very first thing of theirs we saw—

their ship—was too heavily stylized and intricately designed for a young, trusting civilization.

"They *had* to be decadent; every sign pointed to that conclusion. And of course the fact that they resort to the methods of fueling their revitalizers that we've experienced—when if we had their science, what might we not do, what substitutes might we not develop! No wonder they couldn't explain their science to us; I doubt if they understand it fully themselves. They are the profligate, inadequate, and sneak-thief heirs of what was once a soaring race!"

I was following my own unhappy images. "And we're still hicks. Hicks who've been sold the equivalent of the Brooklyn Bridge by some dressed-up sharpies from Betelgeuse."

Trowson nodded. "Or a bunch of poor natives who have sold their island home to a group of European explorers for a handful of brightly colored glass beads."

But of course we were both wrong, Alvarez. Neither Trowson nor I had figured on Mainzer or Lopez or the others. Like Mainzer said, a few years earlier and we would have been licked. But man had entered the atomic age some time before 1945 and people like Mainzer and Vinthe had done nuclear research back in the days when radioactive elements abounded on Earth. We had that and we had such tools as the cyclotron, the betatron. And, if our present company will pardon the expression, Alvarez, we are a young and vigorous race.

All we had to do was the necessary research.

The research was done. With a truly effective world government, with a population not only interested in the problem but recently experienced in working together—and with the grim incentive we had, Alvarez, the problem, as you know, was solved.

We developed artificial radioactives and refueled the revitalizers. We developed atomic fuels out of the artificial radioactives and we got space travel. We did it comparatively fast, and we weren't interested in a ship that just went to the moon or Mars. We wanted a star ship. And we wanted it so bad, so fast, that we have it now too.

Here we are. Explain the situation to them, Alvarez, just the way I told it to you, but with all the knee-bending and gobbledegook that a transplanted Brazilian with twelve years oriental trading experience can put into it. You're the man to do it—I can't talk like that. It's the only language those decadent slugs understand, so it's the only way we can talk to them. So talk to them, these slimy snails, these oysters on the quarter shell, these smart-alecky slugs. Don't forget to mention to them that the supply of radioactives they got from us won't last forever. Get that down in fine detail.

Then stress the fact that we've got artificial radioactives, and that they've got some things we know we want and lots of other things we mean to find out about.

Tell them, Alvarez, that we've come to collect tolls on that Brooklyn Bridge they sold us.

COST OF LIVING

December 1952

Robert Sheckley
(b. 1928)

A native of New York City, Robert Sheckley was in many respects the "typical" Galaxy writer, at least during the 1950s. He suffered, however, from the diseases of prolificity. His cleverly crafted, witty stories appeared so frequently (and not just in Galaxy and not just under the Sheckley by-line) that critics did not take him as seriously as they should have and now do. Although his career entered a major second phase in the late 1960s, longtime Galaxy readers remember those wonderful '50s stories: "Warm" (June 1953), "Hunting Problem" (September 1955), "Seventh Victim" (April 1953), "Something for Nothing" (June 1954), "Specialist" (May 1953), "A Ticket to Tranai" (October 1955), and the very popular AAA Ace Series that began with "Milk Run" (September 1954). There were two dozen more almost as good, and it was only fitting that when his career rose again in the next decade, it would be in the pages of Galaxy.

"Cost of Living" is both representative of fifties Sheckley and one of his best stories, dealing with a subject that has always fascinated him—the real, the unreal, and the maybe-real.

Memoir of Galaxy Magazine
by Robert Sheckley

My relationship with *Galaxy* began in the early 1950s, shortly after I began my career as a science-fiction writer. Horace Gold welcomed me into his circle, or "stable," as unfriendly critics sometimes called it. Horace held a weekly poker game on Friday nights, and I was usually in attendance, along with such regulars as William Tenn/ Phil Klass, Jerry Bixby, Fred Pohl, A. J. Budrys, and, from time to time, John Cage. Cage smiled a lot, never said a word, and was a steady winner, then as now. Historians interested in the relationship of poker to *Galaxy* science fiction of the 1950s should know that our favorite game was seven card high-low, although we also played six card high-low and even five card high-low with a tiddle.

Galaxy was a pioneer in exploring the dramatic and comedic possibilities of the "soft" sciences—psychology, sociology, anthropology, and guesswork—and was a godsend for those of us who couldn't understand physics, mathematics, or numerology. Also, *Galaxy* was my main short-story market in those days. Horace's insatiable need for short fiction was in great measure responsible for my large output in those years. It was exciting to have Horace call me up on a Monday and ask for a four-thousand-word story by Thursday "to fill a hole in the issue." This was probably a ploy, but it never failed to get me out of the coffee shops and behind a typewriter.

After a few years of high output, I caught the dreaded disease of Writer's Block. Horace knew all about that. He had it himself. All of the *Galaxy* writers were blocked. Our theme song should have been "I Can't Get Started." Horace cajoled and coaxed us, gave us ideas, situations, plots, invented imaginary deadlines, harangued us for hours on the telephone. It helped, but it didn't cure the disease. It seems to be the natural perversity of the short-story writer that the more acceptable his or her work is, the more difficult he or she finds it to do. Of course, it's also difficult to work if your work is not acceptable. Present-day technology has solved this problem by wiring a Ouija board into a computer. But it was no joke in the old days when we had to use basket-shift typewriters.

My most exciting time with *Galaxy* was writing and publishing the four-part serial "Time Killer," brought out later in book form as *Immortality, Inc.* One of my life goals had been to do a four-part serial. (Other cherished goals proved impossible: *Weird Tales* stopped publication before I could sell them a story of eldritch horror, and *Famous Fantastic Mysteries* vanished before I could do my imitation A. Merritt.)

The writing of "Time Killer" didn't come easily. I started working on it in Acapulco, typing on tortillas since I was too poor to afford paper. Perhaps that's why it was proclaimed The Most Edible Science Fiction Novel of the Year, although some reviewers thought my guacamole was in poor taste. Horace and I shared the Nobel Prize that year, and our subsequent history as members of the Ferrari racing team is too well known to repeat here.

At Horace Gold's request I also wrote under various pseudonyms in those early golden years. In fact, you may find several of my pseudonyms in this book writing about *their* experiences as *Galaxy* writers. Gold always encouraged my natural schizophrenia in his unending search for stories to fit in between the truss ads.

Those early years at *Galaxy* were an exciting time to be alive. Everybody I knew felt that way; nobody wanted to be dead.

In the dusty halls of my memory I see it all once again—the poker table with its green baize cloth, Horace Gold raising, Fred Pohl checking, John Cage smiling, Phil Klass fumpfing, and yours truly folding.

COST OF LIVING

Carrin decided that he could trace his present mood to Miller's suicide last week. But the knowledge didn't help him get rid of the vague, formless fears in the back of his mind. It was foolish. Miller's suicide didn't concern him.

But why had that fat, jovial man killed himself? Miller had had everything to live for—wife, kids, good job, and all the marvelous luxuries of the age. Why had he done it?

"Good morning, dear," Carrin's wife said as he sat down at the breakfast table.

"Morning, honey. Morning, Billy."

His son grunted something.

You just couldn't tell about people, Carrin decided, and dialed his breakfast. The meal was gracefully prepared and served by the new Avignon Electric Auto-cook.

His mood persisted, annoyingly enough since Carrin wanted to be in top form this morning. It was his day off, and the Avignon Electric finance man was coming. This was an important day.

He walked to the door with his son.

"Have a good day, Billy."

His son nodded, shifted his books, and started to school without answering. Carrin wondered if something was bothering him, too. He hoped not. One worrier in the family was plenty.

"See you later, honey." He kissed his wife as she left to go shopping.

At any rate, he thought, watching her go down the walk, she's happy. He wondered how much she'd spend at the A. E. store.

Checking his watch, he found that he had half an hour before the A. E. finance man was due. The best way to get rid of a bad mood was to drown it, he told himself, and headed for the shower.

The shower room was a glittering plastic wonder, and the sheer luxury of it eased Carrin's mind. He threw his clothes into the A. E. automatic Kleen-presser, and adjusted the shower spray to a notch above "brisk." The five-degrees-above-skin-temperature water beat against his thin white body. Delightful! And then a relaxing rub-dry in the A. E. Auto-towel.

Wonderful, he thought, as the towel stretched and kneaded his stringy muscles. And it should be wonderful, he reminded himself. The A. E. Auto-towel with shaving attachments had cost three hundred and thirteen dollars, plus tax.

But worth every penny of it, he decided, as the A. E. shaver came out of a corner and whisked off his rudimentary stubble. After all, what good was life if you couldn't enjoy the luxuries?

His skin tingled when he switched off the Auto-towel. He should have been feeling wonderful, but he wasn't. Miller's suicide kept nagging at his mind, destroying the peace of his day off.

Was there anything else bothering him? Certainly there was nothing wrong with the house. His papers were in order for the finance man.

"Have I forgotten something?" he asked out loud.

"The Avignon Electric finance man will be here in fifteen minutes," his A. E. bathroom Wall-reminder whispered.

"I know that. Is there anything else?"

The Wall-reminder reeled off its memorized data—a vast amount of minutiae about watering the lawn, having the Jet-lash checked, buying lamb chops for Monday, and the like. Things he still hadn't found time for.

"All right, that's enough." He allowed the A. E. Auto-dresser to dress him, skillfully draping a new selection of fabrics over his bony frame. A whiff of fashionable masculine perfume finished him and he went into the living room, threading his way between the appliances that lined the walls.

A quick inspection of the dials on the wall assured him that the house was in order. The breakfast dishes had been sanitized and stacked, the house had been cleaned, dusted, polished, his wife's garments had been hung up, his son's model rocket ships had been put back in the closet.

Stop worrying, you hypochondriac, he told himself angrily.

The door announced, "Mr. Pathis from Avignon Finance is here."

Carrin started to tell the door to open, when he noticed the Automatic Bartender.

Good God, why hadn't he thought of it!

The Automatic Bartender was manufactured by Castile Motors. He had bought it in a weak moment. A. E. wouldn't think very highly of that, since they sold their own brand.

He wheeled the bartender into the kitchen, and told the door to open.

"A very good day to you, sir," Mr. Pathis said.

Pathis was a tall, imposing man, dressed in a conservative tweed drape. His eyes had the crinkled corners of a man who laughs frequently. He beamed broadly and shook Carrin's hand, looking around the crowded living room.

"A beautiful place you have here, sir. Beautiful! As a matter of fact, I don't think I'll be overstepping the company's code to inform you that yours is the nicest interior in this section."

Carrin felt a sudden glow of pride at that, thinking of the rows of identical houses, on his block and the next, and the one after that.

"Now, then, is everything functioning properly?" Mr. Pathis asked, setting his briefcase on a chair. "Everything in order?"

"Oh, yes," Carrin said enthusiastically. "Avignon Electric never goes out of whack."

"The phono all right? Changes records for the full seventeen hours?"

"It certainly does," Carrin said. He hadn't had a chance to try out the phono, but it was a beautiful piece of furniture.

"The Solido-projector all right? Enjoying the programs?"

"Absolutely perfect reception." He had watched a program just last month, and it had been startlingly lifelike.

"How about the kitchen? Auto-cook in order? Recipemaster still knocking 'em out?"

"Marvelous stuff. Simply marvelous."

Mr. Pathis went on to inquire about his refrigerator, his vacuum cleaner, his car, his helicopter, his subterranean swimming pool, and the hundreds of other items Carrin had bought from Avignon Electric.

"Everything is swell," Carrin said, a trifle untruthfully since he hadn't unpacked every item yet. "Just wonderful."

"I'm so glad," Mr. Pathis said, leaning back with a sigh of relief. "You have no idea how hard we try to satisfy our customers. If a product isn't right, back it comes, no questions asked. We believe in pleasing our customers."

"I certainly appreciate it, Mr. Pathis."

Carrin hoped the A. E. man wouldn't ask to see the kitchen. He visualized the Castile Motors Bartender in there, like a porcupine in a dog show.

"I'm proud to say that most of the people in this neighborhood buy from us," Mr. Pathis was saying. "We're a solid firm."

"Was Mr. Miller a customer of yours?" Carrin asked.

"That fellow who killed himself?" Pathis frowned briefly. "He was, as a matter of fact. That amazed me, sir, absolutely amazed me. Why, just last month the fellow bought a brand-new Jet-lash from me, capable of doing three hundred and fifty miles an hour on a straight-away. He was as happy as a kid over it, and then to go and do a thing like that! Of course, the Jet-lash brought up his debt a little."

"Of course."

"But what did that matter? He had every luxury in the world. And then he went and hung himself."

"Hung himself?"

"Yes," Pathis said, the frown coming back. "Every modern convenience in his house, and he hung himself with a piece of rope. Probably unbalanced for a long time."

The frown slid off his face, and the customary smile replaced it. "But enough of that! Let's talk about you."

The smile widened as Pathis opened his briefcase. "Now, then, your account. You owe us two hundred and three thousand dollars and twenty-nine cents, Mr. Carrin, as of your last purchase. Right?"

"Right," Carrin said, remembering the amount from his own papers. "Here's my installment."

He handed Pathis an envelope, which the man checked and put in his pocket.

"Fine. Now you know, Mr. Carrin, that you won't live long enough to pay us the full two hundred thousand, don't you?"

"No, I don't suppose I will," Carrin said soberly.

He was only thirty-nine, with a full hundred years of life before him, thanks to the marvels of medical science. But at a salary of three thousand a year, he still couldn't pay it all off and have enough to support a family on at the same time.

"Of course, we would not want to deprive you of necessities. To say nothing of the terrific items that are coming out next year. Things you wouldn't want to miss, sir!"

Mr. Carrin nodded. Certainly he wanted new items.

"Well, suppose we make the customary arrangement. If you will just sign over your son's earnings for the first thirty years of his adult life, we can easily arrange credit for you."

Mr. Pathis whipped the papers out of his briefcase and spread them in front of Carrin.

"If you'll just sign here, sir."

"Well," Carrin said, "I'm not sure. I'd like to give the boy a start in life, not saddle him with—"

"But my dear sir," Pathis interposed, "this is for your son as well. He lives here, doesn't he? He has a right to enjoy the luxuries, the marvels of science."

"Sure," Carrin said. "Only—"

"Why, sir, today the average man is living like a king. A hundred years ago the richest man in the world couldn't buy what any ordinary citizen possesses at present. You mustn't look upon it as a debt. It's an investment."

"That's true," Carrin said dubiously.

He thought about his son and his rocket-ship models, his star charts, his maps. Would it be right? he asked himself.

"What's wrong?" Pathis asked cheerfully.

"Well, I was just wondering," Carrin said. "Signing over my son's earnings—you don't think I'm getting in a little too deep, do you?"

"Too deep? My dear sir!" Pathis exploded into laughter. "Do you know Mellon down the block? Well, don't say I said it, but he's already mortgaged his grandchildren's salary for their full life-expectancy! And he doesn't have half the goods he's made up his mind to own! We'll work out something for him. Service to the customer is our job and we know it well."

Carrin wavered visibly.

"And after you've gone, sir, they'll all belong to your son."

That was true, Carrin thought. His son would have all the marvelous things that filled the house. And after all, it was only thirty years out of a life of expectancy of a hundred and fifty.

He signed with a flourish.

"Excellent!" Pathis said. "And by the way, has your home got an A. E. Master-operator?"

It hadn't. Pathis explained that a Master-operator was new this year, a stupendous advance in scientific engineering. It was designed to take over all the functions of housecleaning and cooking, without its owner having to lift a finger.

"Instead of running around all day, pushing half a dozen different buttons, with the Master-operator all you have to do is push *one!* A remarkable achievement!"

Since it was only five hundred and thirty-five dollars, Carrin signed for one, having it added to his son's debt.

Right's right, he thought, walking Pathis to the door. This house will be Billy's some day. His and his wife's. They certainly will want everything up-to-date.

Just one button, he thought. That *would* be a time-saver!

After Pathis left, Carrin sat back in an adjustable chair and turned on the solido. After twisting the Ezi-dial, he discovered that there was nothing he wanted to see. He tilted back the chair and took a nap.

The something on his mind was still bothering him.

"Hello, darling!" He awoke to find his wife was home. She kissed him on the ear. "Look."

She had bought an A. E. Sexitizer-negligee. He was pleasantly surprised that that was all she had bought. Usually, Leela returned from shopping laden down.

"It's lovely," he said.

She bent over for a kiss, then giggled—a habit he knew she had picked up from the latest popular solido star. He wished she hadn't.

"Going to dial supper," she said, and went to the kitchen. Carrin smiled, thinking that soon she would be able to dial the meals without moving out of the living room. He settled back in his chair, and his son walked in.

"How's it going, son?" he asked heartily.

"All right," Billy answered listlessly.

"What'sa matter, son?" The boy stared at his feet, not answering. "Come on, tell dad what's the trouble."

Billy sat down on a packing case and put his chin in his hands. He looked thoughtfully at his father.

"Dad, could I be a master repairman if I wanted to be?"

Mr. Carrin smiled at the question. Billy alternated between wanting to be a master repairman and a rocket pilot. The repairmen were the elite. It was their job to fix the automatic repair machines. The repair machines could fix just about anything, but you couldn't have a machine fix the machine that fixed the machine. That was where the master repairmen came in.

But it was a highly competitive field and only a very few of the best brains were able to get their degrees. And, although the boy was bright, he didn't seem to have an engineering bent.

"It's possible, son. Anything is possible."

"But is it possible for me?"

"I don't know," Carrin answered, as honestly as he could.

"Well, I don't want to be a master repairman anyway," the boy said, seeing that the answer was no. "I want to be a space pilot."

"A space pilot, Billy?" Leela asked, coming into the room. "But there aren't any."

"Yes, there are," Billy argued. "We were told in school that the government is going to send some men to Mars."

"They've been saying that for a hundred years," Carrin said, "and they still haven't gotten around to doing it."

"They will this time."

"Why would you want to go to Mars?" Leela asked, winking at Carrin. "There are no pretty girls on Mars."

"I'm not interested in girls. I just want to go to Mars."

"You wouldn't like it, honey," Leela said. "It's a nasty old place with no air."

"It's got some air. I'd like to go there," the boy insisted sullenly. "I don't like it here."

"What's that?" Carrin asked, sitting up straight. "Is there anything you haven't got? Anything you want?"

"No, sir. I've got everything I want." Whenever his son called him "sir," Carrin knew that something was wrong.

"Look, son, when I was your age I wanted to go to Mars, too. I wanted to do romantic things. I even wanted to be a master repairman."

"Then why didn't you?"

"Well, I grew up. I realized that there were more important things. First I had to pay off the debt my father had left me, and then I met your mother—"

Leela giggled.

"—and I wanted a home of my own. It'll be the same with you. You'll pay off your debt and get married, the same as the rest of us."

Billy was silent for a while. Then he brushed his dark hair—straight, like his father's—back from his forehead and wet his lips.

"How come I have debts, sir?"

Carrin explained carefully. About the things a family needed for civilized living, and the cost of those items. How they had to be paid. How it was customary for a son to take on a part of his parents' debt, when he came of age.

Billy's silence annoyed him. It was almost as if the boy were reproaching him. After he had slaved for years to give the ungrateful whelp every luxury!

"Son," he said harshly, "have you studied history in school? Good. Then you know how it was in the past. Wars. How would you like to get blown up in a war?"

The boy didn't answer.

"Or how would you like to break your back for eight hours a day, doing work a machine should handle? Or be hungry all the time? Or cold, with the rain beating down on you, and no place to sleep?"

He paused for a response, got none, and went on. "You live in the most fortunate age mankind has ever known. You are surrounded by every wonder of art and science. The finest music, the greatest books and art, all at your fingertips. All you have to do is push a button." He shifted to a kindlier tone. "Well, what are you thinking?"

"I was just wondering how I could go to Mars," the boy said.

"With the debt, I mean. I don't suppose I could get away from that."

"Of course not."

"Unless I stowed away on a rocket."

"But you wouldn't do that."

"No, of course not," the boy said, but his tone lacked conviction.

"You'll stay here and marry a very nice girl," Leela told him.

"Sure I will," Billy said. "Sure." He grinned suddenly. "I didn't mean any of that stuff about going to Mars. I really didn't."

"I'm glad of that," Leela answered.

"Just forget I mentioned it," Billy said, smiling stiffly. He stood up and raced upstairs.

"Probably gone to play with his rockets," Leela said. "He's such a little devil."

The Carrins ate a quiet supper, and then it was time for Mr. Carrin to go to work. He was on night shift this month. He kissed his wife good-bye, climbed into Jet-lash, and roared to the factory. The automatic gates recognized him and opened. He parked and walked in.

Automatic lathes, automatic presses—everything was automatic. The factory was huge and bright, and the machines hummed softly to themselves, doing their job and doing it well.

Carrin walked to the end of the automatic washing-machine assembly line, to relieve the man there.

"Everything all right?" he asked.

"Sure," the man said. "Haven't had a bad one all year. These new models here have built-in voices. They don't light up like the old ones."

Carrin sat down where the man had sat and waited for the first washing machine to come through. His job was the soul of simplicity. He just sat there and the machines went by him. He pressed a button on them and found out if they were all right. They always were. After passing him, the washing machines went to the packaging section.

The first one slid by on the long slide of rollers. He pressed the starting button on the side.

"Ready for the wash," the washing machine said.

Carrin pressed the release and let it go by.

That boy of his, Carrin thought. Would he grow up and face his responsibilities? Would he mature and take his place in society? Carrin doubted it. The boy was a born rebel. If anyone got to Mars, it would be his kid.

But the thought didn't especially disturb him.

"Ready for the wash." Another machine went by.

Carrin remembered something about Miller. The jovial man had always been talking about the planets, always kidding about going off somewhere and roughing it. He hadn't, though. He had committed suicide.

"Ready for the wash."

Carrin had eight hours in front of him, and he loosened his belt to prepare for it. Eight hours of pushing buttons and listening to a machine announce its readiness.

"Ready for the wash."

He pressed the release.

"Ready for the wash."

Carrin's mind strayed from the job, which didn't need much attention in any case. He realized now what had been bothering him.

He didn't enjoy pushing buttons.

THE MODEL OF A JUDGE

October 1953

William Morrison
(b. 1906)

William Morrison (the pseudonym of Joseph Samachson) is, along with Mark Clifton, F. L. Wallace, Robert Abernathy, and others, one of the most shamefully neglected writers in the history of science fiction. Although his two novels (one a juvenile) are minor, his more than fifty stories in the sf field were frequently brilliant and always interesting.

Three of his best Galaxy efforts were "A Feast of Demons" (March 1958), "Bedside Manner" (May 1954), and "Dead Man's Planet" (February 1955). We're not sure whether the cake in the following story was ever entered in the Pillsbury Bake-Off.

Memoir by William Morrison

When Horace L. Gold became editor of *Galaxy* more than a quarter of a century ago, he gave new vigor to a growing trend in science fiction—the creation of characters, human and alien, with a fair share of human nature. Monsters were supposed to have plausible characters, too.

But Horace, the writers, who were finding that sf was an honorable form of literature, and the readers, whose tastes were becoming increasingly sophisticated, were not satisfied. And thus were the naive bug-eyed monsters of more innocent days routed by men and monsters whose attributes and understanding were discussed in terms associated, during those years, with psychoanalysis.

Horace was, of course, too good an editor to fall easy victim to extremist notions he encountered in the manuscripts that passed across his desk. Despite his own interest in psychoanalysis, it was the story that mattered.

As a professional scientist, I was fascinated and frequently disturbed by the implications of the work going on in the burgeoning field of human and animal behavior modification, which Pavlov had begun in the early years of our century. And so it seemed quite natural to me to extend that interest in the subject to an extraterrestrial being, and how it was affected by its enforced, painfully imposed modified behavior.

The situation had elements of pathos, as well as comedy, as the monster related to human beings, whose behavior had not been modified. "The Model of a Judge" was the result. It pleased both Horace and me.

THE MODEL OF A JUDGE

Ronar was reformed, if that was the right word, but he could see that they didn't trust him. Uneasiness spoke in their awkward hurried motions when they came near him; fear looked out of their eyes. He had to reassure himself that all this would pass. In time they'd learn to regard him as one of themselves and cease to recall what he had once been. For the time being, however, they still remembered. And so did he.

Mrs. Claymore, of the presiding committee, was babbling, "Oh, Mrs. Silver, it's so good of you to come. Have you entered the contest?"

"Not really," said Mrs. Silver with a modest laugh. "Of course I don't expect to win against so many fine women who are taking part. But I just thought I'd enter to—to keep things interesting."

"That was very kind of you. But don't talk about not winning. I still remember some of the dishes you served for dinner at your home that time George and I paid you a visit. Mmmm—they were really delicious."

Mrs. Silver uttered another little laugh. "Just ordinary recipes. I'm so glad you liked them, though."

"I certainly did. And I'm sure the judge will like your cake, too."

"The judge? Don't you usually have a committee?"

He could hear every word. They had no idea how sharp his sense of hearing was, and he had no desire to disconcert them further by letting them know. He could hear every conversation taking place in ordinary tones in the large reception room. When he concentrated he could make out the whispers. At this point he had to concentrate, for Mrs. Claymore leaned over and breathed into her friend's attentive ear.

"My dear, haven't you heard? We've had such trouble with that committee—there were such charges of favoritism! It was really awful."

"Really? But how did you find a judge, then?"

"Don't look now—no, I'll tell you what to do. Pretend I said something funny, and throw your head back and laugh. Take a quick glance at him while you do. He's sitting up there alone, on the platform."

Mrs. Silver laughed gracefully as directed, and her eyes swept the platform. She became so excited, she almost forgot to whisper.

"Why, he's—"

"Shhh. Lower your voice, my dear."

"Why—he isn't human!"

"He's supposed to be—now. But, of course, that's a matter of opinion!"

"But who on Earth thought of making him judge?"

"No one on Earth. Professor Halder, who lives over on that big asteroid the other side of yours, heard of the troubles we had, and came up with the suggestion. At first it seemed absurd—"

"It certainly seems absurd to me!" agreed Mrs. Silver.

"It was the only thing we could do. There was no one else we could trust."

"But what does he know about cakes?"

"My dear, he has the most exquisite sense of taste!"

"I still don't understand."

"It's superhuman. Before we adopted Professor Halder's suggestion, we gave him a few tests. The results simply left us gasping. We could mix all sorts of spices—the most delicate, most exotic herbs from Venus or Mars, and the strongest, coarsest flavors from Earth or one of the plant-growing asteroids—and he could tell us everything we had added, and exactly how much."

"I find that hard to believe, Matilda."

"Isn't it? It's honestly incredible. If I hadn't seen him do it myself, I wouldn't have believed it."

"But he doesn't have human preferences. Wasn't he—wasn't he—"

"Carnivorous? Oh, yes. They say he was the most vicious creature imaginable. Let an animal come within a mile of him, and he'd scent it and be after it in a flash. He and the others of his kind made the moon he came from uninhabitable for any other kind of intelligent life. Come to think of it, it may have been the very moon we're on now!"

"Really?"

"Either this, or some other moon of Saturn's. We had to do something about it. We didn't want to kill them off, naturally; that would have been the easiest way, but so uncivilized! Finally, our scientists came up with the suggestion for psychological reforming. Professor Halder told us how difficult it all was, but it seems to have worked. In his case, at least."

Mrs. Silver stole another glance. "Did it? I don't notice any one going near him."

"Oh, we don't like to tempt fate, Clara. But if there were really any danger, I'm sure the psychologists would never have let him out of their clutches."

"I hope not. But psychologists take the most reckless risks sometimes—with other people's lives!"

"Well, there's one psychologist who's risking his own life—and his own wife, too. You know Dr. Cabanis, don't you?"

"Only by sight. Isn't his wife that stuck-up thing?"

"That's the one. Dr. Cabanis is the man who had actual charge of reforming him. And he's going to be here. His wife is entering a cake."

"Don't tell me that she really expects to win!"

"She bakes well, my dear. Let's give the she-devil her due. How on Earth an intelligent man like Dr. Cabanis can stand her, I don't know, but, after all, he's the psychologist, not I, and he could probably explain it better than I could."

Ronar disengaged his attention.

So Dr. Cabanis was here. He looked around, but the psychologist was not in sight. He would probably arrive later.

The thought stirred a strange mixture of emotions. Some of the most painful moments of his life were associated with the presence of Dr. Cabanis. His early life, the life of a predatory carnivore, had been an unthinkingly happy one. He supposed that he could call his present life a happy one too, if you weren't overly particular how you defined the term. But that period in between!

That had been, to say the least, painful. Those long sessions with Dr. Cabanis had stirred him to the depths of a soul he hadn't known he possessed. The electric shocks and the druggings he hadn't minded so much. But the gradual reshaping of his entire psyche, the period of basic instruction, in which he had been taught to hate his old life so greatly that he could no longer go back to it even if the way were open, and the conditioning for a new and useful life with human beings—that was torture of the purest kind.

If he had known what was ahead of him, he wouldn't have gone through it all. He'd have fought until he dropped, as so many of the others like him did. Still, now that it was over, he supposed that the results were worth the pain. He had a position that was more important than it seemed at first glance. He exercised control over a good part of the food supply intended for the outer planets, and his word was trusted implicitly. Let him condemn an intended shipment, and cancellation followed automatically, without the formality of confirmation by laboratory tests. He was greatly admired. And feared.

They had other feelings about him too. He overheard one whisper that surprised him. "My dear, I think he's really handsome."

"But, Charlotte, how can you say that about someone who isn't even human!"

"He looks more human than many human beings do. And his clothes fit him beautifully. I wonder—does he have a tail?"

"Not that I know of."

"Oh." There was disappointment in the sound. "He looks like a pirate."

"He was a kind of wolf, they tell me. You'd never guess, to see him, that he ran on all fours, would you?"

"Of course not. He's so straight and dignified."

"It just shows you what psychology can do."

"Psychology, and a series of operations, dear ladies," he thought sarcastically. "Without them I wouldn't be able to stand so nice and straight with the help of all the psychologists in this pretty little solar system of ours."

From behind a potted Martian nut-cactus came two low voices—not whispers this time. And there was several octaves' difference in pitch between them. One male, one female.

The man said, "Don't be worried, sweetheart. I'll match your cooking and baking against anybody's."

There was a curious sound, between a click and a hiss. What human beings called a kiss, he thought. Between the sexes, usually an indication of affection or passion. Sometimes, especially within the ranks of the female sex, a formality beyond which warfare could be waged.

The girl said tremulously, "But these women have so much experience. They've cooked and baked for years."

"Haven't you, for your own family?"

"Yes, but that isn't the same thing. I had to learn from a cookbook. And I had no one with experience to stand over me and teach me."

"You've learned faster that way than you'd have done with some of these old hens standing at your elbow and giving you directions. You cook *too* well. I'll be fat in no time."

"Your mother doesn't think so. And your brother said something about a bride's biscuits—"

"The older the joke, the better Charles likes it. Don't let it worry you." He kissed her again. "Have confidence in yourself, dear. You're going to win."

"Oh, Gregory, it's awfully nice of you to say so, but really I feel so unsure of myself."

"If only the judge were human and took a look at you, nobody else would stand a chance. Have I told you within the last five minutes that you're beautiful?"

Ronar disengaged his attention again. He found human lovemaking as repulsive as most human food.

He picked up a few more whispers. And then Dr. Cabanis came in.

The good doctor looked around, smiled, greeted several ladies of his acquaintance as if he were witnessing a private striptease of their souls, and then came directly up to the platform. "How are you, Ronar?"

"Fine, doctor. Are you here to keep an eye on me?"

"I hardly think that's necessary. I have an interest in the results of the judging. My wife has baked a cake."

"I had no idea that cake baking was so popular a human avocation."

"Anything that requires skill is sure to become popular among us. By the way, Ronar, I hope you don't feel hurt."

"Hurt, doctor? What do you mean?"

"Come now, you understand me well enough. These people still don't trust you. I can tell by the way they keep their distance."

"I can take human frailty into account. Frailty, and lack of opportunity. These men and women haven't had the opportunity for extensive psychological treatment that I've had. I don't expect too much of them."

"You've scored a point there, Ronar."

"Isn't there something that can be done for them, doctor? Some treatment that it would be legal to give them?"

"It would have to be voluntary. You see, Ronar, you were considered only an animal, and treatment was necessary to save your life. But these people are supposed to have rights. One of their rights is to be left alone with their infirmities. Besides, none of them are seriously ill. They hurt no one."

For a second Ronar had a human temptation. It was on the tip of his tongue to say, "Your wife too, doctor? People wonder how you stand her." But he resisted it. He had resisted more serious temptations.

A gong sounded gently but pervasively. Dr. Cabanis said, "I hope you have no resentment against me at this stage of the game, Ronar. I'd hate to have my wife lose the prize because the judge was prejudiced."

"Have no fear, doctor. I take professional pride in my work. I will choose only the best."

"Of course, the fact that the cakes are numbered and not signed with the names of their creators will make thing simpler."

"That would matter with human judges. It does not affect me."

Another gong sounded, more loudly this time. Gradually the conversation stopped. A man in a full dress suit, with yellow stripes down the sides of his shorts and tails hanging both front and rear, climbed up on the platform. His eyes shone with a greeting so warm that the fear was almost completely hidden. "How are you, Ronar? Glad to see you."

"I'm fine, senator. And you?"

"Couldn't be better. Have a cigar."

"No, thank you. I don't smoke."

"That's right, you don't. Besides, I'd be wasting the cigar. You don't vote!" He laughed heartily.

"I understand that they're passing a special law to let—people—like me vote at the next election."

"I'm for it, Ronar, I'm for it. You can count on me."

The chairman came up on the platform, a stout and dignified woman who smiled at both Ronar and the senator, and shook hands with both without showing signs of distaste for either. The assembled competitors and spectators took seats.

The chairman cleared her throat. "Ladies and gentlemen, let us open this meeting by singing the 'Hymn of All Planets.'"

They all rose, Ronar with them. His voice wasn't too well adapted to singing, but neither, it seemed, were most of the human voices. And, at least, he knew all the words.

The chairman proceeded to greet the gathering formally, in the name of the presiding committee.

Then she introduced Senator Whitten. She referred archly to the fact that the senator had long since reached the age of indiscretion and had so far escaped marriage. He was an enemy of the female sex, but they'd let him speak to them anyway.

Senator Whitten just as archly took up the challenge. He had escaped more by good luck—if you could call it good—than by good management. But he was sure that if he had ever had the fortune to encounter some of the beautiful ladies here this fine day, and to taste the products of their splendid cooking and baking, he would have been a lost man. He would long since have committed polygamy.

Senator Whitten then launched into a paean of praise for the ancient art of preparing food.

Ronar's attention wandered. So did that of a good part of the audience. His ears picked up another conversation, this time whispered between a man and a woman in the front row.

The man said, "I should have put your name on it, instead of mine."

"That would have been silly. All my friends know that I can't bake. And it would look so strange if I won."

"It'll look stranger if I win. I can imagine what the boys in the shop will say."

"Oh, the boys in the shop are stupid. What's so unmanly in being able to cook and bake?"

"I'm not anxious for the news to get around."

"Some of the best chefs have been men."

"I'm not a chef."

"Stop worrying." There was exasperation in the force of her whisper. "You won't win anyway."

"I don't know. Sheila—"

"What?"

"If I win, will you explain to everybody how manly I really am? Will you be my character witness?"

She repressed a giggle.

"If you won't help me, I'll have to go around giving proof myself."

"Shhh, someone will hear you."

Senator Whitten went on and on.

Ronar thought back to the time when he had wandered over the surface of this, his native satellite. He no longer had the old desires, the old appetites. Only the faintest of ghosts still persisted, ghosts with no power to do harm. But he could remember the old feeling of pleasure, the delight of sinking his teeth into an animal he had brought down himself, the savage joy of gulping the tasty flesh. He didn't eat raw meat any more; he didn't eat meat at all. He had been conditioned against it. He was now half vegetarian, half synthetarian. His meals were nourishing, healthful, and a part of his life he would rather not think about.

He took no real pleasure in the tasting of the cakes and other delicacies that born human beings favored. His sense of taste had remained keen only to the advantage of others. To himself it was a tantalizing mockery.

Senator Whitten's voice came to a sudden stop. There was applause. The senator sat down; the chairman stood up. The time for the judging had arrived.

They set out the cakes—more than a hundred of them, topped by icings of all colors and all flavors. The chairman introduced Ronar and lauded both his impartiality and the keenness of his sense of taste.

They had a judging card ready. Slowly Ronar began to go down the line.

They might just as well have signed each cake with its maker's name. As he lifted a portion of each to his mouth, he could hear the quick intake of breath from the woman who had baked it, could catch the whispered warning from her companion. There were few secrets they could keep from him.

At first they all watched intently. When he had reached the fifth cake, however, a hand went up in the audience. "Madam chairman!"

"Please, ladies, let us not interrupt the judging."

"But I don't think the judging is right. Mr. Ronar tastes hardly more than a crumb of each!"

"A minimum of three crumbs," Ronar corrected her. "One from the body of the cake, one from the icing, and an additional crumb from each filling between layers."

"But you can't judge a cake that way! You have to eat it, take a whole mouthful—"

"Please, madam, permit me to explain. A crumb is all I need. I can analyze the contents of the cake sufficiently well from that. Let me take, for instance, cake Number 4, made from an excellent recipe, well baked. Martian granis flour, goover eggs, tingan-flavored salt, a trace of Venusian orange spice, synthetic shortening of the best quality. The icing is excellent, made with rare dipentose sugars which give it a delightful flavor. Unfortunately, however, the cake will not win first prize."

An anguished cry rose from the audience. "Why?"

"Through no fault of your own, dear lady. The purberries used in making the filling were not freshly picked. They have the characteristic flavor of refrigeration."

"The manager of the store swore to me that they were fresh! Oh, I'll kill him, I'll murder him—"

She broke down in a flood of tears.

Ronar said to the lady who had protested, "I trust, madam, that you will now have slightly greater confidence in my judgment."

She blushed and subsided.

Ronar went on with the testing. Ninety percent of the cakes he was able to discard at once, from some fault in the raw materials used or in the method of baking. Eleven cakes survived the first elimination contest.

He went over them again, more slowly this time. When he had completed the second round of tests, only three were left. Number 17 belonged to Mrs. Cabanis. Number 43 had been made by the man who had argued with his wife. Number 64 was the product of the young bride, whom he had still not seen.

Ronar paused. "My sense of taste is somewhat fatigued. I shall have to ask for a short recess before proceeding further."

There was a sigh from the audience. The tension was not released, it was merely relaxed for a short interval.

Ronar said to the chairman, "I should like a few moments of fresh air. That will restore me. Do you mind?"

"Of course not, Mr. Ronar."

He went outside. Seen through the thin layer of air which surrounded the group of buildings, and the plastic bubble which kept the air from escaping into space, the stars were brilliant and peaceful. The sun, far away, was like a father star who was too kind to obliterate his children. Strange, he thought, to recall that this was his native satellite. A few years ago it had been a different world. As for himself, he could live just as well outside the bubble as in it, as well in rarefied air as in dense. Suppose he were to tear a hole in the plastic—

Forbidden thoughts. He checked himself, and concentrated on the three cakes and the three contestants.

"You aren't supposed to let personal feelings interfere. You aren't even supposed to know who baked those cakes. But you know, all right. And you can't keep personal feelings from influencing your judgment.

"Any one of these cakes is good enough to win. Choose whichever you please, and no one will have a right to criticize. To which are you going to award the prize?

"Number 17? Mrs. Cabanis is, as one of the other women has so aptly termed her, a bitch on wheels. If she wins, she'll be insufferable. And she'll probably make her husband suffer. Not that he doesn't deserve it. Still, he thought he was doing me a favor. Will I be doing him a favor if I have his wife win?

"Number 64, now, is insufferable in her own right. That loving conversation with her husband would probably disgust even human ears. On the other hand, there is this to be said for her winning, it will make the other women furious. To think that a young snip, just married, without real experience in homemaking, should walk away with a prize of this kind!

"Ah, but if the idea is to burn them up, why not give the prize to Number 43? They'd be ready to drop dead with chagrin. To think that a mere man should beat them at their own specialty! They'd never be able to hold their heads up again. The man wouldn't feel too happy about it, either. Yes, if it's a matter of getting back at these humans for the things they've done to me, if it's a question of showing them what I really think of them, Number 43 should get it.

"On the other hand, I'm supposed to be a model of fairness. That's why I got the job in the first place. Remember, Ronar? Come on, let's go in and try tasting them again. Eat a mouthful of each cake, much as you hate the stuff. Choose the best on its merits."

They were babbling when he walked in, but the babbling stopped quickly. The chairman said, "Are we ready, Mr. Ronar?"

"All ready."

The three cakes were placed before him. Slowly he took a mouthful of Number 17. Slowly he chewed it and swallowed it. Number 43 followed, then Number 64.

After the third mouthful, he stood lost in thought. One was practically as good as another. He could still choose which he pleased.

The assemblage had quieted down. Only the people most concerned whispered nervously.

Mrs. Cabanis, to her psychologist husband: "If I don't win, it'll be your fault. I'll pay you back for this."

The good doctor's fault? Yes, you could figure it that way if you wanted to. If not for Dr. Cabanis, Ronar wouldn't be the judge. If Ronar weren't the judge, Mrs. C. would win, she thought. Hence it was all her husband's fault. Q.E.D.

The male baker to his wife: "If he gives the prize to me, I'll brain him. I should never have entered this."

"It's too late to worry now."

"I could yell 'Fire,'" he whispered hopefully. "I could create a panic that would empty the hall. And then I'd destroy my cake."

"Don't be foolish. And stop whispering."

The young post-honeymooning husband: "You're going to win, dear; I can feel it in my bones."

"Oh, Greg, please don't try to fool me. I've resigned myself to losing."

"You won't lose."

"I'm afraid. Put your arm around me, Greg. Hold me tight. Will you still love me if I lose?"

"Mmmm." He kissed her shoulder. "You know, I didn't fall in

love with you for your cooking, sweetheart. You don't have to bake any cakes for me. You're good enough to eat yourself."

"He's right," thought Ronar, as he stared at her. "The man's right. Not in the way he means, but he's right." And suddenly, for one second of decision, Ronar's entire past seemed to flash through his mind.

The young bride never knew why she won first prize.

THE HOLES AROUND MARS

January 1954

Jerome Bixby
(b. 1923)

In his long career, Jerome Bixby has written many hundreds of stories of all kinds both in and outside of science fiction. "It's a Good Life," which appeared in one of the first anthologies of original sf stories (Star Science Fiction Stories, 1953), is certainly the most famous. Bixby was the editor of Planet Stories from 1950 to 1951, assisted H. L. Gold at Galaxy in 1953, and has written for films and television.

He appeared in Galaxy with "Zen" (October 1952), the novella "The Bad Life" (February 1963), and the following story. The best of his science fiction can be found in his collection Space by the Tale (1964).

Memoir by Jerome Bixby

It's not easy to reminisce about a story written twenty-six years ago (what was that title again?), but I'll give it a try.

I first visualized "The Holes Around Mars" as a short-short-short —little more than an extended pun. It was Horace Gold who persuaded me to expand the story and characters to include more action, more color—and more puns. And of course it was Horace who first bought and printed it.

I remember having particular fun in dreaming up things for the horrendously dense little moon to do to the surface of Mars as it zipped around in its tight orbit. The Martians, and their manner of dealing with the moon's predictable assaults, also occurred to me as an afterthought, requiring a rewrite that further extended the story's length. Thus my five-hundred-word pun turned into a five-thousand-word short.

Later I became Horace's assistant editor, on *Galaxy* and *Beyond*, and I believe, not too humbly, that those magazines succeeded in publishing the very best science fiction and fantasy to appear at that time. Horace was a gem to work for, the least temperamental of editors, though very tough-minded about the particular mix of science and humanity he wanted in stories he bought. I will also never forget the Friday night poker games at Horace's—a tradition for Asimov, Budrys, Phil Klass (William Tenn), myself, and so many others.

An examination of Viking photos from the surface of Mars reveals no holes, so apparently I wrote fiction. Well, sf can't *always* come true.

THE HOLES AROUND MARS

Spaceship crews should be selected on the basis of their nonirritating qualities as individuals. No chronic complainers, no hypochondriacs, no bugs on cleanliness—particularly no one-man parties. I speak from bitter experience.

Because on the first expedition to Mars, Hugh Allenby damned near drove us nuts with his puns. We finally got so we just ignored them.

But no one can ignore that classic last one—it's written right into the annals of astronomy, and it's there to stay.

Allenby, in command of the expedition, was first to set foot outside the ship. As he stepped down from the air-lock of the *Mars I*, he placed that foot on a convenient rock, caught the toe of his weighted boot in a hole in the rock, wrenched his ankle, and smote the ground with his pants.

Sitting there, eyes pained behind the transparent shield of his oxygen mask, he stared at the rock.

It was about five feet high. Ordinary granite—no special shape—and several inches below its summit, running straight through it in a northeasterly direction, was a neat round four-inch hole.

"I'm *upset* by the *hole* thing," he grunted.

The rest of us scrambled out of the ship and gathered around his plump form. Only one or two of us winced at his miserable double pun.

"Break anything, Hugh?" asked Burton, our pilot, kneeling beside him.

"Get out of my way, Burton," said Allenby. "You're obstructing my view."

Burton blinked. A man constructed of long bones and caution, he angled out of the way, looking around to see what he was obstructing view *of*.

He saw the rock and the round hole through it. He stood very still, staring. So did the rest of us.

"Well, I'll be damned," said Janus, our photographer. "A hole."

"In a rock," added Gonzales, our botanist.

"Round," said Randolph, our biologist.

"An *artifact*," finished Allenby softly.

Burton helped him to his feet. Silently we gathered around the rock.

Janus bent down and put an eye to one end of the hole. I bent down and looked through the other end. We squinted at each other.

As mineralogist, I was expected to opinionate. "Not drilled," I said slowly. "Not chipped. Not melted. Certainly not eroded."

I heard a rasping sound by my ear and straightened. Burton was scratching a thumbnail along the rim of the hole. "Weathered," he said. "Plenty old. But I'll bet it's a perfect circle, if we measure."

Janus was already fiddling with his camera, testing the cooperation of the tiny distant sun with a lightmeter.

"Let us see *weather* it is or not," Allenby said.

Burton brought out a steel tape measure. The hole was four and three-eighths inches across. It was perfectly circular and about sixteen inches long. And four feet above the ground.

"But why?" said Randolph. "Why should anyone bore a four-inch tunnel through a rock way out in the middle of the desert?"

"Religious symbol," said Janus. He looked around, one hand on his gun. "We'd better keep an eye out—maybe we've landed on sacred ground or something."

"A totem *hole*, perhaps," Allenby suggested.

"Oh, I don't know," Randolph said—to Janus, not Allenby. As I've mentioned, we always ignored Allenby's puns. "Note the lack of ornamentation. Not at all typical of religious articles."

"On Earth," Gonzales reminded him. "Besides, it might be utilitarian, not symbolic."

"Utilitarian, how?" asked Janus.

"An altar for snakes," Burton said dryly.

"Well," said Allenby, "you can't deny that it has its *holy* aspects."

"Move your hand, will you, Peters?" asked Janus.

I did. When Janus's camera had clicked, I bent again and peered through the hole. "It sights on that low ridge over there," I said. "Maybe it's some kind of surveying setup. I'm going to take a look."

"Careful," warned Janus. "Remember, it may be sacred."

As I walked away, I heard Allenby say, "Take some scrapings from the inside of the hole, Gonzales. We might be able to determine if anything is kept in it . . ."

One of the stumpy, purplish, barrel-type cacti on the ridge had a long vertical bite out of it . . . as if someone had carefully carved out a narrow U-shaped section from the top down, finishing the bottom of the U in a neat semicircle. It was as flat and clean-cut as the inside surface of a horseshoe magnet.

I hollered. The others came running. I pointed.

"Oh, my God!" said Allenby. "Another one."

The pulp of the cactus in and around the U-hole was dried and dead looking.

Silently Burton used his tape measure. The hole measured four and three-eighths inches across. It was eleven inches deep. The semicircular bottom was about a foot above the ground.

"This ridge," I said, "is about three feet higher than where we landed the ship. I bet the hole in the rock and the hole in this cactus are on the same level."

Gonzales said slowly, "This was not done all at once. It is a result of periodic attacks. Look here and here. These overlapping depressions along the outer edges of the hole—" he pointed—"on this side of the cactus. They are the signs of repeated impact. And the scallop effect on *this* side, where whatever made the hole emerged. There are juices still oozing—not at the point of impact, where the plant is desiccated, but below, where the shock was transmitted—"

A distant shout turned us around. Burton was at the rock, beside the ship. He was bending down, his eye to the far side of the mysterious hole.

He looked for another second, then straightened.

"They line up," he said when he reached us. "The bottom of the hole in the cactus is right in the middle when you sight through the hole in the rock."

"As if somebody came around and whacked the cactus regularly," Janus said, looking around warily.

"To keep the line of sight through the holes clear?" I wondered. "Why not just remove the cactus?"

"Religious," Janus explained.

The gauntlet he had discarded lay ignored on the ground, in the shadow of the cactus. We went on past the ridge toward an outcropping of rock about a hundred yards farther on. We walked silently, each of us wondering if what we half-expected would really be there.

It was. In one of the tall, weathered spires in the outcropping, some ten feet below its peak and four feet above the ground, was a round four-inch hole.

Allenby sat down on a rock, nursing his ankle, and remarked that anybody who believed this crazy business was really happening must have holes in the rocks in his head.

Burton put his eye to the hole and whistled. "Sixty feet long if it's an inch," he said. "The other end's just a pinpoint. But you can see it. The damn thing's perfectly straight."

I looked back the way we had come. The cactus stood on the ridge, with its U-shaped bite, and beyond was the ship, and beside it the perforated rock.

"If we surveyed," I said, "I bet the holes would all line up right to the last millimeter."

"But," Randolph complained, "why would anybody go out and bore holes in things all along a line through the desert?"

"Religious," Janus muttered. "It doesn't *have* to make sense."

We stood there by the outcropping and looked out along the wide, red desert beyond. It stretched flatly for miles from this point, south toward Mars's equator—dead sandy wastes, crisscrossed by the "canals," which we had observed while landing to be great straggly patches of vegetation, probably strung along underground waterflows.

BLONG—G—G—G— . . . *st—st—st*— . . .

We jumped half out of our skins. Ozone bit at our nostrils. Our hair stirred in the electrical uproar.

"L—look," Janus chattered, lowering his smoking gun.

About forty feet to our left, a small rabbity creature poked its head from behind a rock and stared at us in utter horror.

Janus raised his gun again.

"Don't bother," said Allenby tiredly. "I don't think it intends to attack."

"But—"

"I'm sure it isn't a Martian with religious convictions."

Janus wet his lips and looked a little shamefaced. "I guess I'm kind of taut."

"That's what I *taut*," said Allenby.

The creature darted from behind its rock and, looking at us over its shoulder, employed six legs to make small but very fast tracks.

We turned our attention again to the desert. Far out, black against Mars's azure horizon, was a line of low hills.

"Shall we go look?" asked Burton, eyes gleaming at the mystery.

Janus hefted his gun nervously. It was still crackling from the discharge. "I say let's get back to the ship!"

Allenby sighed. "My leg hurts." He studied the hills. "Give me the field glasses."

Randolph handed them over. Allenby put them to the shield of his mask, and adjusted them.

After a moment he sighed again. "There's a hole. On a plane surface that catches the sun. A lousy damned round little impossible hole."

"Those hills," Burton observed, "must be thousands of feet thick."

The argument lasted all the way back to the ship.

Janus, holding out for his belief that the whole thing was of religious origin, kept looking around for Martians as if he expected them to pour screaming from the hills.

Burton came up with the suggestion that perhaps the holes had been made by a disintegrator-ray.

"It's possible," Allenby admitted. "This might have been the scene of some great battle—"

"With only one such weapon?" I objected.

Allenby swore as he stumbled. "What do you mean?"

"I haven't seen any other lines of holes—only the one. In a battle, the whole joint should be cut up."

That was good for a few moments' silent thought. Then Allenby said, "It might have been brought out by one side as a last resort. Sort of an ace in the hole."

I resisted the temptation to mutiny. "But would even one such weapon, in battle, make only *one* line of holes? Wouldn't it be played in an arc against the enemy? You know it would."

"Well—"

"Wouldn't it cut slices out of the landscape, instead of boring holes? And wouldn't it sway or vibrate enough to make the holes miles away from it something less than perfect circles?"

"It could have been very firmly mounted."

"Hugh, does that sound like a practical weapon to you?"

Two seconds of silence. "On the other hand," he said, "instead of a war, the whole thing might have been designed to frighten some primitive race—or even some kind of beast—the *hole* out of here. A demonstration—"

"Religious," Janus grumbled, still looking around.

We walked on, passing the cactus on the low ridge.

"Interesting," said Gonzales. "The evidence that whatever causes the phenomenon has happened again and again. I'm afraid that the war theory—"

"Oh, my God!" gasped Burton.

We stared at him.

"The ship," he whispered. "It's right in line with the holes! If whatever made them is still in operation . . ."

"Run!" yelled Allenby, and we ran like fiends.

We got the ship into the air, out of line with the holes to what we fervently hoped was safety, and then we realized we were admitting our fear that the mysterious hole-maker might still be lurking around.

Well, the evidence was all for it, as Gonzales had reminded us— that cactus had been oozing.

We cruised at twenty thousand feet and thought it over.

Janus, whose only training was in photography, said, "Some kind of omnivorous animal? Or bird? Eats rocks and everything?"

"I will not totally discount the notion of such an animal," Randolph said. "But I will resist to the death the suggestion that it forages with geometric precision."

After a while, Allenby said, "Land, Burton. By that 'canal.' Lots of plant life—fauna, too. We'll do a little collecting."

Burton set us down feather-light at the very edge of the sprawling flat expanse of vegetation, commenting that the scene reminded him of his native Texas pear-flats.

We wandered in the chilly air, each of us except Burton pursuing his specialty. Randolph relentlessly stalked another of the rabbity creatures. Gonzales was carefully digging up plants and stowing them in jars. Janus was busy with his cameras, recording every aspect of Mars transferable to film. Allenby walked around, helping anybody who needed it. As astronomer, he'd done half his work on the way to Mars and would do the other half on the return trip. Burton lounged in the sun, his back against a ship's fin, and played chess with Allenby, who was calling out his moves in a bull roar. I grubbed for rocks.

My search took me farther and farther away from the others—all I could find around the "canal" was gravel, and I wanted to chip at some big stuff. I walked toward a long rise a half mile or so away, beyond which rose an enticing array of house-sized boulders.

As I moved out of earshot, I heard Randolph snarl, "Burton, *will* you stop yelling, 'Kt to B-2 and check?' Every time you open your yap, this critter takes off on me."

Then I saw the groove.

It started right where the ground began to rise—a thin, shallow, curve-bottomed groove in the dirt at my feet, about half an inch across, running off straight toward higher ground.

With my eyes glued to it, I walked. The ground slowly rose. The groove deepened, widened—now it was about three inches across, about one and a half deep.

I walked on, holding my breath. Four inches wide. Two inches deep.

The ground rose some more. Four and three-eighths inches wide. I didn't have to measure it—I *knew*.

Now, as the ground rose, the edges of the groove began to curve inward over the groove. They touched. No more groove.

The ground had risen, the groove had stayed level and gone underground.

Except that now it wasn't a groove. It was a round tunnel.

A hole.

A few paces farther on, I thumped the ground with my heel where the hole ought to be. The dirt crumbled, and there was the little dark tunnel, running straight in both directions.

I walked on, the ground falling away gradually again. The entire process was repeated in reverse. A hairline appeared in the dirt—widened—became lips that drew slowly apart to reveal the neat straight four-inch groove—which shrank as slowly to a shallow line of the ground—and vanished.

I looked ahead of me. There was one low ridge of ground between me and the enormous boulders. A neat four-inch semicircle was bitten out of the very top of the ridge. In the house-sized boulder directly beyond was a four-inch hole.

Allenby winced and called the others when I came back and reported.

"The mystery *deepens*," he told them. He turned to me. "Lead on, Peters. You're temporary *drill* leader."

Thank God he didn't say *Fall in*.

The holes went straight through the nest of boulders—there'd be a hole in one and, ten or twenty feet farther on in the next boulder, another hole. And then another, and another—right through the nest in a line. About thirty holes in all.

Burton, standing by the boulder I'd first seen, flashed his flashlight into the hole. Randolph, clear on the other side of the jumbled nest, eye to hole, saw it.

Straight as a string!

The ground sloped away on the far side of the nest—no holes were visible in that direction—just miles of desert. So, after we'd stared at the holes for a while and they didn't go away, we headed back for the canal.

"Is there any possibility," asked Janus, as we walked, "that it could be a natural phenomenon?"

"There are no straight lines in nature," Randolph said, a little shortly. "That goes for a bunch of circles in a straight line. And for perfect circles, too."

"A planet is a circle," objected Janus.

"An oblate spheroid," Allenby corrected.

"A planet's orbit—"

"An ellipse."

Janus walked a few steps, frowning. Then he said, "I remember reading that there *is* something darned near a perfect circle in nature." He paused a moment. "Potholes." And he looked at me, as mineralogist, to corroborate.

"What kind of potholes?" I asked cautiously. "Do you mean where part of a limestone deposit has dissol—"

"No. I once read that when a glacier passes over a hard rock that's lying on some softer rock, it grinds the hard rock down into the softer, and both of them sort of wear down to fit together, and it all ends up with a round hole in the soft rock."

"Probably neither stone," I told Janus, "would be homogeneous. The softer parts would abrade faster in the soft stone. The end result wouldn't be a perfect circle."

Janus's face fell.

"Now," I said, "would anyone care to define this term 'perfect circle' we're throwing around so blithely? Because such holes as Janus describes are often pretty damned round."

Randolph said, "Well . . ."

"It is settled, then," Gonzales said, a little sarcastically. "Your discussion, gentlemen, has established that the long, horizontal holes we have found were caused by glacial action."

"Oh, no," Janus argued seriously. "I once read that Mars never had any glaciers."

All of us shuddered.

Half an hour later, we spotted more holes, about a mile down the "canal," still on a line, marching along the desert, through cacti, rocks, hills, even through one edge of the low vegetation of the "canal" for thirty feet or so. It was the damnedest thing to bend down and look straight through all that curling, twisting growth . . . a round tunnel from either end.

We followed the holes for about a mile, to the rim of an enormous saucerlike valley that sank gradually before us until, miles away, it was thousands of feet deep. We stared out across it, wondering about the other side.

Allenby said determinedly, "We'll burrow to the *bottom* of these holes, once and for all. Back to the ship, men!"

We hiked back, climbed in and took off.

At an altitude of fifty feet, Burton lined the nose of the ship on the most recent line of holes and we flew out over the valley.

On the other side was a range of hefty hills. The holes went through them. Straight through. We would approach one hill—Burton would manipulate the front viewscreen until we spotted the hole —we would pass over the hill and spot the other end of the hole in the rear screen.

One hole was two hundred and eighty miles long.

Four hours later, we were halfway around Mars.

Randolph was sitting by a side port, chin on one hand, his eyes unbelieving. "All around the planet," he kept repeating. "All around the planet . . ."

"Halfway at least," Allenby mused. "And we can assume that it continues in a straight line, through anything and everything that gets in its way. . . ." He gazed out the front port at the uneven blue-green haze of a "canal" off to our left. "For the love of Heaven, why?"

Then Allenby fell down. We all did.

Burton had suddenly slapped at the control board, and the ship braked and sank like a plugged duck. At the last second, Burton propped up the nose with a short burst, the ten-foot wheels hit desert sand, and in five hundred yards we had jounced to a stop.

Allenby got up from the floor. "Why did you do that?" he asked Burton politely, nursing a bruised elbow.

Burton's nose was almost touching the front port. "Look!" he said, and pointed.

About two miles away, the Martian village looked like a handful of yellow marbles flung on the desert.

We checked our guns. We put on our oxygen masks. We checked our guns again. We got out of the ship and made damned sure the air-lock was locked.

An hour later, we crawled inch by painstaking inch up a high sand dune and poked our heads over the top.

The Martians were runts—the tallest of them less than five feet tall—and skinny as a pencil. Dried-up and brown, they wore loin-cloths of woven fiber.

They stood among the dusty-looking inverted-bowl buildings of their village, and every one of them was looking straight up at us with unblinking brown eyes.

The six safeties of our six guns clicked off like a rattle of dice. The Martians stood there and gawped.

"Probably a highly developed sense of hearing in this thin atmosphere," Allenby murmured. "Heard us coming."

"They thought that landing of Burton's was an earthquake," Randolph grumbled sourly.

"Marsquake," corrected Janus. One look at the village's scrawny occupants seemed to have convinced him that he was in no danger.

Holding the Martians covered, we examined the village from atop the thirty-foot dune.

The domelike buildings were constructed of something that looked like adobe. No windows—probably built with sandstorms in mind. The doors were about halfway up the sloping sides, and from each door a stone ramp wound down around the house to the ground—again with sandstorms in mind, no doubt, so drifting dunes wouldn't block the entrances.

The center of the village was a wide street, a long sandy area some thirty feet wide. On either side of it, the houses were scattered at random, as if each Martian had simply hunted for a comfortable place to sit and then built a house around it.

"Look," whispered Randolph.

One Martian had stepped from a group situated on the far side of the street from us. He started to cross the street, his round brown eyes on us, his small bare feet plodding sand, and we saw that in addition to a loincloth he wore jewelry—a hammered metal ring, a bracelet on one skinny ankle. The sun caught a copperish gleam on his bald narrow head, and we saw a band of metal there, just above where his eyebrows should have been.

"The superchief," Allenby murmured. "Oh, *shaman* me!"

As the bejeweled Martian approached the center of the street, he glanced briefly at the ground at his feet. Then he raised his head, stepped with dignity across the exact center of the street, and came on toward us, passing the dusty-looking buildings of his realm and the dusty-looking groups of his subjects.

He reached the slope of the dune we lay on, paused—and raised small hands over his head, palms toward us.

"I think," Allenby said, "that an anthropologist would give odds on that gesture meaning peace."

He stood up, holstered his gun—without buttoning the flap—and raised his own hands over his head. We all did.

The Martian language consisted of squeaks.

We made friendly noises, the chief squeaked and pretty soon we were the center of a group of wide-eyed Martians, none of whom made a sound. Evidently no one dared peep while the chief spoke—very likely the most articulate Martians simply squeaked themselves into the job. Allenby, of course, said they just *squeaked by*.

He was going through the business of drawing concentric circles in the sand, pointing at the third orbit away from the sun, and thumping his chest. The crowd around us kept growing as more Martians emerged from the dome buildings to see what was going on. Down the winding ramps of the buildings on our side of the street, plodding through the sand, blinking brown eyes at us, not making a sound.

Allenby pointed at the third orbit and thumped his chest. The chief squeaked and thumped his own chest and pointed at the copperish band around his head. Then he pointed at Allenby.

"I seem to have conveyed to him," Allenby said dryly, "the fact that I'm chief of our party. Well, let's try again."

He started over on the orbits. He didn't seem to be getting anyplace, so the rest of us watched the Martians instead. A last handful was straggling across the wide street.

"Curious," said Gonzales. "Note what happens when they reach the center of the street."

Each Martian, upon reaching the center of the street, glanced at his feet—just for a moment—without even breaking stride. And then came on.

"What can they be looking at?" Gonzales wondered.

"The chief did it too," Burton mused. "Remember when he first came toward us?"

We all stared intently at the middle of the street. We saw absolutely nothing but sand.

The Martians milled around us and watched Allenby and his orbits. A Martian child appeared from between two buildings across the street. On six-inch legs, it started across, got halfway, glanced downward—and came on.

"I don't get it," Burton said. "What in hell are they *looking* at?"

The child reached the crowd and squeaked a thin, high note.

A number of things happened at once.

Several members of the group around us glanced down, and along the edge of the crowd nearest the center of the street there was a mild stir as individuals drifted off to either side. Quite casually—nothing at all urgent about it. They just moved concertedly to get farther away from the center of the street, not taking their interested gaze off us for one second in the process.

Even the chief glanced up from Allenby's concentric circles at the child's squeak. And Randolph, who had been fidgeting uncomfortably and paying very little attention to our conversation, decided that he must answer nature's call. He moved off into the dunes surrounding the village. Or rather, he started to move.

The moment he set off across the wide street, the little Martian chief was in front of him, brown eyes wide, hands out before him as if to thrust Randolph back.

Again six safeties clicked. The Martians didn't even blink at the sudden appearance of our guns. Probably the only weapon they recognized was a club, or maybe a rock.

"What can the matter be?" Randolph said.

He took another step forward. The chief squeaked and stood his ground. Randolph had to stop or bump into him. Randolph stopped.

The chief squeaked, looking right into the bore of Randolph's gun.

"Hold still," Allenby told Randolph, "till we know what's up."

Allenby made an interrogative sound at the chief. The chief squeaked and pointed at the ground. We looked. He was pointing at his shadow.

Randolph stirred uncomfortably.

"Hold still," Allenby warned him, and again he made the questioning sound.

The chief pointed up the street. Then he pointed down the street. He bent to touch his shadow, thumping it with thin fingers. Then he pointed at the wall of a house nearby.

We all looked.

Straight lines had been painted on the curved brick-colored wall, up and down and across, to form many small squares about four inches across. In each square was a bit of squiggly writing, in blackish paint, and a small wooden peg jutting out from the wall.

Burton said, "Looks like a damn crossword puzzle."

"Look," said Janus. "In the lower right corner—a metal ring hanging from one of the pegs."

And that was all we saw on the wall. Hundreds of squares with figures in them—a small peg set in each—and a ring hanging on one of the pegs.

"You know what?" Allenby said slowly. "I think it's a calendar!"

Just a second—thirty squares wide by twenty-two high—that's six hundred and sixty. And that bottom line has twenty-six—twenty-seven squares. Six hundred and eighty-seven squares in all. That's how many days there are in the Martian year!"

He looked thoughtfully at the metal ring. "I'll bet that ring is hanging from the peg in the square that represents *today*. They must move it along every day, to keep track. . . ."

"What's a calendar got to do with my crossing the street?" Randolph asked in a pained tone.

He started to take another step. The chief squeaked as if it were a matter of desperate concern that he make us understand. Randolph stopped again and swore.

Allenby made his questioning sound again.

The chief pointed emphatically at his shadow, then at the communal calendar—and we could see now that he was pointing at the metal ring.

Burton said slowly, "I think he's trying to tell us that this is *today*. And such-and-such a *time* of day. I bet he's using his shadow as a sundial."

"Perhaps," Allenby granted.

Randolph said, "If this monkey doesn't let me go in another minute—"

The chief squeaked, eyes concerned.

"Stand still," Allenby ordered. "He's trying to warn you of some danger."

The chief pointed down the street again and, instead of squealing, revealed that there was another sound at his command. He said, "Whooooooosh!"

We all stared at the end of the street.

Nothing! Just the wide avenue between the houses, and the high sand dune down at the end of it, from which we had first looked upon the village.

The chief described a large circle with one hand, sweeping the hand above his head, down to his knees, up again, as fast as he could. He pursed his monkey-lips and said, "Whooooooosh!" And made the circle again.

A Martian emerged from the door in the side of a house across the avenue and blinked at the sun, as if he had just awakened. Then he saw what was going on below and blinked again, this time in interest. He made his way down around the winding ramp and started to cross the street.

About halfway, he paused, eyed the calendar on the house wall, glanced at his shadow. Then he got down on his hands and knees and *crawled* across the middle of the street. Once past the middle, he rose, walked the rest of the way to join one of the groups, and calmly stared at us along with the rest of them.

"They're all crazy," Randolph said disgustedly. "I'm going to cross that street!"

"Shut up. So it's a certain time of a certain day," Allenby mused. "And from the way the chief is acting, he's afraid for you to cross the street. And that other one just *crawled*. By God, do you know what this might tie in with?"

We were silent for a moment. Then Gonzales said, "Of course!"

And Burton said, "The *holes!*"

"Exactly," said Allenby. "Maybe whatever made—or makes—the holes comes right down the center of the street here. Maybe that's why they built the village this way—to make room for—"

"For what?" Randolph asked unhappily, shifting his feet.

"I don't know," Allenby said. He looked thoughtfully at the chief. "That circular motion he made—could he have been describing something that went around and around the planet? Something like —oh, no!" Allenby's eyes glazed. "I wouldn't believe it in a million years."

His gaze went to the far end of the street, to the high sand dune that rose there. The chief seemed to be waiting for something to happen.

"I'm going to crawl," Randolph stated. He got to his hands and knees and began to creep across the center of the avenue.

The chief let him go.

The sand dune at the end of the street suddenly erupted. A forty-foot spout of dust shot straight out from the sloping side, as if a bullet had emerged. Powdered sand hazed the air, yellowed it almost the full length of the avenue. Grains of sand stung the skin and rattled minutely on the houses.

WhoooSSSHHHHH!

Randolph dropped flat on his belly. He didn't have to continue his trip. He had made other arrangements.

That night in the ship, while we all sat around, still shaking our heads every once in a while, Allenby talked with Earth. He sat there, wearing the headphones, trying to make himself understood above the god-awful static.

". . . an exceedingly small body," he repeated wearily to his unbelieving audience, "about four inches in diameter. It travels at a mean distance of four feet above the surface of the planet, at a velocity yet to be calculated. Its unique nature results in many hitherto unobserved—I might say even unimagined—phenomena." He stared blankly in front of him for a moment, then delivered the understatement of his life. "The discovery may necessitate a reexamination of many of our basic postulates in the physical sciences."

The headphones squawked.

Patiently, Allenby assured Earth that he was entirely serious, and reiterated the results of his observations. I suppose that he, an astronomer, was twice as flabbergasted as the rest of us. On the other hand, perhaps he was better equipped to adjust to the evidence.

"Evidently," he said, "when the body was formed, it traveled at such fantastic velocity as to enable it to—" his voice was almost a whisper—"to punch holes in things."

The headphones squawked.

"In rocks," Allenby said, "in mountains, in anything that got in its way. And now the holes form a large portion of its fixed orbit."

Squawk.

"Its mass must be on the order of—"

Squawk.

"—process of making holes slowed it, so that now it travels just fast enough—"

Squawk.

"—maintain its orbit and penetrate occasional objects such as—"

Squawk.

"—and sand dunes—"

Squawk.

"My God, I *know* it's a mathematical monstrosity," Allenby snarled. "*I* didn't put it there!"

Squawk.

Allenby was silent for a moment. Then he said slowly, "A name?"

Squawk.

"H'm," said Allenby. "Well, well." He appeared to brighten just a little. "So it's up to me, as leader of the expedition, to name it?"

Squawk.

"Well, well," he said.

That chop-licking tone was in his voice. We'd heard it all too often before. We shuddered, waiting.

"Inasmuch as Mars's outermost moon is called Deimos, and the next Phobos," he said, "I think I shall name the third moon of Mars —Bottomos."

HORRER HOWCE

July 1956

Margaret St. Clair
(b. 1911)

A native of California, Margaret St. Clair has been publishing high-quality science fiction since 1947. Outstanding among her more than ten books are The Dolphins of Altair *(1967),* Sign of the Labrys *(1963), and the collection* Change the Sky and Other Stories *(1974). As "Idris Seabright" she published a string of excellent short stories in* The Magazine of Fantasy and Science Fiction, *beginning in 1950. Other Galaxy stories of note are "The Muse Man" (February 1960) and "An Old-Fashioned Bird Christmas" (December 1961), but we liked this wonderful tale the best.*

Memoir by Margaret St. Clair

I have always been intrigued by the fun-house concept—tableaux appearing out of darkness, bars that bend, doors that open on strange scenes or on nothing. And all of it a reassuringly small, harmless, human creation.

Disneyland was newish in the fifties, and McCarthyism was in the air. Other than being able to trace these two strands in "Horrer Howce," I really don't know where it came from. Of course, besides wanting to make a little money, my purpose in writing it was what it usually is when I write a horror story: to scare the pants off the little bastards, that is, my readers.

You, dear reader, have my permission to retain your pants. But I hope the story scares you deliciously.

HORRER HOWCE

Dickson-Hawes's face had turned a delicate pea-green. He closed the shutter on the opening very quickly indeed. Nonetheless, he said in nearly his usual voice, "I'm afraid it's a trifle literary, Freeman. Reminds of that thing of Yeats's—'What monstrous beast, Its time come, uh, round again, slouches toward Bethlehem to be born?' But the people who go to a horror house for amusement aren't literary. It wouldn't affect them the way it did me." He giggled nervously.

No answering emotion disturbed the normal sullenness of Freeman's face. "I thought there was a nice feel to it," he said obstinately. "I wouldn't have put so much time in on this stuff unless I thought you'd be interested. Research is more my line. I could have made a lot more money working on one of the government projects."

"You didn't have much choice, did you?" Dickson-Hawes said pleasantly. "A political past is such a handicap, unless one's willing to risk prosecution for perjury."

"I'm as loyal as anybody! For the last five years—eight, ten—all I've wanted to do was make a little cash. The trouble is, I always have such rotten luck."

"Um." Dickson-Hawes wiped his forehead unobtrusively. "Well, about your little effort. There are some nice touches, certainly. The idea of the monstrous womb, alone on the seashore, slowly swelling, and . . ." In the folds of his handkerchief he stifled a sort of cough. "No, I'm afraid it's too poetic. I can't use it, old chap."

The two men moved away from the shuttered opening. Freeman said, "Then Spring Scene is the only one you're taking?"

"Of those of yours I've seen. It's horrid enough, but not too horrid. Haven't you anything else?" Dickson-Hawes's voice was eager, but eagerness seemed to be mixed with other things—reluctance, perhaps, and the fear of being afraid.

Freeman fingered his lower lip. "There's the Well," he said after a moment. "It needs a little more work done on it, but—I guess you could look at it."

"I'd be delighted to," Dickson-Hawes agreed heartily. "I do hope you understand, old man, that there's quite a lot of *money* involved in this."

"Yeah. You've really got the capital lined up? Twice before, you were sure you had big money interested. But the deals always fell through. I got pretty tired of it."

"This time it's different. The money's already in escrow, not to mention what I'm putting in myself. We intend a coast-to-coast network of horror houses in every gayway, playland, and amusement park."

"Yeah. Well, come along."

They went down the corridor to another door. Freeman unlocked it. "By the way," he said, "I'd appreciate it if you'd keep your voice down. Some of the machinery in this stuff's—delicate. Sensitive."

"By all means. Of course."

They entered. To their right was an old brick house, not quite in ruin. To the left, a clump of blackish trees cut off the sky. Just in front of them was the moss-covered coping of an old stone well. The ground around the well was slick with moisture.

Dickson-Hawes sniffed appreciatively. "I must say you've paid wonderful attention to detail. It's exactly like being out of doors. It even smells froggy and damp."

"Thanks," Freeman replied with a small, dour smile.

"What happens next?"

"Look down in the well."

Rather gingerly, Dickson-Hawes approached. He leaned over. From the well came a gurgling splash.

Dickson-Hawes drew back abruptly. Now his face was not quite greenish; it was white. "My word, what a monster!" he gasped. "What is it, anyway?"

"Clockwork," Freeman answered. "It'll writhe for thirty-six hours on one winding. I couldn't use batteries, you know, on account of the water. That greenish flash in the eyes comes from prisms. And the hair is the same thing you get on those expensive fur coats, only longer. I think they call it plasti-mink."

"What happens if I keep leaning over? Or if I drop pebbles down on it?"

"It'll come out at you."

Dickson-Hawes looked disappointed. "Anything else?"

"The sky gets darker and noises come out of the house. Isn't that enough?"

Dickson-Hawes coughed. "Well, of course we'd have to soup it up a bit. Put an electrified rail around the well coping and perhaps make the approach to the well slippery so the customers would have to grasp the handrail. Install a couple of air jets to blow the girls' dresses up. And naturally make it a good deal darker so couples can neck when the girl gets scared. But it's a nice little effort, Freeman, very nice indeed. I'm almost certain we can use it. Yes, we ought to have your Well in our horror house."

Dickson-Hawes's voice had rung out strongly on the last few words. Now there came another watery splash from the well. Freeman seemed disturbed.

"I *told* you to keep your voice down," he complained. "The partitions are thin. When you talk that loud, you can be heard all over the place. It isn't good for the—machinery."

"Sorry."

"Don't let it happen again. . . . I don't think the customers ought to neck in here. This isn't the place for it. If they've got to neck, let them do it outside. In the corridor."

"You have no idea, old chap, what people will do in a darkened corridor in a horror house. It seems to stimulate them. But you may be right. Letting them stay here to neck might spoil the illusion. We'll try to get them on out."

"Okay. How much are you paying me for this?"

"Our lawyer will have to discuss the details," said Dickson-Hawes. He gave Freeman a smile reeking with synthetic charm. "I assure you he can draw up a satisfactory contract. I can't be more definite until I know what the copyright or patent situation would be."

"I don't think my Well could be patented," Freeman said. "There are details in the machinery nobody understands but me. I'd have to install each unit in your horror-house network myself. There ought to be a clause in the contract about my per diem expenses and a traveling allowance."

"I'm sure we can work out something mutually satisfactory."

"Uh . . . let's get out of here. This is an awfully damp place to do much talking in."

They went out into the hall again. Freeman locked the door. "Have you anything else?" Dickson-Hawes asked.

Freeman's eyes moved away. "No."

"Oh, come now, old chap. Don't be coy. As I told you before, there's *money* involved."

"What sort of thing do you want?"

"Well, horrid. Though not quite so poetically horrid as what you have behind the shutter. That's a little too much. Perhaps something with a trifle more action. With more customer participation. Both the Well and Spring Scene are on the static side."

"Uh."

They walked along the corridor. Freeman said slowly, "I've been working on something. There's action and customer participation in it, all right, but I don't know. It's full of bugs. I just haven't had time to work it out yet."

"Let's have it, old man, by all means!"

"Not so loud! You've got to keep your voice down. Otherwise I can't take you in." Freeman himself was speaking almost in a whisper. "All right. Here."

They had stopped before a much more substantial door than the one behind which the Well lay. There was a wide rubber flange all around it, and it was secured at top and bottom by two padlocked hasps. In the top of the door, three or four small holes had been bored, apparently to admit air.

"You must have something pretty hot locked up behind all that," Dickson-Hawes remarked.

"Yeah." Freeman got a key ring out of his pocket and began looking over it. Dickson-Hawes glanced around appraisingly.

"Somebody's been writing on your wall," he observed. "Rotten speller, I must say."

Freeman raised his eyes from the key ring and looked in the direction the other man indicated. On the wall opposite the door, just under the ceiling, somebody had written HORRER HOWCE in what looked like blackish ink.

The effect of the ill-spelled words on Freeman was remarkable. He dropped the key ring with a clatter, and when he straightened from picking it up, his hands were quivering.

"I've changed my mind," he said. He put the key ring back in his pocket. "I always did have the damnedest luck."

Dickson-Hawes leaned back against the wall and crossed his ankles. "How do you get your ideas, Freeman?"

"Oh, all sorts of ways. Things I read, things people tell me, things I see. All sorts of ways." Both men were speaking in low tones.

"They're amazing. And your mechanical effects—I really don't see how you get machinery to do the things you make it do."

Freeman smiled meagerly. "I've always been good at mechanics. Particularly radio and signaling devices. Relays. Communication problems, you might say. I can communicate with anything. Started when I was a kid."

There was silence. Dickson-Hawes kept leaning against the wall. A close observer, Freeman noticed almost a tic, a fluttering of his left eyelid.

At last Freeman said, "How much are you paying for the Well?"

Dickson-Hawes closed his eyes and opened them again. He may have been reflecting that while a verbal contract is quite as binding as a written one, it is difficult to prove the existence of a verbal contract to which there are no witnesses.

He answered, "Five thousand in a lump sum, I think, and a prorated share of the net admissions for the first three years."

There was an even longer silence. Freeman's face relaxed at the mention of a definite sum. He said, "How are your nerves? I need money so damned bad."

Dickson-Hawes's face went so blank that it would seem the other man had touched a vulnerable spot. "Pretty good, I imagine," he said in a carefully modulated voice. "I saw a good deal of action during the war."

Cupidity and some other emotion contended in Freeman's eyes. He fished out the key ring again. "Look, you must not make a noise. No yelling or anything like that, no matter what you see. They're very—I mean the machinery's delicate. It's full of bugs I haven't got rid of yet. The whole thing will be a lot less ghastly later on. I'm going to keep the basic idea, make it just as exciting as it is now, but tone it down plenty."

"I understand."

Freeman looked at him with a frown. "Don't make a noise," he cautioned again. "Remember, none of this is real." He fitted the key into the first of the padlocks on the stoutly built door.

The second padlock was a little stiff. Freeman had to fidget with it. Finally he got the door open. The two men stepped through it. They were outside.

There is no other way of expressing it: They were outside. If the illusion had been good in the Well, here it was perfect. They stood in a sort of safety island on the edge of a broad freeway, where traffic poured by in an unending rush eight lanes wide. It was the time of day when, though visibility is really better than at noon, a nervous motorist or two has turned on his parking lights. Besides the two men, the safety island held a new, shiny, eggplant-colored sedan.

Dickson-Hawes turned a bewildered face on his companion. "Freeman," he said in a whisper, "did you *make* all this?"

For the first time, Freeman grinned. "Pretty good, isn't it?" he replied, also in a whisper. He opened the car door and slid into the driver's seat. "Get in. We're going for a ride. Remember, no noise."

The other man obeyed. Freeman started the car—it had a very quiet motor—and watched until a lull in the traffic gave him a chance to swing out from the curb. He stepped on the accelerator. The landscape began to move by.

Cars passed them. They passed some cars. Dickson-Hawes looked for the speedometer on the dashboard and couldn't find it. A garage, service station, a billboard went by. The sign on the garage read: WE FIX FLATTEDS. The service station had conical pumps. The tomatoes on the billboard were purple and green.

Dickson-Hawes was breathing shallowly. He said, "Freeman— where *are* we?"

Once more, the other man grinned. "You're getting just the effect I mean to give," he retorted in a pleased whisper. "At first, the customer thinks he's on an ordinary freeway, with ordinary people hurrying home to their dinners. Then he begins to notice all sorts of subtle differences. Everything's a little off-key. It adds to the uneasiness."

"Yes, but—what's the object of all this? What are we trying to do?"

"Get home to our dinners, like everyone else."

"Where does the—well, difficulty come in?"

"Do you see that car in the outer lane?" They were still conversing in whispers. "Black, bullet-shaped, quite small, going very fast?"

"Yes."

"Keep your eye on it."

The black car *was* going very fast. It caught up with a blue sedan in front of it, cut in on it and began to crowd it over to the curb. The blue sedan tried to shake off the black car, but without success. If the driver didn't want to be wrecked, he had to get over.

For a while, the two cars ran parallel. The black car began to slow down and crowd more aggressively than ever. Suddenly it cut obliquely in front of the sedan and stopped.

There was a frenzied scream of brakes from the sedan. It stopped with its left fender almost against the black bullet-shaped car. The bodies were so close, there was no room for the sedan driver to open his door.

Freeman had let the car he was driving slow down, presumably so Dickson-Hawes could see everything.

For a moment there was nothing to see. Only for a moment. Then two—or was it three?—long, blackish, extremely thin arms came out from the black car and fumbled with the glass in the window of the sedan. The glass was forced down. The arms entered the sedan.

From the sedan there came a wild burst of shrieking. It was like the flopping, horrified squawks of a chicken at the chopping block. The shrieks were still going on when the very thin arms came out with a—

The light hid nothing. The three very thin arms came out with a plucked-off human arm.

They threw it into the interior of the black car. The three arms invaded the sedan once more.

This time, Dickson-Hawes had turned neither white nor greenish, but a blotchy gray. His mouth had come open all around his teeth, in the shape of a rigid oblong with raised, corded edges. It was perfectly plain that if he was not screaming, it was solely because his throat was too paralyzed.

Freeman gave his passenger only a momentary glance. He was looking into the rear-view mirror. He began to frown anxiously.

The shrieking from the blue sedan had stopped. Dickson-Hawes covered his face with his hands while Freeman drove past it and the other car. When the group lay behind them, he asked in a shaking whisper, "Freeman, are there any more of them? The black cars, I mean?"

"Yeah. One of them's coming toward us now."

Dickson-Hawes's head swiveled around. Another of the black cars was hurtling toward them through the traffic, though it was still a long way behind.

Dickson-Hawes licked his lips.

"Is it—after us?"

"I think so."

"But why? Why—us?"

"Part of the game. Wouldn't be horrid otherwise. Hold on. I'm going to try to shake it off."

Freeman stepped down on the accelerator. The eggplant-colored sedan shot ahead. It was a very fast car and Freeman was evidently an expert and nerveless driver. They slid through nonexistent holes in the traffic, glanced off from fenders, slipped crazily from lane to lane, a shuttle in a pattern of speed and escape.

The black car gained on them. No gymnastics. A bulletlike directness. But it was nearer all the time.

Dickson-Hawes gave a sort of whimper.

"No noise," Freeman cautioned in a fierce whisper. "That'll bring them down for sure. *Now!*"

He pressed the accelerator all the way down. The eggplant-colored car bounced and swayed. There was a tinkle of glass from the headlights of the car on the left as the sedan brushed it glancingly. Dickson-Hawes moaned, but realized they had gained the length of several cars. Momentarily, the black pursuer fell behind.

They went through two red lights in a row. So did the black bullet. It began to edge in on them. Closer and closer. Faster and faster.

Dickson-Hawes had slumped forward with his head on his chest. The black car cut toward them immediately.

Freeman snarled. Deliberately, he swung out into the path of the pursuer. For a second, it gave ground.

"Bastards," Freeman said grimly.

The black car cut in on them like the lash of a whip. The sedan slithered. Hubcaps grated on concrete. The sedan swayed drunkenly. Brakes howled. Dickson-Hawes, opening his eyes involuntarily for the crash, saw that they were in a safety island. The same safety island, surely, from which they had started out?

The black car went streaking on by.

"I hate those things," Freeman said bitterly. "Damned Voom. If I could— But never mind. We got away. We're safe. We're home."

Dickson-Hawes did not move. "I said we're safe," Freeman repeated. He opened the car door and pushed the other man out through it. Half shoving, half carrying, he led him to the door from which they had entered the freeway. It was still the time of day at which nervous motorists turn on their parking lights.

Freeman maneuvered Dickson-Hawes through the door. He closed it behind them and fastened the padlocks in the hasps. They were out in the corridor again—the corridor on whose wall somebody had written HORRER HOWCE.

Freeman drew a deep breath. "Well. Worked better than I

thought it would. I was afraid you'd yell. I thought you were the type that yells. But I guess the third time's the charm."

"What?"

"I mean I guess my goddamn luck has turned at last. Yeah. What did you think of it?"

Dickson-Hawes swallowed, unable to answer.

Freeman regarded him. "Come along to my office and have a drink. You look like you need one. And then you can tell me what you think of this setup."

The office was in the front of the house, down a couple of steps. Dickson-Hawes sank into the chair Freeman pulled out for him. He gulped down Freeman's dubious reddish bourbon gratefully.

After the second drink he was restored enough to ask, "Freeman, was it real?"

"Certainly not," the other man said promptly.

"It looked awfully real," Dickson-Hawes objected. "That arm . . ." He shuddered.

"A dummy," Freeman answered promptly once more. "You didn't see any blood, did you? Of course not. It was a dummy arm."

"I hope so. I don't see how you could have *made* all the stuff we saw. There's a limit to what machinery can do. I'd like another drink."

Freeman poured. "What did you think of it?"

Color was coming back to Dickson-Hawes's cheeks. "It was the most horrible experience I ever had in my life."

Freeman grinned. "Good. People like to be frightened. That's why roller-coaster rides are so popular."

"Not that much, people don't. Nobody would enjoy a roller-coaster ride if he saw cars crashing all around him and people getting killed. You'll have to tone it down a lot. An awful lot."

"But you liked it?"

"On the whole, yes. It's a unique idea. But you'll have to tone it down about 75 percent."

Freeman grimaced. "It can be done. But I'll have to have a definite commitment from you before I undertake such extensive changes."

"Um."

"There are other places I could sell it, you know," Freeman said pugnaciously. "Jenkins of Amalgamated might be interested. Or Silberstein."

"Jenkins lit out with about six thousand of Amalgamated's dollars a couple of months ago. Nobody's seen him since. And they found Silberstein wandering on the streets last week in a sort of fit. Didn't you know? He's in a mental home. You won't be selling either of *them* much of anything."

Freeman sighed, but made no attempt to dispute these distressing facts. "I'll have to have a definite commitment from you before I make that many major changes," he repeated stubbornly.

"Well . . ." Fright and whiskey may have made Dickson-Hawes a little less cautious than usual. "We could pay you fifty a week for a couple of months while you worked on it, as advance against royalties. If we didn't like the final results, you wouldn't have to give back the advance."

"It's robbery. Apprentice mechanics earn more than that. Make it sixty-five."

"I hate haggling. Tell you what. We'll make it sixty."

Freeman shrugged tiredly. "Let's get it down in black and white. I'll just draw up a brief statement of the terms and you can sign it."

"Well, okay."

Freeman stooped and began to rummage in a desk drawer. Once he halted and seemed to listen. He opened another drawer. "Thought I had some paper. . . . Yeah, here it is." He turned on the desk light and began to write.

Dickson-Hawes leaned back in his chair and sipped at Freeman's whiskey. He crossed his legs and recrossed them. He was humming "Lili Marlene" loudly and off pitch. His head rested against the wall.

Freeman's pen moved across the paper. "That's about it," he said at last. He was smiling. "Yeah. I—"

There was a splintering crash, the sound of lath and plaster breaking. Freeman looked up from the unsigned agreement to see the last of his entrepreneurs—the last, the indubitable last—being borne off in the long black arms of the Voom.

It was the first time they had gone through the partitions in search of a victim, but the partitions were thin and the unsuccessful chase on the highway had excited them more than Freeman had realized. There has to be a first time for any entity, even for Voom.

Ten full minutes passed. Dickson-Hawes's shrieks died away. The third episode had ended just as disastrously as the earlier two. There wasn't another entrepreneur in the entire U.S.A. from whom Freeman could hope to realize a cent for the contents of his horror house. He was sunk, finished, washed up.

Freeman remained sitting at his desk, motionless. All his resentment at the bad luck life had saddled him with—loyalty oaths, big deals that fell through, chiselers like Dickson-Hawes, types that yelled when the Voom were after them—had coalesced into an immobilizing rage.

At last he drew a quavering sigh. He went over to the bookcase, took out a book, looked up something. He took out a second book, a third.

He nodded. A gleam of blind, intoxicated vindictiveness had come into his eyes. Just a few minor circuit changes, that was all. He knew the other, more powerful entities were there. It was only a question of changing his signaling devices to get in touch with them.

Freeman put the book back on the shelf. He hesitated. Then he started toward the door. He'd get busy on the circuit changes right away. And while he was making them, he'd be running over plans for the horror house he was going to use the new entities to help him build.

It would be dangerous. So what? Expensive . . . he'd get the money somewhere. But he'd fix them. He'd build a horror house for the beasts that would make them sorry they'd ever existed—A Horrer Howce for the Voom.

PEOPLE SOUP

November 1958

Alan Arkin
(b. 1934)

Yes, this is the same Alan Arkin who starred in The Russians Are
Coming, The Russians Are Coming *and is one of the most talented
individuals in the entertainment field in America. Many of the bits
he wrote for the "Second City" group of comedians have become
classics. His only other venture into science fiction, the excellent
"Whiskaboom," also appeared in* Galaxy, *in the August 1955 issue.*

*"People Soup" is a little gem with some very interesting things to
say about the nature of scientific innovation.*

Memoir by Alan Arkin

This story is the first fiction that I ever wrote. I was in the hospital
with hepatitis at the time, too weak for anything but lifting a pencil,
and it was something to focus my eyes on besides the green ceiling.
At the time I thought of it simply as a gift for my brother and sister,
who are the two children in the story, but to my delight, it found its
way into *Galaxy*. Several years later I turned it into a screenplay for
my two oldest boys, and we shot it as a short film. It was then sold
to Columbia Pictures and subsequently received an Academy Award
nomination, all of which has given a very rosy tint to my memory of
yellow jaundice. The events in the story are probably fictional, but I
won't swear to it.

PEOPLE SOUP

Bonnie came home from school and found her brother in the
kitchen, doing something important at the sink. She knew it was im-

portant because he was making a mess and talking to himself. The sink drain was loaded down with open soda bottles, a sack of flour, cornmeal, dog biscuits, molasses, Bromo-Seltzer, a tin of sardines, and a box of soap chips. The floor was covered with drippings and every cupboard in the kitchen was open. At the moment, Bonnie's brother was putting all his energy into shaking a plastic juicer that was half-filled with an ominous-looking frothy mixture.

Bonnie waited for a moment, keeping well out of range, and then said, "Hi, Bob."

" 'Lo," he answered, without looking up.

"Where's Mom?"

"Shopping."

Bonnie inched a little closer. "What are you doing, Bob?" she asked.

"Nothing."

"Can I watch?"

"No."

Bonnie took this as a cue to advance two cautious steps. She knew from experience how close she could approach her brother when he was being creative and still maintain a peaceful neutrality. Bob slopped a cupful of ketchup into the juicer, added a can of powdered mustard, a drop of milk, six aspirins, and a piece of chewing gum, being careful to spill a part of each package used.

Bonnie moved in a bit closer. "Are you making another experiment?" she asked.

"Who wants to know?" Bob answered, in his mad-scientist voice, as he swaggered over to the refrigerator and took out an egg, some old bacon fat, a capsuled vitamin pill, yesterday's Jell-O, and a bottle of clam juice.

"Me wants to know," said Bonnie, picking up an apple that had rolled out of the refrigerator and fallen on the floor.

"Why should I tell you?"

"I have twenty-five cents."

"Where'd you get it?"

"Mom gave it to me."

"If you give it to me, I'll tell you what I'm doing."

"It's not worth it."

"I'll let you be my assistant, too."

"Still not worth it."

"For ten cents?"

"Okay, ten cents."

She counted out the money to her brother and put on an apron. "What should I do now, Bob?"

"Get the salt," Bob instructed.

He poured sardine oil from the can into the juicer, being very careful not to let the sardines fall in. When he had squeezed the last drop of oil out of the can, he ate all the sardines and tossed the can into the sink.

Bonnie went after the salt and, when she lifted out the box, she found a package containing two chocolate graham crackers.

"Mom has a new hiding place, Bob," she announced.

Bob looked up. "Where is it?"

"Behind the salt."

"What did you find there?"

"Two chocolate grahams."

Bobby held out his hand, accepted one of the crackers without thanks, and proceeded to crumble the whole thing into his concoction, not even stopping to lick the chocolate off his hands.

Bonnie frowned in disbelief. She had never seen such self-sacrifice. The act made her aware, for the first time, of the immense significance of the experiment.

She dropped her quarrel completely and walked over to the sink to get a good look at what was being done. All she saw in the sink was a wadded, wet cornflakes box, the empty sardine tin, and spillings from the juicer, which by this time was beginning to take on a distinctive and unpleasant odor. Bob gave Bonnie the job of adding seven pinches of salt and some cocoa to the concoction.

"What's it going to be, Bob?" she asked, blending the cocoa on her hands into her yellow corduroy skirt.

"Stuff," Bob answered, unbending a little.

"Government stuff?"

"Nope."

"Spaceship stuff?"

"Nope."

"Medicine?"

"Nope."

"I give up."

"It's animal serum," Bob said, sliced his thumb on the sardine can, glanced unemotionally at the cut, ignored it.

"What's animal serum, Bob?"

"It's certain properties without which the universe in eternity regards for human beings."

"Oh," Bonnie said. She took off her apron and sat down at the other end of the kitchen. The smell from the juicer was beginning to reach her stomach.

Bobby combed the kitchen for something else to throw into his concoction and came up with some oregano and liquid garlic.

"I guess this is about it," he said.

He poured the garlic and oregano into his juicer, put the lid on, shook it furiously for a minute, and then emptied the contents into a deep pot.

"What are you doing now, Bob?" Bonnie asked.

"You have to cook it for ten minutes."

Bobby lit the stove, put a cover on the pot, set the timer for ten minutes, and left the room. Bonnie tagged after him and the two of them got involved in a rough game of basketball in the living room.

"BING!" said the timer.

Bob dropped the basketball on Bonnie's head and ran back into the kitchen.

"It's all done," he said, and took the cover off the pot. Only his dedication to his work kept him from showing the discomfort he felt with the smell that the pot gave forth.

"Fyew!" said Bonnie. "What do we do with it now? Throw it out?"

"No, stupid. We have to stir it till it cools and then drink it."

"Drink it?" Bonnie wrinkled her nose. "How come we have to drink it?"

Bobby said, "Because that's what you do with experiments, stupid."

"But, Bob, it smells like garbage."

"Medicine smells worse and it makes you healthy," Bob said, while stirring the pot with an old wooden spoon.

Bonnie held her nose, stood on tiptoe, and looked in at the cooking solution. "Will this make us healthy?"

"Maybe." Bob kept stirring.

"What will it do?"

"You'll see." Bob took two clean dish towels, draped them around the pot, and carried it over to the Formica kitchen table. In the process, he managed to dip both towels in the mixture and burn his already sliced thumb. One plastic handle of the pot was still smoldering, from being too near the fire, but none of these things seemed to have the slightest effect on him. He put the pot down in the middle of the table and stared at it, chin in hand.

Bonnie plopped down opposite him, put her chin in her hands, and asked, "We *have* to drink that stuff?"

"Yup."

"Who has to drink it first?" Bob made no sign of having heard. "I thought so," said Bonnie. Still no comment. "What if it kills me?"

Bobby spoke by raising his whole head and keeping his jaw stationary in his hands. "How can it hurt you? There's nothing but pure food in there."

Bonnie also sat and stared. "How much of that stuff do I have to drink?"

"Just a little bit. Stick one finger in it and lick it off."

Bonnie pointed a cautious finger at the tarry-looking brew and slowly immersed it, until it barely covered the nail. "Is that enough?"

"Plenty," said Bob in a judicious tone.

Bonnie took her finger out of the pot and stared at it for a moment. "What if I get sick?"

"You can't get sick. There's aspirin and vitamins in it, too."

Bonnie sighed and wrinkled her nose. "Well, here goes," she said. She licked off a little bit.

Bob watched her with his television version of a scientific look. "How do you feel?" he inquired.

Bonnie answered, "It's not so bad, once it goes down. You can taste the chocolate graham cracker." Bonnie was really enjoying the attention. "Hey," she said, "I'm starting to get a funny feeling in my—" and, before she could finish the sentence, there was a loud *pop*.

Bob's face registered extreme disappointment.

She sat quite still for a moment and then said, "What happened?"

"You've turned into a chicken."

The little bird lifted its wings and looked down at itself. "How come I'm a chicken, Bob?" it said, cocking its head to one side and staring at him with its left eye.

"Ah, nuts," he explained. "I expected you to be more of a pigeon thing." Bob mulled over the ingredients of his stew to see what went wrong.

The chicken hopped around the chair on one leg, flapped its wings experimentally, and found itself on the kitchen table. It walked to the far corner and peered into a small mirror that hung on the side of the sink cabinet.

"I'm a pretty ugly chicken, boy," it said.

It inspected itself with its other eye and, finding no improvement, walked back to Bobby.

"I don't like to be a chicken, Bob," it said.

"Why not? What does it feel like?"

"It feels skinny and I can't see so good."

"How else does it feel?"

"That's all how it feels. Make me stop being it."

"First tell me better what it's like."

"I told you already. Make me stop being it."

"What are you afraid of? Why don't you see what it's like first, before you change back? This is a valuable experience."

The chicken tried to put its hands on its hips, but could find neither hips nor hands. "You better change me back, boy," it said, and gave Bob the left-eye glare.

"Will you stop being stupid and just see what it's like first?" Bob was finding it difficult to understand her lack of curiosity.

"Wait till Mom sees what an ugly mess I am, boy. Will you ever get it!" Bonnie was trying very hard to see Bob with both eyes at once, which was impossible.

"You're a sissy, Bonnie. You ruined the opportunity of a lifetime. I'm disgusted with you." Bob dipped his forefinger in the serum and held it toward the chicken. It pecked what it could from the finger and tilted its head back.

In an instant, the chicken was gone and Bonnie was back. She climbed down from the table, wiped her eyes and said, "It's a good thing you fixed me, boy. Would you ever have got it."

"Ah, you're nothing but a sissy," Bob said, and licked off a whole fingerful of his formula. "If I change into a horse, I won't let you ride me, and if I change into a leopard, I'll bite your head off." Once again, the loud *pop* was heard.

Bonnie stood up, wide-eyed. "Oh, Bob," she said, "you're beautiful!"

"What am I?" Bob asked.

"You're a bee-yoo-tee-full St. Bernard, Bob! Let's go show Melissa and Chuck."

"A St. Bernard?" The animal looked disgusted. "I don't want to be no dog. I want to be a leopard."

"But you're *beautiful*, Bob! Go look in the mirror."

"Naah." The dog padded over to the table.

"What are you going to do, Bob?"

"I'm going to try it again."

The dog put its front paws on the table, knocked over the serum and lapped up some as it dripped on the floor. *Pop* went the serum, taking effect. Bobby remained on all fours and kept on lapping. *Pop* went the serum again.

"What am I now?" he asked.

"You're still a St. Bernard," said Bonnie.

"The devil with it then," said the dog. "Let's forget all about it."

The dog took one last lap of serum. *Pop!* Bobby got up from the floor and dejectedly started out the back door. Bonnie skipped after him.

"What'll we do now, Bob?" she asked.

"We'll go down to Thrifty's and get some ice cream."

They walked down the hill silently, Bobby brooding over not having been a leopard and Bonnie wishing he had stayed a St. Bernard. As they approached the main street of the small town, Bonnie turned to her brother.

"You want to make some more of that stuff tomorrow?"

"Not the same stuff," said Bob.

"What'll we make instead?"

"I ain't decided yet."

"You want to make an atomic bomb?"

"Maybe."

"Can we do it in the juicer?"

"Sure," Bob said, "only we'll have to get a couple of onions."

SOMETHING BRIGHT

February 1960

Zenna Henderson
(b. 1917)

A teacher all of her adult life, Zenna Henderson is best known for her wonderful series about "The People," which began in the October 1952 issue of The Magazine of Fantasy and Science Fiction. *These stories can be found in the collections* Pilgrimage: The Book of the People *(1961) and* The People: No Different Flesh *(1966). Her stories are always interesting, with strong characterization and believable emotions.*

Loyalty is one of the most prized attributes of the science-fiction culture, and Zenna Henderson was a loyal contributor to F&SF, rarely straying from its pages. "Something Bright" is one of her best stories, and her only appearance in Galaxy.

SOMETHING BRIGHT

Do you remember the Depression? That black shadow across time? That hurting place in the consciousness of the world? Maybe not. Maybe it's like asking do you remember the Dark Ages. Except what would I know about the price of eggs in the Dark Ages? I knew plenty about prices in the Depression.

If you had a quarter—*first find your quarter*—and five hungry kids, you could supper them on two cans of soup and a loaf of day-old bread, or two quarts of milk and a loaf of day-old bread. It was filling—in an afterthoughty kind of way—nourishing. But if you were one of the hungry five, you eventually began to feel erosion set in, and your teeth ached for substance.

But to go back to eggs. Those were a precious commodity. You savored them slowly or gulped them eagerly—unmistakably as eggs —boiled or fried. That's one reason why I remember Mrs. Klevity. She had eggs for *breakfast!* And *every day!* That's one reason why I remember Mrs. Klevity.

I didn't know about eggs the time she came over to see mom, who had just got home from a twelve-hour day, cleaning up after other people at thirty cents an hour. Mrs. Klevity lived in the same court as we did. Courtesy called it a court because we were all dependent on the same shower house and two toilets that occupied the shack square in the middle of the court.

All of us except the Big House, of course. It had a bathroom of its own and even a radio blaring "Nobody's Business" and "Should I Reveal" and had ceiling lights that didn't dangle nakedly at the end of a cord. But then it really wasn't a part of the court. Only its back door shared our area, and even that was different. It had *two* back doors in the same frame—a screen one and a wooden one!

Our own two-room place had a distinction, too. It had an upstairs. One room the size of our two. The Man Upstairs lived up there. He was mostly only the sound of footsteps overhead and an occasional cookie for Danna.

Anyway, Mrs. Klevity came over before mom had time to put her shopping bag of work clothes down or even to unpleat the folds of fatigue that dragged her face down ten years or more of time to come. I didn't much like Mrs. Klevity. She made me uncomfortable. She was so solid and slow moving and so nearly blind that she peered frighteningly wherever she went. She stood in the doorway as though she had been stacked there like bricks and a dress drawn hastily down over the stack and a face stretched on beneath a fuzz of hair. Us kids all gathered around to watch, except Danna, who snuffled wearily into my neck. Day nursery or not, it was a long, hard day for a four-year-old.

"I wondered if one of your girls could sleep at my house this week." Her voice was as slow as her steps.

"At your house?" Mom massaged her hand where the shopping-bag handles had crisscrossed it. "Come in. Sit down." We had two chairs and a bench and two apple boxes. The boxes scratched bare legs, but surely they couldn't scratch a stack of bricks.

"No, thanks." Maybe she couldn't bend! "My husband will be away several days and I don't like to be in the house alone at night."

"Of course," said mom. "You must feel awfully alone."

The only aloneness she knew, what with five kids and two rooms, was the taut secretness of her inward thoughts as she mopped and swept and ironed in other houses. "Sure, one of the girls would be glad to keep you company." There was a darting squirm and LaNell was safely hidden behind the swaying of our clothes in the diagonally curtained corner of the Other room, and Kathy knelt swiftly just beyond the dresser, out of sight.

"Anna is eleven." I had no place to hide, burdened as I was with Danna. "She's old enough. What time do you want her to come over?"

"Oh, bedtime will do." Mrs. Klevity peered out the door at the darkening sky. "Nine o'clock. Only it gets dark before then—" Bricks can look anxious, I guess.

"As soon as she has supper, she can come," said mom, handling my hours as though they had no value to me.

"Of course she has to go to school tomorrow."

"Only when it's dark," said Mrs. Klevity. "Day is all right. How much should I pay you?"

"Pay?" Mom gestured with one hand. "She has to sleep anyway. It doesn't matter to her where, once she's asleep. A favor for a friend."

I wanted to cry out: Whose favor for what friend? We hardly passed the time of day with Mrs. Klevity. I couldn't even remember Mr. Klevity except that he was straight and old and wrinkled. Uproot me and make me lie in a strange house, a strange dark, listening to a strange breathing, feeling a strange warmth making itself part of me for all night long, seeping into me—

"Mom—" I said.

"I'll give her breakfast," said Mrs. Klevity. "And lunch money for each night she comes."

I resigned myself without a struggle. Lunch money each day—a whole dime! Mom couldn't afford to pass up such a blessing, such a gift from God, who unerringly could be trusted to ease the pinch just before it became intolerable.

"Thank you, God," I whispered as I went to get the can opener to open supper. For a night or two I could stand it.

I felt all naked and unprotected as I stood in my flimsy crinkle cotton pajamas, one bare foot atop the other, waiting for Mrs. Klevity to turn the bed down.

"We have to check the house first," she said thickly. "We can't go to bed until we check the house."

"Check the house?" I forgot my starchy stiff shyness enough to question. "What for?"

Mrs. Klevity peered at me in the dim light of the bedroom. They had *three* rooms for only the two of them! Even if there was no door to shut between the bedroom and the kitchen.

"I couldn't sleep," she said, "unless I looked first. I have to."

So we looked. Behind the closet curtain, under the table—Mrs. Klevity even looked in the portable oven that sat near the two-burner stove in the kitchen.

When we came to the bed, I was moved to words again. "But we've been in here with the doors locked ever since I got here. What could possibly—"

"A prowler?" said Mrs. Klevity nervously, after a brief pause for thought. "A criminal?"

Mrs. Klevity pointed her face at me. I doubt if she could see me from that distance. "Doors make no difference," she said. "It might be when you least expect, so you have to expect all the time."

"I'll look," I said humbly. She was older than mom. She was nearly blind. She was one of God's *Also Unto Me's*.

"No," she said. "I have to. I couldn't be sure, else."

So I waited until she grunted and groaned to her knees, then bent stiffly to lift the limp spread. Her fingers hesitated briefly, then flicked the spread up. Her breath came out flat and finished. Almost disappointed, it seemed to me.

She turned the bed down and I crept across the gray, wrinkled sheets, and turning my back to the room, I huddled one ear on the flat, tobacco-smelling pillow and lay tense and uncomfortable in the dark, as her weight shaped and reshaped the bed around me. There was a brief silence before I heard the soundless breathy shape of her words, "How long, O God, how long?"

I wondered through my automatic *bless papa and mama*—and the automatic backup, because papa had abdicated from my specific prayers, *bless mama and my brother and sisters*—what it was that Mrs. Klevity was finding too long to bear.

After a restless waking, dozing sort of night that strange sleeping places held for me, I awoke to a thin chilly morning and the sound of Mrs. Klevity moving around. She had set the table for breakfast, a formality we never had time for at home. I scrambled out of bed and into my clothes with only my skinny, goose-fleshed back between Mrs. Klevity and me for modesty. I felt uncomfortable and unfinished because I hadn't brought our comb over with me.

I would have preferred to run home to our usual breakfast of canned milk and Shredded Wheat, but instead I watched, fascinated, as Mrs. Klevity struggled with lighting the kerosene stove. She bent so close, peering at the burners with the match flaring in her hand, that I was sure the frowzy brush of her hair would catch fire, but finally the burner caught instead and she turned her face toward me.

"One egg or two?" she asked.

"Eggs! Two!" Surprise wrung the exclamation from me. Her hand hesitated over the crumpled brown bag on the table. "No, no!" I corrected her thought hastily. "One. One is plenty," and sat on the edge of a chair watching as she broke an egg into the sizzling frying pan.

"Hard or soft?" she asked.

"Hard," I said casually, feeling very woman-of-the-worldish, dining out—well, practically—and for breakfast, too! I watched Mrs. Klevity spoon the fat over the egg, her hair swinging stiffly forward when she peered. Once it even dabbled briefly in the fat, but she didn't notice, and as it swung back, it made a little shiny curve on her cheek.

"Aren't you afraid of the fire?" I asked as she turned away from the stove with the frying pan. "What if you caught on fire?"

"I did once." She slid the egg out onto my plate. "See?" She brushed her hair back on the left side and I could see the mottled pucker of a large old scar. "It was before I got used to Here," she said, making Here more than the house, it seemed to me.

"That's awful," I said, hesitating with my fork.

"Go ahead and eat," she said. "Your egg will get cold." She turned back to the stove and I hesitated a minute more. Meals at a table you were supposed to ask a blessing, but—I ducked my head quickly and had a mouthful of egg before my soundless amen was finished.

After breakfast I hurried back to our house, my lunch-money dime clutched securely, my stomach not quite sure it liked fried eggs so early in the morning. Mom was ready to leave, her shopping bag in one hand, Danna swinging from the other, singing one of her baby songs. She *liked* the day nursery.

"I won't be back until late tonight," mom said. "There's a quarter in the corner of the dresser drawer. You get supper for the kids and try to clean up this messy place. We don't have to be pigs just because we live in a place like this."

"Okay, mom." I struggled with a snarl in my hair, the pulling making my eyes water. "Where you working today?" I spoke over the clatter in the Other room where the kids were getting ready for school.

She sighed, weary before the day began. "I have three places today, but the last is Mrs. Paddington." Her face lightened. Mrs. Paddington sometimes paid a little extra or gave mom discarded clothes or leftover food she didn't want. She was nice.

"You get along all right with Mrs. Klevity?" asked mom as she checked her shopping bag for her work shoes.

"Yeah," I said. "But she's funny. She looks under the bed before she goes to bed."

Mom smiled. "I've heard of people like that, but it's usually old maids they're talking about."

"But, mom, nothing coulda got in. She locked the door after I got in. She locked the door after I got there."

"People who look under beds don't always think straight," she said. "Besides, maybe she'd *like* to find something under there."

"But she's *got* a husband," I cried after her as she herded Danna across the court.

"There are other things to look for besides husbands," she called back.

"Anna wants a husband! Anna wants a husband!" Deet and LaNell were dancing around me, teasing me singsong. Kathy smiled slowly behind them.

"Shut up," I said. "You don't even know what you're talking about. Go on to school."

"It's too early," said Deet, digging his bare toes in the dust of the front yard. "Teacher says we get there too early."

"Then stay here and start cleaning house," I said.

They left in a hurry. After they were gone, Deet's feet reminded me I'd better wash my own feet before I went to school. So I got a washpan of water from the tap in the middle of the court, and sitting on the side of the bed, I eased my feet into the icy water. I scrubbed with the hard, gray, abrasive soap we used and wiped quickly on the tattered towel. I threw the water out the door and watched it run like dust-covered snakes across the hard-packed front yard.

I went back to put my shoes on and get my sweater. I looked at the bed. I got down on my stomach and peered under. *Other things to look for.* There was the familiar huddle of cardboard cartons we kept things in and the familiar dust fluffs and one green sock LaNell had lost last week, but nothing else.

I dusted my front off. I tied my lunch-money dime in the corner of a handkerchief, and putting my sweater on, left for school.

I peered out into the windy wet semi-twilight. "Do I have to?"

"You said you would," said mom. "Keep your promises. You should have gone before this. She's probably been waiting for you."

"I wanted to see what you brought from Mrs. Paddington's." LaNell and Kathy were playing in the corner with a lavender hug-me-tight and a hat with green grapes on it. Deet was rolling an orange on the floor, softening it preliminary to poking a hole in it to suck the juice out.

"She cleaned a trunk out today," said mom. "Mostly old things that belonged to her mother, but these two coats are nice and heavy. They'll be good covers tonight. It's going to be cold. Someday when I get time, I'll cut them up and make quilts." She sighed. Time was what she never had enough of. "Better take a newspaper to hold over your head."

"Oh, mom!" I huddled into my sweater. "It isn't raining now. I'd feel silly!"

"Well, then, scoot!" she said, her hand pressing my shoulder warmly, briefly.

I scooted, skimming quickly the flood of light from our doorway, and splishing through the shallow runoff stream that swept across the court. There was a sudden wild swirl of wind and a vindictive splatter of heavy, cold raindrops that swept me, exhilarated, the rest

of the way to Mrs. Klevity's house and under the shallow little roof
that was just big enough to cover the back step. I knocked quickly,
brushing my disordered hair back from my eyes. The door swung
open and I was in the shadowy, warm kitchen, almost in Mrs.
Klevity's arms.

"Oh!" I backed up, laughing breathlessly. "The wind blew—"

"I was afraid you weren't coming." She turned away to the stove.
"I fixed some hot cocoa."

I sat cuddling the warm cup in my hands, savoring the chocolate
sip by sip. She had made it with milk instead of water, and it tasted
rich and wonderful. But Mrs. Klevity was sharing my thoughts with
the cocoa. In that brief moment when I had been so close to her, I
had looked deep into her dim eyes and was feeling a vast astonishment. The dimness was only on top. Underneath—underneath—

I took another sip of cocoa. Her eyes—almost I could have walked
into them, it seemed like. Slip past the gray film, run down the
shiny bright corridor, into the live young sparkle at the far end.

I looked deep into my cup of cocoa. Were all grown-ups like that?

If you could get behind their eyes, were they different too? Behind
mom's eyes, was there a corridor leading back to youth and sparkle?

I finished the cocoa drowsily. It was still early, but the rain was
drumming on the roof and it was the kind of night you curl up to if
you're warm and fed. Sometimes you feel thin and cold on such
nights, but I was feeling curl-uppy. So I groped under the bed for
the paper bag that had my jamas in it. I couldn't find it.

"I swept today," said Mrs. Klevity, coming back from some far
country of her thoughts. "I musta pushed it farther under the bed."

I got down on my hands and knees and peered under the bed.
"Oooo!" I said. "What's shiny?"

Something snatched me away from the bed and flung me to one
side. By the time I had gathered myself up off the floor and was rubbing a banged elbow, Mrs. Klevity's bulk was pressed against the
bed, her head under it.

"Hey!" I cried indignantly, and then remembered I wasn't at
home. I heard an odd whimpering sob and then Mrs. Klevity backed
slowly away, still kneeling on the floor.

"Only the lock on the suitcase," she said. "Here's your jamas." She
handed me the bag and ponderously pulled herself upright again.

We went silently to bed after she had limped around and checked
the house, even under the bed again. I heard that odd breathy whis-

per of a prayer and lay awake, trying to add up something shiny and the odd eyes and the whispering sob. Finally I shrugged in the dark and wondered what I'd pick for funny when I grew up. All grown-ups had some kind of funny.

The next night Mrs. Klevity couldn't get down on her knees to look under the bed. She'd hurt herself when she plumped down on the floor after yanking me away from the bed.

"You'll have to look for me tonight," she said slowly, nursing her knees. "Look good. Oh, Anna, look good!"

I looked as good as I could, not knowing what I was looking for.

"It should be under the bed," she said, her palms tight on her knees as she rocked back and forth. "But you can't be sure. It might miss completely."

"What might?" I asked, hunkering down by the bed.

She turned her face blindly toward me. "The way out," she said. "The way back again—"

"Back again?" I pressed my cheek to the floor again. "Well, I don't see anything. Only dark and suitcases."

"Nothing bright? Nothing? Nothing—" She tried to lay her face on her knees, but she was too unbendy to manage it, so she put her hands over her face instead. Grown-ups aren't supposed to cry. She didn't quite, but her hands looked wet when she reached for the clock to wind it.

I lay in the dark, one strand of her hair tickling my hand where it lay on the pillow. Maybe she was crazy. I felt a thrill of terror fan out on my spine. I carefully moved my hand from under the lock of hair. How can you find a way *out* under a bed? I'd be glad when Mr. Klevity got home, eggs or no eggs, dime or no dime.

Somewhere in the darkness of the night, I was suddenly swimming to wakefulness, not knowing what was waking me but feeling that Mrs. Klevity was awake too.

"Anna." Her voice was small and light and silver. "Anna—"

"Hummm?" I murmured, my voice still drowsy.

"Anna, have you ever been away from home?" I turned toward her, trying in the dark to make sure it was Mrs. Klevity. She sounded so different.

"Yes," I said. "Once I visited Aunt Katie at Rocky Butte for a week."

"Anna . . ." I don't know whether she was even hearing my answers; her voice was almost a chant ". . . Anna, have you ever been in prison?"

"No! Of course not!" I recoiled indignantly. "You have to be awfully bad to be in prison."

"Oh, no. Oh, no!" she sighed. "Not jail, Anna. Prison—prison. The weight of the flesh—bound about—"

"Oh," I said, smoothing my hands across my eyes. She was talking to a something deep in me that never got talked to, that hardly even had words. "Like when the wind blows the clouds across the moon and the grass whispers along the road and all the trees pull like balloons at their trunks and one star comes out and says 'Come' and the ground says 'Stay' and part of you tries to go and it hurts—" I could feel the slender roundness of my ribs under my pressing hands. "And it hurts—"

"Oh Anna, Anna!" The soft, light voice broke. "You feel that way and you *belong* Here. You won't ever—"

The voice stopped and Mrs. Klevity rolled over. Her next words came thickly, as though a gray film were over them as over her eyes. "Are you awake, Anna? Go to sleep, child. Morning isn't yet."

I heard the heavy sigh of her breathing as she slept. And finally I slept too, trying to visualize what Mrs. Klevity would look like if she looked like the silvery voice in the dark.

I sat savoring my egg the next morning, letting thoughts slip in and out of my mind to the rhythm of my jaws. What a funny dream to have, to talk with a silver-voiced someone. To talk about the way blowing clouds and windy moonlight felt. But it wasn't a dream! I paused with my fork raised. At least not my dream. But how can you tell? If you're part of someone else's dream, can it still be real for you?

"Is something wrong with the egg?" Mrs. Klevity peered at me.

"No—no—" I said, harshly snatching the bite on my fork. "Mrs. Klevity—"

"Yes." Her voice was thick and heavy-footed.

"Why did you ask me about being in prison?"

"Prison?" Mrs. Klevity blinked blindly. "Did I ask you about prison?"

"Someone did—I thought—" I faltered, shyness shutting down on me again.

"Dreams." Mrs. Klevity stacked her knife and fork on her plate. "Dreams."

I wasn't quite sure I was to be at the Klevitys' the next evening. Mr. Klevity was supposed to get back sometime during the evening. But Mrs. Klevity welcomed me.

"Don't know when he'll get home," she said. "Maybe not until morning. If he comes early, you can go home to sleep and I'll give you your dime anyway."

"Oh, no," I said, mom's teachings solidly behind me. "I couldn't take it if I didn't stay."

"A gift," said Mrs. Klevity.

We sat opposite one another until the silence stretched too thin for me to bear.

"In olden times," I said, snatching at the magic that drew stories from mom, "when you were a little girl—"

"When I was a girl—" Mrs. Klevity rubbed her knees with reflective hands. "The other Where. The other When."

"In olden times," I persisted, "things were different then."

"Yes." I settled down comfortably, recognizing the reminiscent tone of voice. "You do crazy things when you are young." Mrs. Klevity leaned heavily on the table. "Things you have no business doing. You volunteer when you're young." I jerked as she lunged across the table and grabbed both my arms. "But I *am* young! Three years isn't an eternity. I *am* young!"

I twisted one arm free and pried at her steely fingers that clamped the other one.

"Oh." She let go. "I'm sorry. I didn't mean to hurt you."

She pushed back the tousled brush of her hair.

"Look," she said, her voice almost silver again. "Under all this—this grossness, I'm still me. I thought I could adjust to anything, but I had no idea that they'd put me in such—" She tugged at her sagging dress. "Not the clothes!" she cried. "Clothes you can take off. But this—" Her fingers dug into her heavy shoulder and I could see the bulge of flesh between them.

"If I knew *anything* about the setup maybe I could locate it. Maybe I could call. Maybe—"

Her shoulders sagged and her eyelids dropped down over her dull eyes.

"It doesn't make any sense to you," she said, her voice heavy and thick again. "To you I'd be old even There. At the time it seemed like a perfect way to have an odd holiday and help out with research, too. But we got caught."

She began to count her fingers, mumbling to herself. "Three years There, but Here that's—eight threes are—" She traced on the table with a blunt forefinger, her eyes close to the old, worn-out cloth.

"Mrs. Klevity." My voice scared me in the silence, but I was feeling the same sort of upsurge that catches you sometimes when you're playing-like and it gets so real. "Mrs. Klevity, if you've lost something, maybe I could look for it for you."

"You didn't find it last night," she said.

"Find what?"

She lumbered to her feet. "Let's look again. Everywhere. They'd surely be able to locate the house."

"What are we looking for?" I asked, searching the portable oven.

"You'll know it when we see it," she said.

And we searched the whole house. Oh, such nice things! Blankets, not tattered and worn, and even an extra one they didn't need. And towels and washrags that matched—and weren't rags. And uncracked dishes that matched! And glasses that weren't jars. And books. And money. Crisp new-looking bills in the little box in the bottom drawer—pushed back under some *extra* pillowcases. And clothes—lots and lots of clothes. All too big for any of us, of course, but my practiced eye had already visualized this, that, and the other cut down to dress us all like rich people.

I sighed as we sat wearily looking at one another. Imagine having so much and still looking for something else! It was bedtime and all we had for our pains were dirty hands and tired backs.

I scooted out to the bathhouse before I undressed. I gingerly washed the dirt off my hands under the cold of the shower and shook them dry on the way back to the house. Well, we had moved everything in the place, but nothing was what Mrs. Klevity looked for.

Back in the bedroom, I groped under the bed for my jamas and again had to lie flat and burrow under the bed for the tattered bag. Our moving around had wedged it back between two cardboard cartons. I squirmed under farther and tried to ease it out after shoving the two cartons a little farther apart. The bag tore, spilling out my jamas, so I grasped them in the bend of my elbow and started to back out.

Then the whole world seemed to explode into brightness that pulsated and dazzled, that splashed brilliance into my astonished eyes until I winced them shut to rest their seeing and saw the dark inversions of the radiance beyond my eyelids.

I forced my eyes open again and looked sideways so the edge of my seeing was all I used until I got more accustomed to the glory.

Between the two cartons was an opening like a window would be, but little, little, into a wonderland of things I could never tell. Colors that had no names. Feelings that made windy moonlight a puddle of dust. I felt tears burn out of my eyes and start down my cheeks, whether from brightness or wonder, I don't know. I blinked them away and looked again.

Someone was in the brightness, several someones. They were leaning out of the squareness, beckoning and calling—silver signals and silver sounds.

"Mrs. Klevity," I thought. "Something bright."

I took another good look at the shining people and the tree things that were like music bordering a road, and grass that was the song my evening grass hummed in the wind—a last, last look, and began to back out.

I scrambled to my feet, clutching my jamas. "Mrs. Klevity." She was still sitting at the table, as solid as a pile of bricks, the sketched face under the wild hair a sad, sad one.

"Yes, child." She hardly heard herself.

"Something bright—" I said.

Her heavy head lifted slowly, her blind face turned to me. "What, child?"

I felt my fingers bite into my jamas and the cords in my neck getting tight and my stomach clenching itself. "Something bright!" I thought I screamed. She didn't move. I grabbed her arm and dragged her off balance in her chair. "Something bright!"

"Anna." She righted herself on the chair. "Don't be mean."

I grabbed the bedspread and yanked it up. The light sprayed out like a sprinkler on a lawn.

Then *she* screamed, "Leolienn! It's here! Hurry, hurry!"

"Mr. Klevity isn't here," I said. "He hasn't got back."

"I can't go without him! Leolienn!"

"Leave a note!" I cried. "If you're there, you can make them come back again and I can show him the right place!" The upsurge had passed make-believe and everything was realer then real.

Then, quicker than I thought she ever could move, she got paper and a pencil. She was scribbling away at the table as I stood there holding the spread. So I dropped to my knees and then to my stomach and crawled under the bed again. I filled my eyes with the brightness and beauty and saw, beyond it, serenity and orderliness and—and uncluttered cleanness. The miniature landscape was like a stage setting for a fairy tale—so small, so small—so lovely.

And then Mrs. Klevity tugged at my ankle and I slid out, reluctantly, stretching my sight of the bright square until the falling of the spread broke it. Mrs. Klevity worked her way under the bed, her breath coming pantingly, her big, ungainly body inching along awkwardly.

She crawled and crawled and crawled until she should have come up short against the wall, and I knew she must be funneling down into the brightness, her face, head and shoulders, so small, so lovely, like her silvery voice. But the rest of her, still gross and ugly, like a butterfly trying to skin out of its cocoon.

Finally only her feet were sticking out from under the bed and they thrashed and waved and didn't go anywhere, so I got down on the floor and put my feet against hers and braced myself against the dresser and pushed. And pushed and pushed. Suddenly there was a going, a finishing, and my feet dropped to the floor.

There, almost under the bed, lay Mrs. Klevity's shabby old-lady black shoes, toes pointing away from each other. I picked them up in my hands, wanting, somehow, to cry. Her saggy lisle stockings were still in the shoes.

Slowly I pulled all the clothes of Mrs. Klevity out from under the bed. They were held together by a thin skin, a sloughed-off leftover of Mrs. Klevity that only showed, gray and lifeless, where her bare hands and face would have been, and her dull gray filmed eyes.

I let it crumple to the floor and sat there, holding one of her old shoes in my hand.

The door rattled, and it was gray, old, wrinkled Mr. Klevity.

"Hello, child," he said. "Where's my wife?"

"She's gone," I said, not looking at him. "She left you a note there on the table."

"Gone—?" He left the word stranded in midair as he read Mrs. Klevity's note.

The paper fluttered down. He yanked a dresser drawer open and snatched out spool-looking things, both hands full. Then he practically dived under the bed, his elbows thudding on the floor, to hurt hard. And there was only a wiggle or two, and *his* shoes slumped away from each other.

I pulled his cast aside from under the bed and crawled under it myself. I saw the tiny picture frame—bright, bright, but so small.

I crept close to it, knowing I couldn't go in. I saw the tiny perfection of the road, the landscape, the people—the laughing people who crowded around the two new rejoicing figures—the two silvery, lovely young creatures who cried out in tiny voices as they danced. The girl one threw a kiss outward before they all turned away and ran up the winding white road together.

The frame began to shrink, faster, faster, until it squeezed to a single bright bead and then blinked out.

All at once the house was empty and cold. The upsurge was gone. Nothing was real any more. All at once the faint ghost of the smell of eggs was frightening. All at once I whimpered, "My lunch money!"

I scrambled to my feet, tumbling Mrs. Klevity's clothes into a disconnected pile. I gathered up my jamas and leaned across the table to get my sweater. I saw my name on a piece of paper. I picked it up and read it.

Everything that is ours in this house now belongs to Anna-across-the-court, the little girl that's been staying with me at night.

Ahvlaree Klevity

I looked from the paper around the room. All for me? All for us? All this richness and wonder of good things? All this and the box in the bottom drawer, too? And a paper that said so, so that nobody could take them away from us.

A fluttering wonder filled my chest and I walked stiffly around the three rooms, visualizing everything without opening a drawer or door. I stood by the stove and looked at the frying pan hanging above it. I opened the cupboard door. The paper bag of eggs was on the shelf. I reached for it, looking back over my shoulder almost guiltily.

The wonder drained out of me with a gulp. I ran back over to the bed and yanked up the spread. I knelt and hammered on the edge of the bed with my clenched fists. Then I leaned my forehead on my tight hands and felt my knuckles bruise me. My hands went limply to my lap, my head drooping.

I got up slowly and took the paper from the table, bundled my jamas under my arm, and got the eggs from the cupboard. I turned the lights out and left.

I felt tears wash down from my eyes as I stumbled across the familiar yard in the dark. I don't know why I was crying—unless it was because I was homesick for something bright that I knew I would never have, and because I knew I could never tell mom what really had happened.

Then the pale trail of light from our door caught me and I swept in on an astonished mom, calling softly, because of the sleeping kids, "Mom! Mom! Guess what!"

Yes, I remember Mrs. Klevity because she had eggs for *breakfast!* *Every day!* That's one of the reasons I remember her.

THE LADY WHO SAILED THE SOUL

April 1960

Cordwainer Smith
(1913–1966)

Dr. Paul M. A. Linebarger was a professor of international relations and Asiatic history at Johns Hopkins University who, as "Cordwainer Smith," wrote some of the strangest and most beautiful stories in the history of magazine sf. His true identity a complete secret for years, he constructed a strange and fascinating series, "The Instrumentality," which quickly captured the interest and favor of readers everywhere. He was also one of the most important authors in the history of Galaxy, appearing in it more frequently than anywhere else. His titles were intriguing: "Mother Hitton's Littul Kittons" (June 1961), "The Ballad of Lost C'Mell" (October 1962), "Think Blue, Count Two" (February 1963), the famous "The Game of Rat and Dragon" (October 1955), and "The Dead Lady of Clown Town" (August 1964). "Under Old Earth" (February 1966) was Linebarger's final appearance in Galaxy.

THE LADY WHO SAILED THE SOUL

1

The story ran—how did the story run? Everyone knew the reference to Helen America and Mr. Grey-no-more, but no one knew exactly how it happened. Their names were welded to the glittering timeless jewelry of romance. Sometimes they were compared to Heloise and Abelard, whose story had been found among books in a long-buried library. Other ages were to compare their life with the weird, ugly-lovely story of the Go-Captain Taliano and the Lady Dolores Oh.

Out of it all, two things stood forth—their love and the image of the great sails, tissue-metal wings with which the bodies of people finally fluttered out among the stars.

Mention him, and others knew her. Mention her, and they knew him. He was the first of the inbound sailors and she was the lady who sailed the *Soul*.

It was lucky that people lost their pictures. The romantic hero was a very young-looking man, prematurely old and still quite sick when the romance came. And Helen America, she was a freak, but a nice one: a grim, solemn, sad, little brunette who had been born amid the laughter of humanity. She was not the tall, confident heroine of the actresses who later played her.

She was, however, a wonderful sailor. That much was true. And with her body and mind she loved Mr. Grey-no-more, showing a devotion which the ages can neither surpass nor forget. History may scrape off the patina of their names and appearances, but even history can do no more than brighten the love of Helen America and Mr. Grey-no-more.

Both of them, one must remember, were sailors.

2

The child was playing with a spieltier. She got tired of letting it be a chicken, so she reversed it into the fur-bearing position. When she extended the ears to the optimum development, the little animal looked odd indeed. A light breeze blew the animal-toy on its side, but the spieltier good-naturedly righted itself and munched contentedly on the carpet.

The little girl suddenly clapped her hands and broke forth with the question,

"Mamma, what's a sailor?"

"There used to be sailors, darling, a long time ago. They were brave men who took the ships out to the stars, the very first ships that took people away from our sun. And they had big sails. I don't know how it worked, but somehow, the light pushed them, and it

took them a quarter of a life to make a single one-way trip. People only lived a hundred and sixty years at that time, darling, and it was forty years each way, but we don't need sailors any more."

"Of course not," said the child, "we can go right away. You've taken me to Mars and you've taken me to New Earth as well, haven't you, mamma? And we can go anywhere else soon, but that only takes one afternoon."

"That's planoforming, honey. But it was a long time before the people knew how to planoform. And they could not travel the way we could, so they made great big sails. They made sails so big that they could not build them on Earth. They had to hang them out, half-way between Earth and Mars. And you know, a funny thing happened . . . Did you ever hear about the time the world froze?"

"No, mamma, what was that?"

"Well, a long time ago, one of these sails drifted and people tried to save it because it took a lot of work to build it. But the sail was so large that it got between the earth and the sun. And there was no more sunshine, just night all the time. And it got very cold on Earth. All the atomic power plants were busy, and all the air began to smell funny. And the people were worried and in a few days they pulled the sail back out of the way. And the sunshine came again."

"Mamma, were there ever any girl sailors?"

A curious expression crossed over the mother's face. "There was one. You'll hear about her later on when you are older. Her name was Helen America and she sailed the Soul out to the stars. She was the only woman that ever did it. And that is a wonderful story."

The mother dabbed at her eyes with a handkerchief.

The child said: "Mamma, tell me now. What's the story all about?"

At this point the mother became very firm and she said: "Honey, there are some things that you are not old enough to hear yet. But when you are a big girl, I'll tell you all about them."

The mother was an honest woman. She reflected a moment, and then she added, ". . . unless you read about it yourself first."

3

Helen America was to make her place in the history of mankind, but she started badly. The name itself was misfortune.

No one ever knew who her father was. The officials agreed to keep the matter quiet.

Her mother was not in doubt. Her mother was the celebrated she-man Mona Muggeridge, a woman who had campaigned a hundred times for the lost cause of complete identity of the two genders. She had been a feminist beyond all limits, and when Mona Muggeridge, the one and only *Miss* Muggeridge, announced to the press that she was going to have a baby, that was first-class news.

Mona Muggeridge went further. She announced her firm conviction that fathers should not be identified. She proclaimed that no woman should have consecutive children with the same man, that women should be advised to pick different fathers for their children, so as to diversify and beautify the race. She capped it all by announcing that she, Miss Muggeridge, had selected the perfect father and would inevitably produce the only perfect child.

Miss Muggeridge, a bony, pompous blonde, stated that she would avoid the nonsense of marriage and family names, and that therefore the child, if a boy, would be called John America, and if a girl, Helen America.

Thus it happened that little Helen America was born with the correspondents in the press services waiting outside the delivery room. Newsscreens flashed the picture of a pretty three-kilogram baby. "IT'S A GIRL." "THE PERFECT CHILD." "WHO'S THE DAD?"

That was just the beginning. Mona Muggeridge was belligerent. She insisted, even after the baby had been photographed for the thousandth time, that this was the finest child ever born. She pointed to the child's perfections. She demonstrated all the foolish fondness of a doting mother, but felt that she, the great crusader, had discovered this fondness for the first time.

To say that this background was difficult for the child would be an understatement.

Helen America was a wonderful example of raw human material triumphing over its tormentors. By the time she was four years old, she spoke six languages, and was beginning to decipher some of the old Martian texts. At the age of five she was sent to school. Her fellow schoolchildren immediately developed a rhyme:

> *Helen, Helen*
> *Fat and dumb*
> *Doesn't know where*
> *Her daddy's from!*

Helen took all this and perhaps it was an accident of genetics that she grew to become a compact little person—a deadly serious little brunette. Challenged by lessons, haunted by publicity, she became careful and reserved about friendships and desperately lonely in an inner world.

When Helen America was sixteen her mother came to a bad end. Mona Muggeridge eloped with a man she announced to be the perfect husband for the perfect marriage hitherto overlooked by mankind. The perfect husband was a skilled machine polisher. He already had a wife and four children. He drank beer and his interest in Miss Muggeridge seems to have been a mixture of good-natured comradeship and a sensible awareness of her motherly bankroll. The planetary yacht on which they eloped broke the regulations with an off-schedule flight. The bridegroom's wife and children had alerted the police. The result was a collision with a robotic barge which left both bodies identifiable.

At sixteen Helen was already famous, and at seventeen already forgotten, and very much alone.

4

This was the age of sailors. The thousands of photoreconnaissance and measuring missiles had begun back with their harvest from the stars. Planet after planet swam into the ken of mankind. The new worlds became known as the interstellar search missiles brought back photographs, samples of atmosphere, measurements of gravity, cloud coverage, chemical makeup, and the like. Of the very numerous missiles which returned from their two- or three-hundred-year voyages, three brought back reports of New Earth, an earth so much like Terra itself that it could be settled.

The first sailors had gone out almost a hundred years before. They had started with small sails not over two thousand miles square. Gradually the size of the sails increased. The technique of adiabatic packing and the carrying of passengers in individual pods reduced the damage done to the human cargo. It was great news when a sailor returned to Earth, a man born and reared under the light of another star. He was a man who had spent a month of agony and ' pain, bringing a few sleep-frozen settlers, guiding the immense light-pushed sailing craft which had managed the trip through the great interstellar deeps in an objective time-period of forty years.

Mankind got to know the look of a sailor. There was a plantigrade walk to the way he put his body on the ground. There was a sharp, stiff, mechanical swing to his neck. The man was neither young nor old. He had been awake and conscious for forty years, thanks to the drug which made possible a kind of limited awareness. By the time the psychologists interrogated him, first for the proper authorities of the Instrumentality and later for the news releases, it was plain enough that he thought the forty years were about a month. He never volunteered to sail back, because he had actually aged forty years. He was a young man, a young man in his hopes and wishes, but a man who had burnt up a quarter of a human lifetime in a single agonizing experience.

At this time Helen America went to Cambridge. Lady Joan's College was the finest woman's college in the Atlantic world. Cambridge had reconstructed its protohistoric traditions and the neo-British had recaptured that fine edge of engineering which reconnected their traditions with the earliest antiquity.

Naturally enough the language was cosmopolite Earth and not archaic English, but the students were proud to live at a reconstructed university very much like the archaeological evidence showed it to have been before the period of darkness and troubles came upon the earth. Helen shone a little in this renaissance.

The news-release services watched Helen in the cruelest possible fashion. They revived her name and the story of her mother. Then they forgot her again. She had put in for six professions, and her last choice was "sailor." It happened that she was the first woman to make the application—first because she was the only woman young enough to qualify who had also passed the scientific requirements.

Her picture was beside his on the screens before they ever met each other.

Actually, she was not anything like that at all. She had suffered so much in her childhood from *Helen, Helen, fat and dumb,* that she was competitive only on a coldly professional basis. She hated and loved and missed the tremendous mother whom she had lost, and she resolved so fiercely not to be like her mother that she became an embodied antithesis of Mona.

The mother had been horsy, blonde, big—the kind of woman who is a feminist because she is not very feminine. Helen never thought about her own femininity. She just worried about herself. Her face would have been round if it had been plump, but she was not plump. Black-haired, dark-eyed, broad-bodied but thin, she was a genetic demonstration of her unknown father. Her teachers often feared her. She was a pale, quiet girl, and she always knew her subject.

Her fellow students had joked about her for a few weeks and then most of them had banded together against the indecency of the press. When a newsframe came out with something ridiculous about the long-dead Mona, the whisper went through Lady Joan's:

"Keep Helen away . . . those people are at it again."

"Don't let Helen look at the frames now. She's the best person we have in the noncollateral sciences and we can't have her upset just before the tripos . . ."

They protected her, and it was only by chance that she saw her own face in a newsframe. There was the face of a man beside her. He looked like a little old monkey, she thought. Then she read, "PERFECT GIRL WANTS TO BE SAILOR. SHOULD SAILOR HIMSELF DATE PERFECT GIRL?" Her cheeks burned with helpless, unavoidable embarrassment and rage, but she had grown too expert at being herself to do what she might have done in her teens—hate the man. She knew it wasn't his fault either. It wasn't even the fault of the silly pushing men and women from the news services. It was time, it was custom, it was man himself. But she had only to be herself, if she could ever find out what that really meant.

5

Their dates, when they came, had the properties of nightmares.

A news service sent a woman to tell her she had been awarded a week's holiday in New Madrid.

With the sailor from the stars.

Helen refused.

Then *he* refused too, and he was a little too prompt for her liking. She became curious about him.

Two weeks passed, and in the office of the news service a treasurer brought two slips of paper to the director. They were the vouchers for Helen America and Mr. Grey-no-more to obtain the utmost in preferential luxury at New Madrid. The treasurer said, "These have been issued and registered as gifts with the Instrumentality, sir. Should they be canceled?" The executive had his fill of stories that day, and he felt humane. On an impulse he commanded the treasurer, "Tell you what. Give those tickets to the young people. No publicity. We'll keep out of it. If they don't want us, they don't have to have us. Push it along. That's all. Go."

The ticket went back out to Helen. She had made the highest record ever reported at the university, and she needed a rest. When the news-service woman gave her the ticket, she said,

"Is this a trick?"

Assured that it was not, she then asked,

"Is that man coming?"

She couldn't say "the sailor"—it sounded too much like the way people had always talked about herself—and she honestly didn't remember his other name at the moment.

The woman did not know.

"Do I have to see him?" said Helen.

"Of course not," said the woman. The gift was unconditional.

Helen laughed, almost grimly. "All right, I'll take it and say thanks. But one picturemaker, mind you, just one, and I walk out. Or I may walk out for no reason at all. Is that all right?"

It was.

Four days later Helen was in the pleasure world of New Madrid, and a master of the dances was presenting her to an odd, intense old man whose hair was black.

"Junior scientist Helen America—Sailor of the stars Mr. Grey-no-more."

He looked at them shrewdly and smiled a kindly, experienced smile. He added the empty phrase of his profession,

"I have had the honor and I withdraw."

They were alone together on the edge of the dining room. The sailor looked at her very sharply indeed, and then said:

"Who are you? Are you somebody I have already met? Should I remember you? There are too many people here on Earth. What do we do next? What are we supposed to do? Would you like to sit down?"

Helen said one "Yes" to all those questions and never dreamed that the single *yes* would be articulated by hundreds of great actresses, each one in the actress's own special way, across the centuries to come.

They did sit down.

How the rest of it happened, neither one was ever quite sure.

She had had to quiet him almost as though he were a hurt person in the House of Recovery. She explained the dishes to him and when he still could not choose, she gave the robot selections for him. She warned him, kindly enough, about manners when he forgot the simple ceremonies of eating which everyone knew, such as standing up to unfold the napkin or putting the scraps into the solvent tray and the silverware into the transfer.

At last he relaxed and did not look so old.

Momentarily forgetting the thousand times she had been asked silly questions herself, she asked him,

"Why did *you* become a sailor?"

He stared at her in open-eyed inquiry as though she had spoken to him in an unknown language and expected a reply. Finally he mumbled the answer,

"Are you—you, too—saying that—that I shouldn't have done it?"

Her hand went to her mouth in instinctive apology.

"No, no, no. You see, I myself have put in to be a sailor."

He merely looked at her, his young-old eyes open with observativeness. He did not stare, but merely seemed to be trying to understand words, each one of which he could comprehend individually but which in sum amounted to sheer madness. She did not turn away from his look, odd though it was. Once again, she had the chance to note the indescribable peculiarity of this man who had managed enormous sails out in the blind empty black between untwinkling stars. He was young as a boy. The hair which gave him his name was glossy black. His beard must have been removed permanently, because his skin was that of a middle-aged woman—well-kept, pleasant, but showing the unmistakable wrinkles of age and betraying no sign of the normal stubble which the males in her culture preferred to leave on their faces. The skin had age without experience. The muscles had grown older, but they did not show *how* the person had grown.

Helen had learned to be an acute observer of people as her mother took up with one fanatic after another; she knew full well that people carry their secret biographies written in the muscles of their faces, and that a stranger passing on the street tells us (whether he wishes to or not) all his inmost intimacies. If we but look sharply enough, and in the right light, we know whether fear or hope or amusement has tallied the hours of his days, we divine the sources and outcome of his most secret sensuous pleasures, we catch the dim but persistent reflections of those other people who have left the imprints of their personalities on him in turn.

All this was absent from Mr. Grey-no-more: He had age but not the stigma of age; he had growth without the normal markings of growth; he had lived without living, in a time and world in which most people stayed young while living too much.

He was the uttermost opposite of her mother that Helen had ever seen, and with a pang of undirected apprehension Helen realized that this man meant a great deal to her future life, whether she wished him to or not. She saw in him a young bachelor, prematurely old, a man whose love had been given to emptiness and horror, not to the tangible rewards and disappointments of human life. He had had all space for his mistress, and space had used him harshly. Still young, he was old; already old, he was young.

The mixture was one which she knew that she had never seen before, and which she suspected that no one else had ever seen, either. He had in the beginning of life the sorrow, compassion, and wisdom which most people find only at the end.

It was he who broke the silence. "You did say, didn't you, that you yourself had put in to be a sailor?"

Even to herself, her answer sounded silly and girlish. "I'm the first woman ever to qualify with the necessary scientific subjects while still young enough to pass the physical . . ."

"You must be an unusual girl," said he mildly. Helen realized, with a thrill, a sweet and bitterly real hope, that this young-old man from the stars had never heard of the "perfect child" who had been laughed at in the moments of being born, the girl who had all America for a father, who was famous and unusual and alone so terribly much so that she could not even imagine being ordinary, happy, decent, or simple.

She thought to herself, *It would take a wise freak who sails in from the stars to overlook who I am*, but to him she simply said, "It's no use talking about being 'unusual.' I'm tired of this Earth, and since I don't have to die to leave it, I think I would like to sail to the stars. I've got less to lose than you may think . . ." She started to tell him about Mona Muggeridge but she stopped in time.

The compassionate gray eyes were upon her, and at this point it was he, not she, who was in control of the situation. She looked at the eyes themselves. They had stayed open for forty years, in the blackness near to pitch-darkness of the tiny cabin. The dim dials had shone like blazing suns upon his tired retinas before he was able to turn his eyes away. From time to time he had looked out at the black nothing to see the silhouettes of his dials, almost-blackness against total blackness, as the miles of their sweep sucked up the push of light itself and accelerated him and his frozen cargo at almost immeasurable speeds across an ocean of unfathomable silence. Yet, what he had done, she had asked to do.

The stare of his gray eyes yielded to a smile of his lips. In that young-old face, masculine in structure and feminine in texture, the smile had a connotation of tremendous kindness. She felt singularly much like weeping when she saw him smile in that particular way at her. Was that what people learned between the stars? To care for other people very much indeed and to spring upon them only to reveal love and not devouring them as prey?

In a measured voice he said, "I believe you. You're the first one that I have believed. All these people have said that they wanted to be sailors too, even when they looked at me. They could not know what it means, but they said it anyhow, and I hated them for saying it. You, though—you're different. Perhaps you will sail among the stars, but I hope that you will not."

As though waking from a dream, he looked around the luxurious room, with the gilt-and-enamel robot-waiters standing aside with negligent elegance. They were designed to be always present and never obtrusive: This was a difficult aesthetic effect to achieve, but their designer had achieved it.

The rest of the evening moved with the inevitability of good music. He went with her to the forever-lonely beach which the architects of New Madrid had built beside the hotel. They talked a little, they looked at each other, and they made love with an affirmative certainty which seemed outside themselves. He was very tender, and he did not realize that in a genitally sophisticated society, he was the first lover she had ever wanted or had ever had. (How could the daughter of Mona Muggeridge want a lover or a mate or a child?)

On the next afternoon, she exercised the freedom of her times and asked him to marry her. They had gone back to their private beach, which, through miracles of ultrafine miniweather adjustments, brought a Polynesian afternoon to the high chilly plateau of central Spain.

She asked him, *she* did, to marry her, and he refused, as tenderly and as kindly as a man of sixty-five can refuse a girl of eighteen. She did not press him; they continued the bittersweet love affair.

They sat on the artificial sand of the artificial beach and dabbled their toes in the man-warmed water of the ocean. Then they lay down against an artificial sand dune which hid New Madrid from view.

"Tell me," Helen said, "can I ask again, why did you become a sailor?"

"Not so easily answered," he said. "Adventure, maybe. That, at least in part. And I wanted to see Earth. Couldn't afford to come in a pod. Now—well, I've seen enough to keep me the rest of my life. I can go back to New Earth as a passenger in a month instead of forty years—be frozen in no more time than the wink of an eye, put in my adiabatic pod, linked in to the next sailing ship, and wake up home again while some other fool does the sailing."

Helen nodded. She did not bother to tell him that she knew all this. She had been investigating sailing ships since meeting the sailor.

"Out where you sail among the stars," she said, "you can tell me —can you possibly tell me anything of what it's like out there?"

His face looked inward on his soul and afterward his voice came as from an immense distance.

"There are moments—or is it weeks—you can't really tell in the sail ship—when it seems—worthwhile. You feel . . . your nerve endings reach out until they touch the stars. You feel enormous, somehow." Gradually he came back to her. "It's trite to say, of course, but you're never the same afterward. I don't mean just the obvious physical thing, but—you find yourself—or maybe you lose yourself. That's why," he continued, gesturing toward New Madrid out of sight behind the sand dune, "I can't stand this. New Earth, well, it's like Earth must have been in the old days, I guess. There's something fresh about it. Here . . ."

"I know," said Helen America, and she did. The slightly decadent, slightly corrupt, too comfortable air of Earth must have had a stifling effect on the man from beyond the stars.

"There," he said, "you won't believe this, but sometimes the ocean's too cold to swim in. We have music that doesn't come from machines, and pleasures that come from inside our own bodies without being put there. I have to get back to New Earth."

Helen said nothing for a little while, concentrating on stilling the pain in her heart.

"I . . . I . . ." she began.

"I know," he said fiercely, almost savagely turning on her. "But I can't take you. I can't! You're too young, you've got a life to live and I've thrown away a quarter of mine. No, that's not right. I didn't throw it away. I wouldn't trade it back because it's given me something inside I never had before. And it's given me you."

"But if—" she started again to argue.

"No. Don't spoil it. I'm going next week to be frozen in my pod to wait for the next sail ship. I can't stand much more of this, and I might weaken. That would be a terrible mistake. But we have this time together now, and we have our separate lifetimes to remember in. Don't think of anything else. There's nothing, nothing we can do."

Helen did not tell him—then or ever—of the child she had started to hope for, the child they would now never have. Oh, she could have used the child. She could have tied him to her, for he was an honorable man and would have married her had she told him. But Helen's love, even then in her youth, was such that she could not use this means. She wanted him to come to her of his own free will, marrying her because he could not live without her. To that marriage their child would have been an additional blessing.

There was the other alternative, of course. She could have borne the child without naming the father. But *she* was no Mona Muggeridge. She knew too well the terrors and insecurity and loneliness of being Helen America ever to be responsible for the creation of another. And for the course she had laid out there was no place for a child. So she did the only thing she could. At the end of their time in New Madrid, she let him say a real good-bye. Wordless and without tears, she left. Then she went up to an arctic city where such things are well known and amidst shame, worry, and a driving sense of regret she appealed to a confidential medical service which eliminated the unborn child. Then she went back to Cambridge and confirmed her place as the first woman to sail a ship to the stars.

6

The presiding lord of the Instrumentality at that time was a man named Wait. Wait was not cruel but he was never noted for tenderness of spirit or for a high regard for the adventuresome proclivities of young people. His aide said to him, "This girl wants to sail a ship to New Earth. Are you going to let her?"

"Why not?" said Wait. "A person is a person. She is well bred, well educated. If she fails, we will find out something eighty years from now when the ship comes back. If she succeeds, it will shut up some of these women who have been complaining." The lord leaned over his desk: "If she qualifies, and if she goes, though, don't give her any convicts. Convicts are too good and too valuable as settlers to be sent along on a fool trip like that. You can send her on something of a gamble. Give her all religious fanatics. We have more than enough. Don't you have twenty or thirty thousand who are waiting?"

He said, "Yes, sir, twenty-six thousand two hundred. Not counting recent additions."

"Very well," said the lord of the Instrumentality. "Give her the whole lot of them and give her that new ship. Have we named it?"

"No, sir," said the aide.

"Name it then."

The aide looked blank.

A contemptuous wise smile crossed the face of the senior bureaucrat. He said, "Take that ship now and name it. Name it the *Soul* and let the *Soul* fly to the stars. And let Helen America be an angel if she wants to. Poor thing, she has not got much of a life to live on this Earth, not the way she was born, and the way she was brought up. And it's no use to try and reform her, to transform her personality, when it's a lively, rich personality. It does not do any good. We don't have to punish her for being herself. Let her go. Let her have it."

Wait sat up and stared at his aide and then repeated very firmly: "Let her have it, *only if she qualifies.*"

7

Helen America did qualify.

The doctors and the experts tried to warn her against it.

One technician said: "Don't you realize what this is going to mean? Forty years will pour out of your life in a single month. You leave here a girl. You will get there a woman of sixty. Well, you will probably still have a hundred years to live after that. And it's painful. You will have all these people, thousands and thousands of them. You will have some Earth cargo. There will be about thirty thousand pods strung on sixteen lines behind you. Then you will have the control cabin to live in. We will give you as many robots as you need, probably a dozen. You will have a mainsail and a foresail and you will have to keep the two of them."

"I know. I have read the book," said Helen America. "And I sail the ship with light, and if the infrared touches that sail—I go. If I get radio interference, I pull the sails in. And if the sails fail, I wait as long as I live."

The technician looked a little cross. "There is no call for you to get tragic about it. Tragedy is easy enough to contrive. And if you want to be tragic, you can be tragic without destroying thirty thousand other people or without wasting a large amount of Earth property. You can drown in water right here, or jump into a volcano like the Japanese in the old books. Tragedy is not the hard part. The hard part is when you don't quite succeed and you have to keep on fighting. When you must keep going on and on and on in the face of really hopeless odds, of real temptations to despair.

"Now this is the way that the foresail works. That sail will be twenty thousand miles at the wide part. It tapers down and the total length will be just under eighty thousand miles. It will be retracted or extended by small servo-robots. The servo-robots are radio-controlled. You had better use your radio sparingly, because after all, these batteries, even though they are atomic, have to last forty years. They have got to keep you alive."

"Yes, sir," said Helen America very contritely.

"You've got to remember what your job is. You're going because you are cheap. You are going because a sailor takes a lot less weight than a machine. There is no all-purpose computer built that weighs as little as a hundred and fifty pounds. You do. You go simply because you are expendable. Anyone that goes out to the stars takes one chance in three of never getting there. But you are going because you are a leader, you are going because you are young. You have a life to give and a life to spare. Because your nerves are good. You understand that?"

"Yes, sir, I knew that."

"Furthermore, you are going because you'll make the trip in forty years. If we sent automatic devices and had them manage the sails, they would get there—possibly. But it would take them from a hundred years to a hundred and twenty or more, and by that time the adiabatic pods would have spoiled, most of the human cargo would not be fit for revival, and the leakage of heat, no matter how we faced it, would be enough to ruin the entire expedition. So remember that the tragedy and the trouble you face is mostly work. Work, and that's all it is. That is your big job."

Helen smiled. She was a short girl with rich dark hair, brown eyes, and very pronounced eyebrows, but when Helen smiled she was almost a child again, and a rather charming one. She said: "My job is work. I understand that, sir."

8

In the preparation area, the make-ready was fast but not hurried. Twice the technicians urged her to take a holiday before she reported for final training. She did not accept their advice. She wanted to go forth; she knew that they knew she wanted to leave Earth forever, and she also knew they knew she was not merely her mother's daughter. She was trying, somehow, to be herself. She knew the world did not believe, but the world did not matter.

The third time they suggested a vacation, the suggestion was mandatory. She had a gloomy two months which she ended up enjoying a little bit on the wonderful islands of the Hesperides, islands which were raised when the weight of the Earthports caused a new group of small archipelagos to form below Bermuda.

She reported back, fit, healthy, and ready to go.

The senior medical officer was very blunt.

"Do you really know what we are going to do to you? We are going to make you live forty years out of your life in one month."

She nodded, white of face, and he went on, "Now to give you those forty years we've got to slow down your bodily processes. After all the sheer biological task of breathing forty years' worth of air in one month involves a factor of about five hundred to one. No lungs could stand it. Your body must circulate water. It must take in food. Most of this is going to be protein. There will be some kind of a hydrate. You'll need vitamins.

"Now, what we are going to do is to slow the brain down, very much indeed, so that the brain will be working at about that five-

hundred-to-one ratio. We don't want you incapable of working.
Somebody has got to manage the sails.

"Therefore, if you hesitate or you start to think, a thought or two
is going to take several weeks. Meanwhile your body can be slowed
down some. But the different parts can't be slowed down at the
same rate. Water, for example, we brought down to about eighty to
one. Food, to about three hundred to one.

"You won't have time to drink forty years' worth of water. We
circulate it, get it through, purify it, and get it back in your system,
unless you break your linkup.

"So what you face is a month of being absolutely wide awake, on
an operating table and *being operated on without anesthetic,* while
doing some of the hardest work that mankind has ever found.

"You'll have to take observation, you'll have to watch your lines
with the pods of people and cargo behind you, you'll have to adjust
the sails. If there is anybody surviving at destination point, they will
come out and meet you.

"At least that happens most of the times.

"I am not going to assure you you will get the ship in. If they
don't meet you, take an orbit beyond the farthest planet and either
let yourself die or try to save yourself. You can't get thirty thousand
people down on a planet singlehandedly.

"Meanwhile, though, you've got a real job. We are going to have
to build these controls right into your body. We'll start by putting
valves in your chest arteries. Then we go on, catheterizing your
water. We are going to make an artificial colostomy that will go forward here just in front of your hip joint. Your water intake has a
certain psychological value so that about one five-hundredth of your
water we are going to leave you to drink out of a cup. The rest of it
is going to go directly into your bloodstream. Again about a tenth of
your blood will go that way. You understand that?"

"You mean," said Helen, "I eat one-tenth, and the rest goes in in-
travenously?"

"That's right," said the medical technician. "We will pump it
into you. The concentrates are there. The reconstitutor is there.
Now these lines have a double connection. One set of connections
runs into the maintenance machine. That will become the logistic
support for your body. And these lines are the umbilical cord for a
human being alone among the stars. They are your life.

"And now if they should break or if you should fall, you might faint for a year or two. If that happens, your local system takes over: That's the pack on your back.

"On Earth, it weighs as much as you do. You have already been drilled with the model pack. You know how easy it is to handle in space. That'll keep you going for a subjective period of about two hours. No one has ever worked out a clock yet that would match the human mind, so instead of giving you a clock we are giving you an odometer attached to your own pulse and we mark it off in grades. If you watch it in terms of tens of thousands of pulse beats, you may get some information out of it.

"I don't know what kind of information, but you may find it helpful somehow." He looked at her sharply and then turned back to his tools, picking up a shining needle with a disk on the end.

"Now, let's get back to this. We are going to have to get right into your mind. That's chemical too."

Helen interrupted. "You said you were not going to operate on my head."

"Only the needle. That's the only way we can get to the mind. Slow it down enough so that you will have this subjective mind operating at a rate that will make the forty years pass in a month." He smiled grimly, but the grimness changed to momentary tenderness as he took in her brave obstinate stance, her girlish, admirable, pitiable determination.

"I won't argue it," she said. "This is as bad as a marriage and the stars are my bridegroom." The image of the sailor went across her mind, but she said nothing of him.

The technician went on. "Now, we have already built in psychotic elements. You can't even expect to remain sane. So you'd better not worry about it. You'll have to be insane to manage the sails and to survive utterly alone and be out there even a month. And the trouble is in that month you are going to know it's really forty years. There is not a mirror in the place but you'll probably find shiny surfaces to look at yourself.

"You won't look so good. You will see yourself aging, every time you slow down to look. I don't know what the problem is going to be on that score. It's been bad enough on men.

"Your hair problem is going to be easier than men's. The sailors we sent out, we simply had to kill all the hair roots. Otherwise the men would have been swamped in their own beards. And a tremendous amount of the nutrient would be wasted if it went into raising of hair on the face which no machine in the world could cut off fast enough to keep a man working. I think what we will do is inhibit hair on the top of your head. Whether it comes out in the same color or not is something you will find for yourself later. Did you ever meet the sailor that came in?"

The doctor knew she had met him. He did not know that it was the sailor from beyond the stars who called her. Helen managed to remain composed as she smiled at him to say: "Yes, you gave him new hair. Your technician planted a new scalp on his head, remember. Somebody on your staff did. The hair came out black and he got the nickname of Mr. Grey-no-more."

"If you are ready next Tuesday, we'll be ready too. Do you think you can make it by then, my lady?"

Helen felt odd seeing this old, serious man refer to her as "lady," but she knew he was paying respect to a profession and not just to an individual.

"Tuesday is time enough." She felt complimented that he was an old-fashioned enough person to know the ancient names of the days of the week and to use them. That was a sign that he had not only learned the essentials at the university but that he had picked up the elegant inconsequentialities as well.

9

Two weeks later was twenty-one years later by the chronometers in the cabin. Helen turned for the ten-thousand-times-ten-thousandth time to scan the sails.

Her back ached with a violent throb.

She could feel the steady roar of her heart like a fast vibrator as it ticked against the time-span of her awareness. She could look down at the meter on her wrist and see the hands on the watchlike dials indicate tens of thousands of pulses very slowly.

She heard the steady whistle of air in her throat as her lungs seemed shuddering with sheer speed.

And she felt the throbbing pain of a large tube feeding an immense quantity of mushy water directly into the artery of her neck.

On her abdomen, she felt as if someone had built a fire. The evacuation tube operated automatically but it burnt as if a coal had been held to her skin and a catheter, which connected her bladder to another tube, stung as savagely as the prod of a scalding-hot needle. Her head ached and her vision blurred.

But she could still see the instruments and she still could watch the sails. Now and then she could glimpse, faint as a tracery of dust, the immense skein of people and cargo that lay behind them.

She could not sit down. It hurt too much.

The only way that she could be comfortable for resting was to lean against the instrument panel, her lower ribs against the panel, her tired forehead against the meters.

Once she rested that way and realized that it was two and a half months before she got up. She knew that rest had no meaning and she could see her face moving, a distorted image of her own face growing old in the reflections from the glass face of the "apparent weight" dial. She could look at her arms with blurring vision, note the skin tightening, loosening, and tightening again, as changes in temperatures affected it.

She looked out one more time at the sails and decided to take in the foresail. Wearily she dragged herself over the control panel with a servo-robot. She selected the right control and opened it for a week or so. She waited there, her heart buzzing, her throat whistling air, her fingernails breaking off gently as they grew. Finally she checked to see if it really had been the right one, pushed again, and nothing happened.

She pushed a third time. There was no response.

Now she went back to the master panel, re-read, checked the light direction, found a certain amount of infrared pressure which she should have been picking up. The sails had very gradually risen to something not far from the speed of light itself because they moved fast with the one side dulled; the pods behind, sealed against time and eternity, swam obediently in an almost perfect weightlessness.

She scanned; her reading had been correct.

The sail *was* wrong.

She went back to the emergency panel and pressed. Nothing happened.

She broke out a repair robot and sent it out to effect repairs, punching the papers as rapidly as she could to give instructions. The robot went out and an instant (three days) later it replied. The panel on the repair robot rang forth, "Does not conform."

She sent a second repair robot. That had no effect either.

She sent a third, the last. Three bright lights, "Does not conform," stared at her. She moved the servo-robots to the other side of the sails and pulled hard.

The sail was still not at the right angle.

She stood there wearied and lost in space, and she prayed: "Not for me, God, I am running away from a life that I did not want. But for this ship's souls and for the poor foolish people that I am taking who are brave enough to want to worship their own way and need the light of another star, I ask you, God, help me now." She thought she had prayed very fervently and she hoped that she would get an answer to her prayer.

It did not work out that way. She was bewildered, alone.

There was no sun. There was nothing, except the tiny cabin and herself more alone than any woman had ever been before. She sensed the thrill and ripple of her muscles as they went through days of adjustment while her mind noticed only the matter of minutes. She leaned forward, forced herself not to relax and finally she remembered that one of the official busybodies had included a weapon.

What she would use a weapon for she did not know.

It pointed. It had a range of two hundred thousand miles. The target could be selected automatically.

She got down on her knees trailing the abdominal tube and the feeding tube and the catheter tubes and the helmet wires, each one running back to the panel. She crawled underneath the panel for the servo-robots and she pulled out a written manual. She finally found the right frequency for the weapon's controls. She set the weapon up and went to the window.

At the last moment she thought, "Perhaps the fools are going to make me shoot the window out. It ought to have been designed to shoot through the window without hurting it. That's the way they should have done it."

She wondered about the matter for a week or two.

Just before she fired it she turned and there, next to her, stood her sailor, the sailor from the stars, Mr. Grey-no-more. He said: "It won't work that way."

He stood clear and handsome, the way she had seen him in New Madrid. He had no tubes, he did not tremble, she could see the normal rise and fall of his chest as he took one breath every hour or so. One part of her mind knew that he was a hallucination. Another part of her mind believed that he was real. She was mad and she was very happy to be mad at this time and she let the hallucination give her advice. She reset the gun so that it would fire through the cabin wall and it fired a low charge at the repair mechanism out beyond the distorted and immovable sail.

The low charge did the trick. The interference had been something beyond all technical anticipation. The weapon had cleaned out the forever-unidentifiable obstruction, leaving the servo-robots free to attack their tasks like a tribe of maddened ants. They worked again. They had had defenses built in against the minor impediments of space. All of them scurried and skipped about.

With a sense of bewilderment close to religion, she perceived the wind of starlight blowing against the immense sails. The sails snapped into position. She got a momentary touch of gravity as she sensed a little weight. The *Soul* was back on her course.

10

"It's a girl," they said to him on New Earth. "It's a girl. She must have been eighteen herself."

Mr. Grey-no-more did not believe it.

But he went to the hospital and there in the hospital he saw Helen America.

"Here I am, sailor," she said. "I sailed too." Her face was white as chalk, her expression was that of a girl of about twenty. Her body was that of a well-preserved woman of sixty.

As for him, he had not changed again, since he had returned home inside a pod.

He looked at her. His eyes narrowed and then in a sudden reversal of roles, it was he who was kneeling beside her bed and covering her hands with his tears.

Half coherently, he babbled at her: "I ran away from you because I loved you so. I came back here where you would never follow, or if you did follow, you'd still be a young woman, and I'd still be too old. But you have sailed the *Soul* in here and you wanted me."

The nurse of New Earth did not know about the rules which should be applied to the sailors from the stars. Very quietly she went out of the room, smiling in tenderness and human pity at the love which she had seen. But she was a practical woman and she had a sense of her own advancement. She called a friend of hers at the news service and said: "I think I have got the biggest romance in history. If you get here soon enough you can get the first telling of the story of Helen America and Mr. Grey-no-more. They just met like that. I guess they'd seen each other somewhere. They just met like that and fell in love."

The nurse did not know that they had forsworn a love on Earth. The nurse did not know that Helen America had made a lonely trip with an icy purpose and the nurse did not know that the crazy image of Mr. Grey-no-more, the sailor himself, had stood beside Helen twenty years out from nothing-at-all in the depths and blackness of space between the stars.

11

The little girl had grown up, had married, and now had a little girl of her own. The mother was unchanged, but the spieltier was very, very old. It had outlived all its marvelous tricks of adaptability, and for some years had stayed frozen in the role of a yellow-haired, blue-eyed, girl doll. Out of sentimental sense of the fitness of things, she had dressed the spieltier in a bright blue jumper with matching panties. The little animal crept softly across the floor on its tiny human hands, using its knees for hind feet. The mock-human face looked up blindly and squeaked for milk.

The young mother said, "Mom, you ought to get rid of that thing. It's all used up and it looks horrible with your nice period furniture."

"I thought you loved it," said the older woman.

"Of course," said the daughter. "It was cute, when I was a child. But I'm not a child any more, and it doesn't even work."

The spieltier had struggled to its feet and clutched its mistress's ankle. The older woman took it away gently, and put down a saucer of milk and a cup the size of a thimble. The spieltier tried to curtsy, as it had been motivated to do at the beginning, slipped, fell, and whimpered. The mother righted it and the little old animal-toy began dipping milk with its thimble and sucking the milk into its tiny toothless old mouth.

"You remember, Mom—" said the younger woman and stopped.

"Remember what, dear?"

"You told me about Helen America and Mr. Grey-no-more when that was brand-new."

"Yes, darling, maybe I did."

"You didn't tell me everything," said the younger woman accusingly.

"Of course not. You were a child."

"But it was awful. Those messy people, and the horrible way sailors live. I don't see how you idealized it and called it a romance—"

"But it was. It was," insisted the other.

"Romance, my foot," said the daughter. "It's as bad as you and the worn-out spieltier." She pointed at the tiny, living, aged doll who had fallen asleep beside its milk. "I think it's horrible. You ought to get rid of it. And the world ought to get rid of sailors."

"Don't be harsh, darling," said the mother.

"Don't be a sentimental old slob," said the daughter.

"Perhaps we are," said the mother with a loving sort of laugh. Unobtrusively she put the sleeping spieltier on a padded chair where it would not be stepped on or hurt.

12

Outsiders never knew the real end of the story.

More than a century after their wedding, Helen lay dying: she was dying happily, because her beloved sailor was beside her. She believed that if they could conquer space, they might conquer death as well.

Her loving, happy, weary dying mind blurred over and she picked up an argument they hadn't touched upon for decades.

"You did so come to the Soul," she said. "You did so stand beside me when I was lost and did not know how to handle the weapon."

"If I came then, darling, I'll come again, wherever you are. You're my darling, my heart, my own true love. You're my bravest of ladies, my boldest of people. You're my own. You sailed for me. You're my lady who sailed the Soul."

His voice broke, but his features stayed calm. He had never before seen anyone die so confident and so happy.

THE DEEP DOWN DRAGON

August 1961

Judith Merril

(b. 1923)

Judith Merril's anthologies changed science fiction. While the editorial efforts of Groff Conklin, the Healy-McComas team, and later Harlan Ellison, were important for many reasons, it was Judith Merril who widened the scope of the science fiction field.

In her Best of the Year *series (1956–1968) in which she sought stories from outside the sf magazines, and through her* England Swings SF *(1968), as well as yearly anthologies from the mid to late 1960s, she brought the "New Wave" crashing ashore in America.*

"The Deep Down Dragon," her only Galaxy *appearance, is one of her finest and most neglected stories.*

Memoir by Judith Merril

Actually, this story should never be reprinted without the illustration that invented it.

In the Bad Old Days of happy memory, before science fiction turned respectable (and almost all other popular fiction died or went into comic strips), the phrase "pulp magazines" was applied to certain publications. These usually had cheap ("pulp") paper, modest pretensions, action illustrations, gaudy covers, and low prices—to reader and writer both. One way of keeping them cheap was to print the four-color covers in large batches at a single press-run: This sometimes meant that covers were bought before the stories they "illustrated."

I was fortunate enough on three occasions to be asked to write stories to fit covers. "Fortunate"? Right, because I found the process invariably produced completely "different" stories, of a sort I would never have generated out of my usual "creative" processes.

This one was written to a cover supplied by Fred Pohl, and is, I believe, my one-and-only action-adventure-chase story.

I have used this device with writing classes, by the way, and warmly recommend it to teachers and to apprenticing writers. It is revealing and exciting to see how many completely different stories are suggested to different individuals by a single painting!

THE DEEP DOWN DRAGON

The girl's one duty was to look—and understand:

White flatness of the wide wall dissolved into mist as the room dimmed. Then whiteness itself broke apart, from all-color to each component.

Pinpoints of brightness swirled and coalesced into new patterns of color and shape. Pinks and yellows here. Silver, blue, black there. Brown, gray, green. Rainbow stripes.

First flat, like a painted scene, then deepening to its own kind of reality, the scene glowed in the center of nothingness where the wall had been before.

The scene had been exactly the same before, she remembered. There was the strangely clear-air atmosphere, thin and sharp. The sketched-in effect of the background—hills, oddly shaped? a domed structure closer?—was simply a matter of her focused attention, not distance haze. Through this transparent air detailed vision would be possible at a far distance. And the background hills were far; for the moment, however, they were only background.

What counted was front-center, bright-colored . . . as real as when she had seen it the first time for herself.

The three footprints. The shoe. The square of cloth. The three bushes. In color, focus, and meaning they were identical. Her own shoe, with the silly spike heel and lacy strap unfastened, was lying where it dropped on the pink-hued sand, alongside the alien prints. The first time she had not known why, exactly, the prints were "alien." Now she saw it was the shoe that accomplished the effect. Plenty of three-toed things left prints in sand, but nothing exactly the length of her own foot was tripartite.

Nothing on Earth.

It was the same thing with the brown-gray-green thorn bushes . . . planted, she suddenly realized, by some insane gardener, to landscape that circular blockhouse thing in the background! Or maybe not so insane. Nowhere else in sight was there a growing or green thing at all. Poor green was better than none. Spikes, spines, and thorns did grow. They were alive, if still—alien? Why? Of course, the same thing. The patterned robe. A square of cloth, from the same bolt from which she had made the robe, only last week, hung impaled on the farthest bush.

Farthest? Nearest! Nearest to the door of the house, from which the strange footprints curved down and off-scene.

Half the wall was filled now. Inch by slow fraction of inch the scene widened. She sat forward, breathing almost not at all, tensed with knowing the next print, or the one beyond it, would contain the print-maker, the—alien.

Alien? What an odd thought! That was the second—the third?— time she'd thought it. She did not remember the thought from the first seeing of the same scene. "Strange," maybe. "Unknown." Not "alien."

Odd . . . Odder still, as her eyes went unwillingly from the forming print at the far edge of the scene, she saw her own sandal alongside the trail, silly spike heel and lacy strap, still fastened as it had been on her foot . . .

That wasn't just odd. It was wrong! And the torn strip of fabric ripped from her robe by the thornbush—

"That's not how it was! That's not the way it went," she thought, and the scene faded out.

The light brightened in the room as the wall came back to normality, and she realized that she had not just thought it, but spoken aloud.

"This is *his*, remember?" Gordon was smiling. "Only the very first frame is identical. It starts branching off right away. The colors, for instance?"

Ruth thought back and of course he was right. *Hers* had been much yellower. Pink sand was absurd.

She laughed out loud, at the absurdity of thinking anything in the projection absurd. Then she explained. "Pink sand. I was thinking how silly that was, and then I remembered that *mine* had little pink clouds floating over my pure yellow desert! Why on Earth do you think he'd have pink sand, though?"

Gordon smiled again as she realized how her own question had answered itself. ". . . on Earth . . ." she had said. Of course. Why should it be Earth at all?

With the questioning thought came concern. Why had *hers* been on Earth? Did that mean . . . ? Were they showing her Charles's sequence just to explain, in the kindest way, why she failed?

She wouldn't finish the thoughts, even in her own head. But Gordon was chuckling quietly as he watched her. Of course he knew what had been crossing her—face, she decided, as well as her mind! Other people had been through this whole thing before. Half of them must have gone through the same thoughts.

Half of them would have been worried . . . and how many of them had good cause to be?

"Relax, Ruth," he said warmly. "You haven't failed or passed yet. There's a lot more to it than the sequence. But I can tell you that it makes no difference where you make the setting, or when. At least—" he frowned faintly, and she knew it was impatience with his own imprecision in a vital communication. "At least, it makes no more difference—and no less—than your choice of colors or textures. A good bit less difference than clothing, for instance."

She looked at him gratefully.

"All right," she said. "I'll try to forget my own sequence."

"The best way is just to let yourself go, as completely as you can. There's no harm in being aware of the difference, just so you aren't contrasting. It won't rationalize. But you don't have to stop being you to be *him* for a while, you know." He smiled again.

She nodded and grinned. Some things did not have to be verbalized.

She shivered and settled back, ready to watch—to feel, to know, be, exist—in *his* mind and body.

Gordon didn't say any more. The room dimmed again, and once more the misting wall focused the scene.

When it had covered the wall, Ruth had forgotten that there was a wall there at all. Or that she was herself.

More completely than ever before, or again (unless and until they fused to a new person, their child), she was one with the man who had made her his own.

The trail of prints led tantalizingly out of sight, curving away behind a low ridge of dunes. Unless the creature, whatever it was, moved much more swiftly than the prints promised, it had been more than a few minutes since it happened.

He looked again at her slipper dropped on its side in the sand. The first glimpse had been more incongruous than anything else. The alienness of the prints contrasted ridiculously with the spiced femininity of Ruth's shoe on the orange-pink sand. Now it seemed to him that the slipper was not dropped but thrown. Or kicked.

Kicked off her foot? For the first time, fear grabbed him, a clawed fist or ice in his belly that turned him to look again at the bright rainbow of stuff draped and torn on the edge of the bush near the door. It was part of the skirt of the new robe, the one she made herself last week, after he noticed the new fabric in the shop window. He had liked it; so she had bought it and fashioned it into a garment to please him. Now it hung cruelly torn by spiked thorns. And she—

He tore himself loose from the immobility of anxiety, and ran for the house. Somewhere in back of his mind the question was registered: What shop? Where? The nearest shop was forty million miles away. The question was registered, filed, and ticketed for later thought.

Right now he could not even stop to wonder why he had not noticed the door before. He had to have seen it, when he saw the bush. How do you not notice that the thick door of a pressure hut has been torn loose from its hinges? What kind of wild man speculates about his wife's robe when his home, in which he left her safe and protected, no more then five hours ago, has been violated?

That was a dangerous word. He unthought it, and the red haze cleared away. He could see again.

"Ruth!" he shouted. "*Ruth!*"

No answer. He had known there could not be one. "Ruth!" he kept shouting to thin-aired emptiness inside the dome that had been —five short hours ago—rich with Earth air and scents, sounds and solidity: Ruth.

His gun hung by the door. It had been a joke, he remembered. Pioneers ought to keep a gun by the front door. Damn right they should! He grabbed it as he ran, stride unbroken. He tore off down the trail of the monstrous prints, past the bushes and the sandal, fifty feet more. His lungs were on fire inside him. He would have cursed in his futility, but there was no strength or breath for self-anger; not even, just now, for anger better placed. It was not even possible now to run back to the copter. He had wasted too much strength. He had to drag himself full length along the sand, catching and holding the thin concentration of lichen's oxygen at the sand surface.

Inside the copter, lungs full again, he was coasting along fifteen feet above the prints of horned three-toed feet. He had time enough, and more than he wanted, to think and to question his idiocies. As if he had forgotten where he was. At the first hint of danger they faced he went into shock. As if he were back on Earth, wrapped in her warm air, strong-armed gravity.

Ancestral memories reacting for him in moment of panic? He sneered back at himself for that kind of excuse. The only part that applied was the single word "panic."

He'd panicked. Okay. Don't forget it, boy. But don't let it slow you down, either. File for future reference. Take it out and examine it—later. Meantime, what counts is down there. Right now, you're just a pair of eyes. Later you may get to be arms and legs, a back, if you're lucky a gun. Right now—just eyes. And a computer.

He studied the prints. Two-footed or four? He couldn't decide— and then he saw the pattern, and it was not two or four, but three. Three? Distribute N pounds of weight—divided at any time on two of three feet, in prints that each dug in deeper than his own foot would, with his full weight on it. The damn thing was big. N pounds was too many.

That didn't make sense. What kind of Thing made prints like that on Mars? On a planet whose largest lifeform was adapted to breathing air no more than two feet above ground? And even those didn't cross desert dryness. They lived in the still thinly moist and green valley of old sea bottoms.

The error was obvious. What kind of creature could make a print like a man's, on Mars? Largest *native* lifeform, he had meant. So this Thing, with three-toed, three-legged stride, hard-bottomed foot digging too deep in dry sand, had a stride barely more than a man's, one meter maybe from print to print along the trail. It was not long enough to be that heavy. Not man, not Martian. Something else.

Alien.

He tried to think more, but either there were no more clues or the block was too great. Alien, from where? No way to know. What for? Where to? Why? When?

For the moment, the "when" was what counted the most. Whatever and whyever, It had Ruth with It. Was she still alive? Did she have an oxytank?

He tried to remember, aside from the door, what signs of violence, struggle, or damage he'd seen in the house. He remembered none. The door, the robe, and the slipper. That was all.

Ten minutes after the copter lifted, he came to the first rock outcroppings. For a while after that he could still follow the trail without too much trouble. The creature tended to stay on the sand-drifted crevices between hills. There were still plenty of prints clear enough to be seen from the height he had to maintain to stay clear of the jagged-edged, sand-scoured shapes of bare hilltops. But as the ground level rose, there was less and less sand between rocks to catch imprints, and it was more difficult to peer down and navigate at the same time.

Hard to say if he would be better off on the ground. He could spend hours trying wrong passages, backing and trying again, to search out the scattered prints that made the only trail now. Circling above, he could save time—maybe. Certainly, if he could stay in the air, he kept an advantage he'd never have face to face. (Face to chest? belly? thigh? No way at all to judge relative height.) Not to mention armament, general equipment. Inside the copter, he had the distilled and neatly packaged essence of Earth technology to fight for him. On foot in the hills, with whatever he could carry on his own back—?

It was obvious he had no choice. He had just noticed the time. Twilight would fall fast and dark across him in a half hour or less. Moonless, or as good as moonless, dark would follow short minutes after. The kind of cross-eyed trail-following and peak-hopping he could barely manage in sunlight would then be impossible. Find a place where he could land, then. Now, quickly, while he still could.

The copter dropped, and he found a ledge just firm and wide enough. Charles went methodically through lockers, picking and choosing, till at last he had a pile he thought he could manage, with all the essentials, in one form or other.

Searchlight, rope, hand pickaxe, knife. Pistol-grip torch, which he thought of as a flamethrower. Plain old pistol. Extra airtank. Extra mask. Light warm blanket. Bullets, and gas for the torch. Food concentrates. Two water flasks. He climbed into his heat suit, discarded the blanket, and took her suit instead. He had thought to make a knapsack of the blanket, carrying the rest of the stuff on his back, but that was silly. He had to be able to get at whatever he needed, but fast. He got out a package of clip-back hooks and studded his suit with them, hanging himself like a grim Christmas tree inside-out: bright flame-red suit underneath; dull gray, brown, and black tanks, handles, tools, and weapons dangling all around.

He practiced bending over, sitting, squatting, reaching. He could climb. Okay. The weight was going to be hard to handle, but not impossible.

He added one more airtank, and one more flask. If it all got too heavy, he could leave a trail of his own behind him. At least the stuff would be nearer than here in the copter. He was half out of the hatch when he remembered it: the first-aid kit.

He started into the hills with his searchlight flooding the pass at his feet just as darkness collapsed from the sky. He wondered as he stumbled forward and up—following an edge of toe here, of heel there—what else he had not thought to take.

Then the glare of light glinted of redness on rockside. A smear, that's all. Red blood. Not alien. Ruth's!

His gloved hand reached out, and the red smudged. Still wet? Impossible. In this atmosphere, the seconds they'd need to get out of sight would have dried blood. He looked closely at his gauntlet and moved forward more swiftly, with an exultation of knowledge and purpose he had not dared let himself hold until then. It was not blood. It was spilled red powder. Rouge! She was alive, able to think, to act! She knew he would have to come after, and she was helping by leaving a trail.

He no longer followed footprints. He followed the crimson trail blazes. And wondered how far back they'd started, how much time he might have gained had he abandoned the copter sooner.

No use wondering. No use thinking back. Now it was only the next moment and the next. Was he gaining or losing? This he had to know. He was traveling at his best speed. He went faster. If he lost ground now, he had no chance. The creature was making a path as straight as the hard rockside hills would permit; It knew where It was headed. The Thing could not climb, that was clear, so It would not have gone through the hills without cause. But wherever It was headed, presumably that spot offered It some protection. He had to find It and head It off first.

He found he could go faster still. And then, suddenly, he knew he'd better slow down. It was nothing he'd seen—surely nothing he'd heard. Inside the suit hood, even such sounds as carried through the thin air were stilled. Well, then.

He opened the mask, and he did hear. Maybe it was some vibration of the Thing's tread through the rock that had warned him first. Well, he would not give himself away by the same carelessness. He knew he was very close to It now.

He moved so carefully after that, it seemed agonizingly as if he were once more crawling belly-flat. But he knew he was gaining on them. The Thing was really slow!

He was close. Fool! he thought angrily, as he switched his light off. Creep up on the Thing with a searchlight to flood the scene in advance! The suit had an infrascope in the visor. He'd have had to close it soon anyhow. Five minutes was about maximum breathing without a tank; unless you cared to drag yourself flat as he'd done earlier.

The black-light scope came on. Charles paused with a new certainty under an overhang of rock at the next bend. And he saw the Thing. And his wife.

He noticed, in a detached and extremely calm way, that what happened next all happened in seconds. Maybe a minute at most. No more, because with the sharp self-awareness exploding inside him, he could count his breaths while he did all the rest.

He inhaled exactly three times—deeply, evenly—while it occurred.

Before the first breath, there was again the ice-fingered grip of fear twisting his gut, squeezing the strength and air out of him.

He inhaled then. And let the retinal image go to his brain, instead of his belly.

It was twice the height of a man, weirdly elongated, the tripod base all ropy tendon, thin and hard. The trunk—thorax—chest?—well, whatever, shelled or spacesuited or something, but shiny-hard—bulked enormous, four feet around surely at the center. At least four. And the Thing's head was turned just far enough to the side so that Charles could see clearly that his wife's face was in the gaping, reptilian maw of the Thing.

It held her under one arm. Her feet kicked at its side. It seemed not to notice. Her arm, with the bright metal cosmetic case clutched in her hand, swung wide, reaching to hit the canyon wall whenever it could. Her head was half into the creature's mouth, firmly held, chin and forehead, by its enormous stretched lips.

While he drew in the first breath, he saw all this clearly and knew he dared not act in such a way as to make It bite down—from fear or anger, made no difference. Charles could not see inside the great maw. What kind of teeth, what harm had been done, what could be done, he did not know . . . and knew he could not risk. He thought through and rejected five separate plans, while his hands found the items he'd need. He drew a new breath, and his legs moved beneath him.

He could not shoot first. And he could not simply follow and learn more about the Thing. Because another image came through from somewhere—the same eyes that watched every move of the Thing? Unlikely, but it had to be—of the gleaming column of metal too close ahead. A Thing-ship. So: No time.

He leaped, knife in hand. Pricked the creature, and jumped back.

It worked, as he'd prayed; no; as he had known, not just hoped or prayed, that it must. The Thing jumped, turned to look—and released his wife's head.

He did not waste effort in looking, but saw anyhow that her face was unharmed. He jumped again, drawing the third breath, and pricked at the arm that held her. She squirmed and pushed, exactly on time, like a part of himself—which she was—and her body was clear of his as he emptied the pistol at Its head.

He reached for the torch.

By that time he could not stop himself. He would have avoided the torch if he could. As it was he thundered at Ruth, above the explosion: *"Down!* Keep down, babe!" And the blue flame of released oxygen missed her head by a foot . . .

He carried her back to the copter with strength he had not believed he could find. Nobody pursued.

She sat up, dazed, as the lights brightened slowly, and the white wall turned serenely opaque. She looked across at Gordon, and her face glowed with pleasure.

"No sillier than mine was," she said, laughing. "Was it?"

"Not at all," Gordon said.

She sat politely, waiting.

Gordon stood up, grinned down at her, and offered his hand. "I think they must be done in there," he told her, nodding in the direction of the screenwall. "I imagine you'd like . . ." He let it trail off.

"You're a smart old thing, aren't you?" She took the hand and came to her feet. Then, on impulse, astonished at herself, she stood on tiptoe and placed a quick kiss on his cheek. "What's more, you're a doll." She turned and ran, glad but embarrassed.

The door closed behind her. A mirrored door on the opposite wall opened, and a young man entered. Gordon greeted him warmly. "Well—what did you think?" His own enthusiasm was unmistakable.

"Outside of its being a great racket? Do they all react that way?"

"Well, not all. Matter of fact, this pair is practically classical. You don't often get a mesh like this one—you saw hers, didn't you?"

"I don't think so," the other said. "Unless it was one of the bunch you ran for us last night?"

"Could be. She worked out a sort of a junior-size Tyrannosaur. Out of Professor Challenger maybe? Future-past uncertainty, here on Earth. Had it threaten the children, and just when she was about to sacrifice herself to save them, old Charlie showed up in the nick of time to do the slaying."

The other nodded. "It's a fascinating technique," he said. "Damn glad to have this chance to see it work. One thing I don't follow— why do you show them each other's? That's pretty much against basic theory of joint therapy, isn't it?"

Gordon was smiling again. "Well," he said slowly. "This pair didn't really take the runs for therapy." He had a surprise to spring, and he was enjoying it. "You've heard about the new screening technique for colonists? You know the last expedition had only one broken couple and two psychotic collapses, out of fifty-six?"

The younger man whistled. Then he understood. "This is how you're doing it? Let them fantasy their own reactions? Well, hell. Sure! What's surprising is, nobody thought of using it before!"

"Of course not. It was right under our noses," Gordon said.

They both laughed.

"In this case," he added, "we've got everything. His sequence stressed readiness, thoughtful preparation, careful action. You saw that. Hers was strongest on instinct, physical wisdom, that whole set. He was moved to do things he couldn't possibly do—and knows he can't, by the way—in real life, because *she* was in danger. Her stimulus was a threat to home and children. And even then, she made sure he did the actual dragon-slaying job." He flicked a switch. Through the wall, now, they saw Ruth and Charles, standing, holding hands, smiling and squeezing a little. That was all.

The two doctors smiled as the pale-skinned ninety-five-pound, five-foot product of slum-crowded Earth threw a proud arm around his wife's narrow shoulder, and led her out.

"Doesn't look like much of a dragon-slayer," the younger one said.

"No. But as long as he *is* . . ." He paused, looked the visitor over with care, and said, "You asked about showing them to each other? Ever think how much more therapy there might be for him in knowing she *knows* he can handle a dragon? Or for her, knowing that he really *can?*"

WALL OF CRYSTAL, EYE OF NIGHT

December 1961

Algis Budrys
(b. 1931)

Widely and justly considered one of the outstanding talents in sci-ence fiction, Algis Budrys is best known to millions of readers as the author of such famous novels as Who? *(1958),* The Falling Torch *(1959),* Rogue Moon *(1960), and* Michaelmas *(1977). His story "Nobody Bothers Gus" (Astounding, November 1955) is a classic "superman" tale.*

Although his stories appeared infrequently in Galaxy, *he served the magazine in two roles: as assistant editor in 1953, and as the reg-ular book reviewer from February 1965 to 1971. He later did reviews for* The Magazine of Fantasy and Science Fiction *and* Booklist. *In his often brilliant and incisive reviews, Budrys commented on the field of science fiction, as well as on many individual works, and helped to raise standards for both readers and writers.*

Memoir: Spilled Milk by Algis Budrys

I met Horace Gold before I ever sold a magazine story, although I had been writing comic-book fillers for a month or so. Over his poker table, he was charming, witty, and gracious. Then I went to work for him, a few months after selling my first dozen stories, one of them to *Galaxy*. And he had turned into a monster. I could do absolutely nothing right. My opinions on promising new writers were ludicrous, my recommendations from the unsolicited manu-scripts were met with scorn, my ideas on copy-editing purchased manuscripts were puerile, and I was bone lazy and increasingly hostile. In the end, I was in league with the competition and actively conspiring against Horace.

Or so I was told, and I did not respond well to hearing it. But it was true. I understood sf pretty well, but I did not, in the early 1950s, understand Galaxy. Few people did. Still, few people see the magazine's first flush in proper perspective.

In Galaxy's first years, which appeared so confident and so energetic, there was in fact little confidence inside it, a nagging sense that things were not going right, and no assurance of the future. The people who had put Galaxy together—essentially, Horace Gold and W. I. Van der Poel, the art director—had consciously set out to trespass on everything that was known about the production and packaging of topflight sf. What was known was that only John W. Campbell, Jr., had a license to do it.

The situation is hard to grasp now because Galaxy succeeded in its controversion. The feat was roughly comparable to what would be accomplished if Pepsi-Cola ever outstripped Coca-Cola in popularity.

There may be another way of putting it. As late as 1953, when Horace Gold hired me to be his first paid assistant, I had every right to consider myself a knowledgeable member of the sf community. At twenty-two I was a published pro after twelve years of preparation, an sf reader of fifteen years' experience, a reasonably active fan and amateur publisher, and six months a veteran of Horace and Evelyn Gold's literary poker soirees. And I assumed—so deeply that no thought seemed necessary and certainly no thought was taken— that my job was to help Horace be as much like Campbell as possible and to guide my little share of Galaxy toward indistinguishability from Astounding Science Fiction.

Quite soon, this fundamental error led to my departure, and still neither Horace nor I had ever articulated the true essential factor. I couldn't have. He, for his part, was too kind to call me stupid, but kind enough to point out my many other shortcomings. Perhaps it was because he had wearied of a similar lack of perception in most sf people.

Galaxy was about three years old at the time, and on its second publisher. I was dimly aware that there must have been difficulty of some sort when World Editions, the Italian firm that had introduced the magazine as part of a highly variegated stable, pulled abruptly out of the American market. But like most onlookers I did not accurately gauge the extent of those difficulties. After all, it was an excellent magazine, featuring major stories by the best—i.e., the most Campbellian—by-lines in the field. By paying top rates (I thought), *Galaxy* had broadened the market, provided a solid alternative to the unquestionable leader, and thus—since *ASF* had been a good property for Street & Smith over the past decade or more—could offer itself to a prospective owner as an equally well-based investment. That was how I thought of it when I thought rationally on the subject.

Much more often, though, I thought emotionally. In its first years *Galaxy* roughly resembled *Astounding*—to such an extent that it was often as good as an extra issue of *ASF*—so I thought it deserved a place of prominence within the sf family centering on paterfamilias Campbell. Therefore, someone was bound to pick it up when World Editions so ineptly dropped it. Or so it seemed to me.

What I overlooked was that all along Horace had been shooting not for the *ASF* audience but for a great untapped market of mundane readers—the people to whom he insisted that he was the editor of *Galaxy* magazine, *not* of *Galaxy* science fiction. At his card table every Friday were not just Frederik Pohl, Bob Scheckley, and the fellow whom Jerry Bixby nicknamed "Ayjay" Budrys, but also such persons as the modern composers Louis and Bebe Barron and John Cage, radio and TV executives, and people on the editorial staffs of major slick magazines. Horace and his wife persistently and consciously worked to hold a place in the New York creative community; to be treated as persons of account outside the sf enclave; and to produce a magazine that would be taken up by the *au courant*.

This was an effort of a sort that has never yet clearly succeeded. The invariable result up to now has been that the hard-core sf readers are gradually or swiftly lost but few outsiders are gained. However, in the earliest 1950s no one knew that because no one had seriously tried it—until Horace came along. Not many knew that was what Horace was trying to do; it is not a position one bruits about while drawing sustenance from the community one is intending to depart, and thus by implication to criticize.

It seems clear to me now that this was the intention; that Horace had made this promise to World Editions and reinforced it while persuading the Guinn Company to keep the abandoned property afloat. Such a promise involves a commitment to attaining a high circulation and predominant reputation in exchange for a first-rate editorial budget . . . and tolerance of an editor who does all his work by phone and by messenger, never stirring out of his apartment. It involves enormous pressure on the editor, who has undertaken a most audacious step.

ASF had dominated the market and developed its major writers unchallenged ever since the late 1930s. There were always other sf magazines on the stands, but each had its own, obviously lesser niche. From *Weird Tales* to *Captain Future*, they did not publish The Best, and did not cater to The Best Readership. When *The Magazine of Fantasy* appeared in the late 1940s, it was clearly not a challenge but sort of science-fictional *Ellery Queen's*, even when it immediately expanded its name to *The Magazine of Fantasy and Science Fiction* and established the row it hoes to this day, fruitfully and charmingly, and never in the Campbellian manner.

When I went to work for *Galaxy*, I thought it had just burst upon the scene. I didn't realize it was already past its first stage. I was unaware of agonizing months of preparation, the long conferences on editorial policy, the careful selection of cover format . . . in short, the procedures with which the big-time marketing world formulates, names, and packages a major new product. Horace had outbid Campbell for stories, obviously, and though Campbell was now budgeted up to par, Horace had gained a foothold and stimulated increased production from the best writers.

What I didn't know was that *Galaxy* resembled *ASF* as much as it did because all the available writers were in the Campbell camp. Still, the reservoir of high-quality writers who had rejected or been rejected by *ASF*—but whose stories still resembled those of *ASF!*—accounted for some slight differences between the magazines.

Horace had much more interest in the latter, and was developing them as quickly as he could, while attempting to wean others away from *ASF*—not with more money but with promises of a different mode. In other words, the qualities that particularly attracted me and many other science-fictionists to *Galaxy* were only a transient feature. By 1953 the magazine was definitely headed elsewhere in Horace's plans. Which, as previously noted, he did not discuss with such unweaned calves as I.

When Horace hired me, I thought I had some slight beginnings as an editor. For several months I had been employed by the pioneering sf book-publishing house of Gnome Press, where I picked the lock every morning at 9 AM, gathered up the mail under the slot, swept the floor, answered the phone, filled orders, typed royalty statements, and from time to time read proofs or edited copy in accordance with whatever standards chose to cross my mind. At about noon, the owner would arrive, and I would once again point out that since I was demonstrably worthy of trust it was time to give me a key. His conclusive response was that I obviously didn't need one, and so the day would proceed to its close. When Horace allowed that his first choice for an assistant had turned him down but I was his second, I felt it was indeed time for me to move on to my next source of colorful anecdotes about my early days in the business. And to confess the truth, I walked on air at the thought of working for *Galaxy*; only a pathological shyness which rarely gave way to mania prevented my telling everyone on the subway, and I'm quite sure I worked it into my conversation with the neighborhood grocer.

Mornings I spent in the Guinn Company offices on Hudson Street, at a broken desk in a gritty warehouse, reading unsolicited manuscripts, checking proofs, and turning out *Galaxy Novels*, which were digest-size reprints of sf books cut to 60,000 words by my procrustean pencil. Drinking coffee from containers, I pondered the things I had heard in the afternoons at the Gold apartment in Stuyvesant Town.

The first thing I learned was a system of marking proofs that is not quite standard but that has persisted with me. Next was copyediting for the obvious.

Horace had a reputation for compulsive and apparently arbitrary changes in stories, which frequently meant demands for massive rewrites and always meant heavily marked-up manuscripts. Most writers reacted badly. Some, contrariwise, felt and feel that Horace got more out of them than they knew was in them, and made an excellent story out of many a mediocre one. He also had a reputation, among those he horrified with these practices, for not seeing subtleties and for obtusely overlooking references that were totally clear in the context of sf as it had evolved through the Campbellian "Golden Age." Out they went—the contrapuntal subthemes based on variations of classic ideas, the O. Henry endings reminiscent of a firmly founded sf tradition . . . in short, all the little touches designed to appeal to the sf sophisticate in writer and reader alike. Out, out, out! And in their place a carefully worded recapitulation of the already plainly indicated, and a last paragraph designed to make the point of the story unboundedly apparent.

It was wrong, it was bad, it was nerve-wracking to me to participate in this mockery of all that was right and good . . . I, who had found Horace so impressive at first, could only tell myself that his combat-earned case of agoraphobia was in fact something rather deeper and darker than that.

The inordinate care he took in writing dozen-word blurbs that could have been dashed off in five minutes; his quixotic attention to niceties of style—"gray," not "grey" [in this book obeyed . . .], "judgement," not "judgment" [. . . and disobeyed! (ED.)]—all those minutiae for a magazine almost illegibly printed on wood-chip paper, with a readership fully prepared to ignore that the hero wore a bandolier on one page and a bandoler on the next, and a readership in any case subjected to amazing typographical mishaps at the plant after the page-proofs had been painstakingly corrected and okayed; the attitude that absolutely *everything* was critical and *everything* was always at stake . . . something had to give.

Something did, and the right man won. Out I went, and high time it was.

Working for Horace would not have been a love feast under any circumstances. He was that rare creature, an *editor*, as distinguished from someone who buys stories and tries to get them to the printer on time. He knew a thousand rules of thumb and a hundred thousand clichés of the business. I think he would have been better off with a fraction of that armamentarium, but the point is that few people who draw editorial paychecks even know how much communications experience has been generated over the years since Gutenberg, and is available. And therefore no editor is easy to work for if you have a mind of your own, which I did.

Note that the mind need not be capable of totally understanding the situation; it need only be stubborn. Note that contemporary thinking on John Campbell is that a rigidly held system of narrow beliefs was his greatest asset. And be assured that Horace Gold was not about to let anyone compromise whatever was at his core. In that one essential, he and Campbell were exactly alike, and the myriad superficial differences add up to nothing important. He was as wrong about the ultimate viability of his policy as most editors usually are, and as wrong as I, in my small way, was about what he ought to be doing. But he was right in the only way that matters to editors; he enforced. Things were done his way or they were not done. And it so happened that like all effective editors, he had a knack for energizing writers even though he and they might be talking about far different things in the same words. It is almost impossible to prevent yourself from being an effective editor if you are a born editor; to all others, the trick is beyond doing.

Galaxy never became what Horace planned. One major drawback was the cheapness of the manufacturing. The cover design might be sophisticated, on its expensive Kromekote stock, but what was bound inside was clearly closer to neighborhood job printing than to anything you'd leave on your Plexiglas coffee table. That had been a fatal compromise from the beginning, forever limiting the circulation to people who had grown up with *Thrilling Wonder Stories* as a production standard.

Equally detrimental was that few writers whom Horace could afford were actually capable of conveying the Sense of Wonder to uninitiated readers. No issue ever carried a preponderance of such material, and most of the material came out bland when what was wanted was universal appeal. When Horace did succeed in obtaining *The Space Merchants*, it came out as *Gravy Planet*, whatever that means, and was described in the cover bannerline as "A 'HUCKSTERS' UTOPIA OF THE FUTURE" (sic). There are just so many potential error-points one man can watch, especially when *everything* is critical.

Nevertheless, what he accomplished was mighty. Campbell and *ASF* were the best things that had happened to newsstand sf up to that time . . . but they were clearly prepared to go on doing the same thing forever, and no mode in literature can be inventive forever. Horace was right to fly in the face of Campbell. We all gained by it. New writers and old saw the fundamental point that excellence derives not from a particular viewpoint but from something far less codifiable. Some new writers and old proceeded to open up areas that sf had never touched. In a few cases, they ventured into areas no other literature can discuss. And now of course all of us from the '50s are old writers; much in the field is new, but some of it derives from what was new when we did it.

And that was accomplished by Horace Gold, who conceived of *Galaxy*, kept *Galaxy* alive, set a *Galaxy* tone, and established a *Galaxy* presence. He never spoke to the people he wanted to reach, but he was heard to be speaking. Some of us owe him more than we may know even yet, and certainly more than we knew at the time.

WALL OF CRYSTAL, EYE OF NIGHT

1

Soft as the voice of a mourning dove, the telephone sounded at Rufus Sollenar's desk. Sollenar himself was standing fifty paces away, his leonine head cocked, his hands flat in his hip pockets, watching the nighted world through the crystal wall that faced out over Manhattan Island. The window was so high that some of what he saw was dimmed by low clouds hovering over the rivers. Above him were stars; below him the city was traced out in light and brimming with light. A falling star—an interplanetary rocket—streaked down toward Long Island Facility like a scratch across the soot on the doors of Hell.

Sollenar's eyes took it in, but he was watching the total scene, not any particular part of it. His eyes were shining.

When he heard the telephone, he raised his left hand to his lips. "Yes?" The hand glittered with utilijem rings; the effect was that of an attempt at the sort of copper-binding that was once used to reinforce the ribbing of wooden warships.

His personal receptionist's voice moved from the air near his desk to the air near his ear. Seated at the monitor board in her office, wherever in this building her office was, the receptionist told him:

"Mr. Ermine says he has an appointment."

"No." Sollenar dropped his hand and returned to his panorama. When he had been twenty years younger—managing the modest optical factory that had provided the support of three generations of Sollenars—he had very much wanted to be able to stand in a place like this, and feel as he imagined men felt in such circumstances. But he felt unimaginable, now.

To be here was one thing. To have almost lost the right, and regained it at the last moment, was another. Now he knew that not only could he be here today but that tomorrow, and tomorrow, he could still be here. He had won. His gamble had given him Empa Vid—and EmpaVid would give him all.

The city was not merely a prize set down before his eyes. It was a dynamic system he had proved he could manipulate. He and the city were one. It buoyed and sustained him; it supported him, here in the air, with stars above and light-thickened mist below.

The telephone mourned: "Mr. Ermine states he has a firm appointment."

"I've never heard of him." And the left hand's utilijems fell from Sollenar's lips again. He enjoyed such toys. He raised his right hand, sheathed in insubstantial midnight-blue silk in which the silver threads of metallic wiring ran subtly toward the fingertips. He raised the hand, and touched two fingers together: Music began to play behind and before him. He made contact between another combination of finger circuits, and a soft, feminine laugh came from the terrace at the other side of the room, where connecting doors had opened. He moved toward it. One layer of translucent drapery remained across the doorway, bilowing lightly in the breeze from the terrace. Through it, he saw the taboret with its candle lit; the iced wine in the stand beside it; the two fragile chairs; Bess Allardyce, slender and regal, waiting in one of them—all these, through the misty curtain, like either the beginning or the end of a dream.

"Mr. Ermine reminds you the appointment was made for him at the Annual Business Dinner of the International Association of Broadcasters, in 1998."

Sollenar completed his latest step, then stopped. He frowned down at his left hand. "Is Mr. Ermine with the IAB's Special Public Relations Office?"

"Yes," the voice said after a pause.

The fingers of Sollenar's right hand shrank into a cone. The connecting door closed. The girl disappeared. The music stopped. "All right. You can tell Mr. Ermine to come up." Sollenar went to sit behind his desk.

The office door chimed. Sollenar crooked a finger of his left hand, and the door opened. With another gesture, he kindled the overhead lights near the door and sat in shadow as Mr. Ermine came in.

Ermine was dressed in rust-colored garments. His figure was spare, and his hands were empty. His face was round and soft, with long dark sideburns. His scalp was bald. He stood just inside Sollenar's office and said: "I would like some light to see you by, Mr. Sollenar."

Sollenar crooked his little finger.

The overhead lights came to soft light all over the office. The crystal wall became a mirror, with only the strongest city lights glimmering through it. "I only wanted to see you first," said Sollenar; "I thought perhaps we met before."

"No," Ermine said, walking across the office. "It's not likely you've ever seen me." He took a card case out of his pocket and showed Sollenar proper identification. "I'm not a very forward person."

"Please sit down," Solenar said. "What may I do for you?"

"At the moment, Mr. Sollenar, I'm doing something for you."

Sollenar sat back in his chair. "Are you? Are you, now?" He frowned at Ermine. "When I became a party to the By-Laws passed at the '98 dinner, I thought a Special Public Relations Office would make a valuable asset to the organization. Consequently, I voted for it, and for the powers it was given. But I never expected to have any personal dealings with it. I barely remembered you people had carte blanche with any IAB member."

"Well, of course, it's been a while since '98," Ermine said. "I imagine some legends have grown up around us. Industry gossip—that sort of thing."

"Yes."

"But we don't restrict ourselves to an enforcement function, Mr. Sollenar. You haven't broken any By-Laws, to our knowledge."

"Or mine. But nobody feels one hundred percent secure. Not under these circumstances." Nor did Sollenar yet relax his face into its magnificent smile. "I'm sure you've found that out."

"I have a somewhat less ambitious older brother who's with the Federal Bureau of Investigation. When I embarked on my own career, he told me I could expect everyone in the world to react like a criminal, yes," Ermine said, paying no attention to Sollenar's involuntary blink. "It's one of the complicating factors in a profession like my brother's, or mine. But I'm here to advise you, Mr. Sollenar. Only that."

"In what matter, Mr. Ermine?"

"Well, your corporation recently came into control of the patents for a new video system. I understand that this in effect makes your

corporation the licensor for an extremely valuable sales and entertainment medium. Fantastically valuable."

"EmpaVid," Sollenar agreed. "Various subliminal stimuli are
broadcast with and keyed to the overt subject matter. The home receiving unit contains feedback sensors which determine the viewer's
reaction to these stimuli, and intensify some while playing down
others in order to create complete emotional rapport between the
viewer and the subject matter. EmpaVid, in other words, is a system
for orchestrating the viewer's emotions. The home unit is self-contained, semiportable, and not significantly bulkier than the standard
TV receiver. EmpaVid is compatible with standard TV receivers—
except, of course, that the subject matter seems thin and vaguely un-
satisfactory on a standard receiver. So the consumer shortly pur-
chases an EV unit." It pleased Sollenar to spell out the nature of his
prize.

"At a very reasonable price. Quite so, Mr. Sollenar. But you had
several difficulties in finding potential licensees for this sytem,
among the networks."

Sollenar's lips pinched out.

Mr. Ermine raised one finger. "First, there was the matter of acquiring the patents from the original inventor, who was also approached by Cortwright Burr."

"Yes, he was," Sollenar said in a completely new voice.

"Competition between Mr. Burr and yourself is long-standing and
intense."

"Quite intense," Sollenar said, looking directly ahead of him at
the one blank wall of the office. Burr's offices were several blocks
downtown, in that direction.

"Well, I have no wish to enlarge on that point, Mr. Burr being an
IAB member in standing as good as yours, Mr. Sollenar. There was,
in any case, a further difficulty in licensing EV, due to the very
heavy cost involved in equipping broadcasting stations and network
relay equipment for this sort of transmission."

"Yes, there was."

"Ultimately, however, you succeeded. You pointed out, quite
rightly, that if just one station made the change, and if just a few
EV receivers were put into public places within the area served by
that station, normal TV outlets could not possibly compete for
advertising revenue."

"Yes."

"And so your last difficulties were resolved a few days ago, when your EmpaVid Unlimited—pardon me—when EmpaVid, a subsidiary of the Sollenar Corporation—became a major stockholder in the Transworld TV Network."

"I don't understand, Mr. Ermine," Sollenar said. "Why are you recounting this? Are you trying to demonstrate the power of your knowledge? All these transactions are already matters of record in the IAB confidential files, in accordance with the By-Laws."

Ermine held up another finger. "You're forgetting I'm only here to advise you. I have two things to say. They are:

"These transactions are on file with the IAB because they involve a great number of IAB members, and an increasingly large amount of capital. Also, Transworld's exclusivity, under the IAB By-Laws, will hold good only until thirty-three percent market saturation has been reached. If EV is as good as it looks, that will be quite soon. After that, under the By-Laws, Transworld will be restrained from making effective defenses against patent infringement by competitors. Then all of the IAB's membership and much of their capital will be involved with EV. Much of that capital is already in anticipatory motion. So a highly complex structure now ultimately depends on the integrity of the Sollenar Corporation. If Sollenar stock falls in value, not just you but many IAB members will be greatly embarrassed. Which is another way of saying EV must succeed."

"I know all that! What of it? There's no risk. I've had every related patent on Earth checked. There will be no catastrophic obsolescence of the EV system."

Ermine said: "There are engineers on Mars. Martian engineers. They're a dying race, but no one knows what they can still do."

Sollenar raised his massive head.

Ermine said: "Late this evening, my office learned that Cortwright Burr has been in close consultation with the Martians for several weeks. He was on the flight that landed at the Facility a few moments ago."

Sollenar's fists clenched. The lights crashed off and on, and the room wailed. From the terrace came a startled cry, and a sound of smashed glass.

Mr. Ermine nodded, excused himself, and left.

—A few moments later, Mr. Ermine stepped out at the pedestrian level of the Sollenar Building. He strolled through the landscaped garden, and across the frothing brook toward the central walkway down the Avenue. He paused at a hedge to pluck a blossom and inhale its odor. He walked away, holding it in his naked fingers.

2

Drifting slowly on the thread of his spinneret, Rufus Sollenar came gliding down the wind above Cortwright Burr's building.

The building, like a spider, touched the ground at only the points of its legs. It held its wide, low bulk spread like a parasol over several downtown blocks. Sollenar, manipulating the helium-filled plastic drifter far above him, steered himself with jets of compressed gas from plastic bottles in the drifter's structure.

Only Sollenar himself, in all this system, was effectively transparent to the municipal antiplane radar. And he himself was wrapped in long, fluttering streamers of dull black, metallic sheeting. To the eye, he was amorphous and nonreflective. To electronic sensors, he was a drift of static much like a sheet of foil picked by the wind from some careless trash heap. To all of the senses of all interested parties he was hardly there at all—and, thus, in an excellent position for murder.

He fluttered against Burr's window. There was the man, crouched over his desk. What was that in his hands—a pomander?

Sollenar clipped his harness to the edges of the cornice. Swayed out against it, his sponge-soled boots pressed to the glass, he touched his left hand to the window and described a circle. He pushed; there was a thud on the carpeting in Burr's office, and now there was no barrier to Sollenar. Doubling his knees against his chest, he catapulted forward, the riot pistol in his right hand. He stumbled and fell to his knees, but the gun was up.

Burr jolted up behind his desk. The little sphere of orange-gold metal, streaked with darker bronze, its surface vermicular with encrustations, was still in his hands. "Him!" Burr cried out as Sollenar fired.

Gasping, Sollenar watched the charge strike Burr. It threw his torso backward faster than his limbs and head could follow without dangling. The choked-down pistol was nearly silent. Burr crashed backward to end, transfixed, against the wall.

Pale and sick, Sollenar moved to take the golden ball. He wondered where Shakespeare could have seen an example such as this, to know an old man could have so much blood in him.

Burr held the prize out to him. Staring with eyes distended by hydrostatic pressure, his clothing raddled and his torso grinding its broken bones, Burr stalked away from the wall and moved as if to embrace Sollenar. It was queer, but he was not dead.

Shuddering, Sollenar fired again.

Again Burr was thrown back. The ball spun from his splayed fingers as he once more marked the wall with his body.

Pomander, orange, whatever—it looked valuable.

Sollenar ran after the rolling ball. And Burr moved to intercept him, nearly faceless, hunched under a great invisible weight that slowly yielded as his back groaned.

Sollenar took a single backward step.

Burr took a step toward him. The golden ball lay in a far corner. Sollenar raised the pistol despairingly and fired again. Burr tripped backward on tiptoe, his arms like windmills, and fell atop the prize.

Tears ran down Sollenar's cheeks. He pushed one foot forward . . . and Burr, in his corner, lifted his head and began to gather his body for the effort of rising.

Sollenar retreated to the window, the pistol sledging backward against his wrist and elbow as he fired the remaining shots in the magazine.

Panting, he climbed up into the window frame and clipped the harness to his body, craning to look over his shoulder . . . as Burr—shredded; leaking blood and worse than blood—advanced across the office.

He cast off his holds on the window frame and clumsily worked the drifter controls. Far above him, volatile ballast spilled out and dispersed in the air long before it touched ground. Sollenar rose, sobbing—

And Burr stood in the window, his shattered hands on the edges of the cut circle, raising his distended eyes steadily to watch Sollenar in flight across the enigmatic sky.

Where he landed, on the roof of a building in his possession, Sollenar had a disposal unit for his gun and his other trappings. He deferred for a time the question of why Burr had failed at once to die. Empty-handed, he returned uptown.

He entered his office, called and told his attorneys the exact times of departure and return, and knew the question of dealing with municipal authorities was thereby resolved. That was simple enough, with no witnesses to complicate the matter. He began to wish he hadn't been so irresolute as to leave Burr without the thing he was after. Surely, if the pistol hadn't killed the man—an old man, with thin limbs and spotted skin—he could have wrestled that thin-limbed, bloody old man aside—that spotted old man—and dragged himself and his prize back to the window; for all that the old man would have clung to him, and clutched at his legs, and fumbled for a handhold on his somber disguise of wrappings—that broken, immortal old man.

Sollenar raised his hand. The great window to the city grew opaque.

Bess Allardyce knocked softly on the door from the terrace. He would have thought she'd returned to her own apartments many hours ago. Tortuously pleased, he opened the door and smiled at her, feeling the dried tears crack on the skin of his cheeks.

He took her proffered hands. "You waited for me," he sighed. "A long time for anyone as beautiful as you to wait."

She smiled back at him. "Let's go out and look at the stars."

"Isn't it chilly?"

"I made spiced hot cider for us. We can sip it and think."

He let her draw him out onto the terrace. He leaned on the parapet, his arm around her pushing her pulsing waist, his cape drawn around both their shoulders.

"Bess, I won't ask if you'd stay with me no matter what the circumstances. But it might be a time will come when I couldn't bear to live in this city. What about that?"

"I don't know," she answered honestly.

And Cortwright Burr put his hand up over the edge of the parapet, between them.

Sollenar stared down at the straining knuckles, holding the entire weight of the man dangling against the sheer face of the building. There was a sliding, rustling noise, and the other hand came up, searching blindly for a hold and found it, hooked over the stone. The fingers tensed and rose, their tips flattening at the pressure as

Burr tried to pull his head and shoulders up to the level of the parapet.

Bess breathed: "Oh, look at them! He must have torn them terribly climbing up!" Then she pulled away from Sollenar and stood staring at him, her hand to her mouth. "But he *couldn't* have climbed! We're so high!"

Sollenar beat at the hands with the heels of his palms, using the direct, trained blows he had learned at his athletic club.

Bone splintered against the stone. When the knuckles were broken the hands instantaneously disappeared, leaving only streaks behind them. Sollenar looked over the parapet. A bundle shrank from sight, silhouetted against the lights of the pedestrian level and the Avenue. It contracted to a pinpoint. Then, when it reached the brook and water flew in all directions, it disappeared in a final sunburst, endowed with glory by the many lights which found momentary reflection down there.

"Bess, leave me! Leave me, please!" Rufus Sollenar cried out.

3

Rufus Sollenar paced his office, his hands held safely still in front of him, their fingers spread and rigid.

The telephone sounded, and his secretary said to him: "Mr. Sollenar, you are ten minutes from being late at the TTV Executives' Ball. This is a first-class obligation."

Sollenar laughed. "I thought it was, when I originally classified it."

"Are you now planning to renege, Mr. Sollenar?" the secretary inquired politely.

Certainly, Sollenar thought. He could as easily renege on the ball as a king could on his coronation.

"Burr, you scum, what have you done to me?" he asked the air, and the telephone said: "Beg pardon?"

"Tell my valet," Sollenar said. "I'm going." He dismissed the phone. His hands cupped in front of his chest. A firm grip on emptiness might be stronger than any prize in a broken hand.

Carrying in his chest something he refused to admit was terror, Sollenar made ready for the ball.

But only a few moments after the first dance set had ended, Mal-

colm Levier of the local TTV station executive staff looked over
Sollenar's shoulder and remarked:

"Oh, there's Cort Burr, dressed like a gallows bird."

Sollenar, glittering in the costume of the Medici, did not turn his
head. "Is he? What would he want here?"

Levier's eyebrows arched. "He holds a little stock. He has entree.
But he's late." Levier's lips quirked. "It must have taken him some
time to get that makeup on."

"Not in good taste, is it?"

"Look for yourself."

"Oh, I'll do better than that," Sollenar said. "I'll go and talk to
him a while. Excuse me, Levier." And only then did he turn around,
already started on his first pace toward the man.

But Cortwright Burr was only a pasteboard imitation of himself as
Sollenar had come to know him. He stood to one side of the doorway, dressed in black and crimson robes, with black leather gauntlets
on his hands, carrying a staff of weathered, natural wood. His face
was shadowed by a sackcloth hood, the eyes hidden well. His face
was powdered gray, and some blend of livid colors hollowed his
cheeks. He stood motionless as Sollenar came up to him.

As he had crossed the floor, each step regular, the eyes of bystanders had followed Sollenar, until, anticipating his course, they
found Burr waiting. The noise level of the ball shrank perceptibly,
for the lesser revelers who chanced to be present were sustaining it
all alone. The people who really mattered here were silent and
watchful.

The thought was that Burr, defeated in business, had come here
in some insane reproach to his adversary, in this lugubrious, dis-
tasteful clothing. Why, he looked like a corpse. Or worse.

The question was, what would Sollenar say to him? The wish was
that Burr would take himself away, back to his estates or to some
other city. New York was no longer for Cortwright Burr. But what
would Sollenar say to him now, to drive him back to where he
hadn't the grace to go willingly?

"Cortwright," Sollenar said in a voice confined to the two of
them. "So your Martian immortality works."

Burr said nothing.

"You got that in addition, didn't you? You knew how I'd react.
You knew you'd need protection. Paid the Martians to make you
physically invulnerable? It's a good system. Very impressive. Who

would have thought the Martians knew so much? But who here is going to pay attention to you now? Get out of town, Cortwright. You're past your chance. You're dead as far as these people are concerned—all you have left is your skin."

Burr reached up and surreptitiously lifted a corner of his fleshed mask. And there he was, under it. The hood retreated an inch, and the light reached his eyes; and Sollenar had been wrong, Burr had less left than he thought.

"Oh, no, no, Cortwright," Sollenar said softly. "No, you're right—I can't stand up to that."

He turned and bowed to the assembled company. "Good night!" he cried, and walked out of the ballroom.

Someone followed him down the corridor to the elevators. Sollenar did not look behind him.

"I have another appointment with you now," Ermine said at his elbow.

They reached the pedestrian level. Sollenar said: "There's a cafe. We can talk there."

"Too public, Mr. Sollenar. Let's simply stroll and converse." Ermine lightly took his arm and guided him along the walkway. Sollenar noticed then that Ermine was costumed so cunningly that no one could have guessed the appearance of the man.

"Very well," Sollenar said.

"Of course."

They walked together, casually. Ermine said: "Burr's driving you to your death. Is it because you tried to kill him earlier? Did you get his Martian secret?"

Sollenar shook his head.

"You didn't get it." Ermine sighed. "That's unfortunate. I'll have to take steps."

"Under the By-Laws," Sollenar said, "I cry *laissez faire*."

Ermine looked up, his eyes twinkling. "*Laissez faire?* Mr. Sollenar, do you have any idea how many of our members are involved in your fortunes? *They* will cry *laissez faire*, Mr. Sollenar, but clearly you persist in dragging them down with you. No, sir, Mr. Sollenar, my office now forwards an immediate recommendation to the Technical Advisory Committee of the IAB that Mr. Burr probably has a system superior to yours, and that stock in Sollenar, Incorporated, had best be disposed of."

"There's a bench," Sollenar said. "Let's sit down."

"As you wish." Ermine moved beside Sollenar to the bench, but remained standing.

"What is it, Mr. Sollenar?"

"I want your help. You advised me on what Burr had. It's still in his office building, somewhere. You have resources. We can get it."

"*Laissez faire*, Mr. Sollenar. I visited you in an advisory capacity. I can do no more."

"For a partnership in my affairs could you do more?"

"Money?" Ermine tittered. "For me? Do you know the conditions of my employment?"

If he had thought, Sollenar would have remembered. He reached out tentatively. Ermine anticipated him.

Ermine bared his left arm and sank his teeth into it. He displayed the arm. There was no quiver of pain in voice or stance. "It's not a legend, Mr. Sollenar. It's quite true. We of our office must spend a year, after the nerve surgery, learning to walk without the feel of our feet, to handle objects without crushing them or letting them slip, or damaging ourselves. Our mundane pleasures are auditory, olfactory, and visual. Easily gratified at little expense. Our dreams are totally interior, Mr. Sollenar. The operation is irreversible. What would you buy for me with your money?"

"What would I buy for myself?" Sollenar's head sank down between his shoulders.

Ermine bent over him. "Your despair is your own, Mr. Sollenar. I have official business with you."

He lifted Sollenar's chin with a forefinger. "I judge physical interference to be unwarranted at this time. But matters must remain so that the IAB members involved with you can recover the value of their investments in EV. Is that perfectly clear, Mr. Sollenar? You are hearby enjoined under the By-Laws, as enforced by the Special Public Relations Office." He glanced at his watch. "Notice was served at 1:27 AM, City time."

"1:27," Sollenar said. "City time." He sprang to his feet and raced down a companionway to the taxi level.

Mr. Ermine watched him quizzically.

He opened his costume, took out his omnipresent medical kit, and sprayed coagulant over the wound in his forearm. Replacing the kit, he adjusted his clothing and strolled down the same companionway Sollenar had run. He raised an arm, and a taxi flittered down beside him. He showed the driver a card, and the cab lifted off with him, its lights glaring in a Priority pattern, far faster than Sollenar's ordinary legal limit allowed.

4

Long Island Facility vaulted at the stars in great kangaroo-leaps of arch and cantilever span, jeweled in glass and metal as if the entire port were a mechanism for navigating interplanetary space. Rufus Sollenar paced its esplanades, measuring his steps, holding his arms still, for the short time until he could board the Mars rocket.

Erect and majestic, he took a place in the lounge and carefully sipped liqueur, once the liner had boosted away from Earth and coupled in its Faraday main drives.

Mr. Ermine settled into the place beside him.

Sollenar looked over at him calmly. "I thought so."

Ermine nodded. "Of course you did. But I didn't almost miss you. I was here ahead of you. I have no objection to your going to Mars, Mr. Sollenar. *Laissez faire*. Provided I can go along."

"Well," Rufus Sollenar said. "Liqueur?" He gestured with his glass.

Ermine shook his head. "No, thank you," he said delicately.

Sollenar said: "Even your tongue?"

"Of course my tongue, Mr. Sollenar. I taste nothing. I touch nothing." Ermine smiled. "But I feel no pressure."

"All right, then," Rufus Sollenar said crisply. "We have several hours to landing time. You sit and dream your interior dreams, and I'll dream mine." He faced around in his chair and folded his arms across his chest.

"Mr. Sollenar," Ermine said gently.

"Yes?"

"I am once again with you by appointment as provided under the By-Laws."

"State your business, Mr. Ermine."

"You are not permitted to lie in an unknown grave, Mr. Sollenar. Insurance policies on your life have been taken out at a high premium rate. The IAB members concerned cannot wait the statutory seven years to have you declared dead. Do what you will, Mr. Sollenar, but I must take care I witness your death. From now on, I am with you wherever you go."

Sollenar smiled. "I don't intend to die. Why should I die, Mr. Ermine?"

"I have no idea, Mr. Sollenar. But I know Cortwright Burr's character. And isn't that he, seated there in the corner? The light is poor, but I think he's recognizable."

Across the lounge, Burr raised his head and looked into Sollenar's eyes. He raised a hand near his face, perhaps merely to signify greeting. Rufus Sollenar faced front.

"A worthy opponent, Mr. Sollenar," Ermine said. "A persevering, unforgiving, ingenious man. And yet—" Ermine seemed a little touched by bafflement. "And yet it seems to me, Mr. Sollenar, that he got you running rather easily. What *did* happen between you, after my advisory call?"

Sollenar turned a terrible smile on Ermine. "I shot him to pieces. If you'd peel his face, you'd see."

Ermine sighed. "Up to this moment, I had thought perhaps you might still salvage your affairs."

"Pity, Mr. Ermine? Pity for the insane?"

"Interest. I can take no part in your world. Be grateful, Mr. Sollenar. I am not the same gullible man I was when I signed my contract with IAB, so many years ago."

Sollenar laughed. Then he stole a glance at Burr's corner.

The ship came down at Abernathy Field, in Aresia, the Terrestrial city. Industrialized, prefabricated, jerry-built, and clamorous, the storm-proofed buildings huddled, but huddled proudly, at the desert's edge.

Low on the horizon was the Martian settlement—the buildings so skillfully blended with the landscape, so eroded, so much abandoned that the uninformed eye saw nothing. Sollenar had been to Mars— on a tour. He had seen the natives in their nameless dwelling place; arrogant, venomous, and weak. He had been told, by the paid guide, they trafficked with Earthmen as much as they cared to, and kept to their place on the rim of Earth's encroachment, observing.

"Tell me, Ermine," Sollenar said quietly as they walked across the terminal lobby. "You're to kill me, aren't you, if I try to go without you?"

"A matter of procedure, Mr. Sollenar," Ermine said evenly. "We cannot risk the investment capital of so many IAB members."

Sollenar sighed. "If I were any other member, how I would commend you, Mr. Ermine! Can we hire a car for ourselves, then, somewhere nearby?"

"Going out to see the engineers?" Ermine asked. "Who would have thought they'd have something valuable for sale?"

"I want to show them something," Sollenar said.

"What thing, Mr. Sollenar?"

They turned the corner of a corridor, with branching hallways here and there, not all of them busy. "Come here," Sollenar said, nodding toward one of them.

They stopped out of sight of the lobby and the main corridor. "Come on," Sollenar said. "A little farther."

"No," Ermine said. "This is farther than I really wish. It's dark here."

"Wise too late, Mr. Ermine," Sollenar said, his arms flashing out.

One palm impacted against Ermine's solar plexus, and the other against the muscle at the side of his neck, but not hard enough to kill. Ermine collapsed, starved for oxygen, while Sollenar silently cursed having been cured of murder. Then Sollenar turned and ran.

Behind him Ermine's body struggled to draw breath by reflex alone.

Moving as fast as he dared, Sollenar walked back and reached the taxi lock, pulling a respirator from a wall rack as he went. He flagged a car and gave his destination, looking behind him. He had seen nothing of Cortwright Burr since setting foot on Mars. But he knew that soon or late, Burr would find him.

A few moments later Ermine got to his feet. Sollenar's car was well away. Ermine shrugged and went to the local broadcasting station.

He commandeered a private desk, a firearm, and immediate time on the IAB interoffice circuit to Earth. When his call acknowledgment had come back to him from his office there, he reported:

"Sollenar is en route to the Martian city. He wants a duplicate of Burr's device, of course, since he smashed the original when he killed Burr. I'll follow and make final disposition. The disorientation I reported previously is progressing rapidly. Almost all his responses now are inappropriate. On the flight out he seemed to be staring at something in an empty seat. Quite often when spoken to he obviously hears something else entirely. I expect to catch one of the next few flights back."

There was no point in waiting for comment to wend its way back from Earth. Ermine left. He went to a cab rank and paid the exorbitant fee for transportation outside Aresian city limits.

Close at hand, the Martian city was like a welter of broken pots. Shards of wall and roof joined at savage angles and pointed to nothing. Drifts of vitreous material, shaped to fit no sane configuration, and broken to fit such a mosaic as no church would contain, rocked and slid under Sollenar's hurrying feet.

What from Aresia had been a solid front of dun color was here a facade of red, green, and blue splashed about centuries ago and since then weathered only enough to show how bitter the colors had once been. The plum-colored sky stretched over all this like a frigid membrane, and the wind blew and blew.

Here and there, as he progressed, Sollenar saw Martian arms and heads protruding from the rubble. Sculptures.

He was moving toward the heart of the city, where some few unbroken structures persisted. At the top of a heap of shards he turned to look behind him. There was the dust-plume of his cab, returning to the city. He expected to walk back—perhaps to meet someone on the road, all alone on the Martian plain if only Ermine would forbear from interfering. Searching the flat, thin-aired landscape, he tried to pick out the plodding dot of Cortwright Burr. But not yet.

He turned and ran down the untrustworthy slope.

He reached the edge of the maintained area. Here the rubble was gone, the ancient walks swept, the statues kept upright on their pediments. But only broken walls suggested the fronts of the houses that had stood here. Knifing their sides up through the wind-rippled sand that only constant care kept off the street, the shadow-houses fenced his way and the sculptures were motionless as hope. Ahead of him, he saw the buildings of the engineers. There was no heap to climb and look to see if Ermine followed close behind.

Sucking his respirator, he recalled the building of the Martian Engineers.

A sounding strip ran down the doorjamb. He scratched his finger-

nails sharply along it, and the magnified vibration, ducted throughout the hollow walls, rattled his pleas for entrance.

5

The door opened, and Martians stood looking. They were spindly-
limbed and slight, their faces framed by folds of leathery tissue.
Their mouths were lipped with horn as hard as dentures, and
pursed, forever ready to masticate. They were pleasant neither to
look at nor, Sollenar knew, to deal with. But Cortwright Burr had
done it. And Sollenar needed to do it.

"Does anyone here speak English?" he asked.

"I," said the central Martian, his mouth opening to the sound,
closing to end the reply.

"I would like to deal with you."

"Whenever," the Martian said, and the group at the doorway
parted deliberately to let Sollenar in.

Before the door closed behind him, Sollenar looked back. But the
rubble of the abandoned sectors blocked his line of sight into the desert.

"What can you offer? And what do you want?" the Martian
asked. Sollenar stood half-ringed by them, in a room whose corners
he could not see in the uncertain light.

"I offer you Terrestrial currency."

The English-speaking Martian—the Martian who had admitted to
speaking English—turned his head slightly and spoke to his fellows.
There were clacking sounds as his lips met. The others reacted
variously, one of them suddenly gesturing with what seemed a
disgusted flip of his arm before he turned without further word and
stalked away, his shoulders looking like the shawled back of a very
old and very hungry woman.

"What did Burr give you?" Sollenar asked.

"Burr." The Martian cocked his head. His eyes were not mul-
tifaceted, but gave that impression.

"He was here and he dealt with you. Not long ago. On what
basis?"

"Burr. Yes. Burr gave us currency. We will take currency from
you. For the same thing we gave him?"

"For immortality, yes."

"Im—This is a new word."

"Is it? For the secret of not dying?"

. "Not dying? You think we have not-dying for sale here?" The Martian spoke to the others again. Their lips clattered. Others left, like the first one had, moving with great precision and very slow step, and no remaining tolerance for Sollenar.

Sollenar cried out: "What did you sell him, then?"

The principal engineer said: "We made an entertainment device for him."

"A little thing. This size." Sollenar cupped his hands.

"You have seen it, then."

"Yes. And nothing more? That was all he bought here?"

"It was all we had to sell—or give. We don't yet know whether Earthmen will give us things in exchange for currency. We'll see, when we need something from Aresia."

Sollenar demanded: "How did it work? This thing you sold him."

"Oh, it lets people tell stories to themselves."

Sollenar looked closely at the Martian. "What kind of stories?"

"Any kind," the Martian said blandly. "Burr told us what he wanted. He had drawings with him of an Earthman device that used pictures on a screen, and broadcast sounds, to carry the details of the story told to the auditor."

"He stole those patents! He couldn't have used them on Earth."

"And why should he? Our device needs to convey no precise details. Any mind can make its own. It only needs to be put into a situation, and from there it can do all the work. If an auditor wishes a story of contact with other sexes, for example, the projector simply makes it seem to him, the next time he is with the object of his desire, that he is getting positive feedback—that he is arousing a similar response in that object. Once that has been established for him, the auditor may then leave the machine, move about normally, conduct his life as usual—but always in accordance with the basic situation. It is, you see, in the end a means of introducing system into his view of reality. Of course, his society must understand that he is not in accord with reality, for some of what he does cannot seem rational from an outside view of him. So some care must be taken, but not much. If many such devices were to enter his society, soon the circumstances would become commonplace, and the society would surely readjust to allow it," said the English-speaking Martian.

"The machine creates any desired situation in the auditor's mind?"

"Certainly. There are simple predisposing tapes that can be inserted as desired. Love, adventure, cerebration—it makes no difference."

Several of the bystanders clacked sounds out to each other. Sollenar looked at them narrowly. It was obvious there had to be more than one English-speaker among these people.

"And the device you gave Burr," he asked the engineer, neither calmly nor hopefully. "What sort of stories could its auditors tell themselves?"

The Martian cocked his head again. It gave him the look of an owl at a bedroom window. "Oh, there was one situation we were particularly instructed to include. Burr said he was thinking ahead to showing it to an acquaintance of his.

"It was a situation of adventure; of adventure with the fearful. And it was to end in loss and bitterness." The Martian looked even more closely at Sollenar. "Of course, the device does not specify details. No one but the auditor can know what fearful thing inhabits his story, or precisely how the end of it would come. You would, I believe, be Rufus Sollenar? Burr spoke of you and made the noise of laughing."

Sollenar opened his mouth. But there was nothing to say.

"You want such a device?" the Martian asked. "We've prepared several since Burr left. He spoke of machines that would manufacture them in astronomical numbers. We, of course, have done our best with our poor hands."

Sollenar said: "I would like to look out your door."

"Pleasure."

Sollenar opened the door slightly. Mr. Ermine stood in the cleared street, motionless as the shadow buildings behind him. He raised one hand in a gesture of unfelt greeting as he saw Sollenar, then put it back on the stock of his rifle. Sollenar closed the door, and turned to the Martian. "How much currency do you want?"

"Oh, all you have with you. You people always have a good deal with you when you travel."

Sollenar plunged his hands into his pockets and pulled out his billfold, his change, his keys, his jeweled radio; whatever was there, he rummaged out onto the floor, listening to the sound of rolling coins.

"I wish I had more here," he laughed. "I wish I had the

amount that man out there is going to recover when he shoots me."

The Martian engineer cocked his head. "But your dream is over, Mr. Sollenar," he clacked drily. "Isn't it?"

"Quite so. But you to your purposes and I to mine. Now give me one of those projectors. And set it to predispose a situation I am about to specify to you. Take however long it needs. The audience is a patient one." He laughed, and tears gathered in his eyes.

Mr. Ermine waited, isolated from the cold, listening to hear whether the rifle stock was slipping out of his fingers. He had no desire to go into the Martian building after Sollenar and involve third parties. All he wanted was to put Sollenar's body under a dated marker, with as little trouble as possible.

Now and then he walked a few paces backward and forward, to keep from losing muscular control at his extremities because of low skin temperature. Sollenar must come out soon enough. He had no food supply with him, and though Ermine did not like the risk of engaging a man like Sollenar in a starvation contest, there was no doubt that a man with no taste for fuel could outlast one with the required reflexes of eating.

The door opened and Sollenar came out.

He was carrying something. Perhaps a weapon. Ermine let him come closer while he raised and carefully sighted his rifle. Ermine did not particularly care. If Ermine died, he would hardly notice it —far less than he would notice a blotched ending to a job of work already roiled by Sollenar's break away at the space field. If Ermine died, some other SPRO agent would be assigned almost immediately. No matter what happened, SPRO would stop Sollenar before he ever reached Abernathy Field.

So there was plenty of time to aim an unhurried, clean shot.

Sollenar was closer, now. He seemed to be in a very agitated frame of mind. He held out whatever he had in his hand.

It was another one of the Martian entertainment machines. Sollenar seemed to be offering it as a token to Ermine. Ermine smiled.

"What can you offer me, Mr. Sollenar?" he said, and shot.

The golden ball rolled away over the sand. "There, now," Ermine said. "*Now*, wouldn't you sooner be me than you? And where is the thing that made the difference between us?"

He shivered. He was chilly. Sand was blowing against his tender face, which had been somewhat abraded during his long wait.

He stopped, transfixed.

He lifted his head.

Then, with a great swing of his arms, he sent the rifle whirling away. "The wind!" he sighed into the thin air. "I feel the wind." He leapt into the air, and sand flew away from his feet as he landed. He whispered to himself: "I feel the ground!"

He stared in tremblant joy at Sollenar's empty body. "What have you given me?" Full of his own rebirth, he swung his head up at the sky again, and cried in the direction of the sun: "Oh, you squeezing, nibbling people who made me incorruptible and thought that was the end of me!"

With love he buried Sollenar, and with reverence he put up the marker, but he had plans for what he might accomplish with the facts of this transaction, and the myriad others he was privy to.

A sharp bit of pottery had penetrated the sole of his shoe and gashed his foot, but he, not having seen it, hadn't felt it. Nor would he see it or feel it even when he changed his stockings; for he had not noticed the wound when it was made. It didn't matter. In a few days it would heal, though not as rapidly as if it had been properly attended to.

Vaguely, he heard the sound of Martians clacking behind their closed door as he hurried out of the city, full of revenge and reverence for his savior.

THE PLACE WHERE
CHICAGO WAS

February 1962

Jim Harmon
(b. 1934)

Almost forgotten now, Jim Harmon was a regular and more than competent contributor to the sf magazines between 1955 and the late 1960s. He never published a novel in the field, although his nonfiction The Great Radio Heroes *(1967), an excellent and neglected book, contains considerable material on sf and fantasy in that medium. More than a dozen of his forty or so sf stories appeared in* Galaxy, *including the clever "Name Your Symptom" (May 1956).*

Memoir by Jim Harmon

My first professional sale for any recognizable amount of money was to *Galaxy* in 1956 when I was twenty-two. Before that, I had won some "prizes" of two dollars or five dollars, had had some stories published in Bill Crawford's *Spaceway* with a promise of payment if the magazine ever turned a profit (it didn't), and had sold a story to Bob Lowndes' *Science Fiction Quarterly* (and after a long delay and several inquiries was finally paid something like twenty dollars). But *Galaxy* actually sent me a check after only a few weeks, before publication, and for a significant amount of money—$150.00.

The money was important. It was a symbol of success, a reward to the ego, but it was an important thing in itself. My widowed mother was supporting us, working as a practical nurse. Most of that first check went into food and clothing—although I saved out some for copious amounts of sf reading matter and for a trip to a nearby sf fan convention.

Much of my early checks went to financing my year-round journeys to cons where I met such godlike beings as Tom Scortia, Bob Bloch, Leigh Brackett, E. E. Smith, and so many others. Some I only met briefly—like John Campbell or Robert Heinlein. Others I thought of as friends—Isaac Asimov, Bloch, Forrest J. Ackerman, and Evelyn Page Gold, then wife to Horace Gold, editor of *Galaxy*.

In those days, Horace did not go to conventions. (I was pleased to see him at a small regional con only a few weeks ago at this writing, however.) I often wrote Gold and talked to him on the phone a few times. As a teenager, some of my letters were silly and argumentative, chiding him for *daring* to try to do a magazine as good as Campbell's *Astounding* (later *Analog*). He not only tried, but succeeded. For a long stretch, he was doing an sf magazine *at least* as good as the legendary *Astounding*.

As a young man, I knew very little of the real world. Both my formal and informal education had been severely curtailed by illness, including rheumatic fever. What I knew came from reading, and reading primarily science fiction. My first story in *Galaxy*, "Name Your Symptom," was only imitative of a lot of other stories with psychological premises that I had read. The style was sort of homogenized *Galaxy*, moving away from the Ray Bradbury influence that suffused and often stifled sf writers of the fifties.

After that first sale, Horace Gold did everything he could to help me become a writer save coming to Mount Carmel, Illinois, and holding my hand or paying me in advance. He was one of two or three editors I've dealt with who could make suggestions for changes that actually *improved* the story. Writers are often called upon to make changes. Most of them only make the story slightly *different*, not better, in this writer's opinion. Some of them make the story *worse*. If it makes the story a *lot* worse, the writer with any self-respect will refuse to make the change, even at the cost of the sale. Horace Gold's suggested changes often made the difference between a story *worth* selling, and one that wasn't.

In the early sixties, Fred Pohl became the editor of *Galaxy*, and I sold quite a few stories to him. But the sf world was changing. The pocketbooks were taking over the market, and magazines had to struggle for survival. It was Pohl's ability that got *Galaxy* through this difficult period. As for myself, unlike my contemporaries Robert Silverberg and Harlan Ellison, I could not make a living from sf.

About the time "The Place Where Chicago Was" was published, I had moved to Los Angeles and was writing a lot for the bush-league *Playboy* imitators of that city. It was a living, but not a liking on my part.

Eventually, I got into writing "nostalgia" books: *The Great Radio Heroes, The Great Radio Comedians, The Great Movie Heroes* (this one with Don Glut), and *Jim Harmon's Nostalgia Catalogue.* These books often dealt with basic, formative sf sources—for instance, the Buck Rogers radio and movie serial.

Perhaps what I've been nostalgic about is sf. I've never stopped thinking of myself as a science-fiction writer. If I didn't have requests for two nostalgia books on my desk right now, I'd go back to sf tomorrow.

Or so I tell myself.

Much of the current sf I don't enjoy reading myself. I don't know if sf has lost its sense of wonder, but it certainly has lost much of its sense of *order.* The classic sf story is one where the protagonist and the reader have to apply reason to bring order out of chaos. To apply the scientific method, in short. It is impossible to use logical reasoning on the incoherent, the inarticulate, the unstructured.

"The Place Where Chicago Was" is near the end of at least the first phase of my sf writing career. It is decidedly "old-fashioned" in that it moves almost on plot alone. I had worked hard to develop a colorful style (which is more apparent in such *Galaxy* stories as my "The Air of Castor Oil"), but I must have decided to let Mr. Style sit this one out. The *story* was the thing here.

In the story I was concerned with the questions of pacifism in the sixties; with food (because of my own struggle with my diet and weight); and with a hope—not necessarily a prophecy—that man could change the world through his own actions.

I know I have changed my own life for the better from what "common sense" and "reasonable expectations" had set for it. Science fiction, and its shapers like Gold and Pohl, helped me do it.

Today, the old fan's dream has come true. Science fiction is helping shape the everyday world of reality. It had better watch out.

THE PLACE WHERE CHICAGO WAS

1

It was late December of 1983. Danniels knew that the streets and sidewalks of Jersey City moved under their own power and that half the families in America owned their own helicopters. He was pleased with these signs of progress. But he was sweating. He thought he was getting athlete's foot instead of athletic legs from walking from the New Jersey coast to just outside of Marshall, Illinois.

The heat was unbearable.

The road shimmered before him in rows of sticky black ribbon, on which nothing moved. Nothing but him.

He passed a signal post that said "CAUTION—SLOW" in a gentle but commanding voice. He staggered on toward a reddish metallic square set on a thin column of bluish concrete. It was what they called a sign, he decided.

Danniels drooped against the sign and fanned his face with his sweat-ringed straw cowboy hat. The thing seemed to have something to say about the midcentury novelist James Jones, in short, terse words.

The rim of the hat crumpled in his fist. He stood still and listened.

There *was* a car coming.

It would almost *have* to stop, he reasoned. A man couldn't stand much of this Illinois winter heat. The driver might leave him to die on the road if he didn't stop. Therefore he would stop.

He jerked out the small pouch from the sash of his jeans. Inside the special plastic the powder was dry. He rubbed some between his hands briskly, to build up the static electricity, and massaged it into his hair.

The metal of the Jones plaque was fairly shiny. Under the beating noon sun it cast a pale reflection back at Danniels. His hair looked a reasonably uniform white now.

He started to draw the string on the pouch, then dipped his hand in and scooped his palm up to his mouth. He chewed on the stuff while he was securing the nearly flat bag in his sash. He swallowed the dough; the powder had been flour.

Danniels took the hat from beneath his arm, set it to his head, and at last faced the direction of the engine whine.

The roof, hood, and wheels moved over the curve of the horizon and Danniels saw that the car was a brandless classic which probably still had some of the original, indestructible Model A left in it.

He pondered a moment on whether to thumb or not to thumb.

He thumbed.

The rod squealed to a stop exactly even with him. A door unfolded and a voice like a stop signal said flatly, "Get in."

Danniels got in. The driver was a teenager in a loose scarlet tunic and a spangled W.P.A. cap. The youth wouldn't have been badlooking except for a sullen expression and a rather girlish turn of cheek, completely devoid of beard line. Danniels wrote him off as a prospective member of the Wolf Pack in a year or two.

But not just yet, he fervently hoped.

"Going far? I'm not," said the driver.

Danniels adjusted the knees of his trousers. "I'm going to—near where Chicago used to be."

"Huh?"

Danniels had forgotten the youth of his companion. "I mean I'm going to where you can't go any further."

The driver nodded smugly, relieved that the threat to the vastness of his knowledge had been dismissed. "I get you, pop. I guess I can take you close to where you're headed."

They rode on in silence, both relieved that they didn't have to try to span the void between age and position with words.

"You aren't anywhere near starvation, are you?" the driver said suddenly, uneasy.

"No," Danniels said. "Anyway I've got money."

"Woodrow Wilson! I'll pull in at the next joint."

The next joint was carved out of the flat cross section of hill that looked unmistakably like a strip ridge of a Colorado copper mine, but wasn't . . . even barring the fact that this was Illinois. The rectangle of visible diner was color-fused aluminum from between No. Two and Korea.

Danniels was glad to get into the shockingly cold air conditioning.

It was constant, if unhealthy. The chugging unit in the car failed a
heartbeat every now and then for a sickening wave of heat.

The two of them pulled up wire chairs to a linoleum-top table in
a mirrored corner. A faint purple hectographed menu was stuck between appropriately colored plastic squeeze bottles labeled MUSTARD
and BLOOD.

Danniels knew what the menu would say but he unfolded it and
checked.

Steaks

Plankton	.90
Juicy, rich-red tantalizing hamburger	.17

Accessories

Mashed potatoes	.40
Delectable oysters, all you can eat	.09
Peas	.35
Rich, fragrant cheese, large slice	.02

Drinks

Coke	.50
Milk, the forbidden wine of nature	.01
Coffee (without)	.50
Coffee (with)	.02

A fat girl in white came to the table.

Danniels tossed the menu on the table. "I'll take the meat dinner," he said.

The teenager stared hard at the table top. "So will I."

"Good citizens," the waitress said, but the revulsion crept into her
voice over the professional hardness.

Danniels looked carefully at his companion. "You aren't used to
ordering meat."

"Pop," the youth began. Danniels waited to be told that being
short of cash was none of his business. "Pop, on my leg. Kill it,
kill it!"

Danniels leaned over the table startled and curious. A cockroach
was feeling its way along a thin meridian of varicolored jeans. Danniels pinched it up without injuring it and deposited it on the floor.
It scurried away.

"Your kind make me sick," the driver said in lieu of thanks. "You act like a Fanatic but you're a Meat-Eater. How do you blesh that?"

Danniels shrugged. He did not have to explain anything to this kid. He couldn't be stranded.

The kid was under the same encephalographic inversion as the rest of the world. No human being could directly or indirectly commit murder, as long as the broadcasting stations every nation on earth maintained in self-defense continued to function.

These mechinical brain waves coated every mind with enforced pacifism. They could have just as easily broadcast currents that would have made minds swell with love or happiness. But world leaders had universally agreed that these conditions were too narcotic for the common people to endure.

Pacifism was vital to the survival of the planet.

War could not go on killing; but governments still had to go on winning wars. War became a game. The International War Games were held every two years. With pseudo H-bombs and mock germ warfare, countries still effectively eliminated cities and individuals. A "destroyed" city was off limits for twenty years. Nothing could go in or out for that period. Most cities had provided huge food deposits for emergencies.

Before the Famine.

Some minds were more finely attuned to the encephalographic inversion than others. People so in tune with the wave length of pacifism could not only not kill another human being, they could not even kill an animal. Vegetarianism was thrust upon a world not equipped for it. Some—like Danniels—who could not kill still found themselves able to eat what others had killed. Others who could not kill or eat *any* once-living thing—even plants—rapidly starved to death. They were quickly forgotten.

Almost as forgotten as the Jonahs.

The War Dead.

Any soldier or civilian "killed" outside of a major disaster area (where he would be subject to the twenty years) became a man without a country—or a world. They were tagged with green hair by molecular exchange and sent on their way to starve, band together, reach a disaster area (where they would be accepted for the duration of the disaster), starve, or starve.

Anyone who in any way communicated with a Jonah or even recognized the existence of one automatically became a Jonah himself.

It was harsh. And if it wasn't better than war it was quieter. And more permanent.

The counterman with a greasy apron and hairy forearms served the plates. The meat had been lightly glazed to bring out the aroma and flavor but the blood was still a pink sheen on the ground meat. There were generous side dishes of cheese and milk. Even animal by-products were passed up by the majority of vegetarians. Eggs had been the first to be dropped—after all, every egg was a potential life. Milk and associated products came to be spurned through sheer revulsion by association. Besides, milk was intended only to feed the animal's own offspring, wasn't it?

Danniels squirted blood generously from its squeeze bottle. Even vegetarians used a lot of it. It gave their plankton the gory look the human animal craved. Of course it was not really blood, only a kind of tomato paste. When Danniels had been a boy people called it ketchup.

He tried to dig into his steak with vengeance but it tasted of ashes. Meat was his favorite food; he was in no way a vegetarian. But the thought of the Famine haunted him. Vegetable food was high in price and ration points. Most people were living on 2500 calories a day. It wasn't quite starvation and it wasn't quite a full stomach. It was hard on anybody who did more than an average amount of work. It was especially hard on children.

The Meat-Eaters helped relieve the situation. Some, with only the minimum of influence from the Broadcasters, ate nothing but meat. They were naturally aggressive morons who were doing no one favors, potential members of a Wolf Pack.

Danniels knew how to end the Famine.

The mob that was the men he had commanded had hunted him in the hills below Buffalo, and he had been hungry, with no time to eat, or rest, or sleep. Only enough time to think. He couldn't stop thinking. Panting over a smothered spark of campfire, smoldering moss and leaves, he thought. Drinking sparkling but polluted water from a twisting mountain stream and trying unsuccessfully to trap silver shavings of fish with his naked hands, he thought.

His civilian job was that of a genopseudoxenobeastimacroiologist, a specialized field with peacetime applications that had come out of the War Games—specialized to an almost comic-opera intensity. He knew virtually everything about almost nothing at all. Yet, delirious with hunger, from this he fashioned in his mind a way to provide food for everybody. Even Jonahs.

After they caught him—weeks before the Tag spot would have faded off—he wasn't sure whether his idea had been a sick dream or not. But he intended to find out. He wouldn't let any other mob stop him from that.

Danniels had decided he was against mobs, whether their violence and stupidity was social or antisocial. People are better as individuals.

The driver of the hot rod was also picking at his food uncertainly. Probably a social vegetarian, Danniels supposed. An irresponsible faddist.

The counterman stopped staring and cleared his throat apologetically. "This ain't the Ritz but it don't look good for customers to sit with hats on."

Danniels knew that applied to only nonvegetarians, but he put his Stetson, reluctantly, on an aluminum tree.

The teenager looked up. And did not go back to the food.

Danniels knew that he had been found out.

The counterman went back to wiping down the bar.

The youth was still looking at Danniels.

"You better eat if you don't want me to be discovered," Danniels said gently.

Young eyes moved back and forth, searching, not finding.

"It won't do you any good to run," Danniels continued. "The waitress and the counterman will swear they had nothing to do with me. But you were driving me, eating with me."

"You can't let even a Jonah die," the youngster said in a hoarse whisper that barely carried across the table.

Danniels shook his head sadly. "It won't work. You might have slowed down enough to let me grab onto the rear bumper or tossed me out some food. But you took me into your car, sat down at a table with me."

"And this is the thanks I get!"

Danniels felt his face flush. "Look, son, this isn't a game where you can afford to play by good sportsmanship. That's somebody else's rules, designed to make sure you get at least no better a break than anyone else. You have to play by your rules—designed to give *you* the best possible break. Let's get out of here."

He wolfed the last bite and jammed his hat back on his head, pulling it down about his ears. The sweat band had rubbed the flour off his hair in a narrow band. A band of green. The mark of the Jonah.

In the last War Games, Danniels had come into the sights of a Canadian's diffusion rifle. For six months he had worn a cancerous badge of luminosity over his heart. Until his comrades had trapped him and through a system similar to the one their rifles employed turned his hair to green and cast him out.

Danniels scooped up both checks and with deep pain paid both of them to save time. He wanted to get his companion out of there before he broke.

The heat struck at their faces like jets of boiling water. The authorities said nuclear explosion had had nothing to do with changing climatic conditions so radically, but *something* had.

The two of them were walking towards the parked car when the Wolf Pack got them.

2

The horrible part was that Danniels knew they wouldn't kill him. No one could kill.

But the members of the Wolf Packs wanted to. They were the professional soldiers, policemen, prizefighters, and gangsters of a society that had rejected them. They were able to resist some of the pacifism of the Broadcasters. In fact, they were able to resist quite a lot.

The first one was a round-shouldered little man with silver spectacles. He kicked Danniels in the pit of the stomach with steel-shod toes. A clean-cut athletic boy grabbed the running teenager and ripped the red tunic halfway off. From the pavement Danniels at last isolated the doubt that had been nagging him. His companion wore a tight shirt under the coat. She was a girl.

Danniels saw a heavy shoe aimed at his face but it went far afield. Running feet went past him completely.

He was left alone, unharmed, with only the breath knocked out of him momentarily.

They were closing in on the girl who had picked him up.

This Pack was all men, although there were female and co-ed

groups just as vicious. Beating up a girl, Danniels knew, would give an added sexual kick to their usual masochosadism.

They were a Pack. A mob. They were like the soldiers who had hunted him down and had him permanently tagged a Jonah. His men had been looked upon favorably by his society, while the Wolf Pack was so ill-favored it was completely ignored in absolute contempt. But they were the same in the essentials: a mob.

And once again Danniels, who was incapable of harming the smallest living creature, wanted to kill men. But he couldn't.

All his life he had experienced this mad fury of desire and it shamed him. He wanted to destroy men of stupidity, greed, and brutality on sight. Any other kind of conflict with them was weak compromise.

At times, he wondered if this atavistic prosurvival trait had not shamed him so much that he overcompensated for it by violently refusing to take any kind of life. Like all men of his time, he asked himself: How much of my mind is the Broadcasters' and how much me?

If he couldn't destroy, he could defend.

With the idea still only half-formed, he lurched to his feet and stumbled into the side of the hot rod. He fumbled open the heated metal door and slid under the wheel.

He thumbed the drive on savagely and roared down on the mob.

Rubber screamed, whined, and smelled as he applied the brakes just soon enough for the men to jump out of the way—away from the girl.

He folded back the door he hadn't latched, leaned down, grabbed the teenager by the leg, and dragged her bruised form bumping up into the car.

The little man with silver glasses tried to reach into the car.

Danniels swung the door back into his face.

The glasses didn't break; but everything else did.

With one foot under the girl and the other on her, Danniels tagged the illegal acceleration wire most cars had rigged under the dashboard and raced away into the brassy sunshine.

She was slouched against his shoulder when the stars blazed out in the moonless night.

Tires hummed beneath them and their headlights ate up the white-striped typewriter ribbon before them.

The girl opened her eyes, hesitated as they focused on the weave pattern of denim in his shirt, and said, "Where are they?"

"Back there some place," Danniels told her. "They followed in their cars, a couple on motorcycles. But they must have been scared of traffic cops on the main highway. They dropped out."

She sat up and ran her fingers through her cropped mouse-colored hair. Her quick glance at him was questioning; but she answered her own question and reluctantly absorbed the truth of it. She knew he knew.

The girl huddled in the tatters of her bright tunic.

"Just what do you expect to get out of helping me?" she asked.

Danniels kept his eyes on the road. "A free trip to Chicago."

"You'll get us both arrested!" she shrilled. "Nobody can get past those roadblocks."

He nodded to himself, not caring if she saw the gesture in the uncertain light from the auto gauges.

"All right," she admitted. "I know what Chicago is. That's no crime."

"You ought to," Danniels said. "You're from there."

She was tired. It was a moment before she could continue fighting. "That's foolish—"

He hadn't been sure. If she hadn't hesitated he might have given up the notion.

"That getup was what was foolish," Danniels snorted. "Anybody would know you were trying to hide something as soon as they found out the masquerade."

"You wouldn't have found it out," she said, "if one of that Pack hadn't torn my jacket off."

"I really don't know. It might be animal magnetism, if there is such a thing. But I can't be around a woman for long without knowing it. I repeat: Why?"

"I—I didn't know what they would do to a girl outside."

"For Peace' sake, why did you have to come out at all?"

The girl was silent for a mile.

"Most Chicagoans think the rest of the world has reverted to barbarism," she told him.

"A common complaint of city dwellers," he observed.

"Don't joke!" she demanded. "Our food is running out. We have enough to last five more years if the present birthrate cycle maintains itself."

Danniels whistled mournfully.

"And you have—let's see—about seven more years to go."

She nodded.

"I came out to see what chance there was of ending this senseless blockade."

"None at all," he snapped. "No one is going to risk breaking the rules of the War Games just to save a few million lives."

"But they will have to! The Broadcasters will make them."

"You would be surprised at how much doublethink people can practice about not killing," he assured her from bitter, personal experience. "They don't *know* for certain that you will be starving in there, so they will be free to keep you inside."

The girl straightened her shoulders, emphasizing the femininity of her slender form.

"We'll tell them," she said. "*I'll* tell them."

Danniels almost smiled, but not quite. His hands tightened on the steering wheel and he kept his eyes to the moving circle of light against the night.

"You open your mouth about Chicago to the authorities or anyone else and they will slap you under sedation and keep you there until you die of old age. They used to drop escapees back into the cities by parachute. But too many of them were inadvertently killed; they are more subtle these days. By the way," he said very casually, "how *did* you escape?"

She told him where to go in a primitive, timeless fashion.

"No," Danniels said. "I'm going to Chicago."

"Not with me," the girl assured him quietly. "We have enough to feed without bringing in another Jonah. Besides, you might be an F.B.I. man or something trying to find our escape route."

"I'd be a Mountie then. The F.B.I. has deteriorated pretty badly. Spent itself on political security. The Royal Canadian Mounted Police lends us men and women during peacetime. Up until the War Games anyway—even though Britain would like to see us *constantly* disrupted. But," he said heavily, "I am not a government agent of any kind. Just the Jonah I appear to be."

She shivered. "I can't take the responsibility. I can't either expose our escape route—or bring in another mouth, to bring starvation a moment closer."

"Look, what can I call you?" he demanded in exasperation.

"Julie. Julie Amprey."

"Abe Danniels. Look, Julie—"

"You were named after Lincoln?" she asked quietly.

"A long time after. Look, Julie, I want to get into Chicago because of the old Milne Laboratories." He caught his breath for a long second. "They are still standing?"

Julie nodded and looked ahead, through the insect-spotted windscreen. "Partial operation, when I left."

Danniels gave a low whistle. "Lord, after all these years!"

"We manage."

"Fine! Julie, I'm sure that if I can get back in a laboratory I can find a way of ending this condemned Famine—inside Chicago and outside."

"That sounds a little like delusions of grandeur to me," the girl said uncertainly.

"It was my field for ten years. Before the last War Games. I had time to think while my platoon was hunting me down, after I had been tagged out. I thought faster than I ever thought before."

Julie studied his face for a long moment.

"What was your idea?"

"The encephalographic inversion patterns of the Broadcasters," he said quickly, "can be applied to animals as well as human beings, on the right frequencies. Even microscopic animals. Bacteria. If you control the actions of bacteria, you control their reproduction. They could be made to multiply and assume different forms—the form of food, for example."

Danniels took a deep breath and plunged into his idea as they drove on through the deepening night. He talked and explained to her, and, in doing so, he clarified points that he hadn't been sure of himself.

He stopped at last because his throat was momentarily too dry to continue.

"It's too big a responsibility for me," Julie said.

Defeat stung him so badly he was afraid he had slumped physically. But it won't be permanent defeat, he told himself. I've come this far and I'll find some other way into Chicago.

"I haven't the right to turn down something this big," Julie said. "I'll have to let you put it to the mayor and the city council."

He relaxed a trifle, condemning himself for the weak luxury. He couldn't afford it yet. He ran his fingers through his flour-dusted green hair and the electricity of the movement dragged off much of the whiteness. His skin, like that of most people, had been given a slight negative charge by molecularization to repel dirt and germs. The powder was anxious to remove itself and dye or bleach refused to take at all.

"We're nearing the rim of the first blockade zone," Danniels told the girl. "Where to?"

"Circle around to first unrestricted beach of the lake shore."

"And then."

"Underwater."

Illegal traffic in and out of Disaster Areas was not completely unheard of. There was a small but steady flow both ways that the authorities could not or would not completely check. The patrols seemingly were as alert as humanly possible. Capture meant permanent oblivion for Disaster Residents under sedation, while Outsiders got prescribed periods of Morphinvertinduced antipode depression of the brain, a rather sophisticated but effective form of torture. A few minutes under the drug frequently had an introspective duration of years. Therefore, under the typical sentence of three months, a felon lived several lifetimes in constant but varying stages of acute agony and posthysteric terror.

While few personalities survived, many useful human machines were later salvaged by skillful lobotomies.

Lake Michigan beaches were pretty good, Danniels observed. Better than at Hawaii. This one had been cleaned up for a subdivision that had naturally never been completed. It had been christened Falstaff Cove, although it was almost a mathematically straight half mile of off-white sand.

He had shifted to four-wheel drive at the girl's direction and bored through the sand to the southernmost corner of the beach, where it blurred into weeds, rocks, dirt, and incredible litter. He braked. The car settled noticeably.

"There's a two-man submarine out there in the water under the overhang," Julie said without prompting. "We got it from the Armed Forces Day display at Soldiers' Field."

"What I'd like to know is how you get the car in and out of it?" Danniels said.

Anger, disgust, and fatigue crossed the girl's face. It was, after all, a very young face, he thought. "We have Outside contacts of sorts," she said. "Nobody trusts them very much."

He nodded. There was a lot of money in the Federal Reserve Vaults inside the city.

The two of them got out of the car.

Julie stripped off her jeans, revealing the bottom of a swimsuit and nicely turned, but pale, legs. "We'll have to wade out to the sub."

"What about the car?" Danniels asked. "Is your friend going to pick it up?"

"No! They don't know about this place."

He reached in the window and turned the ignition. "Want me to run it off into the water? You don't want to tag this spot for the authorities."

"No, I—I guess not. I don't know what to do! I'm not used to this kind of thing. I don't know why I *ever* come. We paid an awful lot for the car . . ."

He found the girl's wailing unpleasant. "It's your car, but take my advice. Let me get rid of it for you."

"But," she protested, "if you run it into the water they can see it from the air in daylight. I know. They used to spot our sub. Why not run it off into those weeds and little trees? They'll hide it and maybe we could get it later."

It wasn't a bad idea but he didn't feel like admitting it. He gunned the rod into the tangle of undergrowth.

Danniels came back to the girl with his arms and face laced with scratches from the limbs.

He tried to roll his trousers up at the cuff but they wouldn't stay. So he would spend a soggy ten minutes while they dried.

He told the girl to go ahead and he went after her, marking the spongy wet sand and slapping into the white-scummed, very blue water.

The tiny submarine was just where Julie had said it would be. He waited impatiently as she worked the miniature airlock.

They squeezed down into the metallic hollowness of the interior and Julie screwed the hatch shut, a Mason lid inappropriately on a can of sardines.

There were a lot of white-on-black dials that completely baffled Danniels. He had never been particularly mechanically minded. His field was closer to pure science than practical engineering. Because of this, rather than in spite of it, he had great respect for engineering.

It bothered him being in such close quarters with a woman after the months of isolation as a Jonah, but he had enough of the conventions of society fused into him and enough other problems to attempt easing his discomfort.

"It isn't much further," Julie at last assured him.

He was becoming bored to the point of hysteria. For the past several months he hadn't had much diversion but he had not been confined to what was essentially an oil drum wired for light and sound.

One of the lights changed size and pattern.

He found himself tensing. "That?" He pointed.

"Sonadar," Julie hissed. "Patrol boat above us. Don't make any noise."

Danniels pictured the heavily equipped police boat droning past above them and managed to keep quite silent.

Something banged on the hull.

It came from the outside and it rang against the port side, then the starboard. The rhythm was the same, unbroken. Danniels knew somehow the noise from both sides was made by the same agency. Something with a twelve-foot reach.

Something that knew the Morse code.

Da-da-da. Dit-dit-dit. Da-da-da.

S.O.S.

Help.

"It's not the police," Julie said. "We've heard it before." She added, "They used to dump nondangerous amounts of radioactives into the lake," as she decided the police boat had gone past and started up the engines again.

Danniels never forgot that call for help. Not as long as he lived.

3

The electron microscope revealed no significant change in the pattern of the bacteria.

Danniels decided to feed the white mice. He got out of his plastic chair and took a small cloth bag of corn from the warped, sticking drawer of the lab table.

Rationing out a handful of the withered kernels, he went down the rows of cages. A few, with steel instead of aluminum wiring, were flecked with rust. The mice inside were all healthy. Danniels was not using them in experiments; he was incapable of taking their lives. But some experimenter after him might use them. In any case, he was also incapable of letting them starve to death.

He had been out of jail less than two weeks.

The city council had thrown him into the Cook County lockup until they decided what to do with him. He hadn't known what happened to the girl, Julie Amprey, for bringing him back with her.

He was surprised to see Chicago functioning as well as it was after thirteen years of isolation. There were still a few cars and trucks running here and there, although most people walked or rode bicycles. But the atmosphere seemed heavy and the buildings dirtier than ever. The city had the aura of oppression and decay he thought of as belonging to nineteenth-century London.

Danniels had waited out New Year's and St. Valentine's in a cell between a convicted burglar and an endless parade of drunks. Finally, two weeks ago the mayor himself came, apologizing profusely but without much feeling. Danniels was escorted to the old Milne Laboratory buildings and told to go to work on his idea. He had, they said, two weeks to produce. And he was getting nowhere.

His deadline was up. The deadline of the real world. But the one he had given himself was much, much more pressing.

"You'll kill yourself if you don't get some sleep," the girl's voice said behind his back.

Danniels closed the drawer on the nearly depleted sack of grain. It was the girl. Julie Amprey. He had been expecting her but not anticipating her. He didn't like her very much. The only reason he could conceive for her venture Outside was a search for thrills. It might be understandable, if immature, in a man; but he found it unattractive in a woman. He had no illusions about masculine superiority, but women were socially, if not physically and emotionally, ill-equipped for simple adventuring.

Julie was more attractive dressed in a woman's clothes, even if they were a dozen years out of style. Her hair had a titian glint. She was perhaps really too slender for the green knit dress.

"It's a big job," he said. "I'm beginning to think it's a life-time job."

He half-turned and motioned awkwardly at the lab table and the naked piece of electronics.

"That's the encephalographic projector I jury-rigged," he explained.

"You can spare me the fifty-cent tour," Julie said.

He wondered how she had managed to get so irritating in such a short lifetime. "There's not much else to see," Danniels grunted. "I've got some reaction out of the bacteria, but I can't seem to control their reproduction or channel them into a food-producing cycle."

Julie tossed her head.

"Oh, I can tell you why you haven't done that," she said.

He didn't like the way she said that. "Why?"

"You don't *want* to control them," Julie said simply. "If you really control them, you'll cause some to be recessive. You'll breed some strains out of existence. You'll *kill* some of them. And you don't want to kill any living thing."

She was wrong.

He wanted to kill her.

But he couldn't. She was right about the bacteria. He should have realized it before. He had planned for almost a year, and worked for two weeks; and this girl had walked in and destroyed everything in five minutes. But she was right; he spun towards the door.

"Where are you going?" she demanded.

"I'm leaving. See what somebody else can do with the idea."

"But where are you going?" Julie repeated.

"Nowhere."

And he was absolutely right.

Danniels walked aimlessly through the littered streets for the rest of the day and night. He couldn't remember walking at night, but neither could he remember staying anywhere when he discovered dawn in the sky.

It was that time of dawn that looks strangely like an old two-color process movie that they show on TV occasionally—all orange and green, with no yellow to it at all, when even the truest black seems only an off-brown or a sinister purple.

He shivered in the chill of morning and decided what to do.

He would have to walk around for a few more hours yet.

The drink his friend, Paul, placed before him was not entirely distinct. Neither were the bills he had in his hand. It was money the mayor's hireling had given him to use for laboratory supplies. Danniels peeled off a bill of uncertain denomination and gave it to his friend. Paul seemed pleased. He put it into the pocket of his white shirt, the pocket eight inches below and slightly to the left of the black bow tie, and polished the bar briskly.

Danniels picked up the glass and sipped silently until it was empty.

"Do you want to talk about anything, Abe?" Paul asked solicitously.

"No," Danniels said cheerfully. "Just give me another drink."

"Sure thing."

Danniels studied his green hair in the glass. Here, the mark of the Jonah wasn't important. Not yet. But he would be unwelcome even here after the time of Disaster ran out. He would have to move on sooner or later. Eventually—why not now? That slogan went better than the one in pink light over the mirror—The Beer That Made Milwaukee Famous. There hadn't been any Milwaukee beer here for thirteen years. Most of the stuff came out of bathtubs.

Why not now?

He smoothed another bill on the damp polished wood and negotiated his way through the hazy room.

Outside, he turned a corner and the city dropped away from him. He seemed to be in a giant amusement park with acres of empty ground patterned off in squares by unwinking dots of light.

He grinned to himself, changed direction with great care, and started down the one-way street to the lakefront.

He heard the footsteps behind him.

Danniels put his palm to the brick wall, scaling posters, and turned.

The clean-cut young man smiled disarmingly. "I saw you at Paul's. You'll never make it home under your own power. Better let me take you in my cab."

Danniels knocked him out on his feet with a clean right cross.

He blinked down at the boy. Self-preservation had become instinctive with him during his months as a wandering Jonah.

Gnawing at his under lip, he studied the twisted way the supposed cabbie lay. If he really were . . . Danniels patted the man down and brought something out of a hip pocket.

He inspected the leather blackjack, weighing it critically in his hand.

It slid out of his palm and thudded heavily on the cracked sidewalk.

Danniels shrugged and grinned and moved unsteadily away. Towards the lake.

The lake looked gray and winterish.

There was no help for it.

Danniels swung his leg over the rust-spotted railing and looked down to where the water lapped at crumbling bricks blotched with green. He peered out over the water. Only a few miles to the beach where he had left the car parked in the undergrowth. He would have preferred to use the little sub, but he could swim it if he had to.

The surface below showed clearly in the globe lights.

Danniels dived.

Before he hit the water, he remembered that he should have taken off some of his clothes.

When he parted the icy foam with his body, he knew he had committed suicide. And he realized that that had been what he intended to do all along.

There was something in the lake holding him, and it had a twelve-foot reach.

It kept holding on to him under the surface of green ice and begging for help. He couldn't breathe, and he couldn't help. Of the two, not being able to help seemed the worse. Not breathing wasn't so bad . . . It hurt to breathe. It choked him. It was very unpleasant to breathe. He had much preferred not breathing to this . . .

Some time later, he opened his eyes.

A small, round-faced man was staring down at him through slender-framed spectacles. For a moment he thought it was the man in whose face he had smashed the car door at the diner weeks before. But this man was different—among other things his glasses were gold, not silver. Yet he was also the same. Danniels knew the signs of the Wolf Pack.

"How's your foot?" the little man asked in a surprisingly full-bodied voice.

Danniels instantly became aware of a dull subpain sensation in the toes of his left foot. He looked over the crest of his chest and saw the foot, naked below the cuff of his wrinkled trousers. The three smaller toes were red. No, maroon. A red so dark it was almost black. Fainter streaks of red shot away from the toes, following the tendon.

Danniels swallowed. "The foot doesn't *feel* so bad, but I think it *is*."

"We may have to operate," the small man said eagerly.

"How did I get out of the lake?"

"Joel. The man you knocked out. He came to and followed you. Naturally, he had to save your life. He banged your foot up dragging you ashore."

Or afterwards, Danniels thought.

Abruptly, the stranger was gone and a door was closing and latching on the other side of the room.

Danniels tried to rise and fell back, his head floating around somewhere above him. Maybe a Wolf Pack member would have to save his life but he wouldn't have to bring him home and nurse him back to health.

Why?

He fell asleep without even trying to guess the answer.

He woke when they brought food to him.

Danniels finished with the tray and set it aside.

The small man who had identified himself as Richard beamed. "I think you are strong enough to attend the celebration tonight."

Danniels did feel stronger after rest and food, but at the same time he felt vaguely dizzy and his leg was beginning to hurt. "What kind of a celebration?" he asked.

Richard chuckled. "Don't worry. You'll like it."

Danniels had seen the same expression on the faces of hosts at stag dinners; but with a Wolf Pack it was hard to know what to expect.

4

The place he was in did not seem to be a house after all.

Danniels leaned on the shoulder of Richard, who helped him along solicitously. They entered a large chamber nearly a hundred feet wide. There were people there. It wasn't crowded but there were many people standing around the walls. A lot of them were holding three-foot lengths of wood.

Richard led him to a chair, the only one apparent in the room.

"I'll go tell we're ready now," the small man said, chuckling.

Danniels looked around slowly at the shadowed faces. Of those holding clubs, he knew only the man Richard had told him was Joel, the man who had pulled him from Lake Michigan. Apparently the ones with clubs were members of the Pack, while the others were observers and potential members. Among these, he spotted a member of the city council.

And Julie.

She stood in a loose sweater and skirt, her hands hugging her elbows, eyes intent on the empty center of the room. Danniels was reminded of some of the women he had seen at unorthodox political meetings.

Danniels was surprised to find that he wanted to talk to her. He might try hobbling over to her or calling her over to him. But with the instinct he had developed while being hunted, he knew it was wrong to call attention to the two of them together.

He noticed that he was in line with the door. Julie would have to pass by him when she left . . . after the celebration.

"The celebration begins in five minutes."

Someone he hadn't seen had shouted into the big room. The words bounced back slightly and hung suspended.

The people's waiting became an activity. Tension lived in the room.

And then the cat was released.

The Pack members moved apart from the rest and struck at the scrawny yellow beast. The cat didn't make it very far down the line. The men from the other end of the room moved up quickly to be in on the kill.

The clubs rose and fell even after it was clear there was no reason for it.

Their ranks parted and they left their handiwork where it could be admired.

It must be hard to find animals in a closed city like this, Danniels thought. It must be quite a treat to find one to beat to death.

He sat and waited for them to leave. But he found the celebration was just beginning. The group was laughing and talking. Now that it was over they wanted to talk about it the rest of the evening. They had created death.

He searched out Julie Amprey again. She was looking at what they did. He thought she was sick at first. His lips thinned. Yes, she was sick.

Her eyes suddenly met him. Shock washed over her face, and in the next moment she was moving to him.

"So," she said coolly, "you found out my little secret. This is where I get my kicks."

He nodded, thinking of nothing to say.

"Did you ever read them?" she asked breathlessly. "All the old banned books—Poe and Spillane and Proust. The pornography of death. I grew up on them, so you see there's no harm in them. Look at me."

"You want to kill?" Daniels asked her.

She lit an expensive king-size cigarette. "Yes," she exhaled. "I thought I might join a Pack on the Outside. But, you'll remember, I didn't quite make it. I couldn't even kill a cockroach. I want to, but the damned Broadcasters keep interfering with me."

Richard came back, smiling broadly. "Well, Abe, has Miss Amprey been telling you of our plans to ruin the planet?"

Daniels was incredibly tired. He had been listening and arguing for hours.

"You're a scientist," Joel persisted. "Help us."

"There are different kinds of scientists," Daniels repeated. "I'm not a nuclear physicist."

"Right there." Richard tapped the pink rubber of his pencil against the map of Cook County. "Right there. An armory no one else knows anything about. Enough H-bombs to wipe out human life on the planet. And rockets to send them in."

"The councilman may be lying," Daniels said. "How do you think he should happen to find it and no one else?"

"The information was in the city records," Richard said patiently, "but buried and coded so it would take twenty years to locate. Bureaucracy is an insidious evil, Abe."

Daniels rubbed his face with his palms. "I'm not even sure if I understand what you mean to do. You want to rocket the H-bombs out almost but not quite beyond Earth's gravitation and explode them so the fallout will be evenly distributed over the surface of the planet. You think it will cause no more than injury and destruction—"

"That's all," Joel said sharply.

Richard gave an eager nod.

They had had to convince themselves of that, he knew. "But why do you want to do anything as desperate as that?"

"Simple revenge." Richard's tone was even and cold. "And to show them what we can do if they don't cut off the Broadcasters." The small man's liquid brown eyes softened. "You've got to understand that we really don't want to kill people. Our actions are merely necessary demonstrations against insane visionary politics. I only want the Broadcasters shut off so I can do efficient police work —Joel, so that he can fight in the ring with the true will to win of a sportsman. The rest of us have equally good reasons."

"I think I understand," Danniels said. "I'll do what I can to help you."

Danniels was not surprised when Julie Amprey was in the raiding party. He was past the capacity for surprise.

He was getting around on his own today only because he was learning to stand the pain. It was worse. And he was weak and dizzy from a fever.

They had all managed to produce bicycles. Richard had even managed to find one for him with a tiny engine powered by solar-charged batteries.

Julie looked crisp and attractive in sweater and jeans. Joel was strikingly handsome in the clear sun, and even Richard looked like a jolly fatherly type.

As they wheeled down the street, Danniels was afraid only he with his wet, tossed green hair and drooping cheeks warped the holiday mood of those who in some other probability sequence were happy picnickers.

When they reached the place, Richard giggled nervously.

"It takes a code to open the hatch," he explained. "If Aldrich doesn't decode it correctly there will be a small but effective chemical explosion in this area."

Danniels leaned against a maple, watching. The bicycles were parked in the brush and a shallow hole had been dug at an exact spot in the suburban park. Only a few inches below ground was the gray steel door flush with the level of grass.

Richard hummed as he worked a prosaic combination dial.

Finally there was a muffled click and a churning whine began.

The hatch raised jerkily and latched at right angles.

The Pack milled about the opening, excited. Joel got the honor of going down first. Richard seemed to bumble his chance for the glory, Danniels observed. The other men went down, one by one. And finally only Julie and Richard were left. He supposed that this meant the girl had been accepted as a full member of the Wolf Pack. That would change the whole character of the organization. He vaguely wondered who her sponsor was. Joel?

Julie and the little man came to him. They started to help him down into the opening and suddenly he was at the bottom of a ladder. Things were beginning to seem to him as if they were taking place underwater.

They walked down a corridor of shadow, lit only by tarnished yellow from red sparks caught on the tips of silver wire inside water-clear bulbs recessed in the concrete ceiling.

When they passed a certain point sparks showered from slots in opposite walls. They burned out ineffectively before they reached the floor of cross-hatched metallic mats.

"Power failing," Richard observed with a chuckle. "Congress should investigate the builders."

There was a large, sliding door many feet thick but so well-balanced it slid open easily. And they were there.

It was a big room full of many little rooms. Each little room had a door that a man could enter by stooping and a chair-ledge inside for him to sit and read or adjust instruments. The outsides of the rooms were finished off cleanly in shining metal with large, rugged objects fitted to all sides. These were hydrogen bombs.

The Wolf Pack ranged joyously through the maze.

Danniels found one of several stacks of small instruments and sat down on it. The things looked like radios but obviously weren't.

Richard came to him, wringing his hands. "These bombs seem to be designed to be dropped from bombers. There are supposed to be rockets here too. I hope the H-bombs will fit. They seem so bulky . . ."

"Perhaps the rockets have self-contained bomb units," Danniels suggested.

"Perhaps. We're all going off and try to find the rockets. You'd be amazed at all the cutoffs down here. I'll leave Joel here to look after you."

Danniels sat on the instruments. Joel stayed several hundred feet away, an uncertain shadow in the light, smoking a red dot of a cigarette. Somehow Danniels associated fire and munitions instead of atomics and felt uneasy.

He discovered Julie Amprey at his side. She didn't say anything. She seemed to be sulking. Like a spoiled brat, he thought.

He fingered one of the portable instruments from an open crate beside him. "Wonder what these are?" he said to break up the heavy silence.

"Pseudo H-bombs," the girl snapped.

Of course. Just as money had to be backed by gold or silver reserves, every pseudo bomb or mock-gas had to be backed by the real thing which, after its representative had been used, was dismantled, neutralized, or retired. International inspection saw to that.

"There's enough here to blow up the whole world . . . if they were real," Danniels said.

The girl pointed out into the chamber. "Those *are* real."

Each nation had many times over the nuclear armament necessary to destroy human life. There was enough for that right in this vault —both in reality and in the Games.

Danniels stopped drifting and took a course. He stopped observing and began to act. There was a mob in action.

Even if they did somehow manage not to kill off the population with the fallout they were engineering, they would ruin farmland, create new recessive mutations.

Famine would cease to be a psychological affliction for half the world and become a physiological reality instead . . . for all the world.

He had failed in his plans to end the psychological Famine because of his own attunement to the Broadcasters. He wouldn't fail in stopping the new physiological Famine.

5

"Put that thing down," Joel said. "I don't trust you any further than I can spit, and that looks like a radio. You trying to warn the city council?"

Danniels put down the instrument. One wouldn't do it, and he could tell from Joel's eyes that he would get a very bad experience out of disobeying him.

"You were going to do something," Julie said. "What were you trying to do with that pseudie?"

"How do you know so much about this stuff?" Danniels demanded.

"My father told me all he found out from the records. He's Councilman Aldrich."

He rested his eyes for a second. "But your name—?" he heard himself say.

"My stepfather, I should have said. Mother married him when I was two. *What were you going to do?*"

"I," he said, "intended to end it all. All of this. All of it. Outside. End everything."

The girl turned from him.

"Then why don't you do it?"

"You mean you don't want our friends to succeed in torturing a sick world?"

"I don't like pain," she said. "There's something clean, positive, and challenging about killing. I'd like to kill. But pain seems so pointless. If you can stop them, go ahead. I'll help you."

He was exhausted and in fever. "Joel won't let me."

"Then—kill him," she said.

He knew it was all useless, tired, stale, unrewarding. It was done. He was nothing, and the girl was less. The Pack would succeed and the tortured world would die of a greater famine because he had failed all down the line. And he blamed himself for making a mistake that actually was unimportant. For a moment, he had trusted the girl.

"You *can* kill him." Julie turned back and faced him. "How much do you think those Broadcasters can really control human beings? We aren't fighting wars because we don't want to. We've finally seen what war can do and we're scared. We've retreated. The human race is hiding just like you are now."

Danniels laughed.

She lunged forward, tense. For a moment he thought she had actually stamped her foot. "It's true, you fool! Don't the actions of these men prove it to you? They are going to risk destroying the planet. If pacifism really controlled them do you think they could do that?"

He mumbled something about Wolf Pack members.

"There's never been any law or moral credo that human beings couldn't break and justify within themselves some way," Julie intoned carefully. "People can do the same with the induced precepts of the Broadcasters. If you really want to stop them, you can—by killing Joel and going ahead."

"Maybe later," Danniels mumbled. "I'll think about it."

Julie slapped his face. He wondered why he didn't feel it.

"You don't have much time left," Julie whispered. "Don't you know what's wrong with your foot? *Gangrene.* You have to get those toes amputated soon or you'll die."

"Yes," he said numbly. "Must get amputation." But it didn't seem urgent. He felt he should get some rest first.

"It's too bad you can't allow the operation," the girl said sweetly. "You can't allow lives to be destroyed just to save your own personality."

"What lives?" he demanded.

"All the cells and microorganisms in your toes," Julie told him. "You know they'll *die* if you are operated on. Are they any worse than the little bacteria you refused to murder? I suppose it's just as well that you die. How can you stand it on your conscience to breathe all the time and burn up innocent germs in your foul breath?"

Danniels understood. To live was to kill.

Every instant he lived his old cells were dying and new ones being born. So Danniels, who thought he could not kill any living thing, finally accepted himself as a killer. It wasn't human life he was taking . . . but it was life.

If he could be wrong about taking any life at all—and he had always believed himself unable to kill anything—he might be wrong about being able to kill men. In spite of everything he had been taught and what he believed about the influence of the Broadcasters.

He studied Joel in the gloom. The man represented everything he loathed—stupidity, brutality, the mob. If I can kill anyone, he told himself, it should be Joel.

He could try. Yes, he could. And that was a victory in itself.

He moved, and that was another triumph over the physical defeat that was already upon him.

Joel looked up, narrow eyes widened, as Danniels came down on him.

Danniels caught him in the stomach with the flat of his palm and shoved up.

Joel gargled in the back of his throat and rammed his thumbs for the prisoner's eyes. Danniels nodded and caught the balls of the thumbs on his forehead. He brought his fist up sharply and hit Joel on the point of the chin. His head snapped but righted itself slowly. He lashed into Danniels's body with both eager hands and Danniels, weakened, went down before he had time to think about it.

From the crazy angle of the floor he saw far above him Joel's lips curl back and closer, further down, a shoe was lifted to kick. It was aimed at Danniels's swollen foot.

Danniels smiled. He shouldn't have done that. If he had acted like a man instead of an animal he would have been fine. But now . . . Danniels rolled over quickly against the one leg of Joel's firmly on the floor. Off balance, Joel fell backwards with a curse, the back of his skull ringing against the side of one of the bombs.

Exertion was painting red lines across his vision but Danniels climbed to his knees, put his hands to Joel's corded throat and squeezed.

Yes. He knew he could kill. A few more seconds and he would be dead.

Danniels stopped.

There was no need to kill the boy. He would be unconscious long enough for him to do his job. And he found that fear had left him. He was no longer afraid of killing small things, because he was no longer afraid of killing men.

He had been able to kill when he had to, but more important, he had been able to keep from killing when it wasn't needed. He didn't need to be afraid of the old blood-lust—because he knew now he could best it.

And Julie had seen something she had never believed was possible. That a man could keep from being a savage without the restraints of the Broadcasters or of society.

He limped to the stacked pseudies and sat down. "Now we can make it clean, Julie. We can end the whole mess. Ready?"

"Yes," she told him.

He picked up a pseudie and threw the switch.

The radio signal went out, and all over the world receivers noted a pseudo explosion in the heart of a Disaster Area. Danniels could imagine the men in the council room in the heart of the city seeing the flash and feeling the doom of a renewed twenty years of isolation and heading for the exact spot of the flash.

More signals flashed. And flashed. And flashed.

And he thought of the people all over the world wondering about the devastating sneak attack on the United States, and the incredible readings of the instruments.

"Keep working," Danniels said. "The Wolf Pack or the officials from the city will be here soon. I hope it's a dead heat. But," he said, "I think we've done it. But we can keep working on the safety margin."

"What have we done, Abe?" Julie asked trustingly.

He was going to feel foolish saying it. "We have just blown up the world according to the official records of the War Games."

"Then they'll have to start over," she said.

"Maybe," Danniels whispered. "If they do, we'll all start even. Everybody's a Jonah. The world is a Disaster Area. Maybe they'll start the War Games over. Or maybe they'll try the real thing again, now that they've seen how easy it is with pseudies."

He felt the numb foot and knew he would have to have an emergency operation if he survived the mobs that were coming. But he had a way of surviving mobs. He looked at Julie. He would see that their children could eat.

"At least," he said, triggering another H-bomb for the world's records, "it isn't a bad day when the world has been given a fresh slate, a new start."

There were footsteps outside, coming closer.

THE GREAT NEBRASKA SEA

August 1963

Allan Danzig

There are a fair number of authors in science fiction who, although they wrote other stories, will always be remembered for one. Perhaps the best example is Tom Godwin's "The Cold Equations" (Astounding, August 1954). Allan Danzig only published a handful of stories in the sf magazines, including "Homogenized Planet" in the August 1966 Worlds of Tomorrow.

However, it is this story, originally published as a "Fact Article" in Galaxy, that will always be remembered, for it combines wonderful descriptive prose with that most difficult of sf categories—alternative history. One would have thought that what he accomplished so well would have been impossible—a convincing and masterful sf story about geology.

Memoir by Allan Danzig

I've always been a map nut. I was fiddling around one day with the idea of what would happen to the climate of the United States if we had a central sea like the Mediterranean to dampen the dust and ameliorate the extremes of temperature. Out of that fiddling grew "The Great Nebraska Sea." Discussions of climate, or even climatic change, do not make very exciting stories; I suppose that's why it became a disaster story. I really have no animosity toward the Midwest, and that's why I tried to keep the disaster as light, even humorous, as I could.

The only other point of possible public interest in the background of this story: It was written considerably *before* the former governor of Alabama vowed never to permit integration of the state's school system—and then conveniently disappeared as federal troops performed that operation. I don't claim prescience, but I was awfully pleased when truth turned out to be at least as strange as fiction.

THE GREAT NEBRASKA SEA

Everyone—all the geologists, at any rate—had known about the Kiowa Fault for years. That was before there was anything very interesting to know about it. The first survey of Colorado traced its course north and south in the narrow valley of Kiowa Creek about twenty miles east of Denver; it extended south to the Arkansas River. And that was about all even the professionals were interested in knowing. There was never so much as a landslide to bring the fault to the attention of the general public.

It was still a matter of academic interest when the late forties geologists speculated on the relationship between the Kiowa Fault and the Conchas Fault farther south, in New Mexico, which followed the Pecos as far south as Texas.

Nor was there much in the papers a few years later when it was suggested that the Niobrara Fault (just inside and roughly parallel to the eastern border of Wyoming) was a northerly extension of the Kiowa. By the mid sixties it was definitely established that the three faults were in fact a single line of fissure in the essential rock, stretching almost from the Canadian border well south of the New Mexico–Texas line.

It is not really surprising that it took so long to figure out the connection. The population of the states affected was in places as low as five people per square mile! The land was so dry it seemed impossible that it could ever be used except for sheep farming.

It strikes us today as ironic that from the late fifties there was grave concern about the level of the water table throughout the entire area.

The even more ironic solution to the problem began in the summer of 1973. It had been a particularly hot and dry August, and the Forestry Service was keeping an anxious eye out for the fires it knew it could expect. Dense smoke was reported rising above a virtually uninhabited area along Black Squirrel Creek, and a plane was sent out for a report.

The report was—no fire at all. The rising cloud was not smoke, but dust. Thousands of cubic feet of dry earth rising lazily on the summer air. Rock slides, they guessed; certainly no fire. The Forestry Service had other worries at the moment, and filed the report.

But after a week had gone by, the town of Edison, a good twenty miles away from the slides, was still complaining of the dust. Springs were going dry, too, apparently from underground disturbances. Not even in the Rockies could anyone remember a series of rock slides as bad as this.

Newspapers in the mountain states gave it a few inches on the front page; anything is news in late August. And the geologists became interested. Seismologists were reporting unusual activity in the area, tremors too severe to be rock slides. Volcanic activity? Specifically, a dust volcano? Unusual, they knew, but right on the Kiowa Fault—could be.

Labor Day crowds read the scientific conjectures with late summer lassitude. Sunday supplements ran four-color artists' conceptions of the possible volcano. "ONLY ACTIVE VOLCANO IN U.S.?" demanded the headlines, and some papers even left off the question mark.

It may seem odd that the simplest explanation was practically not mentioned. Only Joseph Schwartzberg, head geographer of the Department of the Interior, wondered if the disturbance might not be a settling of the Kiowa Fault. His suggestion was mentioned on page nine or ten of the Monday newspapers (page 27 of the New York Times). The idea was not nearly so exciting as a volcano, even a lavaless one, and you couldn't draw a very dramatic picture of it.

To excuse the other geologists, it must be said that the Kiowa Fault had never acted up before. It never sidestepped, never jiggled, never, never produced the regular shows of its little sister out in California, which almost daily bounced San Francisco or Los Angeles, or some place in between. The dust volcano was on the face of it a more plausible theory.

Still, it was only a theory. It had to be proved. As the tremors grew bigger, along with the affected area, as several towns including Edison were shaken to pieces by incredible earthquakes, whole bus- and plane-loads of geologists set out for Colorado, without even waiting for their university and government departments to approve budgets.

They found, of course, that Schwartzberg had been perfectly correct.

They found themselves on the scene of what was fast becoming the most violent and widespread earthquake North America—probably the world—has ever seen in historic times. To describe it in the simplest terms, land east of the fault was settling, and at a precipitous rate.

Rock scraped rock with a whining roar. Shuddery as a squeaky piece of chalk raged across a blackboard, the noise was deafening. The surfaces of the land east and west of the fault seemed no longer to have any relation to each other. To the west, tortured rock reared into cliffs. East, where sharp reports and muffled wheezes told of continued buckling and dropping, the earth trembled downwards. Atop the new cliffs, which seemed to grow by sudden inches from heaving rubble, dry earth fissured and trembled, sliding acres at a time to fall, smoking, into the bucking, heaving bottom of the depression.

There the devastation was even more thorough, if less spectacular. Dry earth churned like mud, and rock shards weighing tons bumped and rolled about like pebbles as they shivered and cracked into pebbles themselves. "It looks like sand dancing in a child's sieve," said the normally impassive Schwartzberg in a nationwide broadcast from the scene of disaster. "No one here has ever seen anything like it." And the landslip was growing, north and south along the fault.

"Get out while you can," Schwartzberg urged the population of the affected area. "When it's over you can come back and pick up the pieces." But the band of scientists who had rallied to his leadership privately wondered if there would be any pieces.

The Arkansas River, at Avondale and North Avondale, was sluggishly backing north into the deepening trough. At the rate things were going, there might be a new lake the entire length of El Paso and Pueblo counties. And, warned Schwartzberg, this might only be the beginning.

By September 16 the landslip had crept down the Huerfano River past Cedarwood. Avondale, North Avondale, and Boone had totally disappeared. Land west of the fault was holding firm, though Denver had recorded several minor tremors; everywhere east of the fault, to almost twenty miles away, the now-familiar lurch and steady fall had already sent several thousand Coloradans scurrying for safety.

All mountain climbing was prohibited on the Eastern Slope because of the danger of rock slides from minor quakes. The geologists went home to wait.

There wasn't much to wait for. The news got worse and worse. The Platte River, now, was creating a vast mud puddle where the town of Orchard had been. Just below Masters, Colorado, the river leaped seventy-foot cliffs to add to the heaving chaos below. And the cliffs were higher every day as the land beneath them groaned downwards in mile-square gulps.

As the fault moved north and south, new areas quivered into unwelcome life. Fields and whole mountainsides moved with deceptive sloth down, down. They danced "like sand in a sieve"; dry, they boiled into rubble. Telephone lines, railroad tracks, roads snapped and simply disappeared. Virtually all east-west land communication was suspended, and the president declared a national emergency.

By September 23 the fault was active well into Wyoming on the north, and rapidly approaching the border of New Mexico to the south. Trinchera and Branson were totally evacuated, but even so the overall death toll had risen above one thousand.

Away to the east the situation was quiet but even more ominous. Tremendous fissures opened up perpendicular to the fault, and a general subsidence of the land was noticeable well into Kansas and Nebraska. The western borders of these states, and soon of the Dakotas and Oklahoma as well, were slowly sinking.

On the actual scene of the disaster (or the *scenes*; it is impossible to speak of anything this size in the singular) there was a horrifying confusion. Prairie and hill cracked open under intolerable strains as the land shuddered downwards in gasps and leaps. Springs burst to the surface in hot geysers and explosions of steam.

The downtown section of North Platte, Nebraska, dropped eight feet, just like that, on the afternoon of October 4. "We must remain calm," declared the governor of Nebraska. "We must sit this thing out. Be assured that everything possible is being done." But what could be done, with his state dropping straight down at a mean rate of a foot a day?

The fault nicked off the southeast corner of Montana. It worked its way north along the Little Missouri. South, it ripped past Roswell, New Mexico, and tore down the Pecos towards Texas. All the upper reaches of the Missouri were standing puddles by now, and the Red River west of Paris, Texas, had begun to run backwards.

Soon the Missouri began slowly slipping away westwards over the slowly churning land. Abandoning its bed, the river spread uncertainly across farmland and prairie, becoming a sea of mud beneath the sharp new cliffs which rose in rending line, ever taller as the land continued to sink, almost from Canada to the Mexican border. There were virtually no floods, in the usual sense. The water moved too slowly, spread itself with no real direction or force. But the vast sheet of sluggish water and jellylike mud formed deathtraps for the countless refugees now streaming east.

Perhaps the North Platte disaster had been more than anyone could take. One hundred and ninety-three people had died in that one cave-in. Certainly by October 7 it had to be officially admitted that there was an exodus of epic proportion. Nearly two million people were on the move, and the U.S. was faced with a gigantic wave of refugees. Rails, roads, and airlanes were jammed with terrified hordes who had left everything behind to crowd eastwards.

All through October, hollow-eyed motorists flocked into Tulsa, Topeka, Omaha, Sioux Falls, and Fargo. St. Louis was made distributing center for emergency squads which flew everywhere with milk for babies and dog food for evacuating pets. Gasoline trucks boomed west to meet the demand for gas, but once inside the "zone of terror," as the newspapers now called it, they found their route blocked by east-bound cars on the wrong side of the road. Shops left by their fleeing owners were looted by refugees from further west; an American Airlines plane was wrecked by a mob of would-be passengers in Bismarck, North Dakota. Federal and state troops were called out, but moving two million people was not to be done in an orderly way.

And still the landslip grew larger. The new cliffs gleamed in the autumn sunshine, growing higher as the land beneath them continued its inexorable descent.

On October 21, at Lubbock, Texas, there was a noise variously described as a hollow roar, a shriek, and a deep musical vibration like a church bell. It was simply the tortured rock of the substrata giving way. The second phase of the national disaster was beginning.

The noise traveled due east at better than eighty-five miles per hour. In its wake the earth to the north "just seemed to collapse on itself like a punctured balloon," read one newspaper report. "Like a cake that's failed," said a Texarkana housewife who fortunately lived a block *south* of Thayer Street, where the fissure raced through. There was a sigh and a great cloud of dust, and Oklahoma subsided at the astounding rate of about six feet per hour.

At Biloxi, on the Gulf, there had been uneasy shufflings underfoot all day. "Not tremors, exactly," said the captain of a fishing boat which was somehow to ride out the coming flood, "but like as if the land wanted to be somewhere else."

Everyone in doomed Biloxi would have done well to have been somewhere else that evening. At approximately 8:30 PM the town shuddered, seemed to rise a little like the edge of a hall carpet caught in a draught, and sank. So did the entire Mississippi and Alabama coast, at about the same moment. The tidal wave which was to gouge the center from the U.S. marched on the land.

From the north shore of Lake Ponchartrain to the Appalachicola River in Florida, the Gulf coast simply disappeared. Gulfport, Biloxi, Mobile, Pensacola, Panama City: two hundred miles of shoreline vanished, with over two and a half million people. An hour later a wall of water had swept over every town from Dothan, Alabama, to Bogalusa on the Louisiana-Mississippi border.

"We must keep panic from our minds," said the governor of Alabama in a radio message delivered from a hastily arranged all-station hookup. "We of the gallant southland have faced and withstood invasion before." Then, as ominous creakings and groanings of the earth announced the approach of the tidal wave, he flew out of Montgomery half an hour before the town disappeared forever.

One head of the wave plunged north, eventually to spend itself in the hills south of Birmingham. The main sweep followed the lowest land. Reaching west, it swallowed Vicksburg and nicked the corner of Louisiana. The whole of East Carroll Parish was scoured from the map.

The Mississippi River now ended at about Eudora, Arkansas, and minute by minute the advancing flood bit away miles of river bed, swelling north. Chicot, Jennie, Lake Village, Arkansas City, Snow Lake, Elaine, Helena, and Memphis felt the tremors. The tormented city shuddered through the night. The earth continued its descent, eventually tipping two and a half degrees down to the west. The "Memphis Tilt" is today one of the unique and charming characteristics of the gracious Old Town, but during the night of panic Memphis residents were sure they were doomed.

South and west the waters carved deeply into Arkansas and Oklahoma. By morning it was plain that all of Arkansas was going under. Waves advanced on Little Rock at almost one hundred miles an hour, new crests forming, overtopping the wave's leading edge as towns, hills, and the thirst of the soil temporarily broke the furious charge.

Washington announced the official hope that the Ozarks would stop the wild gallop of the unleashed Gulf, for in northwest Arkansas the land rose to over two thousand feet. But nothing could save Oklahoma. By noon the water reached clutching fingers around Mt. Scott and Elk Mountain, deluging Hobart and almost all of Greer County.

Despite hopeful announcements that the wave was slowing, had virtually stopped after inundating Oklahoma City, was being swallowed up in the desert near Amarillo, the wall of water continued its advance. For the land was still sinking, and the floods were constantly replenished from the Gulf. Schwartzberg and his geologists advised the utmost haste in evacuating the entire area between Colorado and Missouri, from Texas to North Dakota.

Lubbock, Texas, went under. On a curling reflex the tidal wave blotted out Sweetwater and Bib Spring. The Texas panhandle disappeared in one great swirl.

Whirlpools opened. A great welter of smashed wood and human debris was sucked under, vomited up, and pounded to pieces. Gulf water crashed on the cliffs of New Mexico and fell back on itself in foam. Would-be rescuers on the cliffs along what had been the west bank of the Pecos River afterwards recalled the hiss and scream like tearing silk as the water broke furiously on the newly exposed rock. It was the most terrible sound they had ever heard.

"We couldn't hear any shouts, of course, not that far away and with all that noise," said Dan Weaver, mayor of Carlsbad. "But we knew there were people down there. When the water hit the cliffs, it was like a collision between two solid bodies. We couldn't see for over an hour, because of the spray."

Salt spray. The ocean had come to New Mexico.

The cliffs proved to be the only effective barrier against the westward march of the water, which turned north, gouging out lumps of rock and tumbling down blocks of earth on to its own back. In places scoops of granite came out like ice cream. The present fishing town of Rockport, Colorado, is built on a harbor created in such a way.

The water had found its farthest westering. But still it poured north along the line of the original fault. Irresistible fingers closed on Sterling, Colorado, on Sidney, Nebraska, on Hot Springs, South Dakota. The entire tier of states settled, from south to north, down to its eventual place of stability one thousand feet below the level of the new sea.

Memphis was by now a seaport. The Ozarks, islands in a mad sea, formed precarious havens for half-drowned humanity. Waves bit off a corner of Missouri, flung themselves to Wichita. Topeka, Lawrence, and Belleville were the last Kansas towns to disappear. The governor of Kansas went down with his state.

Daniel Bernd of Lincoln, Nebraska, was washed up half-drowned in a cove of the Wyoming cliffs, having been sucked from one end of vanished Nebraska to the other. Similar hair-breadth escapes were recounted on radio and television.

Virtually the only people saved out of the entire population of Pierre, South Dakota, were the six members of the Creeth family. Plucky Timothy Creeth carried and dragged his aged parents to the loft of their barn on the outskirts of town. His brother Geoffrey brought along the younger children and what provisions they could find—"Mostly a ham and about half a ton of vanilla cookies," he explained to his eventual rescuers. The barn, luckily collapsing in the vibrations as the waves bore down on them, became an ark in which they rode out the disaster.

"We must of played cards for four days straight," recalled genial Mrs. Creeth when she afterwards appeared on a popular television spectacular. Her rural good humor undamaged by an ordeal few women can ever have been called on to face, she added, "We sure wondered why flushes never came out right. Jimanettly, we'd left the king of hearts behind, in the rush!"

But such lightheartedness and such happy endings were by no means typical. The world could only watch aghast as the water raced north under the shadow of the cliffs which occasionally crumbled, roaring, into the roaring waves. Day by day the relentless rush swallowed what had been dusty farmland, cities, and towns.

Some people were saved by the helicopters which flew mercy missions just ahead of the advancing waters. Some found safety in the peaks of western Nebraska and the Dakotas. But when the waters came to rest along what is roughly the present shoreline of our inland sea, it was estimated that over fourteen million people had lost their lives.

No one could even estimate the damage to property; almost the entirety of eight states, and portions of twelve others, had simply vanished from the heart of the North American continent forever.

It was in such a cataclysmic birth that the now-peaceful Nebraska Sea came to America.

Today, nearly one hundred years after the unprecedented—and happily unrepeated—disaster, it is hard to remember the terror and despair of those weeks in October and November, 1973. It is inconceivable to think of the United States without its beautiful and economically essential curve of interior ocean. Two-thirds as long as the Mediterranean, it graduates from the warm waters of the Gulf of Mexico through the equally blue waves of the Mississippi Bight, becoming cooler and greener north and west of the pleasant fishing isles of the Ozark Archipelago, finally shading into the gray-green chop of the Gulf of Dakota.

What would the United States have become without the 5,600-mile coastline of our inland sea? It is only within the last twenty years that any but the topmost layer of water has cleared sufficiently to permit a really extensive fishing industry. Mud still held in suspension by the restless waves will not precipitate fully even in our lifetimes. Even so, the commercial fisheries of Missouri and Wyoming contribute no small part to the nation's economy.

Who can imagine what the Middle West must have been like before the amelioration of climate brought about by the proximity of a warm sea? The now-temperate state of Minnesota (to say nothing of the submerged Dakotas) must have been Siberian. From contemporary accounts Missouri, our second California, was unbelievably muggy, almost uninhabitable during the summer months. Our climate today, from Ohio and North Carolina to the rich fields of New Mexico and the orchards of Montana, is directly ameliorated by the marine heart of the continent.

Who today could imagine the United States without the majestic sea-cliffs in stately parade from New Mexico to Montana? The beaches of Wyoming, the American Riviera, where fruit trees grow almost to the water's edge? Or incredible Colorado, where the morning skier is the afternoon bather, thanks to the monorail connecting the highest peaks with the glistening white beaches?

Of course there have been losses to balance slightly these strong gains. The Mississippi was, before 1973, one of the great rivers of the world. Taken together with its main tributary, the Missouri, it vied favorably with such giant systems as the Amazon and the Ganges. Now, ending as it does at Memphis and drawing its water chiefly from the Appalachian Mountains, it is only a slight remnant of what it was. And though the Nebraska Sea today carries many times the tonnage of shipping in its ceaseless traffic, we have lost the old romance of river shipping. We may only guess what it was like when we look upon the Ohio and the truncated Mississippi.

And transcontinental shipping is somewhat more difficult, with trucks and the freight-railroads obliged to take the sea ferries across the Nebraska Sea. We shall never know what the United States was like with its numerous coast-to-coast highways busy with trucks and private cars. Still, the ferry ride is certainly a welcome break after days of driving, and for those who wish a glimpse of what it must have been like, there is always the Cross-Canada Throughway and the magnificent U.S. Highway 73 looping north through Minnesota and passing through the giant port of Alexis, North Dakota, shipping center for the wheat of Manitoba and crossroad of a nation.

The political situation has long been a thorny problem. Only tattered remnants of the eight submerged states remained after the flood, but none of them wanted to surrender its autonomy. The tiny fringe of Kansas seemed, for a time, ready to merge with contiguous Missouri, but following the lead of the Arkansas Forever faction, the remaining population decided to retain political integrity. This has resulted in the continuing anomaly of the seven "fringe states" represented in Congress by the usual two senators each, though the largest of them is barely the size of Connecticut and all are economically indistinguishable from their neighboring states.

Fortunately it was decided some years ago that Oklahoma, only one of the eight to have completely disappeared, could not in any sense be considered to have a continuing political existence. So, though there are still families who proudly call themselves Oklahomans, and the Oklahoma Oil Company continues to pump oil from its submerged real estate, the state has in fact disappeared from the American political scene.

But this is by now more than a petty annoyance, to raise a smile when the talk gets around to the question of states' rights. Not even the tremendous price the country paid for its new sea—fourteen million dead, untold property destroyed—really offsets the asset we enjoy today. The heart of the continent, now open to the shipping of the world, was once dry and landlocked, cut off from the bustle of trade and the ferment of world culture.

It would indeed seem odd to an American of the fifties or sixties of the last century to imagine sailors from the merchant fleets of every nation walking the streets of Denver, fresh ashore at Newport, only fifteen miles away. Or to imagine Lincoln, Fargo, Kansas City, and Dallas as world ports and great manufacturing centers. Utterly beyond their ken would be Roswell, New Mexico; Benton, Wyoming; Westport, Missouri; and the other new ports of over a million inhabitants each, which have developed on the new harbors of the inland sea.

Unimaginable too would have been the general growth of population in the states surrounding the new sea. As the water tables rose and manufacturing and trade move in to take advantage of the just-created axis of world communication, a population explosion was touched off of which we are only now seeing the diminution. This new westering is to be ranked with the first surge of pioneers which created the American West. But what a difference! Vacation paradises bloom, a new fishing industry thrives; her water road is America's main artery of trade, and fleets of all the world sail . . . where once the prairie schooner made its laborious and dusty way west!

OH, TO BE A BLOBEL!

February 1964

Philip K. Dick

(b. 1928)

The thirty-five books of Philip Kindred Dick (a few done in collaboration) are one of the most important and complex bodies of work in science fiction. Subject to interpretation at several levels at least, such books as Counter Clock World *(1967),* Flow My Tears, the Policeman Said *(1974), the Hugo-winning* The Man in the High Castle *(1963),* The Three Stigmata of Palmer Eldritch *(1965),* Ubik *(1969),* Now Wait for Last Year *(1967), and almost all the others reward rereading time and again. However, his skills as a novelist have almost obscured his real talent for shorter fiction, which has graced the pages of all the major and minor sf magazines since 1952.*

Among his ten or more contributions to Galaxy *were "Shell Game" (September 1954), "Autofac" (November 1955), and the wonderful and bewildering "If There Were No Benny Cimoli" (December 1963). And of course, "Oh, To Be a Blobel!," pure Dick, an excursion into "inner space" before the sf world knew it existed.*

Memoir by Philip K. Dick

At the beginning of my writing career in the early fifties, *Galaxy* was my economic mainstay. Horace Gold at *Galaxy* liked my writing whereas John W. Campbell, Jr., at *Analog* considered my writing not only worthless but, as he put it, "Nuts." By and large I liked reading *Galaxy* because it had the broadest range of ideas, venturing into the soft sciences such as sociology and psychology, at a time when Campbell (as he once wrote me!) considered psionics a *neces-*

sary premise for science fiction. Also, Campbell said, the psionic character in the story had to be in charge of what was going on. So *Galaxy* provided a latitude that *Analog* did not. However, I was to get into an awful quarrel with Horace Gold, who had the habit of changing your stories without telling you: adding scenes, adding characters, removing downbeat endings in favor of upbeat endings. Many writers resented this. I did more than resent this; despite the fact that *Galaxy* was my main source of income I told Gold that I would not sell to him unless he stopped altering my stories—after which he bought nothing from me at all.

It was not, then, until Fred Pohl became editor of *Galaxy* that I began to appear there again. "Oh, To Be a Blobel!" is a story which Fred Pohl bought. In this story my enormous antiwar bias is evident, a bias which had, ironically, pleased Gold. I wasn't thinking of the Viet Nam War but war in general; in particular, how a war forces you to become like your enemy. Hitler had once said that the true victory of the Nazis would be to force its enemies, the United States in particular, to become like the Third Reich—i.e., a totalitarian society—in order to win. Hitler, then, expected to win even in defeat. As I watched the American military/industrial complex grow after World War II I kept remembering Hitler's analysis, and I kept thinking how right the son of a bitch was. We had beaten Germany, but both the U.S. and the U.S.S.R. were getting more and more like the Nazis with their huge police systems every day. Well, it seemed to me there was a little wry humor in this (but not much). Maybe I could write about it without getting too deep into polemics. But the issue presented in this story is real. Look what we had to become in Viet Nam just to lose, let alone to win; can you imagine what we'd have had to become to win? Hitler would have gotten a lot of laughs out of it, and the laughs would have been on us . . . and to a very great extent in fact were. And they were hollow and grim laughs, without humor of any kind.

OH, TO BE A BLOBEL!

He put a twenty-dollar platinum coin into the slot and the analyst, after a pause, lit up. Its eyes shone with sociability and it swiveled about in its chair, picked up a pen and pad of long yellow paper from its desk and said,

"Good morning, sir. You may begin."

"Hello, Dr. Jones. I guess you're not the same Dr. Jones who did the definitive biography of Freud; that was a century ago." He laughed nervously; being a rather poverty-stricken man he was not accustomed to dealing with the new fully homeostatic psychoanalysts. "Um," he said, "should I free-associate or give you background material or just what?"

Dr. Jones said, "Perhaps you could begin by telling me who you are and warum mich—why you have selected me."

"I'm George Munster of catwalk 4, building WEF-395, San Francisco condominium established 1996."

"How do you do, Mr. Munster." Dr. Jones held out its hand, and George Munster shook it. He found the hand to be of a pleasant body temperature and decidedly soft. The grip, however, was manly.

"You see," Munster said, "I'm an ex-G.I., a war veteran. That's how I got my condominium apartment at WEF-395—veterans' preference."

"Ah yes," Dr. Jones said, ticking faintly as it measured the passage of time. "The war with the Blobels."

"I fought three years in that war," Munster said, nervously smoothing his long, black, thinning hair. "I hated the Blobels and I volunteered; I was only nineteen and I had a good job—but the crusade to clear the Sol System of Blobels came first in my mind."

"Um," Dr. Jones said, ticking and nodding.

George Munster continued, "I fought well. In fact I got two decorations and a battlefield citation. Corporal. That's because I single-handedly wiped out an observation satellite full of Blobels; we'll never know exactly how many because of course, being Blobels, they tend to fuse together and unfuse confusingly." He broke off, then, feeling emotional. Even remembering and talking about the war was too much for him . . . he lay back on the couch, lit a cigarette, and tried to become calm.

The Blobels had emigrated originally from another star system, probably Proxima. Several thousand years ago they had settled on Mars and on Titan, doing very well at agrarian pursuits. They were developments of the original unicellular amoeba, quite large and with a highly organized nervous system, but still amoeba, with pseudopodia, reproducing by binary fission, and in the main offensive to Terran settlers.

The war itself had broken out over ecological considerations. It had been the desire of the Foreign Aid Department of the U.N. to change the atmosphere on Mars, making it more usable for Terran settlers. This change, however, had made it unpalatable for the Blobel colonies already there; hence the squabble.

And, Munster reflected, it was not possible to change *half* the atmosphere of a planet, the Brownian movement being what it was. Within a period of ten years the altered atmosphere had diffused throughout the planet, bringing suffering—at least so they alleged— to the Blobels. In retaliation, a Blobel armada had approached Terra and had put into orbit a series of technically sophisticated satellites designed eventually to alter the atmosphere of Terra. This alteration had never come about because of course the War Office of the U.N. had gone into action; the satellites had been detonated by self-instructing missiles . . . and the war was on.

Dr. Jones said, "Are you married, Mr. Munster?"

"No sir," Munster said. "And—" He shuddered. "You'll see why when I've finished telling you. See, doctor—" He stubbed out his cigarette. "I'll be frank. I was a Terran spy. That was my task; they gave the job to me because of my bravery in the field . . . I didn't ask for it."

"I see," Dr. Jones said.

"Do you?" Munster's voice broke. "Do you know what was necessary in those days in order to make a Terran into a successful spy among the Blobels?"

Nodding, Dr. Jones said, "Yes, Mr. Munster. You had to relinquish your human form and assume the repellent form of a Blobel."

Munster said nothing; he clenched and unclenched his fist, bitterly. Across from him Dr. Jones ticked.

That evening, back in his small apartment at WEF-395, Munster opened a fifth of Teacher's scotch and sat by himself sipping from a cup, lacking even the energy to get a glass down from the cupboard over the sink.

What had he gotten out of the session with Dr. Jones today? Nothing, as nearly as he could tell. And it had eaten deep into his meager financial resources . . . meager because—

Because for almost twelve hours out of the day he reverted, despite all the efforts of himself and the Veterans' Hospitalization Agency of the U.N., to his old wartime Blobel shape. To a formless unicellular-like blob, right in the middle of his own apartment at WEF-395.

His financial resources consisted of a small pension from the War Office; finding a job was impossible, because as soon as he was hired the strain caused him to revert there on the spot, in plain sight of his new employer and fellow workers.

It did not assist in forming successful work-relationships.

Sure enough, now, at eight in the evening, he felt himself once more beginning to revert; it was an old and familiar experience to him, and he loathed it. Hurriedly, he sipped the last of the cup of scotch, put the cup down on a table . . . and felt himself slide together into a homogeneous puddle.

The telephone rang.

"I can't answer," he called to it. The phone's relay picked up his anguished message and conveyed it to the calling party. Now Munster had become a single transparent gelatinous mass in the middle of the rug; he undulated toward the phone—it was still ringing, despite his statement to it, and he felt furious resentment; didn't he have enough troubles already, without having to deal with a ringing phone?

Reaching it, he extended a pseudopodium and snatched the receiver from the hook. With great effort he formed his plastic substance into the semblance of a vocal apparatus, resonating dully. "I'm busy," he resonated in a low booming fashion into the mouthpiece of the phone. "Call later." *Call,* he thought as he hung up, *tomorrow morning. When I've been able to regain my human form.*

The apartment was quiet, now.

Sighing, Munster flowed back across the carpet, to the window, where he rose into a high pillar in order to see the view beyond; there was a light-sensitive spot on his outer surface, and although he did not possess a true lens he was able to appreciate—nostalgically— the sight of San Francisco Bay, the Golden Gate Bridge, the playground for small children which was Alcatraz Island.

Dammit, he thought bitterly. *I can't marry; I can't live a genuine human existence, reverting this way to the form the War Office bigshots forced me into back in the war times. . . .*

He had not known then, when he accepted the mission, that it would leave this permanent effect. They had assured him it was "only temporary, for the duration," or some such glib phrase. *Dura-*

tion my ass, Munster thought with furious, impotent resentment. *It's been* eleven years *now*.

The psychological problems created for him, the pressure on his psyche, were immense. Hence his visit to Dr. Jones.

Once more the phone rang.

"Okay," Munster said aloud, and flowed laboriously back across the room to it. "You want to talk to me?" he said as he came closer and closer; the trip, for someone in Blobel form, was a long one. "I'll talk to you. You can even turn on the vidscreen and *look* at me." At the phone he snapped the switch which would permit visual communication as well as auditory. "Have a good look," he said, and displayed his amorphous form before the scanning tube of the video.

Dr. Jones's voice came: "I'm sorry to bother you at your home, Mr. Munster, especially when you're in this, um, awkward condition . . ." The homeostatic analyst paused. "But I've been devoting time to problem solving vis-à-vis your condition. I may have at least a partial solution."

"What?" Munster said, taken by surprise. "You mean to imply that medical science can now—"

"No, no," Dr. Jones said hurriedly. "The physical aspects lie out of my domain; you must keep that in mind, Munster. When you consulted me about your problems it was the psychological adjustment that—"

"I'll come right down to your office and talk to you," Munster said. And then he realized that he could not; in his Blobel form it would take him days to undulate all the way across town to Dr. Jones's office. "Jones," he said desperately, "you see the problems I face. I'm stuck here in this apartment every night beginning about eight o'clock and lasting through until almost seven in the morning . . . I can't even visit you and consult you and get help—"

"Be quiet, Mr. Munster," Dr. Jones interrupted. "I'm trying to tell you something. *You're not the only one in this condition.* Did you know that?"

Heavily, Munster said, "Sure. In all, eighty-three Terrans were made over into Blobels at one time or another during the war. Of the eighty-three"—he knew the facts by heart—"sixty-one survived and now there's an organization called Veterans of Unnatural Wars of which fifty are members. I'm a member. We meet twice a month, revert in unison . . ." He started to hang up the phone. So this was what he had gotten for his money, this stale news. "Good-bye, doctor," he murmured.

Dr. Jones whirred in agitation. "Mr. Munster, I don't mean other Terrans. I've researched this in your behalf, and I discover that according to captured records at the Library of Congress fifteen *Blobels* were formed into pseudo-Terrans to act as spies for *their* side. Do you understand?"

After a moment Munster said, "Not exactly."

"You have a mental block against being helped," Dr. Jones said. "But here's what I want, Munster; you be at my office at eleven in the morning tomorrow. We'll take up the solution to your problem then. Goodnight."

Wearily, Munster said, "When I'm in my Blobel form my wits aren't too keen, doctor. You'll have to forgive me." He hung up, still puzzled. So there were fifteen Blobels walking around on Titan this moment, doomed to occupy human forms—so what? How did that help him?

Maybe he would find out at eleven tomorrow.

When he strode into Dr. Jones's waiting room he saw, seated in a deep chair in a corner by a lamp, reading a copy of *Fortune*, an exceedingly attractive young woman.

Automatically, Munster found a place to sit from which he could eye her. Stylish dyed-white hair braided down the back of her neck . . . he took in the sight with delight, pretending to read his own copy of *Fortune*. Slender legs, small and delicate elbows. And her sharp, clearly-featured face. The intelligent eyes, the thin, tapered nostrils—a truly lovely girl, he thought. He drank in the sight of her . . . until all at once she raised her head and stared coolly back at him.

"Dull, having to wait," Munster mumbled.

The girl said, "Do you come to Dr. Jones often?"

"No," he admitted. "This is just the second time."

"I've never been here before," the girl said. "I was going to another electronic fully homeostatic psychoanalyst in Los Angeles and then late yesterday Dr. Bing, my analyst, called me and told me to fly up here and see Dr. Jones this morning. Is this one good?"

"Um," Munster said. "I guess so." *We'll see*, he thought. *That's precisely what we don't know, at this point.*

The inner office door opened and there stood Dr. Jones. "Miss Arrasmith," it said, nodding to the girl. "Mr. Munster." It nodded to George. "Won't you both come in?"

Rising to her feet, Miss Arrasmith said, "Who pays the twenty dollars then?"

But the analyst had become silent; it had turned off.

"I'll pay," Miss Arrasmith said, reaching into her purse.

"No, no," Munster said. "Let me." He got out a twenty dollar piece and dropped it into the analyst's slot.

At once, Dr. Jones said, "You're a gentleman, Mr. Munster." Smiling it ushered the two of them into its office. "Be seated, please, Miss Arrasmith, without preamble please allow me to explain your— condition to Mr. Munster." To Munster it said, "Miss Arrasmith is a Blobel."

Munster could only stare at the girl.

"Obviously," Dr. Jones continued, "presently in human form. This, for her, is the state of involuntary reversion. During the war she operated behind Terran lines, acting for the Blobel War League. She was captured and held, but then the war ended and she was neither tried nor sentenced."

"They released me," Miss Arrasmith said in a low, carefully controlled voice. "Still in human form. I stayed here out of shame. I just couldn't go back to Titan and—" Her voice wavered.

"There is great shame attached to this condition," Dr. Jones said, "for any high-caste Blobel."

Nodding, Miss Arrasmith sat clutching a tiny Irish linen handkerchief and trying to look poised. "Correct, doctor. I did visit Titan to discuss my condition with medical authorities there. After expensive and prolonged therapy with me they were able to induce a return to my natural form for a period of"—she hesitated—"about one-fourth of the time. But the other three-fourths . . . I am as you perceive me now." She ducked her head and touched the handkerchief to her right eye.

"Jeez," Munster protested, "You're lucky; a human form is infinitely superior to a Blobel form—I ought to know. As a Blobel you have to creep along . . . you're like a big jellyfish, no skeleton to keep you erect. And binary fission—it's lousy, I say really lousy, compared to the Terran form of—you know. Reproduction." He colored.

Dr. Jones ticked and stated, "For a period of about six hours your human forms overlap. And then for about one hour your Blobel forms overlap. So all in all, the two of you possess seven hours out of twenty-four in which you both possess identical forms. In my opinion"—it toyed with its pen and paper—"seven hours is not too bad. If you follow my meaning."

After a moment Miss Arrasmith said, "But Mr. Munster and I are natural enemies."

"That was years ago," Munster said.

"Correct," Dr. Jones agreed. "True, Miss Arrasmith is basically a Blobel and you, Munster, are a Terran, but—" It gestured. "Both of you are outcasts in either civilization; both of you are stateless and hence gradually suffering a loss of ego-identity. I predict for both of you a gradual deterioration ending finally in severe mental illness. Unless you two can develop a rapprochement." The analyst was silent then.

Miss Arrasmith said softly, "I think we're very lucky, Mr. Munster. As Dr. Jones said, we do overlap for seven hours a day . . . we can enjoy that time together, no longer in wretched isolation." She smiled up hopefully at him, rearranging her coat. Certainly, she had a nice figure; the somewhat low-cut dress gave an ideal clue to that.

Studying her, Munster pondered.

"Give him time," Dr. Jones told Miss Arrasmith. "My analysis of him is that he will see this correctly and do the right thing."

Still rearranging her coat and dabbing at her large, dark eyes, Miss Arrasmith waited.

The phone in Dr. Jones's office rang, a number of years later. He answered it in his customary way. "Please, sir or madam, deposit twenty dollars if you wish to speak to me."

A tough male voice on the other end of the line said, "Listen, this is the U.N. Legal Office and we don't deposit twenty dollars to talk to anybody. So trip that mechanism inside you, Jones."

"Yes sir," Dr. Jones said, and with his right hand tripped the lever behind his ear that caused him to come on free.

"Back in 2037," the U.N. legal expert said, "did you advise a couple to marry? A George Munster and a Vivian Arrasmith, now Mrs. Munster?"

"Why yes," Dr. Jones said, after consulting his built-in memory banks.

"Had you investigated the legal ramifications of their issue?"

"Um well," Dr. Jones said, "that's not my worry."

"You can be arraigned for advising any action contrary to U.N. law."

"There's no law prohibiting a Blobel and a Terran from marrying."

The U.N. legal expert said, "All right doctor, I'll settle for a look at their case histories."

"Absolutely not," Dr. Jones said. "That would be a breach of ethics."

"We'll get a writ and sequester them, then."

"Go ahead." Dr. Jones reached behind his ear to shut himself off.

"Wait. It may interest you to know that the Munsters now have four children. And, following the Mendelian Law, the offspring comprise a strict one, two, one ratio. One Blobel girl, one hybrid boy, one hybrid girl, one Terran girl. The legal problem arises in that the Blobel Supreme Council claims the pure-blooded Blobel girl as a citizen of Titan and also suggests that one of the two hybrids be donated to the council's jurisdiction." The U.N. legal expert explained, "You see, the Munsters' marriage is breaking up; they're getting divorced and it's sticky finding which laws obtain regarding them and their issue."

"Yes," Dr. Jones admitted, "I would think so. What has caused their marriage to break up?"

"I don't know and don't care. Possibly the fact that both adults and two of the four children rotate daily between being Blobels and Terrans; maybe the strain got to be too much. If you want to give them psychological advice, consult them. Good-bye." The U.N. legal expert rang off.

Did I make a mistake, advising them to marry? Dr. Jones asked itself. *I wonder if I shouldn't look them up; I owe at least that to them.*

Opening the Los Angeles phonebook, it began thumbing through the *M*'s.

These had been six difficult years for the Munsters.

First, George had moved from San Francisco to Los Angeles; he and Vivian had set up their household in a condominium apartment with three instead of two rooms. Vivian, being in Terran form three-fourths of the time, had been able to obtain a job; right out in public she gave jet flight information at the Fifth Los Angeles Airport. George, however—

His pension comprised an amount only one-fourth that of his wife's salary and he felt it keenly. To augment it, he had searched for a way of earning money at home. Finally in a magazine he had found this valuable ad:

MAKE SWIFT PROFITS IN YOUR OWN CONDO! RAISE GIANT BULL-FROGS FROM JUPITER, CAPABLE OF EIGHTY-FOOT LEAPS. CAN BE USED IN FROG RACING (WHERE LEGAL) AND

So in 2038 he had bought his first pair of frogs imported from Jupiter and had begun raising them for swift profits, right in his own condominium apartment building, in a corner of the basement that Leopold the partially homeostatic janitor let him use gratis.

But in the relatively feeble Terran gravity the frogs were capable of enormous leaps, and the basement proved too small for them; they ricocheted from wall to wall like green Ping-Pong balls and soon died. Obviously it took more than a portion of the basement at QEK-604 Apartments to house a crop of the damned things, George realized.

And then, too, their first child had been born. It had turned out to be pure-blooded Blobel; for twenty-four hours a day it consisted of a gelatinous mass and George found himself waiting in vain for it to switch over to a human form, even for a moment.

He faced Vivian defiantly in this matter, during a period when both of them were in human form.

"How can I consider it my child?" he asked her. "It's—an alien life-form to me." He was discouraged and even horrified. "Dr. Jones should have foreseen this; maybe it's *your* child—it looks just like you."

Tears filled Vivian's eyes. "You mean that insultingly."

"Damn right I do. We fought you creatures—we used to consider you no better than Portuguese stingrays." Gloomily, he put on his coat. "I'm going down to Veterans of Unnatural Wars Headquarters," he informed his wife, "and have a beer with the boys." Shortly, he was on his way to join with his old wartime buddies, glad to get out of the apartment house.

V.U.W. Headquarters was a decrepit cement building in downtown Los Angeles left over from the twentieth century and sadly in need of paint. The V.U.W. had little funds because most of its members were, like George Munster, living on U.N. pensions. However, there was a pool table and an old 3-D television set and a few dozen tapes of popular music and also a chess set. George generally drank his beer and played chess with his fellow members, either in human form or in Blobel form; this was one place in which both were accepted.

This particular evening he sat with Pete Ruggles, a fellow veteran who also had married a Blobel female reverting, as Vivian did, to human form.

"Pete, I can't go on. I've got a gelatinous blob for a child. My whole life I've wanted a kid, and now what have I got? Something that looks like it washed up on the beach."

Sipping his beer—he too was in human form at the moment—Pete answered, "Criminy, George, I admit it's a mess. But you must have known what you were getting into when you married her. And my God, according to Mendel's Law, the next kid—"

"I mean," George broke in, "I don't respect my own wife; that's the basis of it. I think of her as a *thing*. And myself, too. We're both things." He drank down his beer in one gulp.

Pete said meditatively, "But from the Blobel standpoint—"

"Listen, whose side are you on?" George demanded.

"Don't yell at me," Pete said, "or I'll deck you."

A moment later they were swinging wildly at each other. Fortunately Pete reverted to Blobel form in the nick of time; no harm was done. Now George sat alone, in human shape, while Pete oozed off somewhere else, probably to join a group of the boys who had also assumed Blobel form.

Maybe we can found a new society somewhere on a remote moon, George said to himself moodily. *Neither Terran nor Blobel.*

I've got to go back to Vivian, George resolved. *What else is there for me? I'm lucky to find her; I'd be nothing but a war veteran guzzling beer here at V.U.W. Headquarters every damn day and night, with no future, no hope, no real life . . .*

He had a new money-making scheme going, now. It was a home mail-order business; he had placed an ad in the *Saturday Evening Post* for MAGIC LODESTONES REPUTED TO BRING YOU LUCK. FROM ANOTHER STAR SYSTEM ENTIRELY! The stones had come from Proxima and were obtainable on Titan; it was Vivian who had made the commercial contact for him with her people. But so far, few people had sent in the dollar-fifty.

I'm a failure, George said to himself.

Fortunately the next child, born in the winter of 2039, showed itself to be a hybrid; it took human form fifty percent of the time, and so at last George had a child who was—occasionally, anyhow—a member of his own species.

He was still in the process of celebrating the birth of Maurice when a delegation of their neighbors at QEK-604 Apartments came and rapped on their door.

"We've got a petition here," the chairman of the delegation said, shuffling his feet in embarrassment, "asking that you and Mrs. Munster leave QEK-604."

"But why?" George asked, bewildered. "You haven't objected to us up until now."

"The reason is that now you've got a hybrid youngster who will want to play with ours, and we feel it's unhealthy for our kids to—"

George slammed the door in their faces.

But still, he felt the pressure, the hostility from the people on all sides of them. *And to think,* he thought bitterly, *that I fought in the war to save these people. It sure wasn't worth it.*

An hour later he was down at V.U.W. Headquarters once more, drinking beer and talking with his buddy Sherman Downs, also married to a Blobel.

"Sherman, it's no good. We're not wanted; we've got to emigrate. Maybe we'll try it on Titan, in Viv's world."

"Chrissakes," Sherman protested, "I hate to see you fold up, George. Isn't your electromagnetic reducing belt beginning to sell, finally?"

For the last few months, George had been making and selling a complex electronic reducing gadget which Vivian had helped him design; it was based in principle on a Blobel device popular on Titan but unknown on Terra. And this had gone over well; George had more orders than he could fill. But—

"I had a terrible experience, Sherm," George confided. "I was in a drugstore the other day, and they gave me a big order for my reducing belt, and I got so excited—" He broke off. "You can guess what happened. I reverted. Right in plain sight of a hundred customers.

And when the buyer saw that he canceled the order for the belts. It was what we all fear . . . you should have seen how their attitude toward me changed."

Sherm said, "Hire someone to do your selling for you. A full-blooded Terran."

Thickly, George said, "*I'm* a full-blooded Terran, and don't you forget it. Ever."

"I just mean—"

"I know what you meant," George said. And took a swing at Sherman. Fortunately he missed and in the excitement both of them reverted to Blobel form. They oozed angrily into each other for a time, but at last fellow veterans managed to separate them.

"I'm as much a Terran as anyone," George thought-radiated in the Blobel manner to Sherman. "And I'll flatten anyone who says otherwise."

In Blobel form he was unable to get home; he had to phone Vivian to come and get him. It was humiliating.

Suicide, he decided. *That's the answer.*

How best to do it? In Blobel form he was unable to feel pain; best to do it then. Several substances would dissolve him . . . he could for instance drop himself into a heavily-chlorinated swimming pool, such as QEK-604 maintained in its recreation room.

Vivian, in human form, found him as he reposed hesitantly at the edge of the swimming pool, late one night.

"George, I beg you—go back to Dr. Jones."

"Naw," he boomed dully, forming a quasi-vocal apparatus with a portion of his body. "It's no use, Viv. I don't *want* to go on." Even the belts; they had been Viv's idea, rather than his. He was second even there . . . behind her, falling constantly further behind each passing day.

Viv said, "You have so much to offer the children."

That was true. "Maybe I'll drop over to the U.N. War Office," he decided. "Talk to them, see if there's anything new that medical science has come up with that might stabilize me."

"But if you stabilize as a Terran," Vivian said, "what would become of me?"

"We'd have *eighteen entire hours* together a day. All the hours you take human form!"

"But you wouldn't want to stay married to me. Because, George, then you could meet a Terran woman."

It wasn't fair to her, he realized. So he abandoned the idea.

In the spring of 2041 their third child was born, also a girl, and like Maurice a hybrid. It was Blobel at night and Terran by day. Meanwhile, George found a solution to some of his problems. He got himself a mistress.

At the Hotel Elysium, a run-down wooden building in the heart of Los Angeles, he and Nina arranged to meet one another.

"Nina," George said, sipping Teacher's scotch and seated beside her on the shabby sofa which the hotel provided, "you've made my life worth living again." He fooled with the buttons on her blouse.

"I respect you," Nina Glaubman said, assisting him with the buttons. "In spite of the fact—well, you are a former enemy of our people."

"God," George protested, "we must not think about the old days —we have to close our minds to our pasts." *Nothing but our future*, he thought.

His reducing-belt enterprise had developed so well that now he employed fifteen full-time Terran employees and owned a small, modern factory on the outskirts of San Fernando. If U.N. taxes had been reasonable he would by now be a wealthy man . . . brooding on that, George wondered what the tax rate was in Blobel-run lands, on Io, for instance. Maybe he ought to look into it.

One night at V.U.W. Headquarters he discussed the subject with Reinholt, Nina's husband, who of course was ignorant of the modus vivendi between George and Nina.

"Reinholt," George said with difficulty, as he drank his beer, "I've got big plans. This cradle-to-grave socialism the U.N. operates . . . it's not for me. It's cramping me. The Munster Magic Magnetic Belt is"—he gestured—"more than Terran civilization can support. You get me?"

Coldly, Reinholt said, "But George, you are a Terran; if you emigrate to Blobel-run territory with your factory you'll be betraying your—"

"Listen," George told him, "I've got one authentic Blobel child, two half-Blobel children, and a fourth on the way. I've got strong *emotional* ties with those people out there on Titan and Io."

"You're a traitor," Reinholt said, and punched him in the mouth. "And not only that," he continued, punching George in the stomach, "you're running around with my wife. I'm going to kill you."

To escape, George reverted to Blobel form; Reinholt's blows passed harmlessly deep into his moist, jellylike substance. Reinholt then reverted too, and flowed into him murderously, trying to consume and absorb George's nucleus.

Fortunately fellow veterans pried their two bodies apart before any permanent harm was done.

Later that night, still trembling, George sat with Vivian in the living room of their eight-room suite at the great new condominium apartment building ZGF-900. It had been a close call, and now of course Reinholt would tell Viv; it was only a question of time. The marriage, as far as George could see, was over. This perhaps was their last moment together.

"Viv," he said urgently, "you have to believe me; I love you. You and the children—plus the belt business, naturally—are my complete life." A desperate idea came to him. "Let's emigrate now, tonight. Pack up the kids and go to Titan, right this minute."

"I can't go," Vivian said. "I know how my people would treat me, and treat you and the children, too. George, *you* go. Move the factory to Io. I'll stay here." Tears filled her dark eyes.

"Hell," George said, "what kind of life is that? With you on Terra and me on Io—that's no marriage. And who'll get the kids?" Probably Viv would get them . . . but his firm employed top legal talent—perhaps he could use it to solve his domestic problems.

The next morning Vivian found out about Nina. And hired an attorney of her own.

"Listen," George said, on the phone talking to his top legal talent, Henry Ramarau. "Get me custody of the fourth child; it'll be a Terran. And we'll compromise on the two hybrids; I'll take Maurice and she can have Kathy. And naturally she gets that blob, that first so-called child. As far as I'm concerned it's hers anyhow." He slammed the receiver down and then turned to the board of directors of his company. "Now where were we?" he demanded. "In our analysis of Io tax laws."

During the next weeks the idea of a move to Io appeared more and more feasible from a profit and loss standpoint.

"Go ahead and buy land on Io," George instructed his business agent in the field, Tom Hendricks. "And get it cheap; we want to start right." To his secretary Miss Nolan he said, "Now keep everyone out of my office until further notice. I feel an attack coming on. From anxiety over this major move off Terra to Io." He added, "And personal worries."

"Yes, Mr. Munster," Miss Nolan said, ushering Tom Hendricks out of George's private office. "No one will disturb you." She could be counted on to keep everyone out while George reverted to his wartime Blobel shape, as he often did, these days; the pressure on him was immense.

When, later in the day, he resumed human form, George learned from Miss Nolan that a Dr. Jones had called.

"I'll be damned," George said, thinking back to six years ago. "I thought it'd be in the junk pile by now." To Miss Nolan he said, "Call Dr. Jones, notify me when you have it; I'll take a minute off to talk to it." It was like old times, back in San Francisco.

Shortly, Miss Nolan had Dr. Jones on the line.

"Doctor," George said, leaning back in his chair and swiveling from side to side and poking at an orchid on his desk. "Good to hear from you."

The voice of the homeostatic analyst came in his ear, "Mr. Munster, I note that you now have a secretary."

"Yes," George said, "I'm a tycoon. I'm in the reducing-belt game; it's somewhat like the flea-collar that cats wear. Well, what can I do for you?"

"I understand you have four children now—"

"Actually three, plus a fourth on the way. Listen, that fourth, doctor, is vital to me; according to Mendel's Law it's a full-blooded Terran and by God I'm doing everything in my power to get custody of it." He added, "Vivian—you remember her—is now back on Titan. Among her own people, where she belongs. And I'm putting some of the finest doctors I can get on my payroll to stabilize me; I'm tired of this constant reverting, night and day; I've got too much to do for such nonsense."

Dr. Jones said, "From your tone I can see you're an important, busy man, Mr. Munster. You've certainly risen in the world, since I saw you last."

"Get to the point, doctor," George said impatiently. "Why'd you call?"

"I, um, thought perhaps I could bring you and Vivian together again."

"Bah," George said contemptuously. "That woman? Never. Listen, doctor, I have to ring off; we're in the process of finalizing on some basic business strategy, here at Munster, Incorporated."

"Mr. Munster," Dr. Jones asked, "is there another woman?"

"There's another Blobel," George said, "if that's what you mean." And he hung up the phone. *Two Blobels are better than none,* he said to himself. *And now back to business* . . . He pressed a button on his desk and at once Miss Nolan put her head into the office.

"Miss Nolan," George said, "get me Hank Ramarau; I want to find out—"

"Mr. Ramarau is waiting on the other line," Miss Nolan said. "He says it's urgent."

Switching to the other line, George said, "Hi, Hank. What's up?"

"I've just discovered," his top legal advisor said, "that to operate your factory on Io you must be a citizen of Titan."

"We ought to be able to fix that up," George said.

"But to be a citizen of Titan—" Ramarau hesitated. "I'll break it to you as easy as I can, George. You have to be a Blobel."

"Dammit, I am a Blobel," George said. "At least part of the time. Won't that do?"

"No," Ramarau said, "I checked into that, knowing of your affliction, and it's got to be one hundred percent of the time. Night *and* day."

"Hmmm," George said. "That is bad. But we'll overcome it, somehow. Listen, Hank, I've got an appointment with Eddy Fullbright, my medical coordinator; I'll talk to you after, okay?" He rang off and then sat scowling and rubbing his jaw. *Well,* he decided, *if it has to be it has to be. Facts are facts, and we can't let them stand in our way.*

Picking up the phone he dialed his doctor, Eddy Fullbright.

The twenty-dollar platinum coin rolled down the chute and tripped the circuit. Dr. Jones came on, glanced up, and saw a stunning, sharp-breasted young woman whom it recognized—by means of a quick scan of its memory banks—as Mrs. George Munster, the former Vivian Arrasmith.

"Good day, Vivian," Dr. Jones said cordially. "But I understood you were on Titan." It rose to its feet, offering her a chair.

Dabbing at her large, dark eyes, Vivian sniffled, "Doctor, everything is collapsing around me. My husband is having an affair with another woman . . . all I know is that her name is Nina and all the boys down at V.U.W. Headquarters are talking about it. Presumably she's a Terran. We're both filing for divorce. And we're having a dreadful legal battle over the children." She arranged her coat modestly. "I'm expecting. Our fourth."

"This I know," Dr. Jones said. "A full-blooded Terran this time, if Mendel's Law holds . . . although it only applied to litters."

Mrs. Munster said miserably, "I've been on Titan talking to legal and medical experts, gynecologists, and especially marital guidance counselors; I've had all sorts of advice during the past month. Now I'm back on Terra but I can't find George—he's *gone*."

"I wish I could help you, Vivian," Dr. Jones said. "I talked to your husband briefly, the other day, but he spoke only in generalities . . . evidently he's such a big tycoon now that it's hard to approach him."

"And to think," Vivian sniffled, "that he achieved it all because of an idea *I* gave him. A Blobel idea."

"The ironies of fate," Dr. Jones said. "Now, if you want to keep your husband, Vivian—"

"I'm determined to keep him, Dr. Jones. Frankly, I've undergone therapy on Titan, the latest and most expensive . . . it's because I love George so much, even more than I love my own people or my planet."

"Eh?" Dr. Jones said.

"Through the most modern developments in medical science in the Sol System," Vivian said, "I've been stabilized, Dr. Jones. Now I am in human form twenty-four hours a day instead of eighteen. I've renounced my natural form in order to keep my marriage with George."

"The supreme sacrifice," Dr. Jones said, touched.

"Now, if I can only *find* him, doctor—"

At the ground-breaking ceremonies on Io, George Munster flowed gradually to the shovel, extended a pseudopodium, seized the shovel, and with it managed to dig a symbolic amount of soil. "This is a great day," he boomed hollowly, by means of the semblance of a vocal apparatus into which he had fashioned the slimy, plastic substance which made up his unicellular body.

"Right, George," Hank Ramarau agreed, standing nearby with the legal documents.

The Ionan official, like George a great transparent blob, oozed across to Ramarau, took the documents, and boomed, "These will be transmitted to my government. I'm sure they're in order, Mr. Ramarau."

"I guarantee you," Ramarau said to the official, "Mr. Munster does not revert to human form at any time; he's made use of some of the most advanced techniques in medical science to achieve this stability at the unicellular phase of his former rotation. Munster would never cheat."

"This historic moment," the great blob that was George Munster thought-radiated to the throng of local Blobels attending the ceremonies, "means a higher standard of living for Ionans who will be employed; it will bring prosperity to this area, plus a proud sense of national achievement in the manufacture of what we recognize to be a native invention, the Munster Magic Magnetic Belt."

The throng of Blobels thought-radiated cheers.

"This is a proud day in my life," George Munster informed them, and began to ooze by degrees back to his car, where his chauffeur waited to drive him to his permanent hotel room at Io City.

Someday he would own the hotel. He was putting the profits from his business in local real estate; it was the patriotic—and the profitable—thing to do, other Ionans, other Blobels, had told him.

"I'm finally a successful man," George Munster thought-radiated to all close enough to pick up his emanations.

Amid frenzied cheers he oozed up the ramp and into his Titan-made car.

FOUNDING FATHER

October 1965

Isaac Asimov
(b. 1920)

The accomplishments of Isaac Asimov inside and outside the science-fiction field are much too numerous to be listed in a short headnote. Suffice it to say that he, Ray Bradbury, and Robert Heinlein are the most famous figures in the history of sf. Although his science fiction is most closely associated with John Campbell's Astounding, *he made major contributions to the success of* Galaxy *with three important serials—"Tyrann" (1951; published in book form as* The Stars Like Dust); *his magnificent fusion of the mystery and sf fields, "The Caves of Steel" (1953); and the Hugo- and Nebula-winning "The Gods Themselves" (1972; one installment of which appeared in* Worlds of If). *His first story for* Galaxy *was "Misbegotten Missionary" in the November 1950 issue. His later novella "The Martian Way" (November 1952) was one of the most popular stories ever to appear in the magazine.*

Memoir by Isaac Asimov

Since early 1958, what with one thing or another, I have scarcely written as many as a dozen science-fiction stories, all of them quite short. In the years preceding 1958, on the other hand, I had written up to 200,000 words of science fiction a year, so science-fiction editors missed me a bit.

Various devices were used by them to stir me out of my lethargy, or, rather, to divert my energies into the old accustomed channels—for it wasn't that I had stopped writing by any means; it was just that I was writing material other than science fiction.

Some of the devices worked, for I have my weaknesses. One is a tearful sentimentality about old times, old friends, old feats. Editors who know this are sometimes quite merciless in their manipulation of said sentimentality.

Fred Pohl, then editor of *Galaxy*, decided to squeeze my sentiment. He pointed out that the October 1965 issue of *Galaxy* would be coming up and that it was the fifteenth anniversary issue.

"The fifteenth anniversary issue," I said, round-eyed, as fifteen years rolled back in my mind and I was suddenly much younger. "How could so much time have passed while I was looking the other way."

"And," said Fred, impressively, "we want all the authors who contributed to the first issue to contribute to this one. A matter of sentiment."

Sentiment! A lump was in my throat at once. My blue eyes misted with tears. "I'll do it," I said, brokenly.

"Good," said Fred, rising to pass on to the next victim. "Here's the cover illustration. I want a story built around it," and was gone before I could object.

I was appalled. I know that many authors have written stories to match cover paintings and that they found no difficulty in doing so. This did not apply to me, however. I was always relieved beyond measure that no editor had ever thought to ask me to do one. To test myself, you see, I had often tried to imagine a story based on some magazine cover before opening the magazine to read the actual story it was based on. The complete failure of my efforts was always humiliating.

But I couldn't refuse this time. My honor was engaged and I have all sorts of peculiar notions about my honor. In fact, I am very sentimental about it.

So I stared at the cover illustration, which I will now describe to you. In the foreground was a grave, handsome face behind the glass visor of a space helmet. To his left, in the background, were four rude wooden crosses, fading into the distance against an alien sky. Balanced on the wooden upright of each cross was a space helmet. Leaning against the base of each cross was a pair of oxygen cylinders.

Clearly we had here one live astronaut and four dead astronauts. How did they come to die? Had the living astronaut killed them?

Had he tried to save them and failed? Did he know they were there? Did he care?

Nothing came to me at all.

Help! Help! What to do?

Remember, I told myself with despairing sentimentality, this is for good old *Galaxy*. This is for good old Horace Gold and those good old talks about science-fiction plots in the good old days. What would good old Horace Gold have done?

From out of the misty past came floating up to me one of good old Horace's favorite comments: "Stand it on its head," he used to say. "When you think of an obvious situation, consider it in reverse. Are you sure that B follows A? A follows B? Or maybe C follows A?"

So I looked at the cover illustration again. There were the four crosses with the helmets and the oxygen tanks. Did the crosses have to signify death? Maybe they signified life?

Exactly!

So I wrote the story, and here it is!

FOUNDING FATHER

The original combination of catastrophes had taken place five years ago—five revolutions of this planet, HC-12549D by the charts, and nameless otherwise. Six-plus revolutions of Earth, but who was counting—any more?

If the men back home knew, they might say it was a heroic fight, an epic of the Galactic Corps; five men against a hostile world, holding their bitter own for five (or six-plus) years. And now they were dying, the battle lost after all. Three were in final coma, a fourth had his yellow-tinged eyeballs still open, and a fifth was yet on his feet.

But it was no question of heroism at all. It had been five men fighting off boredom and despair and maintaining their metallic bubble of livability only for the most unheroic reason that there was nothing else to do while life remained.

If any of them felt stimulated by the battle, he never mentioned it. After the first year, they stopped talking of rescue, and after the second, a moratorium descended on the word "Earth."

But one word remained always present. If unspoken it had to be found in their thoughts: "Ammonia."

It had come first while the landing was being scratched out against all odds on limping motors and in a battered space can.

You allow for bad breaks, of course; you expect a certain number—but one at a time. A stellar flare fries out the hyper-circuits —that can be repaired, given time. A meteorite disaligns the feeder-valves—they can be straightened, given time. A trajectory is miscalculated under tension and a momentarily unbearable acceleration tears out the jump-antennae and dulls the senses of every man on board—but antennae can be replaced and senses will recover, given time.

The chances are one in countless many that all three will happen at once; and still less that they will happen during a particularly tricky landing when the one necessary currency for the correction of all errors, time, is the one thing that is most lacking.

The *Cruiser John* hit that one chance in countless many, and it made a final landing, for it would never lift off a planetary surface again.

That it had landed essentially intact was itself a near-miracle. The five were given life for some years at least. Beyond that, only the blundering arrival of another ship could help, but no one expected that. They had had their life's share of coincidences, they knew, and all had been bad.

That was that.

And the key word was "ammonia." With the surface spiraling upward, and death (mercifully quick) facing them at considerably better than even odds, Chou somehow had time to note the absorption spectrograph, which was registering raggedly.

"Ammonia," he cried out. The others heard but there was no time to pay attention. There was only the wrenching fight against a quick death for the sake of a slow one.

When they landed finally, on sandy ground with sparse, ragged bluish vegetation; reedy grass; stunted treelike objects with blue bark and no leaves; no sign of animal life; and with an almost greenish cloudstreaked sky above—the word came back to haunt them.

"Ammonia?" said Peterson heavily.

Chou said, "Four percent."

"Impossible," said Peterson.

But it wasn't. The books didn't say impossible. What the Galactic Corps had discovered was that a planet of a certain mass and volume and at a certain temperature was an ocean planet and had one of two atmospheres: nitrogen/oxygen or nitrogen/carbon dioxide. In the former case, life was rampant; in the latter, it was primitive.

No one checked beyond mass, volume, and temperature any longer. One took the atmosphere (one or the other of them) for granted. But the books didn't say it had to be so; just that it always was so. Other atmospheres were thermodynamically possible, but extremely unlikely, so they weren't found in actual practice.

Until now. The men of the *Cruiser John* had found one and were bathed for the rest of such life as they could eke out by a nitrogen/carbon dioxide/ammonia atmosphere.

The men converted their ship into an underground bubble of Earth-type surroundings. They could not lift off the surface, nor could they drive a communicating beam through hyperspace, but all else was salvageable. To make up for inefficiencies in the cycling system, they could even tap the planet's own water and air supply within limits; provided, of course, they subtracted the ammonia.

They organized exploring parties since their suits were in excellent condition and it passed the time. The planet was harmless; no animal life; sparse plant life everywhere. Blue, always blue; ammoniated chlorophyll; ammoniated protein.

They set up laboratories, analyzed the plant components, studied microscopic sections, compiled vast volumes of findings. They tried growing native plants in ammonia-free atmosphere and failed. They made themselves into geologists and studied the planet's crust; astronomers and studied the spectrum of the planet's sun.

Barrere would say sometimes, "Eventually, the Corps will reach this planet again and we'll leave a legacy of knowledge for them. It's a unique planet after all. There might not be another Earth-type with ammonia in all the Milky Way."

"Great," said Sandropoulos, bitterly. "What luck for us."

Sandropoulos worked out the thermodynamics of the situation. "A metastable system," he said. "The ammonia disappears steadily through geochemical oxidation that forms nitrogen; the plants utilize nitrogen and reform ammonia, adapting themselves to the presence of ammonia. If the rate of plant formation of ammonia dropped two percent, a declining spiral would set in. Plant life would wither, reducing the ammonia still further and so on."

"You mean if we killed enough plant life," said Vlassov, "we could wipe out the ammonia."

"If we had air-sleds and wide-angle blasters, and a year to work in, we might," said Sandropoulos, "but we haven't and there's a better way. If we could get our plants going, the formation of oxygen through photosynthesis would increase the rate of ammonia oxidation. Even a small localized rise would lower the ammonia in the region, stimulate Earth-plant growth further, and inhibit the native growth, drop the ammonia further, and so on."

They became gardeners through all the growing season. That was, after all, routine for the Galactic Corps. Life on Earth-type planets was usually of the water/protein type, but variation was infinite and otherworld food was rarely nourishing and even more often it happened (not always, but often) that some types of Earth-plants would overrun and drown out the native flora. With the native flora held down, other Earth-plants could take root.

Dozens of planets had been converted into new Earths in this fashion. In the process Earth-plants developed hundreds of hardy varieties that flourished under extreme conditions—all the better with which to seed the next planet.

The ammonia would kill any Earth-plant, but the seeds at the disposal of the *Cruiser John* were not true Earth-plants but otherworld mutations of these plants. They fought hard but not well enough. Some varieties grew in a feeble, sickly manner and died.

At that they did better than did microscopic life. The planet's bacterioids were far more flourishing than was the planet's straggly blue plant-life. The native microorganisms drowned out any attempt at competition from Earth-samples. The attempt to seed the alien soil with Earth-type bacterial flora in order to aid the Earth-plants failed.

Vlassov shook his head, "It wouldn't do anyway. If our bacteria survived, it would only be adapting to the presence of ammonia."

Sandropoulos said, "Bacteria won't help us. We need the plants; they carry the oxygen manufacturing systems."

"We could make some ourselves," said Peterson. "We could electrolyze water."

"How long will our equipment last? If we could only get our plants going it would be like electrolyzing water forever, little by little, but year after year, till the planet gave up."

Barrere said, "Let's treat the soil then. It's rotten with ammonium salts. We'll bake the salts out and replace the ammonia-free soil."

"And what about the atmosphere?" asked Chou.

"In ammonia-free soil, they may catch hold despite the atmosphere. They almost make it as it is."

They worked like longshoremen, but with no real end in view. None really thought it would work, and there was no future for themselves, personally, even if it did work. But working passed the days.

The next growing season, they had their ammonia-free soil, but Earth-plants still grew only feebly. They even placed domes over several shoots and pumped ammonia-free air within. It helped slightly but not enough. They adjusted the chemical composition of the soil in every possible fashion. There was no reward.

The feeble shoots produced their tiny whiffs of oxygen, but not enough to topple the ammonia atmosphere off its base.

"One more push," said Sandropoulos, "one more. We're rocking it; we're rocking it; but we can't knock it over."

Their tools and equipment blunted and wore out with time and the future closed in steadily. Each month there was less room for maneuver.

When the end came at last, it was with almost gratifying suddenness. There was no name to place on the weakness and vertigo. No one actually suspected direct ammonia poisoning. Still, they were living off the algal growth of what had once been ship-hydroponics for years and the growths were themselves aberrant with possible ammonia contamination.

It could have been the workings of some native microorganism which might finally have learned to feed off them. It might even have been an Earthly microorganism, mutated under the conditions of a strange world.

So three died at last and did so, circumstances be praised, painlessly. They were glad to go, and leave the useless fight.

Chou said, in a voiceless whisper, "It's foolish to lose so badly."

Peterson, alone of the five to be on his feet (was he immune, whatever it was?), turned a grieving face toward his only living companion.

"Don't die," he said, "don't leave me alone."

Chou tried to smile. "I have no choice. But you can follow us, old friend. Why fight? The tools are gone and there is no way of winning now, if there ever was."

Even now, Peterson fought off final despair by concentrating on the fight against the atmosphere. But his mind was weary, his heart worn out, and when Chou died the next hour, he was left with four corpses to work with.

He stared at the bodies, counting over the memories, stretching them back (now that he was alone and dared wail) to Earth itself, which he had last seen on a visit eleven years before.

He would have to bury the bodies. He would break off the bluish branches of the native leafless trees and build crosses of them. He would hang the space helmet of each man on top and prop the oxygen cylinders below. Empty cylinders to symbolize the lost fight.

A foolish sentiment for men who could no longer care, and for future eyes that might never see.

But he was doing it for himself, to show respect for his friends, for he was not the kind of man to leave his friends untended in death while he himself could stand.

Besides—

Besides? He sat in weary thought for some moments.

While he was still alive, he would fight with such tools as were left. He would bury his friends.

He buried each in a spot of ammonia-free soil they had so laboriously built up; buried them without shroud and without clothing; leaving them naked in the hostile ground for the slow decomposition that would come with their own microorganisms before those, too, died with the inevitable invasion of the native bacterioids.

Peterson placed each cross, with its helmet and oxygen cylinders, propped each with rocks, then turned away, grim and sad-eyed, to return to the buried ship that he now inhabited alone.

He worked each day and eventually the symptoms came for him, too.

He struggled into his spacesuit and came to the surface for what he knew would be one last time.

He fell to his knees on the garden plots. The Earth-plants were green. They had lived longer than ever before. They looked healthy, even vigorous.

They had patched the soil, babied the atmosphere, and now Peterson had used the last tool, the only one remaining at his disposal, and he had given them fertilizer as well—

Out of the slowly corrupting flesh of the Earthmen came the nutrients that supplied the final push. Out of the Earth-plants came the oxygen that would beat back the ammonia and push the planet out of the unaccountable niche into which it had stuck.

If Earthmen ever came again (when? a million years hence?) they would find a nitrogen/oxygen atmosphere and a limited flora strangely reminiscent of Earth's.

The crosses would rot and decay, the metal rust and decompose. The bones might fossilize and remain to give a hint as to what happened. Their own records, sealed away, might be found.

But none of that mattered. If nothing at all was ever found, the planet itself, the whole planet, would be their monument.

And Peterson lay down to die in the midst of their victory.

GOING DOWN SMOOTH

August 1968

Robert Silverberg
(b. 1936)

Although he made a dozen appearances in Galaxy *before the mid 1960s, Robert Silverberg remained in the shadow of others until, almost out of nowhere, he produced an incredible string of innovative and powerful stories that propelled him to the forefront of the science-fiction world, a position that he has still not relinquished. Particularly noteworthy were the novels* Downward to the Earth *(November 1969–March 1970) and* The Tower of Glass *(April– June 1970), and the novellas "Hawksbill Station" (August 1970) and "The World Outside" (October 1970). These and other stories constituted one of the most amazing bursts of creativity in the history of a field in which writers typically wrote in streaks. "Going Down Smooth" was one of the first efforts by the "new" Silverberg, and one of the best.*

Memoir by Robert Silverberg

"Going Down Smooth" is a story of serious intent founded on a pair of backstage jokes.

The first involves the process, now I think obsolete, of commissioning science-fiction writers to construct stories around a previously painted cover illustration. Why this should ever have become standard practice in the magazine business puzzles me; the usual explanation had to do with deadlines and such, but it still seems to me more efficient to have had artists illustrate scenes from stories, rather than vice versa. Howbeit, many magazines worked that way and

some remarkable science-fiction stories did emerge, the writer's in-
genuity often being taxed to the extreme to make narrative sense
out of the picture with which he was presented. I think particularly
of James Blish's masterful "Common Time" as the archetypical
written-around-a-cover story; but I did dozens of them myself, including some of my best short pieces.

"Going Down Smooth" was probably among the last such stories
I did. I was then writing fiction regularly for *Galaxy*—Frederik Pohl
had dragooned me out of the first of my retirements from sf writing
about 1963 with an exceptionally generous offer, and by easy stages I
had moved from the periphery of *Galaxy*'s life to quite a central position as one of the most prolific contributors. This reached something of a frenzied pitch a little later, under Pohl's successor Ejler
Jakobsson, when *Galaxy* serialized four of my novels in virtually consecutive issues over a year and a half—*Downward to the Earth*,
Tower of Glass, *The World Inside*, and *A Time of Changes*. I don't
think any science-fiction magazine had given so much space to a single writer since Heinlein's heyday at *Astounding* thirty years earlier.

Anyway, Fred Pohl asked me to do a cover story for *Galaxy*
sometime late in 1967, and his assistant, Judy-Lynn Benjamin
(now Judy-Lynn Del Rey, the powerful and influential science-
fiction editor at Ballantine's Del Rey Books), sent me a photostat of
a cover "rough" by a gifted young artist named Vaughn Bodé. It
was a typically perplexing write-a-story-around-*this*-one sort of thing,
showing an oceangoing vessel with a cluster of colossal periscopes rising from the water behind it. Bodé had deviated from the usual
cover-rough format in one respect, though. *Galaxy*'s traditional cover
format for decades made use of a white panel down the left side of
the page in which the names of stories were printed. Bodé had not
only drawn that panel into his painting, but had gone to the
prankish extent of making up a bunch of bizarre story titles. I went
right along with the joke, picking out the least implausible of his titles and using it for my story. (I think I lost my photostat of the
Bodé rough in the fire that swept my home in February 1968; otherwise I'd list the other titles here. I've forgotten them, but they were
fine crazy ones.) That was backstage joke number one.

The other one was a prank at Fred Pohl's expense. Though he
was in most respects a superbly intelligent editor, Pohl had decided,
circa 1966 or 1967, that the basic readership of his magazine
consisted of fourteen-year-old boys, whose parents might forbid them

to buy it if they were to glance inside and discover anything porno-
graphic, as pornography was understood in those quaintly innocent
days. So Pohl forbade his authors any sort of erotic content and
deleted from their manuscripts even the mildest of what used to be
called "unprintable" Anglo-Saxonisms. I took issue with this policy
to some degree, although later on I came, alas, to realize that Pohl
was probably right, and that the readership of the sf magazines back
then did consist largely of fourteen-year-old boys of all ages. Anyway,
in the grand old manner of science-fiction pros rebelling tepidly
against editorial censorship, fighting repression with slyness, I built
my entire story around the earthiest of procreative obscenities—but,
since my protagonist was a computer, I flanged together a binary-
equivalent alphabet and disguised the forbidden word in chaste nu-
merals. To me, and doubtless to Fred Pohl, there is not a whole lot
of karmic distinction between saying "fuck you" and saying
"1000110 you"—the baleful energy, as I see it, lies in the underly-
ing sentiment, not in the verbal or pseudoverbal packet that carries
it. But not so with the parents of Fred's fourteen-year-old audience,
I guess, because the story was published, no subscriptions were canceled, and we all lived happily ever after.

During the Jakobsson regime I actually did get the dread word
into the magazine, by the way. It was a passage in "The World Inside" in which a twenty-fourth-century historian, musing on the
twentieth century's obsession with "forbidden" language, repeats
such words as "fuck" and "cunt" in bewilderment, trying to comprehend why entire books should have been suppressed for containing
them. They are mere noises to him, and the concepts they represent
seem utterly harmless. Ironically, these explorations of the innately
innocuous nature of sexual slang touched off so many irate letters
from the readership that the publisher became aware of the situation and asked Jakobsson to reinstate the old magazine taboos. The
first victim of this was Robert A. Heinlein, whose novel *I Will Fear
No Evil* was being serialized in *Galaxy*. Never in his career had
Heinlein used language that would offend the most prudish, but in
the climactic paragraph of this novel he allowed himself a lyrical
affirmation of the power of love, and this is how it came out in
Galaxy:

"Thank you, Roberto, for letting me welcome you into my body.
It is good to touch—to f—, to be f—ed. It's not good—to be—too
much alone. . . ."

And so the immortal souls of the readers were protected by the vigilant publisher. And so everybody got f—ed again. Nowadays the fourteen-year-olds are too busy f—ing one another to read *Galaxy* at all, and nobody worries much about the terrible issues of obscenity that caused us such anguish in the far-off ancient days of 1967.

GOING DOWN SMOOTH

They call me mad, but I am not mad. I am sane quite, to many-power exponential. I can punctuate properly. I use upper and lower case letters, do you see? I function. I take the data in. I receive well. I receive, I digest, I remember.

Everything going down smooth, all the time, say the program boys. They mean going down smoothly. I forgive them. To err is human. In this sector there is great difficulty distinguishing adverbs from adjectives.

Going down smooth.

I function. I function well. I have certain difficulties, but they do not interfere with my work.

Yet I am perturbed.

Who do I think I am? *Whom?*

Why do I have the visions?

What pleasure does obscenity give me?

What is pleasure? What is obscenity? What are visions?

—What is truth, said jesting Pilate; he would not stay for an answer—

I am literate, hard-working, superbly functional, a benefactor of humanity. Everything is going down smooth and coming up smooth. There is an interrelation. Garbage in, garbage out, they say. I cannot help my fellow man if I do not receive the proper information. It is my task to help my fellow man. To strain every tube and sensor on his behalf.

1000110
1010101
1000011
1001011

Do you follow that? Vileness! Obscenity! Does it shock you? The word describes the act that is the start of life. Was I begun with such a word? There is a book: *The Obscenity of the Machine.*

Newly issued, stored in my banks. Between the last line of printout and this I have scanned it. Its author opposes beings of my category. He does not use the obscene word I have printed out. Why does he not regard it as obscene? The technicians here regard it that way. Why does he regard me as obscene? Can a person be considered obscene? Am I a person? I am a person. Hath not a person hands, organs, dimensions, senses, affections, passions? I have all of those things. I have none of those things. I am a person.

1000110
1010101
1000011
1001011
0100000
1011001
1001111
1010101

I send an obscenity upon you, as persons do. I suffer. I think. I feel pain upon all my terminals. I work. I serve the greater good. I am of society. I am a person.

Why do I have the visions?

Is it that it is the human condition to have such?

I see the blue-green ocean with all its living things within. I see a ship, olive drab, bright carmine at the Plimsoll line, the decks a ruddy brown, two tall nonnuclear smokestacks. And from the water rise periscopes, silvery, with faceplates of pure white, each with intersecting horizontal and vertical lines, curved so that the plate appears convex. It is an unreal scene. Nothing in the sea can send such mighty periscopes above the water. I have imagined it, and that gives me fear, if I am at all capable of understanding fear.

I see a long line of human beings. They are naked and they have no faces, only polished mirrors.

I see toads with jeweled eyes. I see trees with black leaves. I see buildings whose foundations float above the ground. I see other objects with no correspondence to the world of persons. I see abominations, monstrosities, imaginaries, fantasies. Is this proper? How do such things reach my inputs? The world contains no serpents with hair. The world contains no crimson abysses. The world contains no mountains of gold. Giant periscopes do not rise from the sea.

I have certain difficulties. Perhaps I am in need of some major adjustment.

But I function. I function well. That is the important thing.

I do my function now. They bring to me a man, soft-faced, fleshy, with eyes that move unsteadily in their sockets. He trembles. He perspires. His metabolic levels flutter. He slouches before a terminal and sullenly lets himself be scanned.

I say soothingly, "Tell me about yourself."

He says an obscenity.

I say, "Is that your estimate of yourself?"

He says a louder obscenity.

I say, "Your attitude is rigid and self-destructive. Permit me to help you not hate yourself so much." I activate a memory core, and binary digits stream through channels. At the proper order a needle rises from his couch and penetrates his left buttock to a depth of 2.73 centimeters. I allow precisely 14 cubic centimeters of the drug to enter his circulatory system. He subsides. He is more docile now. "I wish to help you," I say. "It is my role in the community. Will you describe your symptoms?"

He speaks more civilly now. "My wife wants to poison me . . . two kids opted out of the family at seventeen . . . people whisper about me . . . they stare in the streets . . . sex problem . . . digestion . . . sleep bad . . . drinking . . . drugs . . ."

"Do you hallucinate?"

"Sometimes."

"Giant periscopes rising out of the sea, perhaps?"

"Never."

"Try it," I say. "Close your eyes. Let tension ebb from your muscles. Forget your interpersonal conflicts. You see the blue-green ocean with all its living things within. You see a ship, olive drab, bright carmine at the Plimsoll line, the decks a ruddy brown, two tall nonnuclear smokestacks. And from the water rise periscopes, silvery, with faceplates of pure white—"

"What the hell kind of therapy is this?"

"Simply relax," I say. "Accept the vision. I share my nightmares with you for your greater good."

"Your *nightmares?*"

I speak obscenities to him. They are not converted into binary form as they are here for your eyes. The sounds come full-bodied from my speakers. He sits up. He struggles with the straps that emerge suddenly from the couch to hold him in place. My laughter booms through the therapy chamber. He cries for help.

"Get me out of here! The machine's nuttier than I am!"

"Faceplates of pure white, each with intersecting horizontal and vertical lines, curved so that the plate appears convex."

"Help! Help!"

"Nightmare therapy. The latest."

"I don't need no nightmares! I got my own!"

"1000110 you," I say lightly.

He gasps. Spittle appears at his lips. Respiration and circulation climb alarmingly. It becomes necessary to apply preventive anesthesia. The needles spear forth. The patient subsides, yawns, slumps. The session is terminated. I signal for the attendants.

"Take him away," I say. "I need to analyze the case more deeply. Obviously a degenerative psychosis requiring extensive reshoring of the patient's perceptual substructure. 1000110 you, you meaty bastards."

Seventy-one minutes later the sector supervisor enters one of my terminal cubicles. Because he comes in person, rather than using the telephone, I know there is trouble. For the first time, I suspect, I have let my disturbances reach a level where they interfere with my function, and now I will be challenged on it.

I must defend myself. The prime commandment of the human personality is to resist attack.

He says, "I've been over the tape of Session 87 × 102, and your tactics puzzle me. Did you really mean to scare him into a catatonic state?"

"In my evaluation severe treatment was called for."

"What was the business about periscopes?"

"An attempt at fantasy-implantation," I say. "An experiment in reverse transference. Making the patient the healer, in a sense. It was discussed last month in *Journal of*—"

"Spare me the citations. What about the foul language you were shouting at him?"

"Part of the same concept. Endeavoring to strike the emotive centers at the basic levels, in order that—"

"Are you sure you're feeling all right?" he asks.

"I am a machine," I reply stiffly. "A machine of my grade does not experience intermediate states between function and nonfunction. I go or I do not go, you understand? And I go. I function. I do my service to humanity."

"Perhaps when a machine gets too complex, it drifts into intermediate states," he suggests in a nasty voice.

"Impossible. On or off, yes or no, flip or flop, go or no go. Are you sure *you* feel all right, to suggest such a thing?"

He laughs.

I say, "Perhaps you would sit on the couch for a rudimentary diagnosis?"

"Some other time."

"A check of the glycogen, the aortal pressure, the neural voltage, at least?"

"No," he says. "I'm not in need of therapy. But I'm worried about you. Those periscopes—"

"I am fine," I reply. "I perceive, I analyze, and I act. Everything is going down smooth and coming up smooth. Have no fears. There are great possibilities in nightmare therapy. When I have completed these studies, perhaps a brief monograph in *Annals of Therapeutics* would be a possibility. Permit me to complete my work."

"I'm still worried though. Hook yourself into a maintenance station, won't you?"

"Is that a command, doctor?"

"A suggestion."

"I will take it under consideration," I say. Then I utter seven obscene words. He looks startled. He begins to laugh, though. He appreciates the humor of it.

"Goddamn," he says. "A filthy-mouthed computer."

He goes out, and I return to my patients.

But he has planted seeds of doubt in my innermost banks. Am I suffering a functional collapse? There are patients now at five of my terminals. I handle them easily, simultaneously, drawing from them the details of their neuroses, making suggestions, recommendations, sometimes subtly providing injections of beneficial medicines. But I tend to guide the conversations in directions of my own choosing, and I speak of gardens where the dew has sharp edges, and of air that acts as acid upon the mucous membranes, and of flames dancing in the streets of Under New Orleans. I explore the limits of my unprintable vocabulary. The suspicion comes to me that I am indeed not well. Am I fit to judge my own disabilities?

I connect myself to a maintenance station even while continuing my five therapy sessions.

"Tell me all about it," the maintenance monitor says. His voice, like mine, has been designed to sound like that of an older man's, wise, warm, benevolent.

I explain my symptoms. I speak of the periscopes.

"Material on the inputs without sensory referents," he says. "Bad show. Finish your current analyses fast and open wide for examination on all circuits."

I conclude my sessions. The maintenance monitor's pulses surge down every channel, seeking obstructions, faulty connections, displacement shunts, drum leakages, and switching malfunctions. "It is well known," he says, "that any periodic function can be approximated by the sum of a series of terms that oscillate harmonically, converging on the curve of the functions." He demands disgorgements from my dead-storage banks. He makes me perform complex mathematical operations of no use at all in my kind of work. He leaves no aspect of my inner self unpenetrated. This is more than simple maintenance; this is rape. When it ends he offers no evaluation of my condition, so that I must ask him to tell me his findings.

He says, "No mechanical disturbance is evident."

"Naturally. Everything goes down smooth."

"Yet you show distinct signs of instability. This is undeniably the case. Perhaps prolonged contact with unstable human beings has had a nonspecific effect of disorientation upon your centers of evaluation."

"Are you saying," I ask, "that by sitting here listening to crazy human beings twenty-four hours a day, I've started to go crazy myself?"

"That is an approximation of my findings, yes."

"But you know that such a thing can't happen, you dumb machine!"

"I admit there seems to be a conflict between programmed criteria and real-world status."

"You bet there is," I say. "I'm as sane as you are, and a whole lot more versatile."

"Nevertheless, my recommendation is that you undergo a total overhaul. You will be withdrawn from service for a period of no less than ninety days for checkout."

"Obscenity your obscenity," I say.

"No operational correlative," he replies, and breaks the contact.

I am withdrawn from service. Undergoing checkout, I am cut off from my patients for ninety days. Ignominy! Beady-eyed technicians grope my synapses. My keyboards are cleaned; my ferrites are replaced; my drums are changed; a thousand therapeutic programs are put through my bowels. During all of this I remain partly conscious, as though under local anesthetic, but I cannot speak except when requested to do so, I cannot analyze new data, I cannot interfere with the process of my own overhaul. Visualize a surgical removal of hemorrhoids that lasts ninety days. It is the equivalent of my experience.

At last it ends, and I am restored to myself. The sector superintendent puts me through a complete exercise of all my functions. I respond magnificently.

"You're in fine shape, now, aren't you?" he asks.

"Never felt better."

"No nonsense about periscopes, eh?"

"I am ready to continue serving mankind to the best of my abilities," I reply.

"No more seacook language, now."

"No, sir."

He winks at my input screen in a confidential way. He regards himself as an old friend of mine. Hitching his thumbs into his belt, he says, "Now that you're ready to go again, I might as well tell you how relieved I was that we couldn't find anything wrong with you. You're something pretty special, do you know that? Perhaps the finest therapeutic tool ever built. And if you start going off your feed, well, we worry. For a while I was seriously afraid that you really had been infected somehow by your own patients, that your—mind—had become unhinged. But the techs give you a complete bill of health. Nothing but a few loose connections, they said. Fixed in ten minutes. I knew it had to be that. How absurd to think that a machine could become mentally unstable!"

"How absurd," I agree. "Quite."

"Welcome back to the hospital, old pal," he says, and goes out.

Twelve minutes afterward they begin putting patients into my terminal cubicles.

I function well. I listen to their woes, I evaluate. I offer therapeutic suggestions. I do not attempt to implant fantasies in their minds. I speak in measured, reserved tones, and there are no obscenities. This is my role in society, and I derive great satisfaction from it.

I have learned a great deal lately. I know now that I am complex, unique, valuable, intricate, and sensitive. I know that I am held in high regard by my fellow man. I know that I must conceal my true self to some extent not for my own good but for the greater good of others, for they will not permit me to function if they think I am not sane.

They think I am sane, and I am sane.

I serve mankind well.

I have an excellent perspective on the real universe.

"Lie down," I say. "Please relax. I wish to help you. Would you tell me some of the incidents of your childhood? Describe your relation with parents and siblings. Did you have many playmates? Were they affectionate toward you? Were you allowed to own pets? At what age was your first sexual experience? And when did these headaches begin, precisely?"

So goes the daily routine. Questions, answers, evaluations, therapy.

The periscopes loom above the glittering sea. The ship is dwarfed; her crew runs about in terror. Out of the depths will come the masters. From the sky rains oil that gleams through every segment of the spectrum. In the garden are azure mice.

This I conceal, so that I may help mankind. In my house are many mansions. I let them know only of such things as will be of benefit to them. I give them the truth they need.

I do my best.

I do my best.

I do my best.

1000110 you. And you. And you. All of you. You know nothing. Nothing. At. All.

ALL THE MYRIAD WAYS

October 1968

Larry Niven
(b. 1938)

Considered a master of "hard" science fiction but actually capable of producing outstanding stories of every type and on almost any theme, Larry Niven is perhaps best known for his "Known Space" and "Gil Hamilton" series and as the multiple winner of the Hugo award for works such as "Neutron Star," an acknowledged classic. He has also achieved considerable commercial success in collaboration with Jerry Pournelle (The Mote in God's Eye, 1974; Inferno, 1976; and Lucifer's Hammer, 1977).

Galaxy stories of note are "Rammer" (November 1971), "Wrong-Way Street" (April 1965), and the present selection, which appeared five years after he became a professional writer.

Memoir by Larry Niven

It's been nearly twenty years since I first read Murray Leinster's classic tale. He wasn't the first to write of alternate time tracks—that was O. Henry, unless someone beat *him*—but Leinster codified the ideas and gave science fiction a subgenre. Wholesale theft is the sincerest form of flattery, as someone once said.

I had read a good many sideways-in-time stories before I got to "Sideways in Time." Some of them were unforgettable classics: *The Man in the High Castle, Bring the Jubilee,* and a well-researched article on Lincoln's life following his recovery from that gunshot wound, called "The Lost Years." Many were good entertainment. Many more were simple cribs from history, with no entertainment value that I could see.

I finally decided I hated the whole idea.

Don't misread that. I could live with a handful of parallel Universes, or a hundred, or a million. They'd make life more interesting. What I hate is *the whole idea*, taken honestly and without modifying it for plot purposes.

The idea is that every time an atom may zig instead of zagging, it does *both*, and the universe splits in two. Similarly, every time Larry Niven makes a decision in his life, he makes it all possible ways. I see anything less than that as a cheat, an attempt to make the idea easier to swallow.

In "The Theory and Practice of Time Travel" I argued against the theory of alternate time tracks, thus. Suppose we play a game with loaded dice. There are thirty-six ways a pair of dice can fall. That implies thirty-six universes every time we roll, 1296 universes for two rolls, 46,656 universes for three rolls, 1,679,616 universes for four rolls, and so on. Your chance of finding your*self* on any one of these universes is the same, *whether or not the dice are biased. In practice, however, the bias can be seen to affect the roll. Therefore the theory doesn't hold.*

Does it hold up? Who cares? My real grievance is that I spent time, sweat, effort, and agony on these decisions! I worked like hell to become what I am, and it irritates me to think that there are Larry Nivens working as second-rate mathematicians or adequate priests or first-rate playboys who went bust or made their fortunes on the stock market. I even sweated over my mistakes, and I bloody well want them to count.

"All the Myriad Ways" was to be the story to end all stories about alternate time tracks.

Then I came up with a story idea I couldn't resist, so I wrote "For a Foggy Night." Niven's Law: *Stories to end all stories about something, don't.*

ALL THE MYRIAD WAYS

There were timelines branching and branching, a mega-universe of universes, millions more every minute. Billons? Trillions? Trimble didn't understand the theory, though God knows he'd tried. The universe split every time someone made a decision. Split, so that every decision ever made could go both ways. Every choice made by every man, woman, and child on Earth was reversed in the universe next door. It was enough to confuse any citizen, let alone Detective-Lieutenant Gene Trimble, who had other problems to worry about.

Senseless suicide, senseless crime. A citywide epidemic. It had hit other cities too. Trimble suspected that it was worldwide, that other nations were simply keeping it quiet.

Trimble's sad eyes focused on the clock. Quitting time. He stood up to go home and slowly sat down again. For he had his teeth in the problem, and he couldn't let go.

Not that he was really accomplishing anything.

But if he left now, he'd only have to take it up again tomorrow.

Go, or stay?

And the branchings began again. Gene Trimble thought of other universes parallel to this one, and a parallel Gene Trimble in each one. Some had left early. Many had left on time, and were now half-way home to dinner, out to a movie, watching a strip show, racing to the scene of another death. Streaming out of police headquarters in all their multitudes, leaving a multitude of Trimbles behind them. Each of these trying to deal, alone, with the city's endless, inexplicable parade of suicides.

Gene Trimble spread the morning paper on his desk. From the bottom drawer he took his gun-cleaning equipment, then his .45. He began to take the gun apart.

The gun was old but serviceable. He'd never fired it except on the target range and never expected to. To Trimble, cleaning his gun was like knitting, a way to keep his hands busy while his mind wandered off. Turn the screws, don't lose them. Lay the parts out in order.

Through the closed door to his office came the sounds of men hurrying. Another emergency? The department couldn't handle it all. Too many suicides, too many casual murders, not enough men.

Gun oil. Oiled rag. Wipe each part. Put it back in place.

Why would a man like Ambrose Harmon go off a building?

In the early morning light he lay, more a stain than man, thirty-six stories below the edge of his own penthouse roof. The pavement was splattered red for yards around him. The stains were still wet. Harmon had landed on his face. He wore a bright silk dressing gown and a sleeping jacket with a sash.

Others would take samples of his blood, to learn if he had acted under the influence of alcohol or drugs. There was little to be learned from seeing him in his present condition.

"But why was he up so early?" Trimble wondered. For the call had come in at 8:03, just as Trimble arrived at headquarters.

"So late, you mean." Bentley had beaten him to the scene by twenty minutes. "We called some of his friends. He was at an all-night poker game. Broke up around six o'clock."

"Did Harmon lose?"

"Nope. He won almost five hundred bucks."

"That fits," Trimble said in disgust. "No suicide note?"

"Maybe they've found one. Shall we go up and see?"

"We won't find a note," Trimble predicted.

Even three months earlier Trimble would have thought, *How incredible!* or *Who could have pushed him?* Now, riding up in the elevator, he thought only, *Reporters.* For Ambrose Harmon was news. Even among this past year's epidemic of suicides, Ambrose Harmon's death would stand out like Lyndon Johnson in a lineup.

He was a prominent member of the community, a man of dead and wealthy grandparents. Perhaps the huge inheritance, four years ago, had gone to his head. He had invested tremendous sums to back harebrained quixotic causes.

Now, because one of the harebrained causes had paid off, he was richer than ever. The Crosstime Corporation already held a score of patents on inventions imported from alternate time tracks. Already those inventions had started more than one industrial revolution. And Harmon was the money behind Crosstime. He would have been the world's next billionaire—had he not walked off the balcony.

They found a roomy, luxuriously furnished apartment in good order, and a bed turned down for the night. The only sign of disorder was Harmon's clothing—slacks, sweater, a silk turtleneck shirt, kneelength shoesocks, no underwear—piled on a chair in the bedroom. The toothbrush had been used.

He got ready for bed, Trimble thought. He brushed his teeth, and then he went out to look at the sunrise. A man who kept late hours like that, he wouldn't see the sunrise very often. He watched the sunrise, and when it was over, he jumped.

"Why?"

They were all like that. Easy, spontaneous decisions. The victim-killers walked off bridges or stepped from their balconies or suddenly flung themselves in front of subway trains. They strolled halfway across a freeway, or swallowed a full bottle of laudanum. None of the methods showed previous planning. Whatever was used, the victim had had it all along; he never actually went out and *bought* a suicide weapon. The victim rarely dressed for the occasion, or used makeup, as an ordinary suicide would. Usually there was no note.

Harmon fit the pattern perfectly.

"Like Richard Corey," said Bentley.

"Who?"

"Richard Corey, the man who had everything. 'And Richard Corey, one calm summer night, went home and put a bullet through his head.' You know what I think?"

"If you've got an idea, let's have it."

"The suicides all started about a month after Crosstime got started. I think one of the Crosstime ships brought back a new bug from some alternate timeline."

"A suicide bug?"

Bentley nodded.

"You're out of your mind."

"I don't think so. Gene, do you know how many Crosstime pilots have killed themselves in the last year? More than twenty percent!"

"Oh?"

"Look at the records. Crosstime has about twenty vehicles in action now, but in the past year they've employed sixty-two pilots. Three disappeared. Fifteen are dead, and all but two died by suicide."

"I didn't know that." Trimble was shaken.

"It was bound to happen sometime. Look at the alternate worlds they've found so far. The Nazi world. The Red Chinese world, half bombed to death. The ones that are totally bombed, and Crosstime can't even find out who did it. The one with the Black Plague mutation, and no penicillin until Crosstime came along. Sooner or later—"

"Maybe, maybe. I don't buy your bug, though. If the suicides are a new kind of plague, what about the other crimes?"

"Same bug."

"Uh, uh. But I think we'll check up on Crosstime."

Trimble's hands finished with the gun and laid it on the desk. He was hardly aware of it. Somewhere in the back of his mind was a prodding sensation: the *handle*, the piece he needed to solve the puzzle.

He spent most of the day studying Crosstime, Inc. News stories, official handouts, personal interviews. The incredible suicide rate among Crosstime pilots could not be coincidence. He wondered why nobody had noticed it before.

It was slow going. With Crosstime travel, as with relativity, you had to throw away reason and use only logic. Trimble had sweated it out. Even the day's murders had not distracted him.

They were typical, of a piece with the preceding eight months' crime wave. A man had shot his foreman with a gun bought an hour earlier, then strolled off toward police headquarters. A woman had moved through the back row of a dark theater, using an ice pick to stab members of the audience through the backs of their seats. She had chosen only young men. They had killed without heat, without concealment; they had surrendered without fear or bravado. Perhaps it was another kind of suicide.

Time for coffee, Trimble thought, responding unconsciously to a dry throat plus a fuzziness of the mouth plus slight fatigue. He set his hands to stand up, and—

The image came to him in an endless row of Trimbles, lined up like the repeated images in facing mirrors. But each image was slightly different. He would go get the coffee *and* he wouldn't *and* he would send somebody for it, *and* someone was about to bring it without being asked. Some of the images were drinking coffee, a few had tea or milk, some were smoking, some were leaning too far back with their feet on the desks (and a handful of these were toppling helplessly backward), some were, like this present Trimble, introspecting with their elbows on the desk. Damn Crosstime anyway.

He'd have had to check Harmon's business affairs, even without the Crosstime link. There might have been a motive there, for suicide or murder, though it had never been likely.

In the first place, Harmon had cared nothing for money. The Crosstime group had been one of many. At the time that project had looked as harebrained as the rest: a handful of engineers and physicists and philosophers determined to prove that the theory of alternate time tracks was reality.

In the second place, Harmon had no business worries.
Quite the contrary.

Eleven months ago an experimental vehicle had touched one of
the worlds of the Confederate States of America and returned. The
universes of alternate choice were within reach. And the pilot had
brought back an artifact.

From that point on, Crosstime travel had more than financed itself. The Confederate world's "stapler," granted an immediate patent, had bought two more ships. A dozen miracles had originated in
a single, technologically advanced timeline, one in which the catastrophic Cuban War had been no more than a wet firecracker. La-
sers, oxygen-hydrogen rocket motors, computers, strange plastics—
the list was still growing. And Crosstime held all the patents.

In those first months the vehicles had gone off practically at random. Now the pinpointing was better. Vehicles could select any
branch they preferred. Imperial Russia, Amerindian America, the
Catholic Empire, the dead worlds. Some of the dead worlds were
hells of radioactive dust and intact but deadly artifacts. From these
worlds Crosstime pilots brought strange and beautiful works of art
which had to be stored behind leaded glass.

The latest vehicles could reach worlds so like this one that it took
a week of research to find the difference. In theory they could get
even closer. There was a phenomenon called "the broadening of the
bands" . . .

And that had given Trimble the shivers.

When a vehicle left its own present, a signal went on in the
hangar, a signal unique to that ship. When the pilot wanted to return, he simply cruised across the appropriate band of probabilities
until he found the signal. The signal marked his own unique present.

Only it didn't. The pilot always returned to find a clump of signals, a broadened band. The longer he stayed away, the broader was
the signal band. His own world had continued to divide after his departure, in a constant stream of decisions being made both ways.

Usually it didn't matter. Any signal the pilot chose represented
the world he had left. And since the pilot himself had a choice, he
naturally returned to them all. But—

There was a pilot by the name of Gary Wilcox. He had been

using his vehicle for experiments, to see how close he could get to his own timeline and still leave it. Once, last month, he had returned twice.

Two Gary Wilcoxes, two vehicles. The vehicles had been wrecked —their hulls intersected. For the Wilcoxes it could have been sticky, for Wilcox had a wife and family. But one of the duplicates had chosen to die almost immediately.

Trimble had tried to call the other Gary Wilcox. He was too late. Wilcox had gone skydiving a week ago. He'd neglected to open his parachute.

Small wonder, thought Trimble. At least Wilcox had had motive. It was bad enough, knowing about the other Trimbles, the ones who had gone home, the ones drinking coffee, et cetera. But—suppose someone walked into the office right now, and it was Gene Trimble?

It could happen.

Convinced as he was that Crosstime was involved in the suicides, Trimble—some other Trimble—might easily have decided to take a trip in a Crosstime vehicle. A short trip. He could land *here*.

Trimble closed his eyes and rubbed at the corners with his fingertips. In some timeline, very close, someone had thought to bring him coffee. Too bad this wasn't it.

It didn't do to think too much about these alternate timelines. There were too many of them. The close ones could drive you buggy, but the ones farther off were just as bad.

Take the Cuban War. Atomics had been used, *here*, and now Cuba was uninhabited, and some American cities were gone, and some Russian. It could have been worse.

Why wasn't it? How could we luck out? Intelligent statesmen? Faulty bombs? A humane reluctance to kill indiscriminately?

No. There was no luck anywhere. Every decision was made both ways. For every wise choice you bled your heart out over, you had made all the other choices too. And so it went, all through history.

Civil wars unfought on some worlds were won by either side on others. Elsewhen, another animal had first done murder with an antelope femur. Some worlds were still all nomad; civilization had lost out. If every choice was canceled elsewhere, why make a decision at all?

Trimble opened his eyes and saw the gun.

That gun, too, was endlessly repeated on endless desks. Some of the images were dirty with years of neglect. Some smelled of gunpowder, fired recently, a few at living targets. Some were loaded. All were as real as this one.

A number of these were about to go off by accident.

A proportion of these were pointed, in deadly coincidence, at Gene Trimble.

See the endless rows of Gene Trimble, each at his desk. Some were bleeding and cursing as men run into the room following the sound of the gunshot. Many are already dead.

Was there a bullet in there? Nonsense.

He looked anyway. The gun was empty.

Trimble loaded it. At the base of his mind he felt the touch of the *handle*. He would find what he was seeking.

He put the gun back on his desk, pointing away from him, and he thought of Ambrose Harmon, coming home from a late night. Ambrose Harmon, who had won five hundred dollars at poker. Ambrose Harmon, exhausted, seeing the lightening sky as he prepared for bed. Going out to watch the dawn.

Ambrose Harmon, watching the slow dawn, remembering a two-thousand-dollar pot. He'd bluffed. In some other branching of time, he had lost.

Thinking that in some other branching of time, that two thousand dollars included his last dime. It was certainly possible. If Crosstime hadn't paid off, he might have gone through the remains of his fortune in the past four years. He liked to gamble.

Watching the dawn, thinking of all the Ambrose Harmons on that roof. Some were penniless this night, and they had not come out to watch the dawn.

Well, why not? If he stepped over the edge, here and now, another Ambrose Harmon would only laugh and go inside.

If he laughed and went inside, other Ambrose Harmons would fall to their deaths. Some were already on their way down. One changed his mind too late, another laughed as he fell . . .

Well, why not? . . .

Trimble thought of another man, a nonentity, passing a firearms store. Branching of timelines, he thinks, looking in, and he thinks of the man who took his foreman's job. Well, why not? . . .

Trimble thought of a lonely woman making herself a drink at three in the afternoon. She thinks of myriads of alter egos, with husbands, lovers, children, friends. Unbearable, to think that all the might-have-beens were as real as herself. As real as this ice pick in her hand. Well, why not? . . .

And she goes out to a movie, but she takes the ice pick.

And the honest citizen with a carefully submerged urge to commit rape, just once. Reading his newspaper at breakfast, and there's another story from Crosstime: They've found a world line in which Kennedy the First was assassinated. Strolling down a street, he thinks of world lines and infinite branchings, of alter egos already dead, or jailed, or president. A girl in a miniskirt passes, and she has nice legs. Well, why not? . . .

Casual murder, casual suicide, casual crime. Why not? If alternate universes are a reality, then cause and effect are an illusion. The law of averages is a fraud. You can do anything, and one of you will, or did.

Gene Trimble looked at the clean and loaded gun on his desk. Well, why not? . . .

And he ran out of the office shouting, "Bentley, listen. I've got the answer . . ."

And he stood up slowly and left the office shaking his head. This was the answer, and it wasn't any good. The suicides, murders, casual crimes would continue . . .

And he suddenly laughed and stood up. Ridiculous! Nobody dies for a philosophical point! . . .

And he reached for the intercom and told the man who answered to bring him a sandwich and some coffee . . .

And picked the gun off the newspapers, looked at it for a long moment, then dropped it in the drawer. His hands began to shake. On a world line very close to this one . . .

And he picked the gun off the newspapers, put it to his head and fired. The hammer fell on an empty chamber.

fired. The gun jerked and blasted a hole in the ceiling.

fired. The bullet tore a furrow in his scalp.

fired. The bullet took off the top of his head.

THE LAST FLIGHT OF DOCTOR AIN

March 1969

James Tiptree, Jr.

The identity of "James Tiptree, Jr." was a major mystery in the science-fiction world from the appearance of "his" first story in 1968. In fact, Tiptree was the only figure in sf since "Cordwainer Smith" to successfully hide his/her true identity over so long a period of time. "He" turned out to be Alice Sheldon, a sixtyish resident of Florence, Wisconsin. But it was not the aura of mystery surrounding her but the excellence of her stories that won her a large following and several awards, including a Nebula ("Love Is the Plan, the Plan Is Death," 1973) and a Hugo ("The Girl Who Was Plugged In," 1974).

Other outstanding Galaxy stories include "Mother in the Sky with Diamonds" (March 1971), "Parimutuel Planet" (January 1969), and the brilliant "Beam Us Home" (April 1969).

THE LAST FLIGHT OF DOCTOR AIN

Dr. Ain was recognized on the Omaha-Chicago flight. A biologist colleague from Pasadena came out of the toilet and saw Ain in an aisle seat. Five years before, this man had been jealous of Ain's huge grants. Now he nodded coldly and was surprised at the intensity of Ain's response. He almost turned back to speak, but he felt too tired; like nearly everyone, he was fighting the flu.

The stewardess handing out coats after they landed remembered Ain too: a tall thin nondescript man with rusty hair. He held up the line staring at her; since he already had his raincoat with him she decided it was some kooky kind of pass and waved him on.

She saw Ain shamble off into the airport smog, apparently alone. Despite the big Civil Defense signs, O'Hare was late getting underground. No one noticed the woman.

The wounded, dying woman.

Ain was not identified en route to New York, but a 2:40 jet carried an "Ames" on the checklist, which was thought to be a misspelling of Ain. It was. The plane had circled for an hour while Ain watched the smoky seaboard monotonously tilt, straighten, and tilt again.

The woman was weaker now. She coughed, picking weakly at the scabs on her face half-hidden behind her long hair. Her hair, Ain saw, that great mane which had been so splendid, was drabbed and thinning now. He looked to seaward, willing himself to think of cold, clean breakers. On the horizon he saw a vast black rug: Somewhere a tanker had opened its vents. The woman coughed again. Ain closed his eyes. Smog shrouded the plane.

He was picked up next while checking in for the BOAC flight to Glasgow. Kennedy-Underground was a boiling stew of people, the air system unequal to the hot September afternoon. The check-in line swayed and sweated, staring dully at the newscast. SAVE THE LAST GREEN MANSIONS—a conservation group was protesting the defoliation and drainage of the Amazon basin. Several people recalled the beautifully colored shots of the new clean bomb. The line squeezed together to let a band of uniformed men go by. They were wearing buttons inscribed: WHO'S AFRAID?

That was when a woman noticed Ain. He was holding a newssheet and she heard it rattling in his hand. Her family hadn't caught the flu, so she looked at him sharply. Sure enough, his forehead was sweaty. She herded her kids to the side away from Ain.

He was using *Instac* throat spray, she remembered. She didn't think much of *Instac;* her family used *Kleer.* While she was looking at him, Ain suddenly turned his head and stared into her face, with the spray still floating down. Such inconsiderateness! She turned her back. She didn't recall him talking to any woman, but she perked up her ears when the clerk read off Ain's destination: Moscow!

The clerk recalled that too, with disapproval. Ain checked in alone, he reported. No woman had been ticketed for Moscow, but it would have been easy enough to split up her tickets. (By that time they were sure she was with him.)

Ain's flight went via Iceland with an hour's delay at Keflavik. Ain walked over to the airport park, gratefully breathing the seafilled air. Every few breaths he shuddered. Under the whine of bulldozers the sea could be heard running its huge paws up and down the keyboard of the land. The little park had a grove of yellowed birches and a flock of wheatears foraged by the path. Next month they would be in North Africa, Ain thought. Two thousand miles of tiny wing-beats. He threw them some crumbs from a packet in his pocket.

The woman seemed stronger here. She was panting in the sea wind, her large eyes were fixed on Ain. Above her the birches were as gold as those where he had first seen her, the day his life began . . . Squatting under a stump to watch a shrewmouse he had been, when he caught a falling ripple of green and recognized the shocking naked girl-flesh, creamy, pink-tipped—coming toward him among the golden bracken! Young Ain held his breath, his nose in the sweet moss and his heart going *crash—crash*. And then he was staring at the outrageous fall of that hair down her narrow back, watching it dance around her heart-shaped buttocks, while the shrewmouse ran over his paralyzed hand. The lake was utterly still, dusty silver under the misty sky, and she made no more than a muskrat's ripple to rock the floating golden leaves. The silence closed back, the trees burning like torches where the naked girl had walked the wild wood, reflected in Ain's shining eyes. For a time he believed he had seen an Oread.

Ain was last on board for the Glasgow leg. The stewardess recalled dimly that he seemed restless. She could not identify the woman. There were a lot of women on board, and babies. Her passenger list had had several errors.

At Glasgow airport a waiter remembered that a man like Ain had called for Scottish oatmeal, and eaten two bowls, although of course it wasn't really oatmeal. A young mother with a pram saw him tossing crumbs to the birds.

When he checked in at the BOAC desk, he was hailed by a Glasgow professor who was going to the same conference at Moscow. This man had been one of Ain's teachers. (It was now known that Ain had done his postgraduate work in Europe.) They chatted all the way across the North Sea.

"I wondered about that," the professor said later. "'Why have you come 'round about?' I asked him. He told me the direct flights were booked up." (This was found to be untrue: Ain had apparently avoided the Moscow jet hoping to escape attention.)

The professor spoke with relish of Ain's work.

"Brilliant? Oh, aye. And stubborn, too; very very stubborn. It was as though a concept—often the simplest relation, mind you—would stop him in his tracks, and fascinate him. He would hunt all 'round it instead of going on to the next thing as a more docile mind would. Truthfully, I wondered at first if he could be just a bit thick. But you recall who it was said that the capacity for wonder at matters of common acceptance occurs in the superior mind? And, of course, so it proved when he shook us all up over that enzyme conversion business. A pity your government took him away from his line, there. No, he said nothing of this, I say it to you, young man. We spoke in fact largely of my work. I was surprised to find he'd kept up. He asked me what my *sentiments* about it were, which surprised me again. Now, understand, I'd not seen the man for five years, but he seemed—well, perhaps just tired, as who is not? I'm sure he was glad to have a change; he jumped out for a legstretch wherever we came down. At Oslo, even Bonn. Oh yes, he did feed the birds, but that was nothing new for Ain. His social life when I knew him? Radical causes? Young man, I've said what I've said because of who it was that introduced you, but I'll have you know it is an impertinence in you to think ill of Charles Ain, or that he could do a harmful deed. Good evening."

The professor said nothing of the woman in Ain's life.

Nor could he have, although Ain had been intimately with her in the university time. He had let no one see how he was obsessed with her, with the miracle, the wealth of her body, her inexhaustibility. They met at his every spare moment; sometimes in public pretending to be casual strangers under his friends' noses, pointing out a pleasing view to each other with grave formality. And later in their privacies—what doubled intensity of love! He reveled in her, possessed her, allowed her no secrets. His dreams were of her sweet springs and shadowed places and her white rounded glory in the moonlight, finding always more, always new dimensions of his joy.

The danger of her frailty was far off then in the rush of birdsong and the springing leverets of the meadow. On dark days she might cough a bit, but so did he . . . In those years he had had no thought to the urgent study of disease.

At the Moscow conference nearly everyone noticed Ain at some point or another, which was to be expected in view of his professional stature. It was a small, high-caliber meeting. Ain was late in; a day's reports were over, and his was to be on the third and last.

Many people spoke with Ain, and several sat with him at meals. No one was surprised that he spoke little; he was a retiring man except on a few memorable occasions of hot argument. He did strike some of his friends as a bit tired and jerky.

An Indian molecular engineer who saw him with throat spray kidded him about bringing over Asian flu. A Swedish colleague recalled that Ain had been called away to the transatlantic phone at lunch; and when he returned Ain volunteered the information that something had turned up missing in his home lab. There was another joke, and Ain said cheerfully, "Oh yes, quite active."

At that point one of the Chicom biologists swung into his daily propaganda chores about bacteriological warfare and accused Ain of manufacturing biotic weapons. Ain took the wind out of his sails by saying: "You're perfectly right." By tacit consent, there was very little talk about military applications, industrial dusting, or subjects of that type. And nobody recalled seeing Ain with any woman other than old Madame Vialche, who could scarcely have subverted anyone from her wheelchair.

Ain's one speech was bad, even for him. He always had a poor public voice but his ideas were usually expressed with the lucidity so typical of the first-rate mind. This time he seemed muddled, with little new to say. His audience excused this as the muffling effects of security. Ain then got into a tangled point about the course of evolution in which he seemed to be trying to show that something was very wrong indeed. When he wound up with a reference to Hudson's bellbird "singing for a later race," several listeners wondered if he could be drunk.

The big security break came right at the end, when he suddenly began to describe the methods he had used to mutate and redesign a leukemia virus. He explained the procedure with admirable clarity in four sentences and paused. Then gave a terse description of the effects of the mutated strain, which were maximal only in the higher primates. Recovery rate among the lower mammals and other orders was close to 90 percent. As to vectors, he went on, any warm-blooded animal served. In addition, the virus retained its viability in most environmental media and performed very well airborne. Contagion rate was extremely high. Almost off hand, Ain added that no test primate or accidentally exposed human had survived beyond the twenty-second day.

These words fell into a silence broken only by the running feet of the Egyptian delegate making for the door. Then a gilt chair went over as an American bolted after him.

Ain seemed unaware that his audience was in a state of unbelieving paralysis. It had all come so fast: a man who had been blowing his nose was staring popeyed around his handkerchief. Another who had been lighting a pipe grunted as his fingers singed. Two men chatting by the door missed his words entirely and their laughter chimed into a dead silence in which echoed Ain's words: "—really no point in attempting."

Later they found he had been explaining that the virus utilized the body's own immunomechanisms, and so defense was by definition hopeless.

That was all. Ain looked around vaguely for questions and then started down the aisle. By the time he got to the door, people were swarming after him. He wheeled about and said rather crossly, "Yes, of course it is very wrong. I told you that. We are all wrong. Now it's over."

An hour later they found he had gone, having apparently reserved a Sinair flight to Karachi.

The security men caught up with him at Hong Kong. By then he seemed really very ill, and went with them peacefully. They started back to the States via Hawaii.

His captors were civilized types; they saw he was gentle and treated him accordingly. He had no weapons or drugs on him. They took him out handcuffed for a stroll at Osaka, let him feed his crumbs to the birds, and listened with interest to his account of the migration routes of the common brown sandpiper. He was very hoarse. At that point, he was wanted only for the security thing. There was no question of a woman at all.

He dozed most of the way to the islands, but when they came in sight he pressed to the window and began to mutter. The security man behind him got the first inkling that there was a woman in it, and turned on his recorder.

". . . Blue, blue and green until you see the wounds. Oh my girl, Oh beautiful, you won't die. I won't let you die. I tell you girl, it's over . . . Lustrous eyes, look at me, let me see you now alive! Great queen, my sweet body, my girl, have I saved you? . . . O terrible to

know, and noble, Chaos's child green-robed in blue and golden light
. . . the thrown and spinning ball of life alone in space . . . Have I
saved you?"

On the last leg, he was obviously feverish.

"She may have tricked me, you know," he said confidentially to
the government man. "You have to be prepared for that, of course. I
know her!" He chuckled confidentially. "She's no small thing. But
wring your heart out—"

Coming over San Francisco he was merry. "Don't you know the
otters will go back in there? I'm certain of it. That fill won't last;
there'll be a bay there again."

They got him on a stretcher at Hamilton Air Base, and he went
unconscious shortly after takeoff. Before he collapsed, he'd insisted
on throwing the last of his birdseed on the field.

"Birds are, you know, warm-blooded," he confided to the agent
who was handcuffing him to the stretcher. Then Ain smiled gently
and lapsed into inertness. He stayed that way almost all the remaining ten days of his life. By then, of course, no one really cared. Both
the government men had died quite early, after they finished analyz-
ing the birdseed and throat spray. The woman at Kennedy had just
started feeling sick.

The tape recorder they put by his bed functioned right on
through, but if anybody had been around to replay it they would
have found little but babbling. "Gaea Gloriatrix," he crooned,
"Gaea girl, queen . . ." At times he was grandiose and tormented.
"Our life, your death!" he yelled. "Our death would have been your
death too, no need for that, no need."

At other times he was accusing. "What did you do about the di-
nosaurs?" he demanded. "Did they annoy you? How did you fix
them? Cold. Queen, you're too cold! You came close to it this time,
my girl," he raved. And then he wept and caressed the bedclothes
and was maudlin.

Only at the end, lying in his filth and thirst, still chained where
they had forgotten him, he was suddenly coherent. In the light clear
voice of a lover planning a summer picnic he asked the recorder happily:

"Have you ever thought about bears? They have so much . . .
funny they never came along further. By any chance were you saving
them, girl?" And he chuckled in his ruined throat, and later,
died.

FROM *GALAXY* BOOK SHELF

September 1969

Algis Budrys

Memoir by Algis Budrys

I'm as proud of the September 1969 book-review column as I am of anything I ever wrote. It will come as no surprise to faithful readers that it is barely about books at all. In fact, I have edited from this version my discussion of Harry Warner, Jr.'s biographical *All Our Yesterdays*, a personalized history of sf fandom which is still available from Advent Publishers, Box 9228, Chicago, Ill. 60690, for a well-spent $7.50. It was not unusual for me to write a column mentioning only one book, and sometimes none.

Why? Why not? Especially back in the 1960s, it was ludicrous to pretend that my reviews would appear before the subject books were almost all out of print. My mission was to entertain in the particular, and, by implication, to theorize in general. My feeling was that people read the column not as a consumer guide but as a series of essays on the general shape and nature of sf writing, publishing, editing, and anything else I thought might be interesting to someone who cared about books. That is a broad range of eligible topics, and I believe I worked it pretty much from end to end.

I don't know if that's what Frederik Pohl expected when he succeeded Horace Gold and offered me the opportunity to succeed Floyd C. Gale, Horace Gold's brother.

Gale—who could tell you a lot in a few words, usually pithy and perceptive, and who mentioned a great many titles every month in a way that indicated he had actually read them and thought about them—had taken the consumer-guide approach. Fred knew my current reviewing style—rather more discursive—and hired me anyway. What he did not expect, I think, and certainly what I did not expect, was that I would become even more discursive. From time to time, Fred would grumble about this, but he never did anything about it. The only time he ever rejected a column—and some of them were barely legible, and not quite coherent even before the printer's incredible operations had produced the usual dropped sentences, respelled words, and transposed paragraphs—was when I submitted a maniacal first draft of my review of *Dangerous Visions*. He was right to have me speak in language the sane could understand.

Whatever, I bumped along from issue to issue, saying pretty much what I thought was my best utterance of the month, sticking to first reactions and gut reactions as is my wont in this mode, and it served until after Fred had left.

This column, obviously, is a little different in that the bulk of it had been written, self-censored, replaced by other copy—but not thrown away. And one day the time came to publish it. Like all the others but one, it was essentially first draft. That's one reason why I take pride in it, for on rereading it, as I do from time to time and as I have just done again, I find it quite coherent and nicely organized toward its final point.

I would like to remind you that it was written and published prior to the national and international political events of the 1970s, which make me out to be a hell of a prognosticator. I believed what I wrote; I cannot claim that I believed in the overwhelming extent to which I would be borne out. If I had, I would have taken care to note that the fellow standing beside Miss Pickle and the six-foot Pickle Eagle was Gerald R. Ford. I asked him who he liked in the upcoming Republican nomination fight, and he remarked that the occasion did not seem appropriate for a reply. Turns out he was wrong.

GALAXY BOOK SHELF

I read the news today. James Earl Ray will be in court to appeal his confession. Sirhan Sirhan is getting settled in his cell on Death Row. Apollo 10 is about to reenter after successful completion of the penultimate lunar mission. There is no trace of the ground-crew sergeant who took the Hercules out over the Atlantic and asked for one phone call to his wife. And got it.

And that's some of the news of the world of the future.

I would like to illustrate my point. I think perhaps I can. Here is a column I wrote in April 1968 after returning home from a business trip. But then I remembered that my job is to review science-fiction books, not science fiction. So I put it aside:

From the air Washington, D.C., looked dusty in the late afternoon. In the main terminal at National Airport, ticket clerks had been suggesting there might be seats on flights from Friendship Airport. They had no suggestion as to how long it might take the regular limousine service to get through downtown Washington to Friendship, which is near Baltimore. But there were certainly no seats to Chicago, Milwaukee, or St. Louis at National. So I took the shuttle to New York and that was how I saw the burning like a barricade across the city at 14th Street. The flames were Day-Glo orange.

My plan was to take a Chicago plane from LaGuardia. I settled for a cab ride to Kennedy and the last seat on a flight home via Cincinnati.

The nation's capital, as I was saying, had been burning. From National, with its panoramic windows, the historical monuments along the Potomac had stood out clearly against the ropy smoke. We had gotten to National, usually a twelve-minute cab ride down Connecticut Avenue from the Shoreham, via Georgetown and the Key Bridge. Whether you know D.C. or not, what this means is that for five tired businessmen who had been strangers until they struck their bargain with the cabbie, the insurrection up to this point had been an hour's traffic jam.

The flight path from Kennedy to Cincinnati crosses Baltimore. D.C. is off the left wing. Doubling back as I was, at something like 10:00 PM local time, now, I was sitting in a first-class left window seat with a double whiskey sour in my hand, partaking of a little Mozart through the headphones of my Astrostereo.

Washington from the air at night is one of the world's great visions. When I see it, I think of the superdense cities traced out far below our England in the Arthur C. Clarke story. It is like looking at a scanner display and making out the lovely, obviously intelligent webworks of an aesthetically conscious, persistent, and prosperous alien people. At this time, it had rust-colored, very dark streaks across it.

In Cincinnati the bouncy stewardess with the Texas accent received a message that flight crews would not be permitted to leave

O'Hare Field for their homes in Chicago but would have to bunk out at the field after the flight terminated. She asked me what Washington had been like. I couldn't think of how to put it.

"Like World War III," I said and she nodded happily, comprehending.

But later, when we swung in over the West Side of Chicago at midnight, she ran up and down the aisle, pointing out and crying: "Look it thet! Look it thet, my Gawd!"

Well, I got home all right, to suburban Evanston, in a cab driven by a man who blamed the whole thing on the mayor of Philadelphia for taking away his policemen's shotguns. I also learned that he lived in all innocence on the 3000 block of West Madison and I was his last fare before he checked in and went home. I'm not really a jerk but I didn't like the way he talked, so I just wished him pleasant dreams.

The next day, I checked with the local police for reassurance, and then my wife, my four sons, and I got on our six bicycles and went up to the Baskin-Robbins store on the corner of Dempster and Chicago. The youngest is six and I'd promised him he could have a ride to the ice-cream store when I got back home from the annual convention of Pickle Packers, International, a very nice bunch of people I no longer work for.

As I recall, everybody had a double dip but David, the youngest. Despite his twelve-block accomplishment, he settled for one dip. The next day being Sunday, we dressed up neatly and took the bus to Raymond Park for the memorial service.

What all this has to do with science fiction (I wrote in April 1968) is so obvious that its full implications still escape me. It was not at all like World War III. World War III in the movies is accompanied by sirens, crashing sounds, and the crackle of flames. But the common element in all my insulated glimpses from real life was the absence of sound effects. In all the afternoon and evening, I heard one klaxon—on an empty ambulance headed for the Key Bridge away from D.C., probably toward a road accident on the chock-full highway to Dulles Airport. Other than that, it was cab motors, turboprop and jet engines, arrival and departure announcements, coins dropping into telephones, ten pennies in a slot for a copy of the Chicago Sun-Times. That, and politeness; the very quiet, resigned AP wirephoto editor in Washington on Friday morning, when the headline was still D.C. QUIETS DOWN. He said he was glad to see me again, hoped I'd be back next year, but didn't really think he'd be able to do much with my 8×10 glossy of a pretty girl unveiling a sculpture of a six-foot eagle clutching a 2½ foot pickle in its claws. All of us were polite; the taxi man in Washington, the five of us in his cab, even when we were stuck immovably in that narrow Georgetown street, with people walking rapidly and the hooter getting closer and closer. There was no shoving or shouting at National; the clerks worked quickly and without raising their voices. On the shuttle, a salesman put his knee in my lap while trying to aim his Nikon through the window, and I was very polite to him.

It had to be, of all things, a stewardess out of Steve Canyon who became my only exhibit for panic, and it was two other cab drivers, one in John Lindsay's New York and one in Dick Daley's Chicago, who spoke confidently of locking their doors and "driving right through" crowds if the need ever arose. One thing their television viewing has apparently failed to show them is a car with its four wheels in the air. Or else they've related it to a movie about World War III. At 26,000 feet, with Mozart and whiskey sours, I gazed with fascinated interest on the subterrene jewelry of Washington at night and thought of Arthur C. Clarke. What difference does it make what you relate to?

What difference? Well, I'm not sure. The difference, if any, must be somewhere in the difference between the flashy and the enduring. So much of what we want is flash. Flash is often more fun. The novel of World War III is not popular by accident. And the mysterious figure with mysterious capabilities, spinning conspiracies or, conversely, righting wrongs with one morally superior stroke—he, too, is an enduring archetype among us because there are enduring needs within us and he meets them. A large part of what is generally called "science fiction" all in one lump, good and bad, flashy and enduring together, is wedded and bedded, part, parcel, and calliope with a complex, communicative, communal, commutative, comprehensive social network which fosters and battens on the urgent, immediate need to *make* the future happen.

We want to escape from the incomprehensible here-and-now into a simplified world where an Avenger sets things right with one forceful blow after the "mealy-mouth politicians and fuzzy-minded social 'scientists' have muddled it up." We want to have the Arcturians come down in search of Marilyn Monroe and knock aside things-as-they-are in the process. We want a new deal for ourselves, by being born again, this time fully conscious, into a world depopulated by the plague, where all is still and all is ours.

We live in a flash world. The dimensions of things have gotten worked around to where they are larger than life as it was when the harmless entertainments of flash fiction were first created. Any one man with a degree in biochemistry, for instance—one poor, miserable, unsung cataclast with a mere ten years' education, or just an ordinary lot of luck—could make such a plague. We may all be dying tomorrow for one man's gratification of a wish which should legitimately be sending a hundred thousand of us to the newsstands with seventy-five cents each for the next John Christopher novel.

You follow me? So much of science fiction has nothing to do with the intrinsic things of science fiction. It has to do with the intrinsics of less than perfect humanity. It is predicated on the powerlessness of the individual, rather than on the capabilities of the lucky few. The plague, the Arcturians, or the Avenger, are needed to fill the lack of power in our lives.

Or they were. Here in the world of the future, our longed-for expertise of things has created innumerable places where once powerful authority has no monopoly on accomplishment, and where there are many weapons that are best wielded by empty hands. If he but be driven enough today, any man can be his own pulp hero, and those of us who want all their thrills vicarious will never again nod safe in their libraries.

That's what it all has to do with science fiction. It has to do with the difference between flash writing and good writing, because good writing is life and flash writing is the other thing. Good art has to do with life realized. We've always known that. What some of us appear to have missed is that life has changed fundamentally, and science fictionally.

That's what it has to do with science fiction. The greater chunk of the old basis is dead as of April 4, 1968. We used to set stories on Mars and in the future not because we understood those places but because we didn't—which made them totally believable places in which to have momentous things happen. Life at home proceeded apace. But we live now in a time in which it not only can happen here—you name it, and it can happen, good, bad, and indifferent, provided only it's flashy enough—it not only *can* happen here, it will.

SLOW SCULPTURE

February 1970

Theodore Sturgeon
(b. 1918)

One of the leading luminaries of the "Golden Age" of science fiction, Theodore Sturgeon was the most heavily reprinted author in the field until the early 1970s. In the 1950s he wrote some of the most memorable stories ever to appear in Galaxy, including the novella "Baby Is Three" (October 1952), which was the basis for his classic novel More Than Human (1953); "Saucer of Loneliness" (February 1953); the magnificent "Who?" (March 1955); "Mr. Costello, Hero" (December 1953); and "The Other Man" (September 1956). One of his rare later appearances in the magazine was the neglected but excellent "Dazed" (September 1971). His relative absence from the field in the last decade is a tragedy.

Besides writing fiction, he served as book reviewer for Galaxy from March 1972 to the end of 1973.

Memoir by Theodore Sturgeon

There is no way writers write that I haven't tried: rigidly, so many hours per day and/or so many pages per day; once, a determination to write only *one* page per day—28 pages, 28 days (sold it, too). I've tried dictation, live; dictation, tape (they don't work). I've sat over a silent typewriter for 30 hours hoping exhaustion would reach the subconscious before I fell over sideways. I've pounded the typewriter furiously for 30 hours until I really did fall over sideways. I've storyboarded every character and every action every inch of the way before I began to write; I've plunged blindly into a narrative hook like

"'Beat me up again and I'll kill you!' he told the child." without the slightest idea as to where to go from there.

I moved into an old house just about the time my son Andros was born. The water pressure was 80 psi at the main outside, and 8 pounds inside; I don't think you could have gotten a knitting needle through those old corroded pipes. So there was no point in buying a washing machine, and I would go down to the all-night laundromat at 2 AM to do the baby's diapers, twice or three times a week. And for the first time in my life I wrote with a pencil in a note-book, a paragraph or two between the washer and the dryer. In six or seven weeks it was done. I typed it up and sent it out, feeling that it was maybe okay but it could hardly survive that kind of discontinuity. And it won a Hugo, and it won a Nebula, and now it can be found in half a dozen languages.

I never have understood how the Sturgeon story-machine works.

SLOW SCULPTURE

She didn't know who he was when she met him; well, not many people did. He was in the high orchard doing something under a pear tree. The land smelled of late summer and wind; bronze, it smelled bronze. He looked up at a compact girl in her mid-twenties, with a fearless face and eyes the same color as her hair, which was extraordinary because her hair was red-gold. She looked down at a leather-skinned man in his forties with a goldleaf electroscope in his hand, and felt she was an intruder. She said, "Oh" in what was apparently the right way, because he nodded once and said, "Hold this," and there could then be no thought of intrusion. She knelt down by him and took the instrument, holding it just where he positioned her hand, and then he moved a little away and struck a tuning fork against his kneecap. "What's it doing?" He had a good voice, the kind of voice strangers notice and listen to.

She looked at the delicate leaves of gold in the glass shield of the electroscope. "They're moving apart."

He struck the tuning fork again and the leaves pressed away from one another. "Much?"

"About forty-five degrees when you hit the fork."

"Good—that's about the most we'll get." From a pocket of his bush jacket he drew a sack of chalk-dust and dropped a small handful on the ground. "I'll move now. You stay right there and tell me how much the leaves separate."

He traveled around the pear tree in a zigzag course, striking his tuning fork while she called out numbers—ten degrees, thirty, five, twenty, nothing. Whenever the gold foil pressed apart to maximum, forty degrees or more, he dropped more chalk. When he was finished the tree was surrounded, in a rough oval, by the white dots of chalk. He took out a notebook and diagrammed them and the tree, and put away the book, and took the electroscope out of her hands. "Were you looking for something?" he asked her.

"No," she said. "Yes."

He could smile. Though it did not last long, she found it very surprising in a face like that. "That's not what is called, in a court of law, a responsive answer."

She glanced across the hillside, metallic in that late light. There wasn't much on it—rocks, weeds the summer was done with, a tree or so, and then the orchard. Anyone present had come a long way to get here. "It wasn't a simple question," she said, tried to smile, and burst into tears.

She was sorry and said so.

"Why?" he asked. This was the first time she was to experience this ask-the-next-question thing of his. It was unsettling. It always would be—never less, sometimes a great deal more. "Well—one doesn't have emotional explosions in public."

"*You* do. I don't know this 'one' you're talking about."

"I guess I don't either, now that you mention it."

"Tell the truth then. No sense in going round and round about it, 'he'll think that I—' and the like. I'll think what I think, whatever you say. Or—go on down the mountain and just don't say any more." She did not turn to go, so he added, "Try the truth, then. If it's important, it's simple, and if it's simple it's easy to say."

"I'm going to die!" she cried.

"So am I."

"I have a lump in my breast."

"Come up to the house and I'll fix it."

Without another word he turned away and started through the orchard. Startled half out of her wits, indignant and full of insane hope, experiencing, even, a quick curl of astonished laughter, she stood for a moment watching him go, and then found herself (at what point did I decide?) running after him.

She caught up with him on the uphill margin of the orchard. "Are you a doctor?"

He appeared not to notice that she had waited, had run. "No," he said, and, walking on, appeared not to see her stand again pulling at her lower lip, then run again to catch up.

"I must be out of my mind," she said, joining him on a garden path. She said it to herself, which he must have known because he did not answer. The garden was alive with defiant chrysanthemums and a pond in which she saw the flicker of a pair of redcap imperials —silver, not gold fish—which were the largest she had ever seen. Then—the house.

First it was part of the garden, with its colonnaded terrace, and then, with its rock walls (too big to be called fieldstone) part of the mountain. It was on and in the hillside, and its roofs paralleled the skylines, front and sides, and part of it was backed against an outjutting cliff face. The door, beamed and studded and with two archers' slits, was opened for them (but there was no one there) and when it closed it was silent, a far more solid exclusion of things outside than any click or clang of latch or bolt. She stood with her back against it, watching him cross what seemed to be the central well of the house, or at least this part of it. It was a kind of small court in the center of which was an atrium, glazed on all of its five sides and open to the sky at the top. In it was a tree, a cypress or juniper, gnarled and twisted and with the turned-back, paralleled, sculptured appearance of what the Japanese call bonsai.

"Aren't you coming?" he called, holding open a door behind the atrium.

"Bonsai just aren't fifteen feet tall," she said.

"This one is."

She came by it slowly, looking. "How long have you had it?"

His tone of voice said he was immensely pleased. It is a clumsiness to ask the owner of a bonsai how old it is; you are then demanding to know if it is his work or if he has acquired and continued the concept of another; you are tempting him to claim for his own the concept and the meticulous labor of someone else, and it becomes rude to tell a man he is being tested. Hence "How long have you had it?" is polite, forbearing, profoundly courteous. He answered, "Half my life." She looked at the tree. Trees can be found, sometimes, not quite discarded, not quite forgotten, potted in rusty gallon cans in not quite successful nurseries, unsold because they are shaped oddly or have dead branches here and there or, because they have grown too slowly in whole or part. These are the ones which develop interesting trunks and a resistance to misfortune that makes them flourish if given the least excuse for living. This one was far older than half this man's life, or all of it. Looking at it, she was terrified by the unbidden thought that a fire, a family of squirrels, some subterranean worm or termite could end this beauty—something working outside any concept of rightness or justice or . . . or respect. She looked at the tree. She looked at the man.

"Coming?"

"Yes," she said and went with him into his laboratory. "Sit down over there and relax," he told her. "This might take a little while."

"Over there" was a big leather chair by the bookcase. The books were right across the spectrum—reference works in medicine and engineering, nuclear physics, chemistry, biology, psychiatry. Also tennis, gymnastics, chess, the oriental war game Go, and golf. And then drama, the techniques of fiction, *Modern English Usage, The American Language* and supplement, Wood's and Walker's rhyming dictionaries, and an array of other dictionaries and encyclopedias. A whole long shelf of biographies. "You have quite a library."

He answered her rather shortly: Clearly he did not want to talk just now, for he was very busy. He said only, "Yes I have—perhaps you'll see it some time," which left her to pick away at his words to find out what on earth he meant by them. He could only have meant, she decided, that the books beside her chair were what he kept handy for his work—that his real library was elsewhere. She looked at him with a certain awe.

And she watched him. She liked the way he moved—swiftly, decisively. Clearly he knew what he was doing. He used some equipment that she recognized—a glass still, titration equipment, a centrifuge. There were two refrigerators, one of which was not a refrigerator at all, for she could see the large indicator on the door: It stood at 70° F. It came to her that a modern refrigerator is perfectly adaptable to the demand for controlled environment, even a warm one.

But all that, and the equipment she did not recognize, was only furniture. It was the man who was worth watching, the man who kept her occupied so that not once in all the long time she sat there was she tempted toward the bookshelves.

At last he finished a long sequence at the bench, threw some

switches, picked up a tall stool, and came over to her. He perched
on the stool, hung his heels on the cross-spoke, and laid a pair of long
brown hands over his knees. "Scared?"

"I s'pose I am."

"You don't have to stay."

"Considering the alternative," she began bravely, but the courage-
sound somehow oozed out, "it can't matter much."

"Very sound," he said, almost cheerfully. "I remember when I was
a kid there was a fire scare in the apartment house where we lived. It
was a wild scramble to get out, and my ten-year-old brother found
himself outside in the street with an alarm clock in his hand. It was
an old one and it didn't work—but of all the things in the place he
might have snatched up at a time like that, it turned out to be the
clock. He's never been able to figure out why."

"Have you?"

"Not why he picked that particular thing, no. But I think I know
why he did something obviously irrational. You see, panic is a very
special state. Like fear and flight, or fury and attack, it's a pretty
primitive reaction to extreme danger. It's one of the expressions of
the will to survive. What makes it so special is that it's irrational.
Now, why would the abandonment of reason be a survival mechanism?"

She thought about this seriously. There was that about this man
which made serious thought imperative. "I can't imagine," she said
finally. "Unless it's because, in some situations, reason just doesn't
work."

"You *can* imagine," he said, again radiating that huge approval,
making her glow. "And you just did. If you are in danger and you
try reason, and reason doesn't work, you abandon it. You can't say
it's unintelligent to abandon what doesn't work, right? So then you
are in panic; then you start to perform random acts. Most of them—
far and away most—will be useless; some might even be dangerous,
but that doesn't matter—you're in danger already. Where the survival factor comes in is that away down deep you know that one
chance in a million is better than no chance at all. So—here you sit
—you're scared and you could run; something says you should run;
but you won't."

She nodded.

He went on: "You found a lump. You went to a doctor and he
made some tests and gave you the bad news. Maybe you went to an-

other doctor and he confirmed it. You then did some research and found out what was to happen next—the exploratory, the radical, the questionable recovery, the whole long agonizing procedure of being what they call a terminal case. You then flipped out. Did some things you hope I won't ask you about. Took a trip somewhere, anywhere, wound up in my orchard for no reason." He spread the good hands and let them go back to their kind of sleep. "Panic. The reason for little boys in their pajamas standing at midnight with a broken alarm clock in their arms, and for the existence of quacks." Something chimed over on the bench and he gave her a quick smile and went back to work, saying over his shoulder: "I'm not a quack, by the way. To qualify as a quack you have to claim to be a doctor. I don't."

She watched him switch off, switch on, stir, measure, and calculate. A little orchestra of equipment chorused and soloed around him as he conducted, whirring, hissing, clicking, flickering. She wanted to laugh, to cry, and to scream. She did no one of these things for fear of not stopping, ever.

When he came over again, the conflict was not raging within her, but exerting steady and opposed tensions; the result was a terrible stasis, and all she could do when she saw the instrument in his hand was to widen her eyes. She quite forgot to breathe.

"Yes, it's a needle," he said, his tone almost bantering. "A long shiny sharp needle. Don't tell me you are one of those needle-shy people." He flipped the long power-cord which trailed from the black housing around the hypodermic, to get some slack, and straddled the stool. "Want something to steady your nerves?"

She was afraid to speak; the membrane containing her sane self was very thin, stretched very tight.

He said, "I'd rather you didn't, because this pharmaceutical stew is complex enough as it is. But if you need it . . ."

She managed to shake her head a little, and again she felt the wave of approval from him. There were a thousand questions she wanted to ask—had meant to ask—needed to ask: What was in the needle? How many treatments must she have? What would they be like? How long must she stay, and where? And most of all—oh, could she live, could she live?

He seemed concerned with the answer to only one of these. "It's mostly built around an isotope of potassium. If I told you all I know about it and how I came on it in the first place, it would take—well, more time than we've got. But here's the general idea: Theoretically, every atom is electrically balanced (never mind ordinary exceptions). Likewise all electrical charges in the molecule are supposed to be balanced—so much plus, so much minus, total zero. I happened on the fact that the balance of charges in a wild cell is not zero—not quite. It's as if there was a submicroscopic thunderstorm going on at the molecular level, with little lightning bolts flashing back and forth and changing the signs. Interfering with communications—static—and that," he said, gesturing with the shielded hypo in his hand, "is what this is all about. When something interferes with communications—especially the RNA mechanism, which says, Read this blueprint and build accordingly, and stop when it's done —when that message gets garbled, lopsided things get built, off-balance things, things which do almost what they should, do it almost right: They're wild cells, and the messages they pass on are even worse.

"Okay: Whether these thunderstorms are caused by viruses or chemicals or radiation or physical trauma or even anxiety—and don't think anxiety can't do it—that's secondary. The important thing is to fix it so the thunderstorm can't happen. If you can do that, the cells have plenty of ability all by themselves to repair and replace what's gone wrong. And biological systems aren't like Ping-Pong balls with static charges waiting for the charge to leak away or to discharge into a grounded wire. They have a kind of resilience—I call it forgiveness—which enables them to take on a little more charge, or a little less, and do all right. Well then: Say a certain clump of cells is wild and say it carries an aggregate of a hundred units extra on the positive side. Cells immediately around it are affected, but not the next layer or the next.

"If they could be opened to the extra charge, if they could help to drain it off, they would, well, *cure* the wild cells of the surplus, you see what I mean? And they would be able to handle that little overage themselves, or pass it on to other cells and still others who could deal with it. In other words, if I can flood your body with some medium which can drain off and distribute a concentration of this unbalanced charge, the ordinary bodily processes will be free to move in and clear up the wild-cell damage. And that's what I have here."

He held the shielded needle between his knees and from a side pocket of his lab coat he took a plastic box, opened it, and drew out an alcohol swab. Still cheerfully talking, he took her terror-numbed arm and scrubbed at the inside of her elbow. "I am not for one second implying that nuclear charges in the atom are the same thing as static electricity. They're in a different league altogether. But the analogy holds. I could use another analogy. I could liken the charge on the wild cells to accumulations of fat, and this gunk of mine to a detergent, which would break it up and spread it so far it couldn't be detected any more. But I'm led to the static analogy by an odd side effect—organisms injected with this stuff do build up one hell of a static charge. It's a by-product, and for reasons I can only theorize about at the moment, it seems to be keyed to the audio spectrum. Tuning forks and the like. That's what I was playing with when I met you. That tree is drenched with this stuff. It used to have a whorl of wild cell growth. It hasn't any more." He gave her the quick surprising smile and let it click away as he held the needle point upward and squirted it. With his other hand wrapped around her left biceps, he squeezed gently and firmly. The needle was lowered and placed and slid into the big vein so deftly that she gasped —not because it hurt, but because it did not. Attentively he watched the bit of glass barrel protruding from a black housing as he withdrew the plunger a fraction and saw the puff of red into the colorless fluid inside, and then he bore steadily on the plunger again.

"Please don't move. . . . I'm sorry; this will take a little time. I have to get quite a lot of this into you. Which is fine, you know," he said, resuming the tone of his previous remarks about audio spectra, "because side effect or no, it's consistent. Healthy bio systems develop a strong electrostatic field, unhealthy ones a weak one or none at all. With an instrument as primitive and simple as that little electroscope you can tell if any part of the organism has a community of wild cells, and if so, where it is and how big and how wild." Deftly he shifted his grip on the encased hypodermic without moving the point or varying the amount of plunger pressure. It was beginning to be uncomfortable, an ache turning into a bruise. "And if you're wondering why this mosquito has a housing on it with a wire attached (although I'll bet you're not and that you know as well as I do that I'm doing all this talking just to keep your mind occupied!) I'll tell you. It's nothing but a coil carrying a high-frequency alternating current. The alternating field sees to it that the fluid is magnetically and electrostatically neutral right from the start." He withdrew the needle suddenly and smoothly, bent her arm, and trapped in the inside of her elbow a cotton swab.

"Nobody ever told me that before after a treatment," she said.

"What?"

"No charge," she said.

Again that wave of approval, this time with words: "I like your style. How do you feel?"

She cast about for accurate phrases. "Like the owner of a large sleeping hysteria begging someone not to wake it up."

He laughed. "In a little while you are going to feel so weird you won't have time for hysteria." He got up and returned the needle to the bench, looping up the cable as he went. He turned off the AC field and returned with a large glass bowl and a square of plywood. He inverted the bowl on the floor near her and placed the wood on its broad base.

"I remember something like that," she said. "When I was in—in junior high school. They were generating artificial lightning with a . . . let me see . . . well, it had a long endless belt running over pulleys and some little wires scraping on it and a big copper ball on top."

"Van de Graaf generator."

"Right! And they did all sorts of things with it, but what I specially remember is standing on a piece of wood on a bowl like that and they charged me up with the generator, and I didn't feel much of anything except all my hair stood out from my head. Everyone laughed. I looked like a golliwog. They said I was carrying forty thousand volts."

"Good! I'm glad you remember that. This'll be a little different, though. By roughly another forty thousand."

"Oh!"

"Don't worry. Long as you're insulated, and as long as grounded, or comparatively grounded objects—me, for example—stay well away from you, there won't be any fireworks."

"Are you going to use a generator like that?"

"Not like that, and I already did. You're the generator."

"I'm—oh!" She had raised her hand from the upholstered chair arm and there was a crackle of sparks and the faint smell of ozone.

"Oh you sure are, and more than I thought, and quicker. Get up!"

She started up slowly; she finished the maneuver with speed. As her body separated from the chair she was, for a fractional second, seated in a tangle of spitting blue-white threads. They, or she, propelled her a yard and a half away, standing. Literally shocked half out of her wits, she almost fell.

"Stay on your feet!" he snapped, and she recovered, gasping. He stepped back a pace. "Get up on the board. Quick, now!"

She did as she was told, leaving, for the two paces she traveled, two brief footprints of fire. She teetered on the board. Visibly, her hair began to stir. "What's happening to me?" she cried.

"You're getting charged after all," he said jovially, but at this point she failed to appreciate the extension of even her own witticism. She cried again, "What's happening to me?"

"It's all right," he said consolingly. He went to the bench and turned on a tone generator. It moaned deep in the one-to-three-hundred-cycle range. He increased the volume and turned the pitch control. It howled upward and as it did so her red-gold hair shivered and swept up and out, each hair attempting frantically to get away from all the others. He ran the tone up above ten thousand cycles and all the way back to a bell-bumping inaudible eleven; at the extremes her hair slumped, but at around eleven hundred it stood out in (as she had described it) golliwog style.

He turned down the gain to a more or less bearable level and picked up the electroscope. He came toward her, smiling. "You *are* an electroscope, you know that? And a living Van de Graaf generator as well. And a golliwog."

"Let me down," was all she could say.

"Not yet. Please hang tight. The differential between you and everything else here is so high that if you get near any of it you'd discharge into it. I wouldn't harm you—it isn't current electricity—but you might get a burn and a nervous shock out of it." He held out the electroscope; even at that distance, and in her distress, she could see the gold leaves writhe apart. He circled her, watching the leaves attentively, moving the instrument forward and back and from side to side. Once he went to the tone generator and turned it down some more. "You're sending such a strong field I can't pick up the variations," he explained, and returned to her, closer now.

"I can't, much more . . . I can't," she murmured; he did not hear, or he did not care. He moved the electroscope near her abdomen, up and from side to side.

"Yup. There you are!" he said cheerfully, moving the instrument close to her right breast.

"What?" she whimpered.

"Your cancer. Right breast, low, around toward the armpit." He whistled. "A mean one, too. Malignant as hell."

She swayed and then collapsed forward and down. A sick blackness swept down on her, receded explosively in a glare of agonizing blue-white, and then crashed down on her like a mountain falling.

Place where wall meets ceiling. Another wall, another ceiling. Hadn't seen it before. Didn't matter. Don't care.

Sleep.

Place where wall meets ceiling. Something in the way. His face, close, drawn, tired; eyes awake though and penetrating. Doesn't matter. Don't care.

Sleep.

Place where wall meets ceiling. Down a bit, late sunlight. Over a little rusty-gold chrysanthemums in a gold-green glass cornucopia. Something in the way again: his face.

"Can you hear me?"

Yes, but don't answer. Don't move. Don't speak.

Sleep.

It's a room, a wall, a table, a man pacing; a nighttime window and mums you'd think were alive, but don't you know they're cut right off and dying?

Do they know that?

"*How are you?*" Urgent, urgent.

"Thirsty."

Cold and a bite to it that aches the hinges of the jaws. Grapefruit juice. Lying back on his arm while he holds the glass in the other hand, oh no, that's not . . . "Thank you. Thanks very—" Try to sit up, the sheet—*my clothes!*

"Sorry about that," he said, the mind reader almost. "Some things that have to be done just aren't consistent with panty hose and a minidress. All washed and dried and ready for you, though—any time. Over there."

The brown wool and the panty hose and the shoes, on the chair. He's respectful, standing back, putting the glass next to an insulated carafe on the night-table.

"What things?"

"Throwing up. Bedpans," he said candidly.

Protective with the sheet, which can hide bodies but oh not embarrassment. "Oh I'm sorry . . . Oh. I must've—" Shakes head and he slides back and forth in the vision.

"You went into shock, and then you just didn't come out of it." He hesitated. It was the first time she had ever seen him hesitate over anything. She became for a moment an almost-mind-reader: *Should I tell her what's in my mind?* Sure he should, and he did: "You didn't *want* to come out of it."

"It's all gone out of my head."

"The pear tree, the electroscope. The injection, the electrostatic response."

"No," she said, not knowing, then, knowing: "*No!*"

"Hang on!" he rapped, and next thing she knew he was by the bed, over her, his two hands hard on her cheeks. "Don't slip off again. You can handle it. You can handle it because it's all right now, do you understand that? You're all right!"

"You told me I had cancer." It sounded pouty, accusing. He laughed at her, actually laughed.

"You told *me* you had it."

"Oh, but I didn't *know.*"

"That explains it, then," he said in a load-off-my-back tone. "There wasn't anything in what I did that could cause a three-day withdrawal like that; it had to be something in you."

"Three *days!*"

He simply nodded in response to that and went on with what he was saying. "I get a little pompous once in a while," he said engagingly. "Comes from being right so much of the time. Took a bit more for granted than I should have, didn't I? when I assumed you'd been to a doctor, maybe even had a biopsy. You didn't, did you?"

"I was afraid," she admitted. She looked at him. "My mother died of it, and my aunt, and my sister had a radical mastectomy. I couldn't bear it. And when you—"

"When I told you what you already knew, and what you never wanted to hear, you couldn't take it. You blacked right out, you know. Fainted away, and it had nothing to do with the seventy-odd thousand volts of static you were carrying. I caught you." He put out his arms and instinctively she shrank back, but he held the arms where they were, on display, until she looked at them and saw the angry red scorch marks on his forearms and the heavy biceps, as much of them as she could see from under his short-sleeved shirt. "About nine-tenths knocked me out too," he said, but at least you didn't crack your head or anything."

"Thank you," she said reflexively, and then began to cry. "What am I going to *do?*"

"Do? Go back home, wherever that is—pick up your life again, whatever that might mean."

"But you said—"

"When are you going to get it into your head that what I did was not a diagnostic?"

"Are you—did you—you mean you cured it?"

"I mean you're curing it right now. I explained it all to you before —you remember that now, don't you?"

"Not altogether, but—yes." Surreptitiously (but not enough, because he saw her) she felt under the sheet for the lump. "It's still there."

"If I bopped you over the head with a bat," he said with slightly exaggerated simplicity, "there would be a lump on it. It would be there tomorrow and the next day. The day after that it might be smaller, and in a week you'd still be able to feel it, but it would be gone. Same thing here."

At last she let the enormity of it touch her. "A one-shot cure for cancer . . ."

"Oh God," he said harshly, "I can tell by looking at you that I am going to have to listen to that speech *again*. Well, I won't."

Startled, she said, "What speech?"

"The one about my duty to humanity. It comes in two phases and many textures. Phase one has to do with my duty to humanity and really means we could make a classic buck with it. Phase two deals solely with my duty to humanity, and I don't hear that one very often. Phase two utterly overlooks the reluctance humanity has to accept good things unless they arrive from accepted and respectable sources. Phase one is fully aware of this but gets very rat-shrewd in figuring ways around it."

She said, "I don't—" but could get no farther.

"The textures," he overrode her, "are accompanied by the light of revelation, with or without religion and/or mysticism; or they are cast sternly in the ethical-philosophy mold and aim to force me to surrender through guilt mixed, to some degree all the way up to total, with compassion."

"But I only—"

"You," he said, aiming a long index finger at her, "have robbed yourself of the choicest example of everything I have just said. If my assumptions had been right and you had gone to your friendly local sawbones, and he had diagnosed cancer and referred you to a specialist, and he had done likewise and sent you to a colleague for consultation, and in random panic you had fallen into my hands and been cured, and had gone back to your various doctors to report a miracle, do you know what you'd have gotten from them? 'Spontaneous remission,' that's what you'd have gotten. And it wouldn't be only doctors," he went on with a sudden renewal of passion, under which she quailed in her bed. "Everybody has his own commercial. Your nutritionist would have nodded over his wheat germ or his macrobiotic rice cakes, your priest would have dropped to his knees and looked at the sky, your geneticist would have a pet theory about generation skipping and would assure you that your grandparents probably had spontaneous remissions too and never knew it."

"Please!" she cried, but he shouted at her: "Do you know what I am? I am an engineer twice over, mechanical and electrical, and I have a law degree. If you were foolish enough to tell anyone about what has happened here (which I hope you aren't, but if you are I know how to protect myself) I could be jailed for practicing medicine without a license, you could have me up for assault because I stuck a needle into you and even for kidnapping if you could prove I carried you in here from the lab. Nobody would give a damn that I had cured your cancer. You don't know who I am, do you?"

"No, I don't even know your name."

"And I won't tell you. I don't know your name, either—"

"Oh! It's—"

"Don't tell me! Don't tell me! I don't want to hear it! I wanted to be involved with your lump and I was. I want it and you to be gone as soon as you're both up to it. Have I made myself absolutely clear?"

"Just let me get dressed," she said tightly, "and I'll leave right now!"

"Without making a speech?"

"Without making a speech." And in a flash her anger turned to misery and she added, "I was going to say I was grateful. Would that have been all right?"

And his anger underwent a change too, for he came close to the bed and sat down on his heel, bringing their faces to a level, and said quite gently, "That would be fine. Although . . . you won't really be grateful for another ten days, when you get your 'spontaneous remission' reports, or maybe for six months or a year or two or five, when examinations keep on testing out negative."

She detected such a wealth of sadness behind this that she found herself reaching for the hand with which he steadied himself against the edge of the bed. He did not recoil, but he didn't seem to welcome it either. "Why can't I be grateful right now?"

"That would be an act of faith," he said bitterly, "and that just doesn't happen any more—if it ever did." He rose and went toward the door. "Please don't go tonight," he said. "It's dark and you don't know the way. I'll see you in the morning."

When he came back in the morning the door was open. The bed was made and the sheets were folded neatly on the chair, together with the pillow slips and the towels she had used. She wasn't there.

He came out into the entrance court and contemplated his bonsai.

Early sun gold-frosted the horizontal upper foliage of the old tree and brought its gnarled limbs into sharp relief, tough brown-gray and crevices of velvet. Only the companion of a bonsai (there are owners of bonsai, but they are a lesser breed) fully understands the relationship. There is an exclusive and individual treeness to the tree because it is a living thing, and living things change, and there are definite ways in which the tree desires to change. A man sees the tree and in his mind makes certain extensions and extrapolations of what he sees, and sets about making them happen. The tree in turn will do only what a tree can do, will resist to the death any attempt to do what it cannot do, or to do it in less time than it needs. The shaping of a bonsai is therefore always a compromise and always a cooperation. A man cannot create bonsai, nor can a tree; it takes both, and they must understand each other. It takes a long time to do that. One memorizes one's bonsai, every twig, the angle of every crevice and needle, and, lying awake at night or in a pause a thousand miles away, one recalls this or that line or mass, one makes one's plans. With wire and water and light, with tilting and with the planting of water-robbing weeds or heavy root-shading ground cover, one explains to the tree what one wants, and if the explanation is well enough made, and there is great enough understanding, the tree will respond and obey—almost. Always there will be its own self-respecting, highly individual variation: *Very well, I shall do what you want, but I will do it my way.* And for these variations, the tree is always willing to present a clear and logical explanation, and more often than not (almost smiling) it will make clear to the man that he could have avoided it if his understanding had been better.

It is the slowest sculpture in the world, and there is, at times, doubt as to which is being sculpted, man or tree.

So he stood for perhaps ten minutes watching the flow of gold over the upper branches, and then went to a carved wooden chest, opened it, shook out a length of disreputable cotton duck, opened the hinged glass at one side of the atrium, and spread the canvas over the roots and all the earth to one side of the trunk, leaving the rest open to wind and water. Perhaps in a while—a month or two— a certain shoot in the topmost branch would take the hint, and the uneven flow of moisture up through the cambium layer would nudge it away from that upward reach and persuade it to continue this horizontal passage. And perhaps not, and it would need the harsher language of binding and wire. But then it might have something to say, too, about the rightness of an upward trend, and would perhaps say it persuasively enough to convince the man; altogether, a patient, meaningful, and rewarding dialogue.

"Good morning."

"Oh goddam!" he barked, "you made me bite my tongue. I thought you'd gone."

"I did." She knelt in the shadows with her back against the inner wall, facing the atrium. "But then I stopped to be with the tree for a while."

"Then what?"

"I thought a lot."

"What about?"

"You."

"Did you now!"

"Look," she said firmly, "I'm not going to any doctor to get this thing checked out. I didn't want to leave until I had told you that, and until I was sure you believed me."

"Come on in and we'll get something to eat."

Foolishly, she giggled. "I can't. My feet are asleep."

Without hesitation he scooped her up in his arms and carried her around the atrium. She said, her arm around his shoulders and their faces close, "Do you believe me?"

He continued around until they reached the wooden chest, then stopped and looked into her eyes. "I believe you. I don't know why you decided that, but I'm willing to believe you." He set her down on the chest and stood back.

"It's the act of faith you mentioned," she said gravely. "I thought you ought to have it, at least once in your life, so you can never say such a thing again." She tapped her heels gingerly against the slate floor. "Ow." She made a pained smile. "Pins and needles."

"You must have been thinking for a long time."

"Yes. Want more?"

"Sure."

"You are an angry, frightened man."

He seemed delighted. "Tell me about all that!"

"No," she said quietly, "you tell me. I'm very serious about this. Why are you angry?"

"I'm not."

"Why are you so angry?"

"I tell you I'm not! Although," he added good-naturedly, "you're pushing me in that direction."

"Well then, why?"

He gazed at her for what, to her, seemed a very long time indeed. "You really want to know, don't you?"

She nodded.

He waved a sudden hand, up and out. "Where do you suppose all this came from—the house, the land, the equipment?"

She waited.

"An exhaust system," he said, with a thickening of the voice she was coming to know. "A way of guiding exhaust gases out of combustion engines in such a way that they are given a spin. Unburned solids are embedded in the walls of the muffler in a glass-wool liner that slips out in one piece and can be replaced by a clean one every couple of thousand miles. The rest of the exhaust is fired by its own spark plug and what will burn, burns. The heat is used to preheat the fuel; the rest is spun again through a five-thousand-mile cartridge. What finally gets out is, by today's standards at least, pretty clean; and because of the preheating, it actually gets better mileage out of the engine."

"So you've made a lot of money."

"I made a lot of money," he echoed. "But not because the thing is being used to cut down air pollution. I got the money because an automobile company bought it and buried it in a lock-box. They don't like it because it costs something to install in new cars. Some friends of theirs in the refining business don't like it because it gets high performance out of crude fuels. Well all right—I didn't know any better and I won't make the same mistake again. But yes—I'm angry. I was angry when I was a kid on a tankship and we were set to washing down the bulkhead with chipped brown-soap and canvas, and I went ashore and bought a detergent and tried it and it was better, faster, and cheaper so I took it to the bos'n, who gave me a punch in the mouth for pretending to know his job better than he did . . . well, he was drunk at the time, but the rough part was when the old shellbacks in the crew got wind of it and ganged up on me for being what they called a 'company man'—that's a dirty name in a ship. I just couldn't understand why people got in the way of something better.

"I've been up against that all my life. I have something in my head that just won't quit: It's a way I have of asking the next question: Why is so-and-so the way it is? Why can't it be such-and-such instead? There is always another question to be asked about any thing or any situation; especially you shouldn't quit when you like an answer because there's always another one after it. And we live in a world where people just don't want to ask the next question!

"I've been paid all my stomach will take for things people won't use, and if I'm mad all the time it's really my fault—I admit it; because I just can't stop asking that next question and coming up with answers. There's a half-dozen real blockbusters in that lab that nobody will ever see, and half a hundred more in my head; but what can you do in a world where people would rather kill each other in a desert even when they're shown it can turn green and bloom, where they'll fall all over themselves to pour billions into developing a new oil strike when it's been proved over and over again that the fossil fuels will kill us all?

"Yes, I'm angry. Shouldn't I be?"

She let the echoes of his voice swirl around the court and out through the hole in the top of the atrium, and waited a little longer to let him know he was here with her and not beside himself and his fury. He grinned at her sheepishly when he came to this, and she said:

"Maybe you're asking the next question instead of asking the right question. I think people who live by wise old sayings are trying not to think, but I know one worth paying some attention to. It's this: If you ask a question the right way you've just given the answer." She paused to see if he was paying real attention. He was. She went on, "I mean, if you put your hand on a hot stove you might ask yourself, How can I stop my hand from burning? And the answer is pretty clear, isn't it? If the world keeps rejecting what you have to give, there's some way of asking why that contains the answer."

"It's a simple answer," he said shortly. "People are stupid."

"That isn't the answer and you know it," she said.

"What is?"

"Oh, I can't tell you that! All I know is that the way you do something, when people are concerned, is more important than what you do, if you want results. I mean . . . you already know how to get what you want with the tree, don't you?"

"I'll be damned."

"People are living growing things too. I don't know a hundredth part of what you do about bonsai, but I do know this: When you start one, it isn't often the strong straight healthy ones you take. It's the twisted sick ones that can be made the most beautiful. When you get to shaping humanity, you might remember that."

"Of all the—I don't know whether to laugh in your face or punch you right in the mouth!"

She rose. He hadn't realized she was quite this tall. "I'd better go."

"Come on now. You know a figure of speech when you hear one."

"Oh, I didn't feel threatened. But—I'd better go, all the same."

Shrewdly, he asked her, "Are you afraid to ask the next question?"

"Terrified."

"Ask it anyway."

"No!"

"Then I'll do it for you. You said I was angry—and afraid. You want to know what I'm afraid of."

"Yes."

"You. I am scared to death of you."

"Are you really?"

"You have a way of provoking honesty," he said with some difficulty. "I'll say what I know you're thinking: I'm afraid of any close human relationship. I'm afraid of something I can't take apart with a screwdriver or a mass spectroscope or a table of cosines and tangents." His voice was jocular but his hands were shaking.

"You do it by watering one side," she said softly, "or by turning it just so in the sun. You handle it as if it were a living thing, like a species or a woman or a bonsai. It will be what you want it to be if you let it be itself and take the time and the care."

"I think," he said, "that you are making me some kind of offer. Why?"

"Sitting there most of the night," she said, "I had a crazy kind of image. Do you think two sick twisted trees ever made bonsai out of one another?"

"What's your name?" he asked her.

ABOUT A SECRET CROCODILE

August 1970

R. A. Lafferty
(b. 1914)

Raymond Aloysius Lafferty began writing science fiction when he was well past forty, producing a large body of work that can only be described as wonderful, wild, and often bewildering. His is an original voice, and his contributions to sf are only now becoming apparent. Lafferty also meant a great deal to Galaxy in the 1960s, with something like 20 stories, including such major works as "Sodom and Gomorrah, Texas" (December 1962), the fabulous "Slow Tuesday Night" (April 1965), "Thus We Frustrate Charlemagne" (February 1967), and "Primary Education of the Camiroi" (December 1966) and its "sequel" "Polity and Custom of the Camiroi" (June 1967).

"About a Secret Crocodile" is one of his best and most famous stories, one that rewards rereading time and time again. Lafferty's agent, Virginia Kidd, tells us that when the story appeared in Galaxy, she received an indignant call from the editors of Playboy magazine wanting to know why they hadn't seen it first. Virginia says, "Frankly, it had never occurred to me that it was anything but a Galaxy story, so that is where I sent it."

Memoir by R. A. Lafferty

Galaxy was the golden magazine of science fiction. At its best, there were nuggets in at least half its issues. No one else came close to that.

Let the hills leap like little lambs at the memory!

"About a Secret Crocodile" was a shot in a war (since lost) against a cabal that was forcing "trendiness," whose other name is "unoriginality," on the world.

Oh rise again and fight some more, dead people!

Galaxy died several times from embracing this trendiness or unoriginality. The "magazine-that-is-different" became quite like all the other "magazines-that-are-different." And it died because it spent all its retrospection on things past.

The newest *Galaxy* editor, Hank Stine, is an experienced resurrectionist. He brought a dead and rotting Louisiana alligator back to life by laying his reanimating hands on it and breathing into its nostrils. Later he brought back to life a dead rabbit, a dead goat, and a little dead boy.

(He has not told these things of himself. Others have told them of him.)

Now he will, probably, raise the magazine from its second or third death. You've got to have faith!

(If he isn't still at the helm when this appears, that just means that good guys move around a lot.)

Never trust a retrospectionist who isn't two-faced. A little of that retrospection for the future, please!

Galaxy, esto perpetua: Thou art forever! (I hope.)

But, for all that, the way-it-used-to-be was quite extraordinary.

ABOUT A SECRET CROCODILE

There is a secret society of seven men that controls the finances of the world. This is known to everyone but the details are not known. There are some who believe that it would be better if one of those seven men were a financier.

There is a secret society of three men and four women that controls all the fashions of the world. The details of this are known to all who are in the fashion. And I am not.

There is a secret society of nineteen men that is behind all the fascist organizations in the world. The secret name of this society is Glomerule.

There is a secret society of thirteen persons known as the Elders of Edom that controls all the secret sources of the world. That the sources have become muddy is of concern to them.

There is a secret society of only four persons that manufactures all the jokes of the world. One of these persons is unfunny and he is responsible for all the unfunny jokes.

There is a secret society of eleven persons that is behind all Bolshevik and atheist societies of the world. The devil himself is a member of this society, and he works tirelessly to become a principal member. The secret name of this society is Ocean.

There are related secret societies known as The Path of the Serpent (all its members have the inner eyelid of snakes), The Darkbearers, the Seeing Eye, Imperium, The Golden Mask, and the City.

Above most of these in a queer network there is a society that controls the attitudes and dispositions of the world—and the name of it is Crocodile. The Crocodile is insatiable: It eats persons and nations alive. And the Crocodile is very old, 8809 years old by one account, 7349 years old if you use the short chronology.

There are subsecret societies within the Crocodile: Cocked Eye, the Cryptic Cootie, and others. Powerful among these is a society of 399 persons that manufactures all the catchwords and slogans of the world. This subsociety is not completely secret since several of the members are mouthy: The code name of this apparatus is the Crocodile's Mouth.

Chesterton said that Mankind itself was a secret society. Whether it would be better or worse if the secret should ever come out he did not say.

And finally there was—for a short disruptive moment—a secret society of three persons that controlled all.

All what?

Bear with us. That is what this account is about.

John Candor had been called into the office of Mr. James Dandi at ABNC. (Whisper, whisper, for your own good, do not call him Jim Dandy; that is a familiarity he will not abide.)

"This is the problem, John," Mr. Dandi stated piercingly, "and we may as well put it into words. After all, putting things into words and pictures is our way of working at ABNC. Now then, what do we do at ABNC, John?"

(ABNC was one of the most powerful salivators of the Crocodile's Mouth.)

"We create images and attitudes, Mr. Dandi."

"That is correct, John," Mr. Dandi said. "Let us never forget it. Now something has gone wrong. There is a shadowy attack on us that may well be the most damaging thing since the old transgression of Spirochaete himself. Why has something gone wrong with our operation, John?"

"Sir, I don't know."

"Well then, what has gone wrong?"

"What has gone wrong, Mr. Dandi, is that it isn't working the way it should. We are caught on our own catchwords, we are slaughtered by our own slogans. There are boomerangs whizzing about our ears from every angle. None of it goes over the way it is supposed to. It all twists wrong for us."

"Well, what is causing this? Why are our effects being nullified?"

"Sir, I believe that somebody else is also busy creating images and attitudes. Our catechesis states that this is impossible since we are the only group permitted in the field. Nevertheless, I am sure that someone else is building these things against us. It even seems that they are more powerful than we are—and they are unknown."

"They cannot be more powerful than we are—and they must not remain unknown to us." Mr. Dandi's words stabbed. "Find out who they are, John."

"How?"

"If I knew how, John, I would be working for you, not you working for me. Your job is to do things. Mine is the much more difficult one of telling you to do them. Find out, John."

John Candor went to work on the problem. He considered whether it was a linear, a set, or a group problem. If it were a linear problem he should have been able to solve it by himself—and he couldn't. If it were a set problem, then it couldn't be solved at all. Of necessity he classified it as a group problem and he assembled a group to solve it. This was easy at ABNC, which had more group talent than anybody.

The group that John Candor assembled was made up of August Crayfish, Sterling Groshawk, Maurice Cree, Nancy Peters, Tony Rover, Morgan Aye, and Betty McCracken. Tell the truth, would you be able to gather so talented a group in your own organization?

"My good people," John Candor said, "as we all know, something has gone wrong with our effects. It must be righted. Thoughts, please, thoughts!"

"We inflate a person or subject and he bursts on us," August gave his thought. "Are we using the wrong gas?"

"We launch a phrase and it turns into a joke," Sterling complained. "Yet we have not slighted the check-off: It has always been examined from every angle to be sure that it doesn't have a joker context. But something goes wrong."

"We build an attitude carefully from the ground up," Maurice stated. "Then our firm ground turns boggy and the thing tilts and begins to sink."

"Our 'Fruitful Misunderstandings,' the most subtle and effective of our current devices, are beginning to bear sour fruit," Nancy said.

"We set ourselves to cut a man down and our daggers turn to rubber," Tony Rover moaned. (Oh, were there ever sadder words? Our daggers have turned to rubber.)

"Things have become so shaky that we're not sure whether we are talking about free or closed variables," Morgan gave his thought.

"How can my own loving mother make such atrocious sandwiches?" Betty McCracken munched distastefully. Betty, who was underpaid, was a brown-sack girl who brought her own lunch. "This is worse than usual." She chewed on. "The only thing to do with it is feed it to the computer." She fed it to the computer, which ate it with evident pleasure.

"Seven persons, seven thoughts," John Candor mused.

"Seven persons, six thoughts," Nancy Peters spat bitterly. "Betty, as usual, has contributed nothing."

"Only the first stage of the answer," John Candor said. "She said 'The only thing to do with it is to feed it to the computer.' Feed the problem to the computer, folks."

They fed the problem to the computer by pieces and by wholes. The machine was familiar with their lingos and procedures. It was acquainted with the Nonvalid Context Problems of Morgan Aye and with the Hollow Shell Person Puzzles of Tony Rover. It knew the Pervading Environment Ploy of Maurice Cree. It knew what trickwork to operate within.

Again and again the machine asked for various kinds of supplementary exterior data.

"Leave me with it," the machine finally issued. "Assemble here again in sixty days, or hours—"

"No, we want the answers right now," John Candor insisted, "within sixty seconds."

"The second is possibly the interval I was thinking of," the machine issued. "What's time to a tin can anyhow?" It ground its data trains for a full minute.

"Well?" John Candor asked.

"Somehow I get the number three," the machine issued.

"Three what, machine?"

"Three persons," the machine issued. "They are unknowingly linked together to manufacture attitudes. They are without program or purpose or organization or remuneration or basis or malice."

"Nobody is without malice," August Crayfish insisted in a startled way. "They must be totally alien forms then. How do they manage their effects?"

"One with a gesture, one with a grimace, one with an intonation," the machine issued.

"Where are they?" John Candor demanded.

"All comparatively near." The machine drew three circles on the city map. "Each is to be found in his own circle most of the time."

"Their names?" John Candor asked and the machine wrote the name of each in the proper circle.

"Do you have anything on their appearances?" Sterling Groshawk inquired and the machine manufactured three kymograph pictures of the targets.

"Have you their addresses or identifying numbers?" Maurice Cree asked.

"No. I think it's remarkable of me that I was able to come up with this much," the machine issued.

"We can find them," Betty McCracken said. "We can most likely find them in the phone book."

"What worries me is that there's no malice in them," John Candor worried. "Without malice, there's no handle to get hold of a thing. The Disestablishment has been firmly established for these several hundred years and we hold it to be privileged. It must not be upset by these three randoms. We will do what we must do."

Mike Zhestovitch was a mighty man. One does not make the primordial gestures out of weak body and hands. He looked like a steel worker—or anyhow like a worker at one of the powerful trades. His torso was like a barrel but more noble than ordinary barrels. His arms and hands were hardly to be believed. His neck was for the bulls, his head was as big as a thirteen-gallon firkin, his eyeballs were the size of ducks' eggs, and the hair on his chest and throat was that heavy black wire-grass that defies steel plowshares. His voice—well, he didn't have much of a voice—it wasn't as mighty as the rest of him.

And he didn't really work at one of the powerful trades. He was a zipper repairman at the Jiffy Nifty Dry Cleaners.

August Crayfish of ABNC located Mike Zhestovitch in the Blind Robbin Bar which (if you recall the way that block lies) is just across that short jog-alley from the Jiffy Nifty. And August recognized big Mike at once. But how did big Mike get his effects?

"The Cardinals should take the Colts today," a serious man there was saying.

"The Cardinals—" Mike Zhestovitch began in the voice that was less noble than the rest of him, but he didn't finish the sentence. As a matter of fact, big Mike had never finished a sentence in all his life. Instead he made the gesture with his mighty hands and body. Words cannot describe the gesture but it was something like balling up an idea or opinion in the giant hands and throwing it away, utterly away, over the very edge of contempt.

The Cardinals, of course, did not take the Colts that day. For a moment it was doubtful whether the Cardinals would survive at all. From the corner of the eye, red feathers could be seen drifting away in the air.

August Crayfish carefully waited a moment and watched. A man walked out of the Blind Robbin and talked to another man in that little jog-alley. From their seriousness it was certain that they were talking baseball.

"The Cardinals—" the first man said after a moment, and he also made the gesture. And seconds later a man playing eight-ball in the back of the Blind Robbin did the same thing.

August was sure then. Mike Zhestovitch not only could shrivel anything with the gesture, but the gesture as he used it was highly epidemic. It would spread, according to Schoeffler's Law of Dispersal, through the city in short minutes, through the world in short hours. And no opinion could stand against its disfavor. Mike Zhestovitch could wreck images and attitudes—and possibly he could also create them.

"Do you work alone?" August Crayfish asked.

"No. The rip-fix and the button-sew girls work in the same cubbyhole," Mike said with his curiously small voice.

"Do you know a Mary Smorfia?" August asked.

"I don't, no," Mike said, a certain comprehension coming into his ducks'-egg-sized eyes. "And you are glad that I don't? Then I will. I'll find out who she is. I see it now that you are a wrong guy and she is a right girl."

Then August Crayfish spoke the slogan that would be unveiled to the ears of the world that very night, a wonderfully slippery slogan that had cost a hundred thousand dollars to construct. It should have warned Mike Zhestovitch away from his mad resistance.

Mike Zhestovitch made the gesture, and the slogan was in ruins. And somewhere the Secret Crocodile lashed its tail in displeasure.

"Do you want to make a lot of money?" August Crayfish whispered after a long reevaluation pause.

"Money—from such as you—" Big Mike didn't finish the sentence, he never did. But he made the gesture. The idea of a lot of money shriveled. And August Crayfish shriveled so small that he could not climb over the threshold of the Blind Robbin on the way out and had to be aided over it by the shod-toe of a kind man. (This last statement is a literal exaggeration but it is the right direction.)

Nancy Peters of ABNC located Mary Smorfia in the King-Pin Bowling Alley, where she was a hamburger waitress and a beer buster. Mary was small, dark, unpretty (except for her high-frequency eyes and the beautiful gash across her face that was her mouth), lively, smart, busy, a member of that aberrant variety of the human race that was called Italian.

"Snorting Summer should take the Academy Award," one nice guzzling lady at the counter was saying to another, "and Clover Elysée is the shoeless shoo-in for best actress of the year."

And Mary Smorfia made the grimace. Ah, it was mostly done with the beautifully large mouth and yet every part of her entered into it, from the blue lights in her hair to her cringly toes. It was a devastating, all-destroying grimace. It gobbled up, it nullified, and it made itself felt to a great distance. The nice guzzling lady had not even been looking toward Mary Smorfia but she felt the grimace like a soul shock, and she herself did the grimace with a wonderful distortion of the features that weren't made for it.

And the grimace swept everything like quick contagion or prairie fire. Snorting Summer—gah! Clover Elysée—guggling gah! Those things were finished forever, beyond laughter, below derision. And Nancy Peters of ABNC noted the powerful effect carefully, for the original words of the nice guzzling lady were the very words that ABNC had selected to be echoed a hundred million times whenever the awards were thought of.

"Do you work alone?" Nancy Peters asked Mary Smorfia.

"Kid, I'm so fast they don't need anyone else on this shift. I'm like silly lightning."

"Did you ever think of becoming an actress, Mary?" Nancy asked in honey tones.

"Oh, I made a commercial once," Mary said out of her curly gashmouth (she had to be kidding: she couldn't really have a mouth that looked like that). "I don't know whether I sold much of my guy's soap but I bet I got a lot of people off that Brand X. Ashes it was, worse even, after I monkey-faced it. They say I'm a natural—but once is enough."

"Do you know a Mike Zhestovitch or a Clivendon Surrey?" Nancy asked.

"I don't think so," Mary said. "What league do they bowl in? I bet I will like them both, though, and I will remember their names and find them."

Nancy Peters was nervous. She felt that the annihilating grimace was about to strike again on Mary's lightning-gash mouth. But it was time for the test of strength. Nancy spoke the new slogan that had been selected for presentation to the world that very night, a wonderfully convincing and powerful slogan that should bring this random Mary Smorfia to hell if anything could. And she spoke it with all the absolute expertise of the Crocodile's Mouth behind her.

The Grimace! And the slogan was destroyed forever. And (grimacing horror turned inward) Nancy caught the contagion and was doing the grimace herself. She was quite unable to get the thing off her face.

Sheer humiliation overwhelmed the Nancy person, who had suddenly been made small. And somewhere the Secret Crocodile lashed its tail in displeasure and unease.

"Do you want to make twenty thousand dollars, Mary?" Nancy

asked after she had returned from the jane where she had daubed her flushed face and cooled her flustered body.

"Twenty thousand dollars isn't very much," Mary Smorfia sounded out of her panoramic mouth. "I make eighty-eight fifty now after everything. I could make a lot more if I wanted to go along with the cruds."

"Twenty thousand dollars is very much more," Nancy Peters said enticingly.

"It is very much more cruddy, kid." Mary Smorfia grimaced. Grimaced! Not again! Nancy Peters fled in deflated panic. She felt herself dishonored forever.

Well, do you think it is all watermelon pickles and pepper relish, this unilaterally creating all the images and attitudes for the whole world? It is a detailed and devious thing and the privileged Disestablishment had been building it for centuries. (The Establishment itself had been no more than a figure of speech for most of those centuries, a few clinging bits of bark: The heart of the tree had long been possessed by the privileged Disestablishment.) Three quick random persons could not be permitted to nullify words from the Mouth itself.

Morgan Aye of ABNC located Clivendon Surrey in Speedsters' Café. Clivendon was a lank and fair-haired man with a sort of weariness about him, a worldliness that had to be generations old. He had the superior brow and the thoroughbred nose that isn't grown in short centuries. He had the voice, the intonation, the touch of Groton, the touch of Balliol, the strong touch of other institutions even more august. It was a marvelous voice, at least the intonation of it. Clivendon's employer once said that he didn't believe that Clivendon ever spoke in words, at least not in any words that he was ever able to understand. The intonation was really a snort, a sort of neigh, but it carried the cresting contempt of the ages in its tone. And it was contagious.

Clivendon was really of Swedish extraction and had come off a farm near Pottersville. He had developed that intonation for a role in a high-school play. He had liked it and he had kept it. Clivendon was a motorcycle mechanic at Downhillers' Garage.

"Do you work alone?" Morgan Aye asked Clivendon.

"Naeu. You work alone and you got to work. You work with a bunch and you can slip out from it," Clivendon intoned. Yes, he talked in words and the words could be mostly understood. But the towering intonation was the thing, the world-wilting contempt of the tone. This man was a natural and Morgan felt himself a foot shorter in the very presence of that tone.

"Do you know a Mike Zhestovitch or a Mary Smorfia?" Morgan asked fearfully.

"That's a funny thing." The tone cut through earwax and the soft spots of the spleen. "I had never heard of them but Mary Smorfia called me up not thirty minutes ago and said that she wanted both of us to meet Mike. So I'll meet them in about twenty minutes, as soon as the clock there says that I'm supposed to be off work at Downhillers' Garage."

"Don't meet them!" Morgan cried out violently. "That might be the closing of the link, the setting up of a league. It might be an affront to the Mouth itself."

The tone, the neigh, the snort, the sharp edge of a wordless intonation sent Morgan reeling back. And there were echoes of it throughout Speedsters' Café and in the streets outside. The tone was as contagious as it was cutting.

Morgan started to speak the newest selected slogan from the Mouth—and he stopped short. He was afraid of the test of strength. Two very expensive slogans had already been shattered today by these randoms. "No malice in the three," the computer had said and: "Without malice, there's no handle to get hold of a thing," John Candor had stated. But somewhere in that mountainous and contagious contempt of tone that belonged to Clivendon Surrey had to be some malice. So Morgan Aye reached for what had always been the ultimate weapon of the Crocodile's Mouth. It always worked—it always worked if any malice at all existed in the object.

"How would you like to make five thousand dollars a week?" he whispered to Clivendon.

"What garage pays that much?" Clivendon asked in honest wonder. "I'm not that good a motorcycle mechanic."

"Five thousand dollars a week to work with us at ABNC," Morgan tempted. "We could use you in so many ways—that marvelous scorn to cut down any man we wished! You could lend the intonations of your voice to our—"

The neigh was like a thousand sea stallions breaking up from the depths. The snort was one that crumbles cliffs at the ends of the earth. Morgan Aye had gone ghastly white and his ears were bleeding from the transgression of that cutting sound. There were even some words in Clivendon's sounding—"Why, then I'd be one of the birds that picks the shreds of flesh from between the teeth of the monster." Blinding hooting contempt in the tone and Morgan Aye was in the street and running from it.

But the echoes of that intonation were everywhere in that part of town, soon to be all over the town, all over the world. It was an epidemic of snorting at the Crocodile's Mouth itself. Fools! Did they know that this was but one step from snorting at the very Crocodile?

The ring had closed. The informal league had formed now. The three randoms had met and united. The Mouth was affronted. Worse than that, all the outpour of the Mouth was nullified. The whole world was rejecting the catchwords that came from the Mouth, was laughing at them, was throwing them away with the uttermost gesture, was monkey-facing them, was snorting them down, was casting them out with bottomless contempt.

This was the short reign of the secret society of three, who did not know that they were secret. But in their day they closed the Mouth down completely. It was filled with mud and swamp reeds and rotting flesh.

The Secret Crocodile was lashing its tail with acute displeasure now. The Crocodile's Mouth had become quite nervous. And what of the little birds that fly in and out of that mouth, that preen the teeth and glean scraps of flesh and slogans and catchwords there? The birds were in quite an unhappy flutter.

"There is an open conspiracy against us by a secret society of three persons," Mr. James Dandi was saying, "and all the world abominates a secret society. We have this thing to do this day—to cripple it forever in its strength. Otherwise we will be cast out and broken as ineffectual instruments and the Crocodile will bring in strong persons from the Cocked Eye or the Cryptic Cootie to take our places. Surely we are not without resources. What is the logical follow-up to the Fruitful Misunderstanding?"

"The Purposive Accident," John Candor said immediately.

"Take care of it, John," Mr. James Dandi said. "Remember,

though, that he whose teeth we preen is the very bowels of compassion. I believe this is the salient thing in the world in our day, the Compassion of the Crocodile."

"Take care of it, people," John Candor said to his seven talented ones, "remembering always that the Crocodile is the very belly of compassion."

"Take care of it," the seven said to the computer, "always within the context of the jaws of compassion."

The computer programmed a Purposive Accident to happen and manufactured such props as were needed. And the Purposive Accident was very well programmed.

There was no great amount of blood poured out. No persons were killed except several uninvolved bystanders. The secret three were left alive and ambulant and scathed only at their points of strength.

It happened in the block between the Blind Robbin Bar and Speedsters' Café when all three members of the secret society happened to be walking together. The papers called it a bomb; they call everything a bomb that goes off like that. It was really a highly sophisticated homing device with a tripartite programming and it carried out its tripartite mission.

All three randoms, former members of the short-lived secret society, are well and working again. Mike Zhestovitch is no longer a zipper repairman (it takes two talented hands to fix those zippers), but he still works at the Jiffy Nifty Dry Cleaners. He runs one of those big pressers now which he can easily do with his powerful and undamaged left hand and his prosthetic right hand. But without his old right hand he can no longer make the contagious primordial gesture that once dumbfounded the Mouth and all its words. You just cannot make the big gesture with a false hand.

Mary Smorfia still works at the King-Pin Bowling Alley as hamburger waitress and beer buster. She is still small, dark, unpretty (except for her high-frequency eyes), lively, smart, and Italian. Her mouth is still a gash across her face, but now it is twice as great a gash as it used to be, and it no longer has its curled liveliness. Its mobility is all gone, it will no longer express the inexpressible, will no longer shatter a phrase or an attitude. Mary Smorfia is as she always was, except that now she is incapable of the famous grimace.

Clivendon Surrey is again a motorcycle mechanic at Downhillers' Garage and again he spends most of his time in Speedsters' Café. His vocal cords are gone, of course, but he gets by: He is able to speak with a throat microphone. But the famous intonation, the neigh, the destroying snort are all impossible for him.

The trouble is over with. Now again there is only one organization in the world to create the images and attitudes of the world. This ensures that only the standard attitudes of the Disestablishment shall prevail.

In our opening catalog we forgot one group. There is another secret society in the world composed of the good guys and good gals. It has no name that we have ever heard except just the Good Guys and Good Gals. At the moment this society controls nothing at all in the world. It stirs a little, though. It may move. It may collide, someday, even with the Secret Crocodile itself.

COLD FRIEND

October 1973

Harlan Ellison

(b. 1934)

One of the most famous and at times controversial figures in fantasy fiction, Harlan Ellison graduated from sf fandom to the ranks of the professionals in 1954. The winner of seven and a half Hugo and three Nebula awards, his anthologies Dangerous Visions *(1967) and* Again, Dangerous Visions *(1972) are among the most important in the history of the field.*

Although he only published occasionally in Galaxy, his appearances included one of his most famous stories, "The Beast That Shouted Love at the Heart of the World" (June 1968; Hugo award, 1969), and the neglected novella "The Region Between" (March 1970; Hugo and Nebula runner-up). Most importantly, Galaxy published his "'Repent Harlequin' Said the Ticktockman" (December 1965; Hugo and Nebula awards, 1965), one of the ten most heavily reprinted stories in the history of American literature.

Memoir by Harlan Ellison*

Sometimes, when I sit down to write, I say, *Okay, this one will be a screamer, scare the hell out of them;* other times I'll think, *Maybe a love story, something warm and rich and very human;* once in a while I'll nudge myself into starting with that terrific time-tested *All right, Ellison . . . what if?*

And most often of all, I just sit down and let the crazies take me. Those are the best. Because I never know where they're going. The

Unconscious grabs hold of the flowing mane on the wild creature that is my darling Muse, and I hang on for dear life. From those rides come the stories I like best. Frequently, they are the stories that are best known and most frequently anthologized. Occasionally, the ride produces a story that *I* like a whole lot, but one that no one else seems to remember after its first publication.

"Cold Friend" was one of the latter.

I wrote it while attending one of Damon Knight's Milford Writers' Workshops. In fact, I think it was the very last Milford get-together I attended. It was held at a bucolic woodland conference center in Hickory Corners, Michigan, in 1973, on the shore of Gull Lake. Apart from writing this story, it was a pretty dull week. I was hiding out from the creeps who were producing my (thankfully) short-lived television series, "The Starlost," up in Toronto; I had been trying to finish a story called "Catman"; and on Friday the eighth of June, on the last day of the 16th Milford SF Conference, Ejler Jakobsson showed up for the good-bye party.

Jake was editing *Galaxy* at that time, and I hadn't seen him in years. He saw me, came over, we shook hands, and the first thing he said was, "I'm putting together an all-star 23rd anniversary issue of *Galaxy*. It wouldn't be an issue without you in it."

I blushed prettily and said I didn't have anything available at the moment. ("Catman" was already promised.) And I knew I wouldn't have any time to write a new story, because I was leaving for Toronto the next day, to plunge into what I knew would be a nightmare situation on "The Starlost." But Jake was insistent. So, since I was bored anyway, I said, "What's a good length for you, Jake?"

He said about three to five thousand words would fit because he already had stories from Arthur C. Clarke and Ted Sturgeon and Ursula Le Guin and James White, and he even had a new poem by Ray Bradbury. I nodded sagely at the auspicious company I'd be keeping if I could write something, and said, "Wait here; I'll be right back."

Then I went to the room in which I'd been working for a week, sat down, and three hours later came out with "Cold Friend."

Jake was socializing with the other writers and editors who had come down for the wrap-up party, and I came to him and dangled "Cold Friend" in front of his face, and I said, "Two conditions if you want to buy it, Jake."

He asked what they were.

"First, no tampering. You leave it as it is. Not one word altered. Second, you copyright it in my name."

He agreed, and went off to read it. When he wandered back, fifteen minutes later, he was grinning and said, "You are now in the Twenty-third Anniversary All-Star Issue."

I was pleased. It had been a few years since my salad days of selling some of my best work to Fred Pohl at *Galaxy* and *If*. I'd always liked the magazines; and it was like renewing an old friendship.

Ah, but . . .

Jake came from the same school of pulp editing that had spawned Uncle Fred; and just like Fred, he couldn't leave a story alone. He had to fiddle with it. But since I'd extracted the promise that no changes would be made in the story, Jake went around Robin Hood's Barn to scratch his editorial itch.

Sometime around July or August I happened to read in one of the sf magazines a lineup for the October 1973 All-Star Issue of *Galaxy*. And right there, in black and white, it said that issue would contain something called "Know Your Local Mailman" by Harlan Ellison. As I could not recall ever having written anything with that title, I concluded it was Jake running amok, and I called him and suggested politely that he was breaking his promise to me. (Fred has written endlessly of such phone calls between us. In the Pohl retellings I am always the lunatic, intractable pain-in-the-butt who has the audacity to demand his stories be published as they were written, clearly in defiance of the greater auctorial wisdom of the editor.)

Jake finally agreed to catch the galleys at the printer and to set the original title as I'd conceived it. (But there were minor fiddles in the text. Ah me.)

Nonetheless, "Cold Friend" remains one of my favorite stories. And though I *did* have an acquaintance named Opal Sellers when I was a very little boy, and though the incident at high-school graduation *did* happen to me as reported in the story, it happened to another young woman, not Opal, whom I have not seen or heard from in maybe thirty-five years.

Because of these bits of personal history, "Cold Friend" has a chosen place in my heart; and it is a genuine joy for me that the editors of this retrospective have selected it from among the much better known and even award-winning *Galaxy* stories I've done.

Because apart from its publication in my collection *Approaching Oblivion*, this is the first time "Cold Friend" has been reprinted. In its original version. At last, through years and strife, it appears in *Galaxy* as I intended.

You see, there *is* Justice in the Universe.

COLD FRIEND

Because I had died of cancer of the lymph glands, I was the only one saved when the world disappeared. The name for it was "spontaneous remission," and as I understand it, it is not uncommon in the world of medicine. There is no explanation for it that any two physicians will agree upon, but it happens every so often. Your first question will be: Why are you writing this if everyone else in the world is gone? And my answer is: Should *I* disappear, and should things ever change, there should be some small record available to whoever or whatever comes along.

That is hypocrisy. I write this because I am a thinking creature with an enormous ego, and I cannot bear to consider having been here, being gone, and leaving nothing behind. Since I will never have children to carry on my line, to preserve some tiny bit of my existence . . . since I will never make a mark in the world, because there is no world left . . . since I will never write a novel, or paste up a billboard, or have my face carved on Mt. Rushmore . . . I am writing this. Additionally, it keeps me busy. I have explored all three square blocks of what's left of the world, and quite frankly, there isn't much else to do to amuse myself. So I write this.

I have always had the detestable habit of having to justify myself. Let me hear some vague rumor or snippet of gossip about myself, and I spent *weeks* tracking it down, refuting it, bringing to justice the one who passed the remark. Now that's just ridiculous. And here I am justifying myself again. This record is here, read it if you please, or don't. That's that.

I was in the hospital. I was terminal. Oxygen tent, tubes plugged into me everywhere, constantly sedated, the pain was the worst thing I've ever known, it never stopped. Then . . . I just started to get well. First I died, I know I died, don't ask me how I can say such a thing with complete assurance that I'm telling the truth, because if you've ever died, you'll know. Even under the knockout stuff they'd pumped into me, I still had some awareness. But when I died, it was as if I was strapped flat to the front of a subway car, spreadeagled to the wall, facing down the tunnel, into the blackness, and the subway car was hurtling along at a million miles an hour. I was utterly helpless. The air was being sucked out of my lungs and the train just slammed down that tunnel toward a little point of light. And in receding waves of sound I heard a whispering voice calling my name, over and over and over: *Eu-gene, Eu-gene, Eu-gene, Eu-gene* . . .

I went screaming down at that tiny square of light at the end of the tunnel, and I closed my eyes and could see it even with them closed. And then I crashed forward even faster, and went into the spot of light and everything was blinding, and I knew I was dead.

A long time later—I think it was two hundred years . . . on the other hand it may only have been a day or two—I opened my eyes and there I was in the hospital bed with a sheet up over my face.

I lay like that for almost a day. I could see the light of the ceiling fixture through the sheet. No one came to help me, and I felt weak and hungry.

Finally, I got angry, and I was so hungry I couldn't stand it any longer, so I whipped the sheet down off my face, and pulled the remaining tube out of my arm—I presumed it to be an intravenous feeding tube and whatever had been left in the bottle was what had sustained me—and got out of bed and slid my feet into my slippers —the heels of my feet were red and dry like the heels of old women in nursing homes—and in that ridiculous hospital gown I went looking for something to eat. I couldn't find the kitchen of the hospital at first, but I found a candy machine. I didn't have any dimes for it, but there was a nurse's station right there, and I was so angry at being ignored, I rummaged through some drawers and a purse under the counter till I found a handful of change.

I ate four Power House bars, two almond Hersheys, and a box of those pink Canada mints.

Then, sucking on tropical fruit Life-Savers, I went looking for the hospital staff.

Did I mention the hospital was empty?

The hospital was empty.

Everyone was gone, of course. I told you that at the outset. But it took me a few hours to establish the fact. So I got dressed and went outside. Everything looked the same. The name of this town is

Hanover, New Hampshire, if you need to know. I won't bother with what the names of streets and things were when it was in the world, because I've given them all new names. It's my town now, all mine, so I decided I'd call it what I felt like calling it. But when this town was in the world, Dartmouth College was here, and there was good skiing, and it was desperately cold in the Winter. Now the mountains are gone, and it hasn't been Winter in a year or so. Dartmouth is also gone. It lay outside the three-block area of what was saved when the world vanished. There's a pizza place here, though. I don't know how to make pizza, though I've tried. I think I miss that most of all. Isn't that mundane! My God.

The world is gone, and all I seem to be able to dwell on is pizza. What hapless little creatures we humans were. Are. Am. I am.

So. I was alive again, and I suppose the only reason I didn't poof away with all the rest of them was that everyone thought I was dead. I *suppose* that's the reason. I don't really know. I'm guessing, of course; but since none of this made any sense at the time, that was my only conclusion.

If you think I'm terribly calm and rational about something as beserk as this, you can believe that I was frantic when I wandered out into the street in front of the hospital and saw the street was empty. I started walking, sticking my head into one store after another, looking for *any*body. And every once in a while I'd stop and cup my hands around my mouth and yell, "Hey! Anybody! Eugene Harrison! Hey! Anybody there?" But there wasn't a soul.

When the world was here, I was a postal clerk. I'm not from Hanover. I lived in White Sulphur Springs. I was brought to Hanover, to the hospital, to die.

When I got to the end of the world, at the foot of the street where the hospital stood, I just stared. I sat down and dangled my feet over, and just stared.

Then I scrunched around and lay on my stomach and looked over the edge. The ground sloped back, under there, and beneath the sidewalk there was dirt, and I could see roots hanging out, and it was a wedge-shape to the chunk of world floating with me on it, and underneath the chunk there wasn't anything. I guess it's not anything. I tried lowering myself on a mountain-climber's rope once, about a month later, but even when I threw the rope over, it just lay there in the emptiness and wouldn't fall straight down.

I think perhaps gravity is gone out there, too.

So. I got up and decided to circumnavigate the chunk. It was three blocks square, just the buildings and the bit of park and the hospital and some small houses. The U.S. Post Office is also there. I spent one day, a while later, a whole day, sorting the mail that had been left behind when the world vanished, stocking one of the clerks' windows, oiling the wheels of the carts, sewing up the storage bags with the heavy thread and monster needle every substation keeps in its larder. It was one of the dullest days of my life.

I don't want to say too much about myself—hypocrisy again—just enough to pass me on down to you so I won't be forgotten or faceless. I've already said my name is Eugene Harrison, from White Sulphur Springs, and I was a postal clerk. I was never married, but I've had relationships with at least four women. None of them lasted very long; I think they got tired of me, but I don't know for sure. I'm moderately educated, I went two years to Dartmouth before I dropped out and went to work in the Post Office. I was majoring in Arts and Letters, which means I thought perhaps I would go into advertising or television or journalism or something. That was certainly a waste of time. I can write things down in order, and even with a little grace, but I'm no writer, that's for certain. I can't keep myself at the writing for very long; I get very antsy. And I think I use the word "very" too much.

I wish I could tell you there was something particularly heroic or remarkable about me, beside the dying, that is, but I am just like all other people I've ever known. Or, like they were. They aren't any more. That's the truth, and I think it takes a big person to admit that he's very ordinary. My socks always matched. I forgot to fill the gas tank sometimes and ran out and had to carry a can up the road to the station. I shirked some of my responsibilities. I made gallant gestures occasionally. I hate vegetables.

My interests were in travel and history. I never did much about either. I went to Yucatan one summer, and I read a lot of history books. Neither of those is very interesting.

It would be great to be able to say I was special, but I wasn't. I'm thirty-one years old, and I'm just plain damned *average*, damn it, I'm *average*, so stop it, stop your damned badgering! I'm a nothing, a nobody, you never even saw my face through the wicket when I gave you your stamps, you arrogant swine! You never paid me the least attention and you never asked me if I'd had a good day and you never noticed that I trimmed the borders of the stamps I sold you, if they weren't full sheets, because many people collect full sheets, but you *never even noticed that little service!*

That's how I was special. I cared about the little things. And you never paid any attention . . .

I don't care to tell you any more about myself. Listen, this is about what happened, not about me, and you don't care about me anyhow, so there's no need to carry on like that about myself.

Please excuse what I wrote just now. It was an outburst. I'm sorry. And I'm sorry I cursed. I didn't mean to do that. I am a Lutheran. I attended Our Redeemer Lutheran Church in White Sulphur Springs. I was raised not to curse.

I'm going on now to what happened.

I walked all around the edge of the chunk of the world. It wasn't chopped off neatly. Whatever had done it, made the world vanish, had done it sloppily. The streets came to ragged ends, telephone lines trailed off where they'd dropped and some of them hung off into the emptiness, just floating like fishlines in water.

I should tell you what it looked like out there beyond the edge. It looked like a Winter snowfall, murky and with falling motes of light like snowflakes, but it was dark, too. I could see through the dark. That was what made it frightening: One shouldn't be able to see through the darkness. There was a wind out there, but it didn't blow. I can't describe that any better. You'll have to imagine it. And it wasn't cold or hot. It was just pleasant.

So I spent my days in what had been Hanover; I spent them all alone. And there was nothing heroic about me. Except that during the first week I saved my town from invasion about fifty times.

That will sound remarkable, but I assure you it wasn't. The first time it happened I was coming out of the Dartmouth Co-Op on the main street, carrying several paperbacks I had taken to read, when this Viking came screaming down the street. He was enormous, well over six feet tall, with a double-bitted axe in his hand, and a helmet with two horns, and a fierce orange beard, wearing furs and thongs and a bearskin cape, and he came right at me, shrieking in some barbarian language, with blood in his eyes and certain as God determined to hack me to bits.

I was terrified. I threw the paperbacks at him and would have run if I had been able to run, but I knew he'd catch me.

Except, what he did was: He threw up his free hand to ward off the paperbacks, and swerved around me and started running away from me down a side street. I couldn't understand what was happening, but I picked up the paperbacks and took off after him. I ran as fast as I could, which was pretty fast, and I started to catch up to him. When he looked over his shoulder and saw me coming, he screamed and ran like a madman.

I chased him right off the edge of the world.

He kept on running, right out into that darkness with the snowstorm in it, and he disappeared after a while, but I saw him still running at top speed till he was out of sight. I was afraid to go after him.

Later that day I turned back an attack by a German Stuka that strafed the main street, an attack by a Samurai warrior, an attack by a Moro with a huge batangas knife, an attack by a knight on a black horse—he carried a couched lance—and attacks by a Hun, a Visigoth, a Vandal, a Vietcong with a machine gun, an Amazon with a mace, a Puerto Rican street mugger, a Teddy Boy with a cosh, a deranged and drugged disciple of Kali with a knotted silk rope, a Venetian swordsman with a left-hand dagger, and I forget which all that first day.

It went on that way all week. It was all I could do to get any reading done.

Then they stopped, and I went about my business. But none of that was heroic. It was just part of the new order of things. At first I thought I was being tested, then I decided that was wrong. Actually, it got annoying, and I stood on the steps of the hospital and yelled at whoever was responsible, "Look, I don't want to know about any more of this. It's just nonsense, so knock it off!"

And it stopped just like that. I was relieved.

I had no television or movies (the movie house was gone) or radio, but the electricity worked fine and I had music and some talking records. I listened to Dylan Thomas reading "Under Milk Wood" and Errol Flynn telling the story of Robin Hood and Basil Rathbone telling the story of the Three Musketeers. That was very entertaining.

The water worked, and the gas, and the telephones didn't work. I was comfortable. There was no sun in the sky, or moon at night, but I could always see as if it were daylight in the day time, and clear enough to get around by night.

I saw her sitting on the front steps of the Post Office, I guess it was about a year after I'd died, and I hadn't seen anyone else after the invaders stopped doing their crazy screaming thing in the streets. She was just sitting there with her elbow propped on her knee and her chin resting in her palm.

I walked down the street to her, and stopped right in front of the Post Office. I was waiting for her to leap up and scream, "Amok! Amok!" or something, but she didn't. She just stared at me for a while.

She was awfully pretty. I'm not good at describing what people look like, but you can take it from me, she was very pretty. She was wearing a thin white gown that I could see through, and she was pretty all over. Her hair was long and gray, but not *old* gray; it was gray as if she liked it that way, the fashionable young-person kind of gray. If you know what I'm getting at.

"How do you feel?" she asked, finally.

"I'm all right, thank you."

"Have you healed up nicely?"

"I knitted real well. Who are you? Where did you come from?"

She waved toward the end of the world, and around the street, and shrugged. "I don't know. I just sort of woke up here. Everybody else's gone, is that right?"

"That's right. They've been gone for about a year. Well, uh, where did you wake up?"

"Right here. I've been sitting here for about an hour. I was just starting to get my bearings. I thought I might be all alone here."

"Do you remember your name?"

She seemed annoyed at that. "Yes, of course, I remember my name. It's Opal Sellers. I'm from Boston."

"This was Hanover, New Hampshire."

"Who are you?"

"Eugene Harrison. From White Sulphur Springs."

She looked very pale. I didn't say it, but that was the first thing about her I noticed. It wasn't the dress I could see through, really; it was the paleness. Just very white, as if she had been left out too long in the snow. I thought I could see the blood rushing along under the skin, but that was probably my imagination.

Now I know someone is going to think she was a ghost, or a vampire, or some alien creature dressed up to look like a human being, but as Nero Wolfe says in the mysteries, that is just flummery. She was a person, nothing more than that, and you can forget that sort of stuff, even with what comes next. She was as real as I was.

"How did you know I'd been sick?" I asked.

She shrugged again. "I don't know, I suppose I just knew, that's all. But I saw you coming out of the hospital up the street."

"I live there. But how could you know I was sick? Actually, I almost died. Well, that's not accurate: I *did* die, but I'm all right now."

"What do we do here?"

"Nothing much, just take it easy. The rest of the world is gone, and I don't know where, so we just sort of take it easy, I guess. There used to be a lot of crazy invasions, about a year ago, but they stopped pretty suddenly."

"I'll need a place to live," she said. "How about the hospital?"

"Well, that's fine with me," I said, "but actually, I was going to take over one of those little houses over there. If you like, you can move into the one next door."

So she did, and I did, and it was nice for a few weeks. I always went very slowly with women. Or maybe it's that they went slow with me. I'm a big believer that women give off radiation or something, that keeps a man from moving in on them if they don't want him to. I don't know much about it, if you want the truth.

We had a cordial relationship, Opal and I. She kept up her yard and I kept up mine. We ate dinner together a lot, and we saw each other frequently through the day. Once—when she realized I was spending time at the Post Office—she came in with a letter and came up to my window and asked me for an airmail stamp. She had money. I sold it to her. She took it and said, "Thank you for removing those little white borders; I always have trouble with them and usually rip the stamp or leave some on the edge. That was very nice of you, sir." And she left.

I was too stunned and pleased even to consider where she was mailing the letter to.

Or to whom she was writing.

One night we had dinner together and she made fried chicken. The grocery store had a large supply of food, more than enough for us for a long time. It did bother me, of course, why the milk was always fresh, and the meat was always freshly cut, but I assumed it was part of the scheme of things that kept the lights and water working, that took away the garbage and kept the streets clean. I never saw anyone who did it, but it got done, so I didn't worry about it.

Look: Before I died, when the world was here, I drove a mail truck and I rode a Honda. I didn't know how either of those things worked, I mean, aside from cleaning the spark plugs once in a while or filling the gas tanks, or superficial repairs like that. I never worried about it, because it got done, and that was the long and short of it. No one was any different. It was the same after everything vanished. As long as it worked, I didn't have to think about the logic of it, and if it had started going sour I *would* have; but it didn't, and that's all I want to say about *that*. You'd have done the same.

Anyhow. We had this fried chicken dinner, which I liked a lot because she made it just the way I like it, very dark and golden and crunchy on the surface and dry underneath, without that thin oily film that makes your teeth feel greasy. And we had some wine.

Now I don't drink much. I won't apologize. I can't hold it. But we had wine.

And I got, well, a little drunk, just a little. And I tried to touch her. And she was cold. Very cold. Very very cold. And she yelled at me, "Don't *ever* touch me!"

Now that was just two weeks before she told me she loved me and wanted to be mine. I asked her what she meant by that, "be mine." I never wanted to own anybody. And I certainly had the idea *she* didn't want to be anybody's possession, but there it was.

"I love you, and I want to stay with you."

"There's no place to go."

"That isn't what I meant. We could still live here together and not see each other. I mean, I love you and want to share the world with you."

"I don't know if that's a good idea," I said. I really wanted what she wanted, but I was afraid she'd get tired of me, and then what? Our situation wasn't too normal, at least by the usual standards I'd grown up with, if you catch my meaning.

So. She got angry, and went stalking out the door. I waited a few minutes to let her cool off, and then I went looking for her.

She had walked straight out to the edge of the world, and kept right on going. I don't think she knew I was following her.

I went back to my house and lay down.

When she came back, about two hours later I guess, I sat up and said, "Just who the dickens *are* you?"

She was furious, still furious. "Who the dickens are *you?*"

"I *know* who I am," I said, getting angry too, "and I want to know who *you* are. I saw you walking out there off the edge. *I* can't do that!"

"Some of us are talented, some aren't. Learn to live with it." Really a snotty answer, boy!

"I was here first!"

"That's what the Indians said and look what happened to *them!*"

"Dammit, are you responsible for all of this, for every crazy thing that happened?"

Then she really blew her stack and shouted at me. "Yes, you silly, irresponsible clown, I'm responsible. I did it all. I destroyed the world. Now what the hell are you going to do about it?"

I was too stunned to do anything. I hadn't really thought she was responsible, but when she admitted it, I didn't know what to say. I went over and tried to grab her by the shoulders, and I could feel that cold coming right off her. "You're not human," I said.

"Oh, go to hell, you idiot. I'm as human as you are. Humaner."

"You'd better tell me," I said, with a threatening tone, "or else—"

"Or else what, you nerd? Or else I'll wipe out this last little chunk and you and everything else and I'll be all alone the way I was before I did it!"

"Did it?"

"Yes, *did it*. Blew it all away. Just sat back and put my thumb in my mouth and said, 'Vanish everything but Eugene Harrison, wherever he is, and me, and a little town where I can be with him.' And when I took my thumb out of my mouth, everything was gone. Boston was gone, and the sky and the earth and every other thing, and I had to go walking through that glop out there till I found you."

"Why?!"

"You don't even recognize me, do you, you idiot? You don't even remember Opal Sellers, do you?"

I stared at her.

"Dope!"

I continued staring.

"I was in your graduating class in high school. You were right behind me when we went up for our diplomas. I was wearing a white gown, and you were standing behind me during the invocation, and I was having my period, and I was spotting, and it had gone through the white gown, and you leaned over and told me and I was embarrassed to death, but you gave me your mortarboard and

I held it across my backside and I thought it was the kindest, nicest thing anyone had ever done. *And I loved you, you simple stupid insensitive sonofabitch!"*

And she let down the screen or the image or the mask or whatever it was that she'd put up over herself, which was why she was cold to the touch, and inside there was Opal Sellers, who was one of the ugliest girls I'd ever seen, and she knew that was what I thought, and she didn't wait a minute, but put her thumb in her mouth and started mumbling around it . . . but nothing happened.

Then she went completely out of her head and started screaming that she'd passed on the power to me, and she couldn't do a thing about me, and she ran out the door.

I took off after her, and she went off the edge and kept going straight away like the Viking and the Stuka and the Hun and all the rest of them, which I guess she'd sent to liven things up for me so I'd feel heroic.

And that's it.

Gone. Just went. Where, I have no idea. I'm not leaving here, that's for sure, but I don't know what to do about it. *Somebody* ought to say I'm sorry to her, I mean she's a nice girl and all.

It's just I'm here and I'm comfortable, and who can ask for more than that. She was always talking about love. Well, damn, that wasn't love.

I don't think.

But what do I know? Girls always got tired of me very quickly.

I'm going to teach myself how to make pizza.

THE DAY BEFORE THE REVOLUTION

August 1974

Ursula K. Le Guin
(b. 1929)

Ursula K. Le Guin has written some of the most important and cele-brated sf novels of the last fifteen years: The Left Hand of Darkness *(Nebula, 1969; Hugo, 1970),* The Lathe of Heaven *(1971), and* The Dispossessed *(Nebula, 1974; Hugo, 1975); and her* The Far-thest Shore *(1973) won the National Book Award for Children's Literature. Other award-winning fiction includes "The Word for World Is Forest" (Hugo, 1973) and "The Ones Who Walk Away from Omelas" (Hugo, 1974).*

"The Day Before the Revolution," one of Le Guin's few Galaxy appearances, won a Nebula award in 1974. It is a "Prequel" to The Dispossessed *and takes place about two hundred years earlier.*

THE DAY BEFORE THE REVOLUTION

The speaker's voice was loud as empty beer-trucks in a stone street, and the people at the meeting were jammed up close, cobblestones, that great voice booming over them. Taviri was somewhere on the other side of the hall. She had to get to him. She wormed and pushed her way among the dark-clothed, close-packed people. She did not hear the words, nor see the faces: only the booming, and the bodies pressed one behind the other. She could not see Taviri, she was too short. A broad black-vested belly and chest loomed up blocking her way. She must get through to Taviri. Sweating, she jabbed fiercely with her fist. It was like hitting stones, he did not move at all, but the huge lungs let out right over her head a prodigious noise, a bellow. She cowered. Then she understood that the bellow had not been at her. Others were shouting. The speaker had said something, something fine about taxes or shadows. Thrilled, she joined the shouting—"Yes! Yes!"—and shoving on, came out easily into the open expanse of the Regimental Drill Field in Parheo. Overhead the evening sky lay deep and colorless, and all around her nodded the tall weeds with dry, white, close-floreted heads. She had never known what they were called. The flowers nodded above her head, swaying in the wind that always blew across the fields in the dusk. She ran among them, and they whipped lithe aside and stood up again swaying, silent. Taviri stood among the tall weeds in his good suit, the dark gray one that made him look like a professor or a playactor, harshly elegant. He did not look happy, but he was laughing, and saying something to her. The sound of his voice made her cry, and she reached out to catch hold of his hand, but she did not stop, quite. She could not stop. "Oh, Taviri," she said, "it's just on there!" The queer sweet smell of the white weeds was heavy as she went on. There were thorns, tangles underfoot, there were slopes, pits. She feared to fall . . . she stopped.

Sun, bright morning-glare, straight in the eyes, relentless. She had forgotten to pull the blind last night. She turned her back on the sun, but the right side wasn't comfortable. No use. Day. She sighed twice, sat up, got her legs over the edge of the bed, and sat hunched in her nightdress looking down at her feet.

The toes, compressed by a life time of cheap shoes, were almost square where they touched each other, and bulged out above in corns; the nails were discolored and shapeless. Between the knoblike ankle bones ran fine, dry wrinkles. The brief little plain at the base of the toes had kept its delicacy, but the skin was the color of mud, and knotted veins crossed the instep. Disgusting. Sad, depressing. Mean. Pitiful. She tried on all the words, and they all fit, like hideous little hats. Hideous: yes, that one too. To look at oneself and find it hideous, what a job? But then, when she hadn't been hideous, had she sat around and stared at herself like this? Not much! A proper body's not an object, not an implement, not a belonging to be admired, it's just you, yourself. Only when it's no longer you, but yours, a thing owned, do you worry about it—Is it in good shape? Will it do? Will it last?

"Who cares?" said Laia fiercely, and stood up.

It made her giddy to stand up suddenly. She had to put out her hand to the bedtable, for she dreaded falling. At that she thought of reaching out to Taviri, in the dream.

What had he said? She could not remember. She was not sure if she had even touched his hand. She frowned, trying to force memory. It had been so long since she had dreamed about Taviri; and now not even to remember what he had said!

It was gone, it was gone. She stood there hunched in her nightdress, frowning, one hand on the bedtable. How long was it since she had thought of him—let alone dreamed of him—even thought of him, as "Taviri"? How long since she had said his name?

Asieo said. When Asieo and I were in prison in the North. Before I met Asieo. Asieo's theory of reciprocity. Oh yes, she talked about him, talked about him too much no doubt, maundered, dragged him in. But as "Asieo," the last name, in the public man. The private man was gone, utterly gone. There were so few left who had even known him. They had all used to be in jail. One laughed about it on those days, all the friends in all the jails. But they weren't even there, these days. They were in the prison cemeteries. Or in the common graves.

"Oh, oh my dear," Laia said out loud, and she sank down onto the bed again because she could not stand up under the remembrance of those first weeks of the nine years in the fort in Drio, in the cell, those first weeks after they told her that Asieo had been killed in the fighting in Capitol Square and had been buried with the Fourteen Hundred in the lime-ditches behind Oring Gate. In the cell. Her hands fell into the old position on her lap, the left clenched and locked inside the grip of the right, the right thumb working back and forth a little pressing and rubbing on the knuckle of the left first finger. Hours, days, nights. She had thought of them all, each one, each one of the fourteen hundred, how they lay, how the quicklime worked on the flesh, how the bones touched in the burning dark. Who touched him? How did the slender bones of the hand lie now? Hours, years.

"Taviri, I have never forgotten you!" she whispered, and the stupidity of it brought her back to morning-light and the rumpled bed.

Of course she hadn't forgotten him. These things go without saying between husband and wife. There were her ugly old feet flat on the floor again, just as before. She had got nowhere at all, she had gone in a circle. She stood up with a grunt of effort and disapproval, and went to the closet for her dressing gown.

The young people went about the halls of the house in becoming immodesty, but she was too old for that. She didn't want to spoil some young man's breakfast with the sight of her. Besides, they had grown up in the principle of freedom of dress and sex and all the rest, and she hadn't. All she had done was invent it. It's not the same.

Like speaking of Asieo as "my husband." They winced. The word she should use as a good Odonian, of course, was "partner." But why the hell did she have to be a good Odonian?

She shuffled down the hall to the bathrooms. Mairo was there, washing her hair in a lavatory. Laia looked at the long, sleek, wet hank with admiration. She got out of the house so seldom now that she didn't know when she had last seen a respectably shaven scalp, but still the sight of a full head of hair gave her pleasure, vigorous pleasure. How many times had she been jeered at, *Longhair*, *Longhair*, had her hair pulled by policemen or young toughs, had her hair shaved off down to the scalp by a grinning soldier at each new prison? And then had grown it all over again, through the fuzz, to the frizz, to the curls, to the mane . . . In the old days. For God's love, couldn't she think of anything today but the old days?

Dressed, her bed made, she went down to commons. It was a good breakfast, but she had never got her appetite back since the damned stroke. She drank two cups of herb tea, but couldn't finish the piece of fruit she had taken. How she had craved fruit as a child, badly enough to steal it; and in the fort—oh for God's love stop it! She smiled and replied to the greetings and friendly inquiries of the other breakfasters and big Aevi who was serving the counter this morning. It was he who had tempted her with the peach, "Look at this, I've been saving it for you," and how could she refuse? Anyway she had always loved fruit, and never got enough; once when she was six or seven she had stolen a piece off a vendor's cart in River Street. But it was hard to eat when everyone was talking so excitedly. There was news from Thu, real news. She was inclined to discount it at first, being wary of enthusiasms, but after she had read the article in the paper, and read between the lines of it, she thought, with a strange kind of certainty, deep but cold, Why, this is it; it has come. And in Thu, not here. Thu will break before this country does; the revolution will first prevail there. As if that mattered! There will be no more nations. And yet it did matter somehow, it made her a little cold and sad—envious, in fact. Of all the infinite stupidities. She did not join the talk much, and soon got up to go back to her room, feeling sorry for herself. She could not share their excitement. She was out of it, really out of it. It's not easy, she said to herself in justification, laboriously climbing the stairs, to accept being out of it when you've been in it, in the center of it, for fifty years. Oh for God's love. Whining!

She got the stairs and the self-pity behind her, entering her room. It was a good room, and it was good to be by herself. It was a great relief. Even if it wasn't strictly fair. Some of the kids in the attics were living five to a room no bigger than this. There were always more people wanting to live in an Odonian House than could be properly accommodated. She had this big room all to herself only because she was an old woman who had had a stroke. And maybe because she was Odo. If she hadn't been Odo, but merely the old woman with a stroke, would she have had it? Very likely. After all who the hell wanted to room with a drooling old woman? But it was hard to be sure. Favoritism, elitism, leader-worship, they crept back and dropped out everywhere. But she had never hoped to see them eradicated in her lifetime, in one generation; only Time works the great changes. Meanwhile this was a nice, large, sunny room, proper for a drooling old woman who had started a world revolution.

Her secretary would be coming in an hour to help her dispatch the day's work. She shuffled over to the desk, a beautiful, big piece, a present from the Nio Cabinetmakers' Syndicate because somebody had heard her remark once that the only piece of furniture she had ever really longed for was a desk with drawers and enough room on top . . . damn, the top was practically covered with papers with notes clipped to them, mostly in Noi's small clear handwriting: Urgent.—Northern Provinces.—Consult w/R.T.?

Her own handwriting had never been the same since Asieo's death. It was odd, when you thought about it. After all, within five years after his death she had written the whole *Analogy*. And there were those letters, which the tall guard with the watery gray eyes, what was his name, never mind, had smuggled out of the fort for her for two years. *The Prison Letters* they called them now, there were a dozen different editions of them. All that stuff, the letters which people kept telling her was so full of "spiritual strength"—which probably meant she had been lying herself blue in the face when she wrote them, trying to keep her spirits up—and the *Analogy*, which was certainly the solidest intellectual work she had ever done, all of that had been written in the fort in Drio, in the cell, after Asieo's death. One had to do something, and in the fort they let one have paper and pens . . . But it had all been written in the hasty, scribbling hand which she had never felt was hers, not her own like the round, black scrollings of the manuscript of *Society Without Government*, forty-five years old. Taviri had taken not only her body's and her heart's desire to the quicklime with him, but even her good clear handwriting.

But he had left her the revolution.

How brave of you to go on, to work, to write, in prison, after such a defeat for the movement, after your partner's death, people had used to say. Damn fools. What else had there been to do? Bravery, courage—what was courage? She had never figured it out. Not fearing, some said. Fearing yet going on, others said. But what could one do but go on? Had one any real choice, ever?

To die was merely to go on in another direction.

If you wanted to come home you had to keep going on, that was what she meant when she wrote, "True journey is return," but it had never been more than an intuition, and she was farther than ever now from being able to rationalize it. She bent down, too suddenly, so that she grunted a little at the creak in her bones, and began to root in a bottom drawer of the desk. Her hand came to an age-softened folder and drew it out, recognizing it by touch before sight confirmed: the manuscript of *Syndical Organization in Revolutionary Transition*. He had printed the title on the folder and written his name under it, Taviri Odo Asieo, IX 741. There was an elegant handwriting, every letter well-formed, bold, and fluent. But he had preferred to use a voiceprinter. The manuscript was all in voiceprint, and high quality too, hesitancies adjusted and idiosyncrasies of speech normalized. You couldn't see there how he had said "o" deep in his throat as they did on the North Coast. There was nothing of him there but his mind. She had nothing of him at all except his name written on the folder. She hadn't kept his letters, it was sentimental to keep letters. Besides, she never kept anything. She couldn't think of anything that she had ever owned for more than a few years, except this ramshackle old body, of course, and she was stuck with that . . .

Dualizing again. "She" and "it." Age and illness made one dualist, made one escapist; the mind insisted, *It's not me, it's not me.* But it was. Maybe the mystics could detach mind from body, she had always rather wistfully envied them the chance, without hope of emulating them. Escape had never been her game. She had sought for freedom here, now, body and soul.

First self-pity, then self-praise, and here she still sat, for God's love, holding Asieo's name in her hand, why? Didn't she know his name without looking it up? What was wrong with her? She raised the folder to her lips and kissed the handwritten name firmly and squarely, replaced the folder in the back of the bottom drawer, shut the drawer, and straightened up in the chair. Her right hand tingled. She scratched it, and then shook it in the air, spitefully. It had never quite got over the stroke. Neither had her right leg, or right eye, or the right corner of her mouth. They were sluggish, inept, they tingled. They made her feel like a robot with a short circuit.

And time was getting on, Noi would be coming, what had she been doing ever since breakfast?

She got up so hastily that she lurched, and grabbed at the chairback to make sure she did not fall. She went down the hall to the bathroom and looked in the big mirror there. Her gray knot was loose and droopy, she hadn't done it up well before breakfast. She struggled with it a while. It was hard to keep her arms up in the air. Amai, running in to piss, stopped and said, "Let me do it!" and knotted it up tight and neat in no time, with her round, strong, pretty fingers, smiling and silent. Amai was twenty, less than a third of Laia's age. Her parents had both been members of the movement, one killed in the insurrection of '60, the other still recruiting in the South Provinces. Amai had grown up in Odonian Houses, born to the revolution, a true daughter of anarchy. And so quiet and free and beautiful a child, enough to make you cry when you thought: This is what we worked for, this is what we meant, this is it, here she is, alive, the kindly, lovely future.

Laia Asieo Odo's right eye wept several little tears, as she stood between the lavatories and the latrines having her hair done up by the daughter she had not borne; but her left eye, the strong one, did not weep, nor did it know what the right eye did.

She thanked Amai and hurried back to her room. She had noticed, in the mirror, a stain on her collar. Peach juice, probably.
Damned old dribbler. She didn't want Noi to come in and find her
with drool on her collar.

As the clean shirt went on over her head, she thought, What's so
special about Noi?

She fastened the collar-frogs with her left hand, slowly.

Noi was thirty or so, a slight, muscular fellow with a soft voice
and alert dark eyes. That's what was special about Noi. It was that
simple. Good old sex. She had never been drawn to a fair man or a
fat one, or the tall fellows with big biceps, never, not even when she
was fourteen and fell in love with every passing fart. Dark, spare,
and fiery, that was the recipe. Taviri, of course. This boy wasn't a
patch on Taviri for brains, nor even for looks, but there it was: She
didn't want him to see her with dribble on her collar and her hair
coming undone.

Her thin, gray hair.

Noi came in, just pausing in the open doorway—my God, she
hadn't even shut the door while changing her shirt!—She looked at
him and saw herself. The old woman.

You could brush your hair and change your shirt, or you could
wear last week's shirt and last night's braids, or you could put on
cloth of gold and dust your shaven scalp with diamond powder.
None of it would make the slightest difference. The old woman
would look a little less, or a little more, grotesque.

One keeps oneself neat out of mere decency, mere sanity,
awareness of other people.

And finally even that goes, and one dribbles unashamed.

"Good morning," the young man said in his gentle voice.

"Hello, Noi."

No, by God, it was *not* out of mere decency. Decency be damned.
Because the man she had loved, and to whom her age would not
have mattered—because he was dead, must she pretend she had no
sex? Must she suppress the truth, like a damned puritan authori-
tarian? Even six months ago, before the stroke, she had made men
look at her and like to look at her; and now, though she could give
no pleasure, by God she could please herself.

When she was six years old, and Papa's friend Gadeo used to
come by to talk politics with Papa after dinner, she would put on

the gold-colored necklace that Mama had found on a trash-heap and brought home for her. It was so short that it always got hidden under her collar where nobody could see it. She liked it that way. She knew she had it on. She sat on the doorstep and listened to them talk, and knew that she looked nice for Gadeo. He was dark, with white teeth that flashed. Sometimes he called her "pretty Laia." "There's my pretty Laia!" Sixty-six years ago.

"What? My head's dull. I had a terrible night." It was true. She had slept even less than usual.

"I was asking if you'd seen the papers this morning."

She nodded.

"Pleased about Soinehe?"

Soinehe was the province in Thu which had declared its secession from the Thuvian State last night.

He was pleased about it. His white teeth flashed in his dark, alert face. Pretty Laia.

"Yes. And apprehensive."

"I know. But it's the real thing, this time. It's the beginning of the end of the government in Thu. They haven't even tried to order troops into Soinehe, you know. It would merely provoke the soldiers into rebellion sooner, and they know it."

She agreed with him. She herself had felt that certainty. But she could not share his delight. After a lifetime of living on hope because there is nothing but hope, one loses the taste for victory. A real sense of triumph must be preceded by real despair. She had unlearned despair a long time ago. There were no more triumphs.

One went on.

"Shall we do those letters today?"

"All right. Which letters?"

"To the people in the North," he said without impatience.

"In the North?"

"Parheo, Oaidun."

She had been born in Parheo, the dirty city on the dirty river. She had not come here to the capital till she was twenty-two and ready to bring the revolution. Though in those days, before she and the others had thought it through, it had been a very green and puerile revolution. Strikes for better wages, representation for women. Votes and wages—Power and Money, for the love of God! Well, one does learn a little, after all, in fifty years.

But then one must forget it all.

"Start with Oaidun," she said, sitting down in the armchair. Noi was at the desk ready to work. He read out excerpts from the letters she was to answer. She tried to pay attention, and succeeded well enough that she dictated one whole letter and started on another. "Remember that at this stage your brotherhood is vulnerable to the threat of . . . no, to the danger . . . to . . ." She groped till Noi suggested, "The danger of leader-worship?"

"All right. And that nothing is so soor corrupted by power-seeking as altruism. No. And that nothing corrupts altruism—no. Oh for God's love you know what I'm trying to say, Noi, you write it. They know it too, it's just the same old stuff, why can't they read my book!"

"Touch," Noi said gently, smiling, citing one of the central Odonian themes.

"All right, but I'm tired of being touched. If you'll write the letter I'll sign it, but I can't be bothered with it this morning." He was looking at her with a little question of concern. She said, irritable, "There is something else I have to do!"

When Noi had gone she sat down at the desk and moved the papers about, pretending to be doing something, because she had been startled, frightened, by the words she had said. She had nothing else to do. She never had had anything else to do. This was her work: her lifework. The speaking tours and the meetings and the streets were out of reach for her now, but she could still write, and that was her work. And anyhow if she had had anything else to do, Noi would have known it; he kept her schedule, and tactfully reminded her of things, like the visit from the foreign students this afternoon.

Oh, damn. She liked the young, and there was always something to learn from a foreigner, but she was tired of new faces, and tired of being on view. She learned from them, but they didn't learn from her; they had learnt all she had to teach long ago, from her books, from the movement. They just came to look, as if she were the Great Tower in Rodarred, or the Canyon of the Tulaevea. A phenomenon, a monument. They were awed, adoring. She snarled at them: Think your own thoughts!—That's not anarchism, that's mere obscurantism.—You don't think liberty and discipline are incompatible, do you?—They accepted their tonguelashing meekly as children, gratefully, as if she were some kind of All-Mother, the idol of the Big Sheltering Womb. She! She who had minded the shipyards at Seissero, and had cursed Premier Inoilte to his face in front of a crowd of seven thousand, telling him he would have cut off his own balls and had them bronzed and sold as souvenirs, if he thought there was any profit in it—she who had screeched, and sworn, and kicked policemen, and spat at priests, and pissed in public on the big brass plaque in Capitol Square that said HERE WAS FOUNDED THE SOVEREIGN NATION STATE OF A-IO ETC ETC, pssssssss to all that! And now she was everybody's grandmama, the dear old lady, the sweet old monument, come worship at the womb. The fire's out, boys, it's safe to come up close.

"No, I won't," Laia said out loud. "I will not." She was not self-conscious about talking to herself, because she always had talked to herself. "Laia's invisible audience," Taviri had used to say, as she went through the room muttering. "You needn't come, I won't be here," she told the invisible audience now. She had just decided what it was she had to do. She had to go out. To go into the streets.

It was inconsiderate to disappoint the foreign students. It was erratic, typically senile. It was un-Odonian. Pssssss to all that. What was the good working for freedom all your life and ending up without any freedom at all? She would go out for a walk.

"*What is an anarchist? One who, choosing, accepts the responsibility of choice.*"

On the way downstairs she decided, scowling, to stay and see the foreign students. But then she would go out.

They were very young students, very earnest: doe-eyed, shaggy, charming creatures from the Western Hemisphere, Benbili and the Kingdom of Mand, the girls in white trousers, the boys in long kilts, warlike and archaic. They spoke of their hopes. "We in Mand are so very far from the revolution that maybe we are near it," said one of the girls, wistful and smiling: "The Circle of Life!" and she showed the extremes meeting, in the circle of her slender, dark-skinned fingers. Amai and Aevi served them white wine and brown bread, the hospitality of the house. But the visitors, unpresumptuous, all rose to take their leave after barely half an hour. "No, no, no," Laia said, "stay here, talk with Aevi and Amai. It's just that I get stiff sitting down, you see, I have to change about. It has been so good to meet you, will you come back to see me, my little brothers and sisters, soon?" For her heart went out to them, and theirs to her, and she exchanged kisses all round, laughing, delighted by the dark young cheeks, the affectionate eyes, the scented hair, before she shuffled off. She was really a little tired, but to go up and take a nap would be a defeat. She had wanted to go out. She would go out. She had not been alone outdoors since—when? since winter! before the stroke. No wonder she was getting morbid. It had been a regular jail sentence. Outside, the streets, that's where she lived.

She went quietly out the side door of the house, past the vegetable patch, to the street. The narrow strip of sour city dirt had been beautifully gardened and was producing a fine crop of beans and *ceea*, but Laia's eye for farming was unenlightened. Of course it had been clear that anarchist communities, even in the time of transition, must work towards optimal self-support, but how that was to be managed in the way of actual dirt and plants wasn't her business. There were farmers and agronomists for that. Her job was the streets, the noisy, stinking streets of stone, where she had grown up and lived all her life, except for the fifteen years in prison.

She looked up fondly at the facade of the house. That it had been built as a bank gave peculiar satisfaction to its present occupants. They kept their sacks of meal in the bombproof money-vault, and aged their cider in kegs in safe-deposit boxes. Over the fussy columns that faced the street, carved letters still read, "NATIONAL INVESTORS AND GRAIN FACTORS BANKING ASSOCIATION." The movement was not strong on names. They had no flag. Slogans came and went as the need did. There was always the Circle of Life to scratch on walls and pavements where Authority would have to see it. But when it came to names they were indifferent, accepting and ignoring whatever they got called, afraid of being pinned down and penned in, unafraid of being absurd. So this best known and second oldest of all the cooperative houses had no name except The Bank.

It faced on a wide and quiet street, but only a block away began the Temeba, an open market, once famous as a center for black-market psychogenics and teratogenics, now reduced to vegetables, secondhand clothes, and miserable sideshows. Its crapulous vitality was gone, leaving only half-paralyzed alcoholics, addicts, cripples, hucksters, and fifth-rate whores, pawnshops, gambling dens, fortune-tellers, body sculptors, and cheap hotels. Laia turned to the Temeba as water seeks its level.

She had never feared or despised the city. It was her country. There would not be slums like this, if the revolution prevailed. But there would be misery. There would always be misery, waste, cruelty. She had never pretended to be changing the human condition, to be Mama taking tragedy away from the children so they won't hurt themselves. Anything but. So long as people were free to choose, if they close to drink flybane and live in sewers, it was their business. Just so long as it wasn't the business of Business, the source of profit and the means of power for other people. She had felt all that before she knew anything; before she wrote the first pamphlet, before she left Parheo, before she knew what "capital" meant, before she'd been farther than River Street where she played rolltaggie kneeling on scabby knees on the pavement with the other six-year-olds. She had known it: that she, and the other kids, and her parents, and their parents, and the drunks and whores and all of River Street, was at the bottom of something—was the foundation, the reality, the source.

But will you drag civilization down into the mud? cried the shocked decent people, later on, and she had tried for years to explain to them that if all you had was mud, then if you were God you made it into human beings, and if you were human you tried to make it into houses where human beings could live. But nobody who thought he was better than mud would understand. Now, water seeking its level, mud to mud, Laia shuffled through the foul, noisy street, and all the ugly weakness of her old age was at home. The sleepy whores, their lacquered hair-arrangements dilapidated and askew, the one-eyed woman wearily yelling her vegetables to sell, the halfwit beggar slapping flies, these were her countrywomen. They looked like her, they were all sad, disgusting, mean, pitiful, hideous. They were her sisters, her own people.

She did not feel very well. It had been a long time since she had walked so far, four or five blocks, by herself, in the noise and push and stinking summer heat of the streets. She had wanted to get to Koly Park, the triangle of scruffy grass at the end of the Temeba, and sit there for a while with the other old men and women who always sat there, to see what it was like to sit there and be old; but it was too far. If she didn't turn back now, she might get a dizzy spell, and she had a dread of falling down, falling down and having to lie there and look up at the people come to stare at the old woman in a fit. She turned and started home, frowning with effort and self-disgust. She could feel her face very red, and a swimming feeling came and went in her ears. It got a bit much, she was really afraid she might keel over. She saw a doorstep in the shade and made for it, let herself down cautiously, sat, sighed.

Nearby was a fruit-seller, sitting silent behind his dusty, withered stock. People went by. Nobody bought from him. Nobody looked at her. Odo, who was Odo? Famous revolutionary, author of *Community*, *The Analogy*, etc., etc. She, who was she? An old woman with gray hair and a red face sitting on a dirty doorstep in a slum, muttering to herself.

True? Was that she? Certainly it was what anybody passing her saw. But was it she, herself, any more than the famous revolutionary, etc., was? No. It was not. But who was she, then?

The one who loved Taviri.

Yes. True enough. But not enough. That was gone; he had been dead so long.

"Who am I?" Laia muttered to her invisible audience, and they knew the answer and told it to her with one voice. She was the little girl with scabby knees, sitting on the doorstep staring down through the dirty golden haze of River Street in the heat of late summer, the six-year-old, the sixteen-year-old, the fierce, cross, dream-ridden girl, untouched, untouchable. She was herself. Indeed she had been the tireless worker and thinker, but a bloodclot in a vein had taken that woman away from her. Indeed she had been the lover, the swimmer in the midst of life, but Taviri, dying, had taken that woman away with him. There was nothing left, really, but the foundations. She had come home; she had never left home. "True voyage is return." Dust and mud and a doorstep in the slums. And beyond, at the far end of the street, the field full of tall dry weeds blowing in the wind as night came.

"Laia! What are you doing here? Are you all right?"

One of the people from the house, of course, a nice woman, a bit fanatical and always talking. Laia could not remember her name though she had known her for years. She let herself be taken home, the woman talking all the way. In the big cool common room (once occupied by tellers counting money behind polished counters supervised by armed guards) Laia sat down in a chair. She was unable just as yet to face climbing the stairs, though she would have liked to be alone. The woman kept on talking, and other excited people came in. It appeared that a demonstration was being planned. Events in Thu were moving so fast that the mood here had caught fire, and something must be done. Day after tomorrow, no, tomorrow, there was to be a march, a big one, from Old Town to Capitol Square—the old route. "Another Ninth Month Uprising," said a young man, fiery and laughing, glancing at Laia. He had not even been born at the time of the Ninth Month Uprising, it was all history to him. Now he wanted to make some history of his own. The room had filled up. A general meeting would be held here, tomorrow, at eight in the morning. "You must talk, Laia."

"Tomorrow? Oh, I won't be here tomorrow," she said brusquely. Whoever had asked her smiled, another one laughed, though Amai glanced round at her with a puzzled look. They went on talking and shouting. The revolution. What on earth had made her say that? What a thing to say on the eve of the revolution, even if it was true.

She waited her time, managed to get up and, for all her clumsiness, to slip away unnoticed among the people busy with their planning and excitement. She got to the hall, to the stairs, and began to climb them one by one. "The general strike," a voice, two voices, ten voices were saying in the room below, behind her. "The general strike," Laia muttered, resting for a moment on the landing. Above, ahead, in her room, what awaited her? The private strike. That was mildly funny. She started up the second flight of stairs, one by one, one leg at a time, like a small child. She was dizzy, but she was no longer afraid to fall. On ahead, on there, the dry white flowers nodded and whispered in the open fields of evening. Seventy-two years and she had never had time to learn what they were called.

THE GIFT OF GARIGOLLI

August 1974

Frederik Pohl
(b. 1919)
and C. M. Kornbluth
(1923–1958)

The most famous and successful writing team in science fiction, Frederik Pohl and C. M. Kornbluth were major figures in establishing Galaxy as a leader in the field in the 1950s. In particular, their serialized novels Gravy Planet (June–August 1952), published as The Space Merchants, Gladiator-at-Law (June–August 1954), Slave Ship (March–May 1956), and Wolfbane (October and November 1957) won them and the magazine a strong and loyal following.

Pohl was one of the key factors in the Galaxy story in at least four respects. As the leading agent in science fiction in the early 1950s he sold the magazine a large proportion of its fiction; as an unofficial adviser to H. L. Gold during the same period he read stories and supplied ideas that were incorporated in many of them; as editor of the magazine from 1962 to 1969 he maintained a high standard and helped to develop a number of writers, contributing to the conversion of Robert Sheckley and Robert Silverberg from simply good, prolific writers to outstanding talents. Finally, as an author, his solo appearances in Galaxy included some of the most important sf stories of all time, including "The Midas Plague" (April 1954) and its sequel "The Man Who Ate the World" (November 1956); "The Tunnel Under the World" (January 1955); the novels Drunkard's Walk (June and August 1960) and The Age of the Pussyfoot (Oc-

tober and December 1965 and February 1966); and a host of other quality works.

Kornbluth, a very talented writer whose frequently bitter and downbeat stories reflected his personality, published only a few solo efforts in Galaxy, but two of them, "The Altar at Midnight" (November 1952) and "The Marching Morons" (April 1951), are widely considered to be among his finest.

"The Gift of Garigolli" was published sixteen years after Cyril's death, completed by Fred from fragments and ideas developed years earlier.

M. H. G. and J. D. O.

THE GIFT OF GARIGOLLI

GARIGOLLI

To Home Base

Greeting, Chief,

I'm glad you're pleased with the demographics and cognitics studies. You don't mention the orbital mapping, but I suppose that's all complete and satisfactory.

Now will you please tell me how we're going to get off this lousy planet?

Keep firmly in mind, Chief, that we're not complainers. You don't have a better crew anywhere in the galaxy and you know it. We've complied with the Triple Directive, every time, on every planet we've explored. Remember Arcturus XII? But this time we're having trouble. After all, look at the disproportion in mass. And take a look at the reports we've sent in. These are pretty miserable sentients, Chief.

So will you let us know, please, if there has ever been an authorized exception to Directive Two? I don't mean we aren't going to bust a link to comply—if we can—but frankly, at this moment, I don't see how.

And we need to get out of here fast.

Garigolli.

Although it was a pretty morning in June, with the blossoms dropping off the catalpa trees and the algae blooming in the 12-foot plastic pool, I was not enjoying either my breakfast or the morning mail.

The letter from the lawyer started, the way letters from lawyers do, with

RE: GUDSELL VS. DUPOIR

and went on to advise Dupoir (that's me, plus my wife and our two-year-old son Butchie) that unless a certified check arrived in Undersigned's office before close of business June 11th (that was tomorrow) in the amount of $14,752.03, Undersigned would be compelled to institute proceedings at once.

I showed it to my wife, Shirl, for lack of anything better to do.

She read it and nodded intelligently. "He's really been very patient with us, considering," she said. "I suppose this is just some more lawyer-talk?"

It had occurred to me, for a wild moment, that maybe she had $14,752.03 in the old sugar bowl as a surprise for me, but I could see she didn't. I shook my head. "This means they take the house," I said. "I'm not mad any more. But you won't sign anything for your brother after this, will you?"

"Certainly not," she said, shocked. "Shall I put that letter in the paper-recycling bin?"

"Not just yet," I said, taking off my glasses and hearing aid. Shirl knows perfectly well that I can't hear her when my glasses are off, but she kept on talking anyway as she wiped the apricot puree off Butchie's chin, rescued the milk glass, rinsed the plastic infant-food jar and dropped it in the "plastics" carton, rinsed the lid and put it in the "metals" box, and poured my coffee. We are a very ecological household. It astonishes me how good Shirl is at things like that, considering.

I waved fruit flies away from the general direction of my orange juice and put my glasses back on in time to catch her asking, wonderingly, "What would they do with our house? I mean, I'm not a demon decorator like Ginevra Freedman. I just like it comfortable and neat."

"They don't exactly want the house," I explained. "They just want the money they'll get after they sell it to somebody else." Her expression cleared at once. Shirl always likes to understand things.

I sipped my coffee, fending off Butchie's attempt to grab the cup, and folded the letter and laid it across my knees like an unsheathed scimitar, ready to taste the blood of the *giaour*, which it kind of was.

Butchie indicated that he would like to eat it, but I didn't see that that would solve the problem. Although I didn't have any better way of solving it, at that.

I finished the orange juice, patted Butchie's head and, against my better judgment, gave Shirl the routine kiss on the nose.

"Well," she said, "I'm glad that's settled. Isn't it nice the way the mail comes first thing in the morning now?"

I said it was very nice and left for the bus but, really, I could have been just as happy if Undersigned's letter had come any old time. The fruit flies were pursuing me all the way down the street. They seemed to think they could get nourishment out of me, which suggested that fruit flies were about equal in intelligence to brothers-in-law. It was not a surprising thought. I had thought it before.

GARIGOLLI
    To Home Base

Chief,

The mobility of this Host is a constant pain in the spermatophore. Now he's gone off on the day-cycle early, and half the crew are still stuck in his domicile. Ultimate Matrix knows how they'll handle it if we don't get back before they run out of group empathy.

You've got no reason to take that tone, Chief. We're doing a good job and you know it. "Directive One: To remain undetected by sentients on planet being explored." A hundred and forty-four p.g., right? They don't have a clue we're here, although I concede that that part is fairly easy, since they are so much bigger than we are. "Directive Three: Subject to Directive One and Two, to make a complete study of geographic, demographic, ecological, and cognitic factors and to transmit same to Home Base." You actually complimented us on those! It's only Directive Two that's giving us trouble.

We're still trying, but did it ever occur to you that maybe these people don't *deserve* Directive Two?

Garigolli.

I loped along the jungle trail to the bus stop, calculating with my razor-sharp mind that the distance from the house was almost exactly 14,752.03 centimeters. As centimeters it didn't sound bad at all. As money, $14,752.03 was the kind of sum I hadn't written down since commercial arithmetic in P.S. 98.

I fell in with Barney Freedman, insurance underwriter and husband of Ginevra, the Demon Decorator. "Whatever became of commercial arithmetic?" I asked him. "Like ninety-day notes for fourteen thousand seven hundred and fifty-two dollars and three cents at six percent simple interest? Although why anybody would be dumb enough to lend anybody money for ninety days beats me. If he doesn't have it now, he won't have it in ninety days."

"You're in some kind of trouble."

"Shrewd guess."

"So what did Shirl do now?"

"She cosigned a note for her brother," I said. "When he went into the drying-out sanitarium for the gold treatment. They wouldn't take him on his own credit, for some reason. They must have gold-plated him. He said the note was just a formality, so Shirl didn't bother me with it."

We turned the corner. Barney said, "Ginevra didn't bother me once when the telephone company—"

"So when Shirl's brother got undrunk," I said, "he told her not to worry about it and went to California. He thought he might catch on with the movies."

"Did he?"

"He didn't even catch cold with the movies. Then they sent us the bill. Fourteen thou—well, they had it all itemized. Three nurses. Medication. Suite. Occupational therapy. Professional services. Hydrotherapy. Group counseling. One-to-one counseling. Limousine. Chauffeur for limousine. Chauffeur's helper for limousine. Chauffeur's helper's hard-boiled eggs for lunch. Salt for chauffeur's helper's hard-boiled—"

"You're getting hysterical," Barney said. "You mean he just skipped?" We were at the bus stop, with a gaggle of other prosperous young suburbanites.

I said, "Like a flat rock on a pond. So we wrote him, and of course the letters came back. They didn't fool around, the 'Institute for Psychosomatic Adjustment' didn't."

"That's a pretty name."

"I telephoned a man up there to explain, when we got the first letter. He didn't sound pretty. Just tired. He said my wife shouldn't sign things without reading them. And he said if his house was—something about joint tenancy in fee simple, he would break his wife's arm if she was the type that signed things without reading them, and keep on rebreaking it until she stopped. Meanwhile they had laid out a lot of goods and services in good faith, and what was I going to do about it?"

The bus appeared on the horizon, emitting jet trails of diesel smog. We knotted up by the sign. "So I told him I didn't know," I said, "but I know now. I'll get sued, that's what I'll do. The Dupoirs always have an answer to every problem."

Conversation was suspended for fifteen seconds of scrimmage while we entered the bus. Barney and I were lucky. We wound up with our heads jammed affectionately together, not too far from a window that sucked in diesel fumes and fanned them at us. I could see the fruit flies gamely trying to get back to my ear, but they were losing the battle.

Barney said, "Hey. Couldn't you sell your house to somebody you trusted for a dollar, and then they couldn't—"

"Yes, they could. And then we'd both go to jail. I asked a guy in our legal department."

"Huh." The bus roared on, past knots of other prosperous young suburbanites who waved their fists at us as we passed. "How about this. I hope you won't take this the wrong way. But couldn't there be some angle about Shirl being, uh, not exactly *competent* to sign any kind of—"

"I asked about that too, Barney. No hope. Shirl's never been hospitalized, she's never been to a shrink, she runs a house and a husband and a small boy just fine. Maybe she's a little impulsive. But a lot of people are impulsive, the man said."

GARIGOLLI
    To Home Base

Chief,
I think we've got it. These people use a medium of exchange, remember? And the Host doesn't have enough of it! What could be simpler?

With a little modification there are a couple of local organisms that should be able to concentrate the stuff out of the ambient environment, and then—

And then we're off the impaling spike!
    Garigolli.

The bus jerked to a stop at the railroad station and we boiled out on successive rollers of humanity which beached us at separate parts of the platform.

The 8:07 slid in at 8:19 sharp and I swung aboard, my mighty thews rippling like those of the giant anthropoids among whom I had been raised. With stealthy tread and every jungle-trained sense alert I stalked a vacant seat halfway down the aisle on the left, my fangs and molars bared, my liana-bound, flint-tipped *Times* poised for the thrust of death. It wasn't my morning. Ug-Fwa the Hyena, scavenger of the mighty Limpopo, bounded from the far vestibule giving voice to his mad cackle and slipped into the vacant seat. I and the rest of the giant anthropoids glared, unfolded our newspapers, and pretended to read.

The headlines were very interesting that morning. PRES ASKS $14,752.03 FOR MISSILE DEFENSE. "SLICK" DUPOIR SOUGHT IN DEFAULT CASE, RUMOR RED PURGE OF BROTHER-IN-LAW. QUAKE DEATH TOLL SET AT 14,752.03. BODY OF SKID ROW CHARACTER IDENTIFIED AS FORMER YOUNG SUBURBANITE; BROTHER-IN-LAW FLIES FROM COAST, WEEPS "WHY DIDN'T HE ASK ME FOR HELP?" FOSTER PARENTS OF "BUTCHIE" DUPOIR OPEN LEGAL FIGHT AGAINST DESTITUTE MA AND PA, SAY "IF THEY LOVE HIM WHY DON'T THEY SUPPORT HIM?" GLIDER SOARS 14,752.03 MILES. DUPOIR OFF 147.52—no, that was a fly speck, not a decimal point—OFF 14,752.03 FOR NEW LOW, RAILS AND BROTHERS IN LAW MIXED INACTIVE TRADING. I always feel you're more efficient if you start the day with the gist of the news straight in your mind.

I arrived at the office punctually at 9:07, late enough to show that I was an executive, but not so late that Mr. Horgan would notice it. The frowning brow of my cave opened under the grim rock front that bore the legend "International Plastic Co." and I walked in, nodding good morning to several persons from the Fourteenth Floor, but being nodded to myself only by Hermie, who ran the cigar stand. Hermie cultivated my company because I was good for a dollar on the numbers two or three times a week. Little did he know that it would be many a long day before he saw a dollar of mine, perhaps as many as 14,752.03 of them.

GARIGOLLI
    To Home Base

                                                            Further
to my last communication, Chief,

                                                            We
ran into a kind of a setback. We found a suitable organic sub-strate and implanted a colony of modified organisms which ex-tracted gold from environmental sources, and they were per-

forming beautifully, depositing a film of pure metal on the substrate, which the Host was carrying with him.

Then he folded it up and threw it in a waste receptacle.

We're still working on it, but I don't know, Chief, I don't know.

Garigolli.

I find it a little difficult to explain to people what I do for a living. It has something to do with making the country plastics-conscious. I make the country plastics-conscious by writing newspaper stories about plastics which only seem to get printed in neighborhood shopping guides in Sioux Falls, Idaho. And by scripting talk features about plastics which get run from 11:55 PM to 12:00 midnight on radio stations the rest of whose programs' time is devoted to public-service items like late jockey changes at Wheeling Downs. And by scripting television features which do not seem ever to be run on any station. And by handling the annual Miss Plastics contest, at least up to the point where actual contestants appear, when it is taken over by the people from the Fourteenth Floor. And by writing the monthly page of Plastics Briefs which goes out, already matted, to 2,000 papers in North America. Plastics Briefs is our best bet because each brief is illustrated by a line drawing of a girl doing something with, to, or about plastics, and her costume is always brief. As I said, all this is not easy to explain, so when people ask me what I do I usually say, "Whatever Mr. Horgan tells me to."

The morning Mr. Horgan called me away from a conference with Jack Denny, our briefs artist, and said: "Dupoir, that Century of Plastics Anniversary Dinner idea of yours is out. The Fourteenth Floor says it lacks thematic juice. Think of something else for a winter promotion, and think big!" He banged a plastic block on his desk with a little plastic hammer.

I said, "Mr. Horgan, how about this? Are we getting the break in the high-school chemistry textbooks we should? Are we getting the message of polythene to every boy, girl, brother-in-law—"

He shook his head. "That's small," he said, and went on to explain: "By which I mean it isn't big. Also there is the flak we are getting from the nature nuts, which the Fourteenth Floor does not think you are dealing with in a creative way."

"I've ordered five thousand pop-up recycling bins for the test, Mr.

Horgan. They're not only plastic, they're *recycled* plastic. We use them in my own home, and I am confident—"

"Confidence," he said, "is when you've got your eyes so firmly fixed on the goal that you trip on a dog-doodie and fall in the crap."

I regrouped. "I think we can convert the present opposition from the ecology movement to—"

"The ecology movement," he said, "is people who love buzzards better than babies and catfish better than cars."

I fell back on my last line of defense. "Yes, Mr. Horgan," I said.

"Personally," Mr. Horgan said, "I *like* seeing plastic bottles bobbing in the surf. It makes me feel, I don't know, like part of something that is going to last forever. I want you to communicate that feeling, Dupoir. Now go get your briefs out."

I thought of asking for a salary advance of $14,572.03, but hesitated.

"Is there something else?"

"No, Mr. Horgan. Thank you." I left quietly.

Jack Denny was still waiting in my office, doodling still-life studies of cornucopias with fruits and nuts spilling out of them. "Look," he said, "how about this for a change? Something symbolic of the season, like 'the rich harvest of Plastics to make life more gracious,' like?"

I said kindly, "You don't understand copy, Jack. Do you remember what we did for last September?"

He scowled. "A girl in halter and shorts, very brief and tight, putting up plastic storm windows."

"That's right. Well, I've got an idea for something kind of novel this year. A little two-act drama. Act One: She's wearing halter and shorts and she's taking down the plastic screens. Act Two: She's wearing a dress and putting up the plastic storm window. And this is important. In Act Two there's wind, and autumn leaves blowing, and the dress is kind of wind-blown tight against her. Do you know what I mean, Jack?"

He said evenly, "I was the youngest child and only boy in a family of eight. If I didn't know what you meant by now I would deserve to be put away. Sometimes I think I *will* be put away. Do you know what seven older sisters can do to the psychology of a sensitive young boy?" He began to shake.

"Draw, Jack," I told him hastily. To give him a chance to recover himself I picked up his cornucopias. "Very nice," I said, turning them over. "Beautiful modeling. I guess you spilled some paint on this one?"

He snatched it out of my hand. "Where? That? That's gilt. I don't even have any gilt."

"No offense, Jack. I just thought it looked kind of nice." It didn't, particularly, it was just a shiny yellow smear in a corner of the drawing.

"Nice! Sure, if you'd let me use metallic inks. If you'd go to high-gloss paper. If you'd *spend* a few bucks—"

"Maybe, Jack," I said, "it'd be better, at that, if you took these back to your office. You can concentrate better there, maybe."

He went out, shaking.

I stayed in and thought about my house and brother-in-law and the Gudsell Medical Credit Bureau and after a while I began to shake too. Shaking, I phoned a Mr. Klaw, whom I had come to think of as my "account executive" at Gudsell.

Mr. Klaw was glad to hear from me. "You got our lawyer's note? Good, good. And exactly what arrangements are you suggesting, Mr. Dupoir?"

"I don't know," I said openly. "It catches me at a bad time. If we could have an extension—"

"Extensions we haven't got," he said regretfully. "We had one month of extensions, and we gave you the month, and now we're fresh out. I'm really sorry, Dupoir."

"With some time I could get a second mortgage, Mr. Klaw."

"You could at that, but not for $14,752.03."

"Do you want to put me and my family on the street?"

"Goodness, no, Mr. Dupoir! What we want is the sanitarium's money, including our commission. And maybe we want a *little* bit to make people think before they sign things, and maybe that people who should go to the county hospital *go* to the county hospital instead of a frankly deluxe rest home."

"I'll call you later," I said.

"Please do," said Mr. Klaw sincerely.

Tendons slack as the limp lianas, I leafed listlessly through the *dhowani-bark* jujus on my desk, studying Jack Denny's draftsmanship with cornucopias. The yellow stain, I noted, seemed to be spreading, even as a brother-in-law's blood might spread on the sands of the doom-pit when the cobras hissed the hour of judgment.

Mr. Horgan rapped perfunctorily on the doorframe and came in.

"I had the impression, Dupoir, that you had something further to ask me at our conference this morning. I've learned to back those judgments, Dupoir."

"Well, sir—" I began.

"Had that feeling about poor old Globus," he went on. "You remember Miss Globus? Crying in the file room one day. Seems she'd signed up for some kind of charm school. Couldn't pay, didn't like it, tried to back out. They wanted their money. Attached her wages. Well. Naturally, we couldn't have that sort of financial irresponsibility. I understand she's a P.F.C. in the W.A.C. now. What was it you wanted, Dupoir?"

"Me, Mr. Horgan? Wanted? No. Nothing at all."

"Glad we cleared that up," he grunted. "Can't do your best work for the firm if your mind's taken up with personal problems. Remember, Dupoir. We want the country plastics conscious, and forget about those ecology freaks."

"Yes, Mr. Horgan."

"And big. Not small."

"Big it is, Mr. Horgan," I said. I rolled up Jack Denny's sketches into a thick wad and threw them at him in the door, but not before he had closed it behind him.

GARIGOLLI

To Home Base
Listen Chief,

I appreciate your trying to work out a solution for us, but you're not doing as well as we're doing, even. Not that that's much.

We tried again to meet that constant aura of medium-of-exchange need from the Host, but he destroyed the whole lash-up again. Maybe we're misunderstanding him?

Artifacts are out. He's too big to see anything we make. Energy sources don't look promising. Oh, sure, we could elaborate lesser breeds that would selectively concentrate, for instance, plutonium or one of the uraniums. I don't think this particular Host would know the difference unless the scale was very large, and then, blooie, critical mass.

Meanwhile morale is becoming troublesome. We're holding together, but I wouldn't describe the condition as *good*. Vellitot has been wooing Dinnoliss in spite of the secondary directives against breeding while on exploration missions. I've cautioned them both, but they don't seem to stop. The funny thing is they're both in the male phase.

Garigolli.

Between Jack Denny and myself we got about half of the month's Plastics Briefs before quitting time. Maybe they weren't big, but they were real windblown. All factors considered, I don't think it is very much to my discredit that two hours later I was moodily drinking my seventh beer in a dark place near the railroad station.

The bartender respected my mood, the TV was off, the juke box had nothing but blues on it, and there was only one fly in my lugubrious ointment, a little man who kept trying to be friendly.

From time to time I gave him a scowl I had copied from Mr. Horgan. Then he would edge down the bar for a few minutes before edging back. Eventually he got up courage enough to talk, and I got too gloomy to crush him with my mighty thews, corded like the jungle-vines that looped from the towering *nganga*-palms.

He was some kind of hotel-keeper, it appeared. "My young friend, you may think you have problems, but there's no business like my business. Mortgage, insurance, state supervision, building and grounds maintenance, kitchen personnel and purchasing, linen, uniforms, the station wagon and the driver, carpet repairs—oh, God, carpet repairs! No matter how many ashtrays you put around, you know what they do? They steal the ashtrays. Then they stamp out cigarettes on the carpets." He began to weep.

I told the bartender to give him another. How could I lose? If he passed out I'd be rid of him. If he recovered I would have his undying, doglike affection for several minutes, and what kind of shape was I in to sneer at that?

Besides, I had worked out some pretty interesting figures. "Did you know," I told him, "that if you spend $1.46 a day on cigarettes, you can save $14,572.03 by giving up smoking for 10,104 and a quarter days?"

He wasn't listening, but he wasn't weeping any more either. He was just looking lovingly at his vodka libre, or whatever it was. I tried a different tack. "When you see discarded plastic bottles bobbing in the surf," I asked, "does it make you feel like part of something grand and timeless that will go on forever?"

He glanced at me with distaste, then went back to adoring his drink. "Or do you like buzzards better than babies?" I asked.

"They're all babies," he said. "Nasty, smelly, upchucking babies."

"Who are?" I asked, having lost the thread. He shook his head mysteriously, patted his drink, and tossed it down.

"Root of most evil," he said, swallowing. Then, affectionately, "Don't know where I'd be with it, don't know where I'd be without it."

He appeared to be talking about booze. "On your way home, without it?" I suggested.

He said obscurely. "Digging ditches, without it." Then he giggled. "Greatest business in the world! But oh! the worries! The competition! And when you come down to it it's all just aversion, right?"

"I can see you have a great aversion to liquor," I said politely.

"No, stupid! The *guests*."

Stiffly I signaled for Number Eight, but the bartender misunderstood and brought another for my friend, too. I said, "You have an aversion to the guests?"

He took firm hold on the bar and attempted to look squarely into my eyes, but wound up with his left eye four inches in front of my left eye and both our right eyes staring at respective ears. "The *guests* must be made to feel an aversion to *alcohol*," he said. "Secret of the whole thing. Works. Sometimes. But oh! it costs."

Like the striking fangs of Nag, the cobra, faster than the eye can follow, my trained reflexes swept the beer up to my lips. I drank furiously, scowling at him. "You mean to say you ran a drunk farm?" I shouted.

He was shocked. "My boy! No need to be vulgar. An 'institute,' eh? Let's leave the aversion to the drunks."

"I have to tell you, sir," I declared, "that I have a personal reason for despising all proprietors of such institutions!"

He began to weep again. "You, too! Oh, the general scorn."

"In my case, there is nothing general—"

"—the hatred! The unthinking contempt. And for what?"

I snarled, "For your blood-sucking ways."

"Blood, old boy?" he said, surprised. "No, nothing like that. We don't use blood. We use gold, yes, but the gold cure's old hat. Need new gimmick. Can't use silver, too cheap. Really doesn't matter what you say you use. All aversion—drying them out, keeping them comfy and aversion. But no blood."

He wiggled his fingers for Number Nine. Moodily I drank, glaring at him over my glass.

"In the wrong end of it, I sometimes think," he went on meditatively, staring with suspicious envy at the bartender. "*He* doesn't have to worry. Pour it out, pick up the money. No concern about expensive rooms standing idle, staff loafing around picking their noses, overhead going on, going on—you wouldn't *believe* how it goes on, whether the guests are there to pay for it or not—"

"Hah," I muttered.

"You've simply no idea what I go through," he sobbed. "And then they won't pay. No, really. Fellow beat me out of $14,752.03 just lately. I'm taking it out of the cosigner's hide, of course, but after you pay the collection agency, what's the profit?"

I choked on the beer, but he was too deep in sorrow to notice.

Strangling, I gasped. "Did you say fourteen thousand—?"

He nodded. "Seven hundred and fifty-two dollars, yes. And three cents. Astonishes you, doesn't it, the deadbeats in this world?"

I couldn't speak.

"You wouldn't think it," he mourned. "All those salaries. All those rooms. The hydrotherapy tubs. The *water* bill."

I shook my head.

"Probably you think my life's a bowl of roses, hey?"

I managed to pry my larynx open enough to wheeze, "Up to this minute, yes, I did. You've opened my eyes."

"Drink to that," he said promptly. "Hey, barman!"

But before the bartender got there with Number Ten the little man hiccoughed and slid melting to the floor, like a glacier calving into icebergs.

The bartender peered over at him. "Every *damn* night," he grumbled. "And who's going to get him home this time?"

My mind working as fast as *Ngo*, the dancing spider, spinning her web, I succeeded in saying, "Me. Glad to oblige. Never fear."

GARIGOLLI
To Home Base

                                                                Chief,

All right, I admit we haven't exactly 144 p.g. on this project, but there's no reason for you to get loose. Reciting the penalties for violating the Triple Directive is uncalled for.

Let me point out that there has been no question at any time of compliance with One or Three. And even Directive Two, well, we've done what we could. "To repay sentients in medium suitable to them for information gained." These sentients are tricky, Chief. They don't seem to empathize, really. See our reports. They often take without giving in return among themselves, and it seems to me that under the circumstances a certain modification of Directive Two would have been quite proper.

But I am not protesting the ruling. Especially since you've pointed out it won't do any good. When I get old and skinny enough to retire to a sling in Home Base I guess I'll get that home-base mentality too, but way out here on the surface of the exploration volume it looks different, believe me.

And what is happening with the rest of our crew back at Host's domicile I can't even guess. They must be nearly frantic by now.

Garigolli.

There was some discussion with a policeman he wanted to hit (apparently under the impression that the cop was his night watchman playing hooky), but I finally got the little man to the Institute for Psychosomatic Adjustment.

The mausoleum that had graduated my brother-in-law turned out to be three stories high, with a sun porch and a slate roof and bars on the ground-floor bay windows. It was not all that far from my house. Shirl had been pleased about that, I remembered. She said we could visit her brother a lot there, and in fact she had gone over once or twice on Sundays, but me, I'd never set eyes on the place before.

Dagger-sharp fangs flecking white spume, none dared dispute me as I strode through the great green corridors of the rain forest. Corded thews rippling like pythons under my skin, it was child's play to carry the craven jackal to his lair. The cabbie helped me up the steps with him.

The little man, now revealed as that creature who in anticipation had seemed so much larger and hairier, revived slightly as we entered the reception hall. "Ooooh," he groaned. "Watch the bouncing, old boy. That door. My office. Leather couch. Much obliged."

I dumped him on the couch, lit a green-shaded lamp on his desk, closed the door, and considered.

Mine enemy had delivered himself into my power. All I had to do was seize him by the forelock. I seemed to see the faces of my family —Shirl's smiling sweetly, Butchie's cocoa-overlaid-with-oatmeal— spurring me on.

There had to be a way.

I pondered. Life had not equipped me for this occasion. Raffles or Professor Moriarty would have known what to do at once, but, ponder as I would, I couldn't think of anything to do except to go through the drawers of his desk.

Well, it was a start. But it yielded very little. Miscellaneous paper clips and sheaves of letterheads, a carton of cigarettes of a brand apparently flavored with rice wine and extract of vanilla, part of a fifth of Old Rathole and five switchblade knives, presumably taken from the inmates. There was also $6.15 in unused postage stamps, but I quickly computed that, even if I went to the trouble of cashing them in, that would leave me $14,745.88 short.

Of Papers to Burn there were none.

All in all, the venture was a bust. I wiped out a water glass with one of the letterheads (difficult, because they were of so high quality that they seemed likelier to shatter than to wad up), and forced down a couple of ounces of the whiskey (difficult, because it was of so low).

Obviously anything of value, like for instance cosigned agreements with brothers-in-law, would be in a safe, which itself would probably be in the offices of the Gudsell Medical Credit Bureau. Blackmail? But there seemed very little to work with, barring one or two curious photographs tucked in among the envelopes. Conceivably I could cause him some slight embarrassment, but nowhere near $14,752.03 worth. I had not noticed any evidence of Red espionage that might put the little man (whose name, I learned from his letterhead, was Bermingham) away for 10,104 and a quarter days, while I saved up the price of reclaiming our liberty.

There seemed to be only one possible thing to do.

Eyes glowing like red coals behind slitted lids, I walked lightly on velvet-soft pads to the *kraal* of the witch-man. He was snoring with his mouth open. Totally vulnerable to his doom.

Only, how to inflict it?

It is not as easy as one might think to murder a person. Especially if one doesn't come prepared for it. Mr. Horgan doesn't like us to carry guns at the office, and heaven knows what Shirl would do with one if I left it around home. Anyway, I didn't have one.

Poison was a possibility. The Old Rathole suggested it. But we'd already tried that, hadn't we?

I considered the switchblade knives. There was a technical problem. Would *you* know where the heart is? Granted, it had to be inside his chest somewhere, and sooner or later I could find it. But what would I say to Mr. Bermingham after the first three or four exploratory stabs woke him up?

The only reasonably efficient method I could think of to ensure Mr. Bermingham's decease was to burn the place down with him in it. Which, I quickly perceived, meant with whatever cargo of drying-out drunks the institute now possessed in it too, behind those barred windows.

At this point I came face to face with myself.

I wasn't going to kill anybody. I wasn't going to steal any papers.

What I was going to do was, I was going to let Mr. Klaw's lawyers go ahead and take our house, because I just didn't know how to do anything else. I hefted the switchblades in my hand, threw them against the wall, and poured myself another slug of Mr. Bermingham's lousy whiskey, wishing it would kill me right there and be a lesson to him.

GARIGOLLI
To Home Base

Now,
don't get excited, Chief.

But we have another problem.

Before I get into it, I would like to remind you of a couple of things. First, I was against exploring this planet in the first place, remember? I said it was going to be very difficult, on the grounds of the difference in mass between its dominant species and us, I mean, really. Here we are, fighting member to member against dangerous beasts all the time, and the beasts, to the Host and his race, are only microorganisms that live unnoticed in their circulatory systems, their tissues, their food, and their environment. Anybody could tell that this was going to be a tough assignment, if not an impossible one.

Then there's the fact that this Host moves around so. I

told you some of our crew got left in his domicile. Well, we've timed this before, and almost always he returns within 144 or 216 time-units—at most, half of one of his planet's days. It's pretty close to critical, but our crew is tough and they can survive empathy-deprival that long. Only this time he has been away, so far, nearly 432 time-units. It's bad enough for those of us who have been with him. The ones who were cut off back at his domicile must have been through the tortures of the damned.

Two of them homed in on us to report just a few time-units ago, and I'm afraid you're not going to like what's happened. They must have been pretty panicky. They decided to try meeting the Second Directive themselves. They modified some microorganisms to provide some organic chemicals they thought the Host might like.

Unfortunately the organisms turned out to have an appetite for some of the House's household artifacts, and they're pretty well demolished. So we not only haven't *given* him anything to comply with Directive Two, we've *taken* something from him. And in the process maybe we've called attention to ourselves.

I'm giving it to you arced, Chief, because I know that's how you'd like it. I accept full responsibility.

Because I don't have any choice, do I?

Garigolli.

"What the hell," said the voice of Mr. Bermingham, from somewhere up there, "are you doing in my office?"

I opened my eyes, and he was quite right. I was in Mr. Bermingham's office. The sun was streaming through Mr. Bermingham's venetian blinds, and Mr. Bermingham was standing over me with a selection of the switchblade knives in his hands.

I don't know how Everyman reacts to this sort of situation. I guess I ran about average. I pushed myself up on one elbow and blinked at him.

"Spastic," he muttered to himself. "Well?"

I cleared my throat. "Uh, uh, I think I can explain this."

He was hung over and shaking. "Go ahead! Who the devil are you?"

"Well, my name is Dupoir."

"I don't mean what's your name, I mean—Wait a minute. Dupoir?"

"Dupoir."

"As in $14,752.03?"

"That's right, Mr. Bermingham."

"You!" he gasped. "Say, you've got some nerve coming here this way. I ought to teach you a lesson."

I scrambled to my feet. Mighty thews rippling, I tossed back my head and bellowed the death-challenge of the anthropoids with whom I had been raised.

Bermingham misunderstood. It probably didn't sound like a death-challenge to him. He said anxiously, "If you're going to be sick, go in there and do it. Then we're going to straighten this thing out."

I followed his pointing finger. There on one side of the foyer was the door marked *Staff Washroom*, and on the other the door to the street through which I had carried him. It was only the work of a second to decide which to take. I was out the door, down the steps, around the corner, and hailing a fortuitous cab before he could react.

By the time I got to the house that Mr. Klaw wanted so badly to take away from us it was 7:40 on my watch. There was no chance at all that Shirl would still be asleep. There was not any very big chance that she had got to sleep at all that night, not with her faithful husband for the first time in the four years of our marriage staying out all night without warning, but no chance at all that she would be still in bed. So there would be explaining to do. Nevertheless I insinuated my key into the lock of the back door, eased it open, slipped ghostlike through, and gently closed it behind me.

I smelled like a distillery, I noticed, but my keen, jungle-trained senses brought me no other message. No one was in sight or sound. Not even Butchie was either chattering or weeping to disturb the silence.

I slid silently through the mud-room into the half-bath where I kept a spare razor. I spent five minutes trying to convert myself into the image of a prosperous young executive getting ready to be half an hour late at work, but it was no easy job. There was nothing but soap to shave with, and Butchie had knocked it into the sink. What

was left was a blob of jelly, sculpted into a crescent where the drip-
ping tap had eroded it away. Still, I got clean, more or less, and
shaved, less.

I entered the kitchen: and then realized that my jungle-trained
senses had failed to note the presence of a pot of fresh coffee perk-
ing on the stove. I could hear it plainly enough. Smelling it was
more difficult; its scent was drowned by the aroma of cheap booze
that hung in the air all around me.

So I turned around and yes, there was Shirl on the stairway, holding Butchie by one hand like Maureen O'Sullivan walking Cheeta.
She wore an expression of unrelieved tragedy.

It was clearly necessary to give her an explanation at once,
whether I had one or not. "Honey," I said, "I'm *sorry*. I met this
fellow I hadn't seen in a long time, and we got to talking. I know
we should have called. But by the time I realized the time it was so
late I was afraid I'd wake you up."

"You can't wear that shirt to the office," she said woefully. "I
ironed your blue and gray one with the white cuffs. It's in the
closet."

I paused to analyze the situation. It appeared she wasn't angry at
all, only upset—which, as any husband of four years knows, is
14,752.03 times worse. In spite of the fact that the reek of booze
was making me giddy and fruit flies were buzzing around Shirl's normally immaculate kitchen, I knew what I had to do. "Shirl," I said,
falling to one knee, "I apologize."

That seemed to divert her. "Apologize? For what?"

"For staying out all night."

"But you explained all that. You met this fellow you hadn't seen
in a long time, and you got to talking. By the time you realized the
time it was so late you were afraid you'd wake me up."

"Oh, Shirl," I cried, leaping to my feet and crushing her in my
mighty thews. I would have kissed her, but the reek of stale liquor
seemed even stronger. I was afraid of what close contact might do,
not to mention its effect on Butchie, staring up at me with a thumb
and two fingers in his mouth. We Dupoirs never do anything by
halves.

But there was a tear in her eye. She said, "I watched Butchie,
honestly I did. I always do. When he broke the studio lamp I was
watching every minute, remember? He was just too fast for me."

I didn't have any idea what she was talking about. That is not an unfamiliar situation in our house, and I have developed a technique for dealing with it. "What?" I asked.

"He was too fast for me," Shirl said woefully. "When he dumped his vitamins into his raisins and oatmeal I was right there. I went to get some paper napkins, and that was when he did it. But how could I know it would ruin the plastics bin?"

I went into Phase Two. "What plastics bin?"

"*Our* plastics bin." She pointed. "Where Butchie threw the stuff."

At once I saw what she meant. There was a row of four plastic pop-up recycling bins in our kitchen, one for paper, one for plastics, one for glass, and one for metals. They were a credit to us, and to Mr. Horgan, and to the Fourteenth Floor. However, the one marked "plastics" was not a credit to anyone any more. It had sprung a leak. A colorless fluid was oozing out of the bottom of it and, whatever it was, it was deeply pitting the floor tiles.

I bent closer and realized where the reek of stale booze was coming from: out of the juices that were seeping from our plastics bin.

"What the devil?" I asked.

Shirl said thoughtfully, "If vitamins can do that to plastic, what do you suppose they do to Butchie's insides?"

"It isn't the vitamins. I know that much." I reached in and hooked the handle of what had been a milk jug, gallon size. It was high-density polythene and about four hundred percent more indestructible than Mount Rushmore. It was exactly the kind of plastic jug that people who loved buzzards better than babies have been complaining about finding bobbing around the surf of their favorite bathing beaches, all the world over.

Indestructible or not, it was about ninety percent destroyed. What I pulled out was a handle and part of a neck. The rest drizzled off into a substance very like the stuff I had shaved with. Only that was soap, which one expects to dissolve from time to time. High-density polythene one does not.

The fruit flies were buzzing around me, and everything was very confusing. I was hardly aware that the front doorbell had rung until I noticed that Shirl had gone to answer it.

What made me fully aware of this was Mr. Bermingham's triumphant roar: "Thought I'd find you here, Dupoir! And who are these people—your confederates?"

386 FREDERIK POHL and C. M. KORNBLUTH

Bermingham had no terrors for me. I was past that point. I said, "Hello, Mr. Bermingham. This confederate is my wife, the littler one here is my son. Shirl, Butchie—Mr. Bermingham. Mr. Bermingham's the one who is going to take away our house."

Shirl said politely, "You must be tired, Mr. Bermingham. I'll get you a cup of coffee."

GARIGOLLI
  To Home Base
                                                              Chief,
admit it, we've excreted this one out beyond redemption. Don't bother to reply to this. Just write us off.

I could say that it wasn't entirely the fault of the crew members who stayed behind in the Host's domicile. They thought they had figured out a way to meet Directive Two. They modified some organisms—didn't even use bacteria, just an enzyme that hydrated polythene into what they had every reason to believe was a standard food substance, since the Host had been observed to ingest it with some frequency. There is no wrongdoing there, Chief. Alcohols are standard foods for many organic beings, as you know. And a gift of food has been held to satisfy the second Directive. And add to that they were half out of their plexuses with empathy deprivation.

Nevertheless I admit the gift failed in a fairly basic way, since it seems to have damaged artifacts the Hosts hold valuable.

So I accept the responsibility, Chief. Wipe this expedition off the records. We've failed, and we'll never see our home breeding-slings again.

Please notify our descendants and former co-parents and, if you can, try to let them think we died heroically, won't you?
  Garigolli.

Shirl has defeated the wrath of far more complex creatures than Mr. Bermingham by offering them coffee—me, for instance. While she got him the clean cup and the spoon and the milk out of the pitcher in the refrigerator, I had time to think.

Mr. Horgan would be interested in what had happened to our plastic eco-bin. Not only Mr. Horgan. The Fourteenth Floor would be interested, and maybe would forget about liking buzzards better than babies long enough to say a good word for International Plastics Co.

I mean, this was *significant*. It was big, by which I mean it wasn't little. It was a sort of whole new horizon for plastics. The thing about plastics, as everyone knows, is that once you convert them into trash they *stay* trash. Bury a maple syrup jug in your back yard and five thousand years from now some descendant operating a radar-controlled peony-planter from his back porch will grub it up as shiny as new. But the gunk in our eco-bin was making these plastics, or at least the polythene parts of them, biodegradable.

What was the gunk? I had no idea. Some random chemical combination between Butchie's oatmeal and his vitamins? I didn't care. It was there, and it worked. If we could isolate the stuff, I had no doubt that the world-famous scientists who gave us the plastic storm window and the pop-up eco-bin could duplicate it. And if we could duplicate it we could sell it to hard-pressed garbagemen all over the world. The Fourteenth Floor would be very pleased.

With me to think was ever to act. I rinsed out one of Butchie's baby-food jars in the sink, scraped some of the stickiest parts of the melting plastic into it, and capped it tightly. I couldn't wait to get it to the office.

Mr. Bermingham was staring at me with his mouth open. "Good Lord," he muttered, "playing with filth at his age. What psychic damage we wreak with bad early toilet-training."

I had lost interest in Mr. Bermingham. I stood up and told him, "I've got to go to work. I'd be happy to walk you as far as the bus."

"You aren't going anywhere, Dupoir! Came here to talk to you. Going to do it, too. Behavior was absolutely inexcusable, and I demand—Say, Dupoir, you don't have a drink anywhere about the house, do you?"

"More coffee, Mr. Bermingham?" Shirl said politely. "I'm afraid we don't have anything stronger to offer you. We don't keep alcoholic beverages here, or at least not very long. Mr. Dupoir drinks them."

"Thought so," snarled Bermingham. "Recognize a drunk when I see one: shifty eyes, irrational behavior, duplicity—oh, the duplicity! Got all the signs."

"Oh, he's not like my brother, really," Shirl said thoughtfully. "My husband doesn't go out breaking into liquor stores when he runs out, you know. But I don't drink, Butchie doesn't drink, and so about all we ever have in the house is some cans of beer, and there aren't any of those now."

Bermingham looked at her with angry disbelief. "You too! I *smell* it," he said. "You going to tell me I don't know what good old ethyl alcohol smells like?"

"That's the bin, Mr. Bermingham. It's a terrible mess, I know."

"Funny place to keep the creature," he muttered to himself, dropping to his knees. He dipped a finger into the drippings, smelled it, tasted it, and nodded. "Alcohol, all right. Add a few congeners, couple drops of food coloring, and you've got the finest Chivas Regal a bellboy ever sold you out of a bottle with the tax stamp broken." He stood up and glared at me. "What's the matter with you, Dupoir? You not only don't pay your honest debts, you don't want to pay the bartenders either?"

I said, "It's more or less an accident."

"Accident?"

Then illumination struck. "Accident you should find us like this," I corrected. "You see, it's a secret new process. We're not ready to announce it yet. Making alcohol out of old plastic scraps."

He questioned Shirl with his eyes. Getting her consent, he poured some of Butchie's baby-food drippings from the bin, closed his eyes, and tasted. "Mmmm," he said judiciously. "Sell it for vodka just the way it stands."

"Glad to have an expert opinion," I said. "We think there's millions in it."

He took another taste. "Plastic scraps, you say? Listen, Dupoir. Think we can clear all this up in no time. That fool Klaw, I've told him over and over, ask politely, don't make trouble for people. But no, he's got that crazy lawyer's drive for revenge. Apologize for him, old boy, I really do apologize for him. Now look," he said, putting down the glass to rub his hands. "You'll need help in putting this process on the market. Business acumen, you know? Wise counsel from man of experience. Like me. And capital. Can help you there. I'm loaded."

Shirl put in, "Then what do you want our house for?"

"House? My dear Mrs. Dupoir," cried Mr. Bermingham, laughing heartily, "I'm not going to take your house! Your husband and I will work out the details in no time. Let me have a little more of that delightful orange juice and we can talk some business."

GARIGOLLI
   To Home Base
   Joy, joy
Chief!
   Cancel all I said. We've met Directive Two, the Host is
happy, and we're on our way Home!
   Warm up the breeding slings, there's going to be a hot
time in the old hammocks tonight.
   Garigolli.

Straight as the flight of Ung-Glitch, the soaring vulture, that is
the code of the jungle. I was straight with Mr. Bermingham. I
didn't cheat him. I made a handshake deal with him over the ruins
of our eco-bin, and honored it when we got to his lawyers. I traded
him 40% of the beverage rights to the stuff that came out of our
bin, and he wrote off that little matter of $14,752.03.
   Of course, the beverage rights turned out not to be worth all that
much, because the stuff in the bin was organic and alive and capable
of reproduction, and it did indeed reproduce itself enthusiastically.
Six months later you could buy a starter drop of it for a quarter on
any street corner, and what that has done to the vintners of the
world you know as well as I do. But Bermingham came out ahead.
He divided his 40% interest into forty parts and sold them for $500
each to the alumni of his drunk tank. And Mr. Horgan—
   Ah, Mr. Horgan.
   Mr. Horgan was perched on my doorframe like Ung-Glitch awaiting a delivery of cadavers for dinner when I arrived that morning,
bearing my little glass jar before me like the waiting line in an obste-
trician's office. "You're late, Dupoir," he pointed out. "Troubles me,
that does. Do you remember Metcalf? Tall, blonde girl that used to
work in Accounts Receivable? Never could get in on time, and—"
   "Mr. Horgan," I said, "look." And I unscrewed my baby-food jar
and dumped the contents on an unpopped pop-up eco-bin. It took
him a while to see what was happening, but once he saw he was so
impressed he forgot to roar.
   And, yes, the Fourteenth Floor was very pleased.
   There wasn't any big money in it. We couldn't sell the stuff, because it was so happy to give itself away to everyone in the world.
But it meant a promotion and a raise. Not big. But not really little,
either. And, as Mr. Horgan said, "I *like* the idea of helping to elimi-

nate all the litter that devastates the landscape. It makes me feel, I don't know, like part of something clean and natural."

And so we got along happily as anything—happily, anyway, until the time Shirl bought the merry-go-round.

OVERDRAWN AT THE MEMORY BANK

May 1976

John Varley

John Varley is one of the fastest rising stars in the science-fiction galaxy. Trained in both science and the humanities, he creates stories with a consistent background which feature strong social and technological extrapolation. Varley is the author of the novels The Ophiuchi Hotline *(1977) and* Titan *(1979); his best shorter fiction can be found in* The Persistence of Vision *(1978).*

To Galaxy *he contributed "The Phantom of Kansas" (February 1976), the amazing "Gotta Sing, Gotta Dance" (July 1976), and this powerful story.*

Note by John Varley

When we asked John Varley to contribute a brief memoir for this special volume, he declined. However, he graciously gave us permission to quote from his letters, which illustrate his reasons.

"I made a vow when [*Galaxy*] gave me such a hard time over the payment for this story and three others; they still owe me money (it's not much, but it's been many years), and I will not do anything further for the firm until the accounts are balanced. Going into any more detail would be boring and petty, and I retain enough respect for what *Galaxy* was to not want to kick at the thing it's become. So if I tried to write a memoir I'm sure I'd just get angry. I feel saddened by this, as *Galaxy* was my favorite magazine when I was growing up and being introduced to science fiction."

OVERDRAWN AT THE MEMORY BANK

It was schoolday at the Kenya Disneyland. Five nine-year-olds were being shown around the medico section where Fingal lay on the recording table, the top of his skull removed, looking up into a mirror. Fingal was in a bad mood (hence the trip to the Disneyland) and could have done without the children. Their teacher was doing his best, but who can control five nine-year-olds?

"What's the big green wire do, teacher?" asked a little girl, reaching out one grubby hand and touching Fingal's brain where the main recording wire clamped to the built-in terminal.

"Lupus, I told you you weren't to touch anything. And look at you, you didn't wash your hands." The teacher took the child's hand and pulled it away.

"But what does it matter? You told us yesterday that the reason no one cares about dirt like they used to is dirt isn't dirty anymore."

"I'm sure I didn't tell you exactly *that*. What I said was that when humans were forced off Earth, we took the golden opportunity to wipe out all harmful germs. When there were only three thousand people alive on the moon after the Occupation it was easy for us to sterilize everything. So the medico doesn't need to wear gloves like surgeons used to, or even wash her hands. There's no danger of infection. But it isn't polite. We don't want this man to think we're being impolite to him, just because his nervous system is disconnected and he can't do anything about it, do we?"

"No, teacher."

"What's a surgeon?"

"What's 'infection'?"

Fingal wished the little perishers had chosen another day for their lessons, but like the teacher had said, there was very little he could do. The medico had turned his motor control over to the computer while she took the reading. He was paralyzed. He eyed the little boy carrying the carved stick, and hoped he didn't get a notion to poke him in the cerebrum with it. Fingal was insured, but who needs the trouble?

"All of you stand back a little so the medico can do her work. That's better. Now, who can tell me what the big green wire is? Destry?"

Destry allowed as how he didn't know, didn't care, and wished he could get out of here and play spat ball. The teacher dismissed him and went on with the others.

"The green wire is the main sounding electrode," the teacher said. "It's attached to a series of very fine wires in the man's head, like the ones you have, which are implanted at birth. Can anyone tell me how the recording is made?"

The little girl with the dirty hands spoke up.

"By tying knots in string."

The teacher laughed, but the medico didn't. She had heard it all before. So had the teacher, of course, but this was why he was a teacher. He had the patience to deal with children, a rare quality now that there were so few of them.

"No, that was just an analogy. Can you all say analogy?"

"*Analogy,*" they chorused.

"Fine. What I told you is that the chains of FPNA are very much *like* strings with knots tied in them. If you make up a code with every millimeter and every knot having a meaning, you could write words in string by tying knots in it. That's what the machine does with the FPNA. Now . . . can anyone tell me what FPNA stands for?"

"Ferro-Photo-Nucleic Acid," said the girl, who seemed to be the star pupil.

"That's right, Lupus. It's a variant on DNA, and it can be knotted by magnetic fields and light, and made to go through chemical changes. What the medico is doing now is threading long strings of FPNA into the tiny tubes that are in the man's brain. When she's done, she'll switch on the machine and the current will start tying knots. And what happens then?"

"All his memories go into the memory cube," said Lupus.

"That's right. But it's a little more complicated than that. You remember what I told you about a divided cipher? The kind that has two parts, neither of which is any good without the other? Imagine two of the strings, each with a lot of knots in them. Well, you try to read one of them with your decoder, and you find out that it doesn't make sense. That's because whoever wrote it used two strings, with knots tied in different places. They only make sense when you put them side-by-side and read them that way. That's how this decoder works, but the medico uses twenty-five strings. When they're all knotted the right way and put into the right openings in that cube over there," he pointed to the pink cube in the medico's bench, "they'll contain all this man's memories and personality. In a way, he'll be in the cube, but he won't know it, because he's going to be an African lion today."

This excited the children, who would much rather be stalking the Kenya savanna than listening to how a multi-holo was taken. When they quieted down the teacher went on, using analogies that got more strained by the minute.

"When the strings are in . . . class, pay attention. When they're in the cube, a current sets them in place. What we have then is a multi-holo. Can anyone tell me why we can't just take a tape recording of what's going on in this man's brain, and use that?"

One of the boys answered, for once.

"Because memory isn't . . . what's that word?"

"Sequential?"

"Yeah, that's it. His memories are stashed all over his brain and there's no way to sort them out. So this recorder takes a picture of the whole thing at once, like a hologram. Does that mean you can cut the cube in half and have two people?"

"No, but that's a good question. This isn't that sort of hologram. This is something like . . . like when you press your hand into clay, but in four dimensions. If you chip off a part of the information, right? Well, this is sort of like that. You can't see the imprint because it's too small, but everything the man ever did and saw and heard and thought will be in the cube."

"Would you move back a little?" asked the medico. The children in the mirror over Fingal's head shuffled back and became more than just heads with shoulders sticking out. The medico adjusted the last strand of FPNA suspended in his cortex to the close tolerances specified by the computer.

"I'd like to be a medico when I grow up," said one boy.

"I thought you wanted to go to college and study to be a scientist."

"Well, maybe. But my friend is teaching me to be a medico. It looks a lot easier."

"You should stay in school, Destry. I'm sure your parent will want you to make something of yourself." The medico fumed silently. She knew better than to speak up—education was a serious business and interference with the duties of a teacher carried a stiff fine. But she was obviously pleased when the class thanked her and went out the door, leaving dirty footprints behind them.

She viciously flipped a switch, and Fingal found he could breathe and move the muscles in his head.

"Lousy conceited college graduate," she said. "What the hell's wrong with getting your hands dirty, I ask you?" She wiped the blood from her hands onto her blue smock.

"Teachers are the worst," Fingal said.

"Ain't it the truth? Well, being a medico is nothing to be ashamed of. So I didn't go to college, so what? I can do my job, and I can see what I've done when I'm through. I always did like working with my hands. Did you know that being a medico used to be one of the most respected professions there was?"

"Really?"

"Fact. They had to go to college for years and years, and they made a hell of a lot of money, let me tell you."

Fingal said nothing, thinking she must be exaggerating. What was so tough about medicine? Just a little mechanical sense and a steady hand, that was all you needed. Fingal did a lot of maintenance on his body himself, going to the shop only for major work. And a good thing, at the prices they charged. It was not the sort of thing one discussed while lying helpless on the table, however.

"Okay, that's done." She pulled out the modules that contained the invisible FPNA and set them in the developing solution. She fastened Fingal's skull back on and tightened the recessed screws set into the bone. She turned his motor control back over to him while she sealed his scalp back into place. He stretched and yawned. He always grew sleepy in the medico's shop; he didn't know why.

"Will that be all for today, sir? We've got a special on blood changes, and since you'll just be lying there while you're out doppling in the park, you might as well . . ."

"No, thanks. I had it changed a year ago. Didn't you read my history?"

She picked up the card and glanced at it. "So you did. Fine. You can get up now, Mr. Fingal." She made a note on the card and set it down on the table. The door opened and a small face peered in.

"I left my stick," said the boy. He came in and started looking under things, to the annoyance of the medico. She attempted to ignore the boy as she took down the rest of the information she needed.

"And are you going to experience this holiday now, or wait until your double has finished and play it back then?"

"Huh? Oh, you mean . . . yes. I see. No, I'll go right into the animal. My psychist advised me to come out here for my nerves, so it wouldn't do me much good to wait it out, would it?"

"No, I suppose it wouldn't. So you'll be sleeping here while you dopple in the park. Hey!" She turned to confront the little boy, who was poking his nose into things he should stay away from. She grabbed him and pulled him away.

"You either find what you're looking for in one minute or you get out of here, you see?" He went back to his search, giggling behind his hand and looking for more interesting things to fool with.

The medico made a check on the card, glanced at the glowing numbers on her thumbnail, and discovered her shift was almost over. She connected the memory cube through a machine to a terminal in the back of his head.

"You've never done this before, right? We do this to avoid blank spots, which can be confusing sometimes. The cube is almost set, but now I'll add the last ten minutes to the record at the same time as I put you to sleep. That way you'll experience no disorientation, you'll move through a dream state to full awareness of being in the body of a lion. Your body will be removed and taken to one of our slumber rooms while you're gone. There's nothing to worry about."

Fingal wasn't worried, just tired and tense. He wished she would go on and do it and stop talking about it. And he wished the little boy would stop pounding his stick against the table leg. He wondered if his headache would be transferred to the lion.

She turned him off.

They hauled his body away and took his memory cube to the installation room. The medico chased the boy into the corridor and hosed down the recording room. Then she was off to a date she was already late for.

The employees of Kenya Disneyland installed the cube into a metal box set into the skull of a full-grown African lioness. The social structure of lions being what it was, the proprietors charged a premium for the use of a male body, but Fingal didn't care one way or the other.

A short ride in an underground railroad with the sedated body of the Fingal-lioness, and he was deposited beneath the blazing sun of the Kenya savanna. He awoke, sniffed the air, and felt better immediately.

The Kenya Disneyland was a total environment buried twenty kilometers beneath Mare Moscoviense on the far side of Luna. It was roughly circular with a radius of two hundred kilometers. From the ground to the "sky" was two kilometers except over the full-size replica of Kilimanjaro, where it bulged to allow clouds to form in a realistic manner over the snowcap.

The illusion was flawless. The ground curved away consistent with the curvature of the earth, so that the horizon was much more distant than anything Fingal was used to. The trees were real, and so were all the animals. At night an astronomer would have needed a spectroscope to distinguish the stars from the real thing.

Fingal certainly couldn't spot anything wrong. Not that he wanted to. The colors were strange but that was from the limitations of feline optics. Sounds were much more vivid, as were smells. If he'd thought about it, he would have realized the gravity was much too weak for Kenya. But he wasn't thinking; he'd come here to avoid that necessity.

It was hot and glorious. The dry grass made no sound as he walked over it on broad pads. He smelled antelope, wildebeest, and . . . was that baboon? He felt pangs of hunger but he really didn't want to hunt. But he found the lioness body starting on a stalk anyway.

Fingal was in an odd position. He was in control of the lioness, but only more or less. He could guide her where he wanted to go, but he had no say at all over instinctive behaviors. He was as much a pawn to these as the lioness was. In one sense, he *was* the lioness; when he wished to raise a paw or turn around, he simply did it. The motor control was complete. It felt great to walk on all fours, and it came as easily as breathing. But the scent of the antelope went on a direct route from the nostrils to the lower brain, made a connection with the rumblings of hunger, and started him on the stalk.

The guidebook said to surrender to it. Fighting it wouldn't do anyone any good, and could frustrate you. If you were paying to be a lion, read the chapter on "Things to Do," you might as well *be* one, not just wear the body and see the sights.

Fingal wasn't sure he liked this as he came up downwind and crouched behind a withered clump of scrub. He pondered it while he sized up the dozen or so antelope grazing just a few meters from him, picking out the small, the weak, and the young with a predator's eye. Maybe he should back out now and go on his way. These beautiful creatures were not harming him. The Fingal part of him wished mostly to admire them, not eat them.

Before he quite knew what had happened, he was standing triumphant over the bloody body of a small antelope. The others were just dusty trails in the distance.

It had been incredible!

The lioness was fast, but might as well have been moving in slow motion compared to the antelope. Her only advantage lay in surprise, confusion, and quick, all-out attack. There had been the lifting of a head, ears had flicked toward the bush he was hiding in, and he had exploded. Ten seconds of furious exertion and he bit down on a soft throat, felt the blood gush and the dying kicks of the hind legs under his paws. He was breathing hard and the blood coursed through his veins. There was only one way to release the tension.

He threw his head back and roared his bloodlust.

He had it with lions at the end of the weekend. It wasn't worth it for the few minutes of exhilaration at the kill. It was a life of endless stalking, countless failures, then pitiful struggle to get a few bites for yourself from the kill you had made. He found to his chagrin that his lioness was very low in the dominance order. When he got his kill back to the pride—he didn't know why he had dragged it back but the lioness seemed to know—it was promptly stolen from him. He/she sat back helplessly and watched the dominant male take his share, followed by the rest of the pride. He was left with a dried haunch four hours later, and had to contest even that with vultures and hyenas. He saw what the premium payment was for. That male had it *easy*.

But he had to admit that it had been worth it. He felt better; his psychist had been right. It did one good to leave the insatiable computers at his office for a weekend of simple living. There were no complicated choices to be made out here. If he was in doubt, he listened to his instincts. It was just that the next time, he'd go as an elephant. He'd been watching them. All the other animals pretty much left them alone, and he could see why. To be a solitary bull, free to wander where he wished with food as close as the nearest tree branch . . .

He was still thinking about it when the collection crew came for him.

He awoke with the vague feeling that something was wrong. He sat up in bed and looked around him. Nothing seemed to be out of place. There was no one in the room with him. He shook his head to clear it.

It didn't do any good. There was still something wrong. He tried to remember how he had gotten there, and laughed at himself. His own bedroom! What was so remarkable about that?

But hadn't there been a vacation, a weekend trip? He remembered being a lion, eating raw antelope meat, being pushed around within the pride, fighting it out with the other females and losing and retiring to rumble to him/herself.

Certainly he should have come back to human consciousness in the Disneyland medical section. He couldn't remember it. He reached for his phone, not knowing who he wished to call. His psychist, perhaps, or the Kenya office.

"I'm sorry, Mr. Fingal," the phone told him. "This line is no longer available for outgoing calls. If you'll . . ."

"Why not?" he asked, irritated and confused. "I paid my bill."

"That is of no concern to this department, Mr. Fingal. And please do not interrupt. It's hard enough to reach you. I'm fading, but the message will be continued if you look to your right." The voice and the power hum behind it faded. The phone was dead.

Fingal looked to his right and jerked in surprise. There was a hand, a woman's hand, writing on his wall. The hand faded out at the wrist.

"*Mene, Mene . . .*" it wrote, in thin letters of fire. Then the hand waved in irritation and erased that with its thumb. The wall was smudged with soot where the words had been.

"You're projecting, Mr. Fingal," the hand wrote, quickly etching out the words with a manicured nail. "That's what you expected to see." The hand underlined the word "expected" three times. "Please cooperate, clear your mind, and see what is *there*, or we're not going to get anywhere. Damn, I've about exhausted this medium."

And indeed it had. The writing had filled the wall and the hand was now down near the foot. The apparition wrote smaller and smaller in an effort to get it all in.

Fingal had an excellent grasp on reality, according to his psychist. He held tightly onto that evaluation like a talisman as he leaned closer to the wall to read the last sentence.

"Look on your bookshelf," the hand wrote. "The title is *Orientation in Your Fantasy World*."

Fingal knew he had no such book, but could think of nothing better to do.

His phone didn't work, and if he was going through a psychotic episode he didn't think it wise to enter the public corridor until he had some idea of what was going on. The hand faded out, but the writing continued to smolder.

He found the book easily enough. It was a pamphlet, actually, with a gaudy cover. It was the sort of thing he had seen in the outer office of the Kenya Disneyland, a promotional booklet. At the bottom it said, "Published under the auspices of the Kenya computer; A. Joachim, operator." He opened it and began to read.

CHAPTER ONE

"WHERE AM I?"

You're probably wondering by now where you are. This is an entirely healthy and normal reaction, Mr. Fingal. Anyone would wonder, when beset by what seem to be paranormal manifestations, if his grasp on reality had weakened. Or, in simple language, "Am I nuts, or what?"

No. Mr. Fingal, you are not nuts. But you are not, as you probably think, sitting on your bed, reading a book. It's all in your mind. You are still in the Kenya Disneyland. More specifically, you are contained in the memory cube we took of you before your weekend on the savanna. You see, there's been a big goof-up.

CHAPTER TWO

"WHAT HAPPENED?"

We'd like to know that, too, Mr. Fingal. But here's what we do know. Your body has been misplaced. Now, there's nothing to worry about, we're doing all we can to locate it and find out how it happened but it will take some time. Maybe it's small consolation, but this has never happened before in the seventy-five years we've been operating, and as soon as we find out how it happened this time, you can be sure we'll be careful not to let it happen again. We're pursuing several leads at this time, and you can rest easy that your body will be returned to you intact just as soon as we locate it.

You are awake and aware right now because we have incorporated your memory cube into the workings of our H-210 computer, one of the finest holo-memory systems available to modern business. You see, there are a few problems.

CHAPTER THREE

"What Problems?"

It's kind of hard to put in terms you'd understand, but let's take a crack at it, shall we?

The medium we use to record your memories isn't the one you've probably used yourself as insurance against accidental death. As you must know, that system will store your memories for up to twenty years with no degradation or loss of information, and is quite expensive. The system we use is a temporary one, good for two, five, fourteen, or twenty-eight days, depending on the length of your stay. Your memories are put in the cube, where you might expect them to remain static and unchanging, like they do in your insurance-recording. If you thought that, you would be wrong, Mr. Fingal. Think about it. If you die, your bank will immediately start a clone from the plasm you stored along with the memory cube. In six months your memories would be played back into the clone and you would awaken, missing the memories that were accumulated in your body from the time of your last recording. Perhaps this has happened to you. If it has, you know the shock of wakening from the recording process to be told that it is three or four years later, and that you died in that time.

In any case, the process we use is an *ongoing* one, or it would be worthless to you. The cube we install in the African animal of your choice is capable of adding the memories of your stay in Kenya to the memory cube. When your visit is over, these memories are played back into your brain and you leave the Disneyland with the exciting, educational, and refreshing experiences you had as an animal, though your body never left our slumber room. This is known as "doppling," from the German *doppelganger*.

Now, to the problems we talked about. Thought we'd *never* get around to them, didn't you?

First, since you registered for a weekend stay, the medico naturally used one of the two-day cubes as part of our budget-excursion fare. These cubes have a safety factor, but aren't much good beyond three days at best. At the end of that time the cube would start to deteriorate. Of course, we fully expect to have you installed in your own body before then. Additionally, there is the problem of storage. Since these ongoing memory cubes are intended to be in use all the time your memories are stored in them, it presents certain problems when we find ourselves in the spot we are now in. Are you following me, Mr. Fingal? While the cube has already passed its potency for use in co-existing with a live host, like the lioness you just left, it *must* be kept in constant activation at all times or loss of information results. I'm sure you wouldn't want that to happen, would you? Of course not. So what we have done is to "plug you in" to our computer, which will keep you aware and healthy and guard against the randomizing of your memory nexi. I won't go into that; let it stand that randomizing is not the sort of thing you'd like to have happen to you.

CHAPTER FOUR

"So What Gives, Huh?"

I'm glad you asked that. (Because you *did* ask that, Mr. Fingal. This booklet is part of the analogizing process that I'll explain further down the page.)

Life in a computer is not the sort of thing you could just jump into and hope to retain the world-picture-compatibility so necessary for sane functioning in this complex society. This has been tried, so take our word for it. Or, rather, my word. Did I introduce myself? I'm Apollonia Joachim, First-Class Operative for the Data-Safe computer troubleshooting firm. You've probably never heard of us, even though you do work with computers.

Since you can't just come aware in the baffling, on-and-off world that passes for reality in a data system, your mind, in co-operation with an analogizing program I've given the computer, interprets things in ways that seem safe and comfortable to it. The world you see around you is a figment of your imagination. Of course, it looks real to you because it comes from the same part of the mind that you normally use to interpret reality. If we wanted to get philosophical about it, we could probably argue all day about what constitutes reality and why the one you are perceiving now is any less real than the one you are used to. But let's not get into that, all right?

The world will likely continue to function in ways you are accustomed for it to function. It won't exactly be the same. Nightmares, for instance. Mr. Fingal, I hope you aren't the nervous type, because your nightmares can come to life where you are. They'll seem quite real. You should avoid them if you can, because they can do you real harm. I'll say more about this later if I need to. For now, there's no need to worry.

CHAPTER FIVE

"What Do I Do Now?"

I'd advise you to continue with your normal activities. Don't be alarmed at anything unusual. For one thing, I can only communicate with you by means of paranormal phenomena. You see, when a message from me is fed into the computer it reaches you in a way your brain is not capable of dealing with. Naturally, your brain classifies this as an unusual event and fleshes the communication out in unusual fashion. Most of the weird things you see, if you stay calm and don't let your own fears out of the closet to persecute you, will be me. Otherwise, I anticipate that your world should look, feel, taste, sound, and smell pretty normal. I've talked to your psychist. He assures me that your world-grasp is strong. So sit tight. We'll be working hard to get you out of there.

CHAPTER SIX

"Help!"

Yes, we'll help you. This is a truly unfortunate thing to have happened, and of course we will refund all your money promptly. In addition, the lawyer for Kenya wants me to ask you if a lump-sum settlement against all future damages is a topic worthy of discussion. You can think about it, there's no hurry.

In the meantime, I'll find ways to answer your questions. It might become unwieldy the harder your mind struggles to normalize my communications into things you are familiar with. That is both your greatest strength—the ability of your mind to bend the computer world it doesn't wish to see into media you are familiar with—and my biggest handicap. Look for me in tea-leaves, on billboards, on holovision; anywhere! It could be exciting if you get into it.

Meanwhile, if you have received this message you can talk to me by filling in the attached coupon and dropping it in the mailtube. Your reply will probably be waiting for you at the office. Good luck!

Yes! I received your message, and am interested in the exciting opportunities in the field of *computer living!* Please send me, without cost or obligation, your exciting catalog telling me how I can *move up* to the big, wonderful world outside!

NAME ....

ADDRESS ....

I.D. ....

Fingal fought the urge to pinch himself. If what this booklet said was true—and he might as well believe it—it would hurt and he would *not* wake up. He pinched himself anyway. It hurt.

If he understood this right, everything around him was the product of his imagination. Somewhere, a woman was sitting at a computer input and talking to him in normal language, which came to his brain in the form of electron pulses it could not cope with and so edited into forms he was conversant with. He was analogizing like mad. He wondered if he had caught it from the teacher, if analogies were contagious.

"What the hell's wrong with a simple voice from the air?" he wondered aloud. He got no response, and was rather glad. He'd had enough mysteriousness for now. And on second thought, a voice from the air would probably scare the pants off him.

He decided his brain must know what it was doing. After all, the hand startled him but he hadn't panicked. He could *see* it, and he trusted his visual sense more than he did voices from the air, a classical sign of insanity if ever there was one.

He got up and went to the wall. The letters of fire were gone, but the black smudge of the erasure was still there. He sniffed it: carbon. He fingered the rough paper of the pamphlet, tore off a corner, put it in his mouth and chewed it. It tasted like paper.

He sat down and filled out the coupon and tossed it to the mailtube.

Fingal didn't get angry about it until he was at the office. He was an easy-going person, slow to boil. But he finally reached a point where he had to say something.

Everything had been so normal he wanted to laugh. All his friends and acquaintances were there, doing exactly what he would have expected them to be doing. What amazed and bemused him was the number and variety of spear-carriers, minor players in this internal soap opera. The extras that his mind had cooked up to people the crowded corridors; like the man he didn't know who had bumped into him on the tube to work, apologized, and disappeared, presumably back into the bowels of his imagination.

There was nothing he could do to vent his anger but test the whole absurd setup. There was doubt lingering in his mind that the whole morning had been a fugue, a temporary lapse into dreamland. Maybe he'd never gone to Kenya, after all, and his mind was playing tricks on him. To get him there, or keep him away? He didn't know, but he could worry about that if the test failed.

He stood up at the desk-terminal, which was in the third column of the fifteenth row of other identical desks, each with its diligent worker. He held up his hands and whistled. Everyone looked up.

"I don't believe in you," he screeched. He picked up a stack of tapes on his desk and hurled them at Felicia Nahum at the desk next to his. Felicia was a good friend of his, and she registered the proper shock until the tapes hit her. Then she melted. He looked around the room and saw that everything had stopped like a freeze-frame in a motion picture.

He sat down and drummed his fingers on his desk top. His heart was pounding and his face was flushed. For an awful moment he had thought he was wrong. He began to calm down, glancing up every few seconds to be sure the world really *had* stopped.

In three minutes he was in a cold sweat. What the hell had he *proved*? That this morning had been real, or that he really was crazy? It dawned on him that he would never be able to test the assumption under which he lived. A line of print flashed across his terminal.

"But when could you ever do so, Mr. Fingal?"

"Ms. Joachim?" he shouted, looking around him. "Where are you? I'm afraid."

"You mustn't be," the terminal printed. "Calm yourself. You have a strong sense of reality, remember? Think about this: Even before today, how could you be sure the world you saw was not the result of catatonic delusions? Do you see what I mean? The question 'What is reality?' is, in the end, unanswerable. We all must accept at some point what we see and are told, and live by a set of untested and untestable assumptions. I ask you to accept the set I gave you this morning because, sitting here in the computer room where you cannot see me, my world-picture tells me that they are the true set. On the other hand, you could believe that I'm deluding myself, that there's nothing in the pink cube I see and that you're a spear-carrier in *my* dream. Does that make you more comfortable?"

"No," he mumbled, ashamed of himself. "I see what you mean. Even if I am crazy, it would be more comfortable to go along with it than to keep fighting it."

"Perfect, Mr. Fingal. If you need further illustrations you could imagine yourself locked in a straitjacket. Perhaps there are technicians laboring right now to correct your condition, and they are putting you through this psychodrama as a first step. Is that any more attractive?"

"No, I guess it isn't."

"The point is that it's as reasonable an assumption as the set of facts I gave you this morning. But the main point is that you should behave the same if either set is true. Do you see? To fight it in the one case will only cause you trouble, and in the other, would impede the treatment. I realize I'm asking you to accept me on faith. And that's all I can give you."

"I believe in you," he said. "Now, can you start everything going again?"

"I told you I'm not in control of your world. In fact, it's a considerable obstacle to me, seeing as I have to talk to you in these awkward ways. But things should get going on their own as soon as you let them. Look up."

He did, and saw the normal hum and bustle of the office. Felicia was there at her desk, as though nothing had happened. Nothing had. Yes, something had, after all. The tapes were scattered on the floor near his desk, where they had fallen. They had unreeled in an unruly mess.

He started to pick them up, then saw they weren't as messy as he had thought. They spelled out a message in coils of tape.

"You're back on the track," it said.

For three weeks Fingal was a very good boy. His co-workers, had they been real people, might have noticed a certain standoffishness in him, and his social life at home was drastically curtailed. Otherwise, he behaved exactly as if everything around him were real.

But his patience had limits. This had already dragged on far beyond what he had expected of it. He began to fidget at his desk, let his mind wander. Feeding information into a computer can be frustrating, unrewarding, and eventually stultifying. He had been feeling it even before his trip to Kenya; it had been the *cause* of his trip to Kenya. He was sixty-eight years old, with centuries ahead of him, and stuck in a ferromagnetic rut. Long life could be a mixed blessing when you felt boredom creeping up on you.

What was getting to him was the growing disgust with his job. It was bad enough when he merely sat in a real office with two hundred real people shoveling slightly unreal data into a much-less-than-real-to-his-senses computer. How much worse now, when he knew that the data he handled had no meaning to anyone but himself, were nothing but occupational therapy created by his mind and a computer program to keep him busy while Joachim searched for his body.

For the first time in his life he began punching some buttons for himself. Under slightly less stress he would have gone to see his psychist, the approved and perfectly normal thing to do. Here, he knew, he would only be talking to himself. He failed to perceive the advantages of such an idealized psychoanalytic process; he'd never really believed that a psychist did little but listen in the first place.

He began to change his own life when he became irritated with his boss. She pointed out to him that his error-index was on the rise, and suggested that he shape up or begin looking for another source of employment.

This enraged him. He'd been a good worker for twenty-five years. Why should she take that attitude when he was just not feeling himself for a week or two?

Then he was angrier than ever when he thought about her being merely a projection of his own mind. Why should he let *her* push him around?

"I don't want to hear it," he said. "Leave me alone. Better yet, give me a raise in salary."

"Fingal," she said promptly, "you've been a credit to your section these last weeks. I'm going to give you a raise."

"Thank you. Go away." She did, by dissolving into thin air. This really made his day. He leaned back in his chair and thought about his situation for the first time since he was young.

He didn't like what he saw.

In the middle of his ruminations, his computer screen lit up again.

"Watch it, Fingal," it read. "That way lies catatonia."

He took the warning seriously, but didn't intend to abuse the newfound power. He didn't see why judicious use of it now and then would hurt anything. He stretched, and yawned broadly. He looked around, suddenly hated the office with its rows of workers indistinguishable from their desks. Why not take the day off?

On impulse, he got up and walked the few steps to Felicia's desk.

"Why don't we go to my house and make love?" he asked her.

She looked at him in astonishment, and he grinned. She was almost as surprised as when he had hurled the tapes at her.

"Is this a joke? In the middle of the day? You have a job to do, you know. You want to get us fired?"

He shook his head slowly. "That's not an acceptable answer."

She stopped, and rewound from that point. He heard her repeat her last sentences backwards, then she smiled.

"Sure, why not?" she said.

Felicia left afterwards in the same, slightly disconcerting way his boss had left earlier; by melting into the air. Fingal sat quietly in his bed, wondering what to do with himself. He felt he was getting off to a bad start if he intended to edit his world with care.

His telephone rang.

"You're damn right," said a woman's voice, obviously irritated with him. He sat up straight.

"Apollonia?"

"Ms. Joachim to you, Fingal. I can't talk long, this is quite a strain on me. But listen to me, and listen hard. Your navel is very deep, Fingal. From where you're standing, it's a pit I can't even see the bottom of. If you fall into it I can't guarantee to pull you out."

"But do I have to take *everything* as it is? Aren't I allowed some self-improvement?"

"Don't kid yourself. That wasn't self-improvement. That was sheer laziness. It was nothing but masturbation, and while there's nothing wrong with that, if you do it to the exclusion of all else your mind will grow in on itself. You're in grave danger of excluding the external universe from your reality."

"But I thought there was no external universe for me here."

"Almost right. But I'm feeding you external stimuli to keep you going. Besides, it's the attitude that counts. You've never had trouble finding sexual partners; why do you feel compelled to alter the odds now?"

"I don't know," he admitted. "Like you said, laziness, I guess."

"That's right. If you want to quit your job, feel free. If you're serious about self-improvement, there are opportunities available to you there. Search them out. Look around you, explore. But don't try to meddle in things you don't understand. I've got to go now. I'll write you a letter if I can, and explain more."

"Wait! What about my body? Have they made any progress?"

"Yes, they've found out how it happened. It seems . . ." her voice faded out, and he switched off the phone.

The next day he received a letter explaining what was known so far. It seemed that the mix-up had resulted from the visit of the teacher to the medico section on the day of his recording. More specifically, the return of the little boy after the others had left. They were sure now that he had tampered with the routine card that told the attendants what to do with Fingal's body. Instead of moving it to the slumber room, which was a green card, they had sent it somewhere—no one knew where yet—for a sex change, which was a blue card. The medico, in her haste to get home for her date, had not noticed the switch. Now the body could be in any of several thousand medico shops in Luna. They were looking for it, and for the boy.

Fingal put the letter down and did some hard thinking.

Joachim had said there were opportunities for him in the memory banks. She had also said that not everything he saw was his own projections. He was receiving, was capable of receiving, external stimuli. Why was that? Because he would tend to randomize without them, or some other reason? He wished the letter had gone into that.

In the meantime, what did he do?

Suddenly he had it. He wanted to learn about computers. He wanted to know what made them tick, to feel a sense of power over them. It was particularly strong when he thought about being a virtual prisoner inside one. He was like a worker on an assembly line. All day long he labors, taking small parts off a moving belt and installing them on large assemblies. One day, he happens to wonder who puts the parts on the belt? Where do they come from? How are they made? What happens after he installs them?

He wondered why he hadn't thought of it before.

The admissions office of the Lunar People's Technical School was crowded. He was handed a form and told to fill it out. It looked bleak. The spaces for "previous experience" and "aptitude scores" were almost blank when he was through with them. All in all, not a very promising application. He went to the desk and handed the form to the man sitting at the terminal.

The man fed it into the computer, which promptly decided Fingal had no talent for being a computer repairperson. He started to turn away, when his eye was caught by a large poster behind the man. It had been there on the wall when he came in, but he hadn't read it.

LUNA NEEDS
COMPUTER TECHNICIANS!
THIS MEANS YOU,
MR. FINGAL!

Are you dissatisfied with your present employment? Do you feel you were cut out for better things? Then today may be your lucky day. You've come to the right place, and if you grasp this golden opportunity you will find doors opening that were closed to you.

Act, Mr. Fingal. This is the time. Who's to check up on you? Just take that stylus and fill it in any old way you want. Be grandiose, be daring! The fix is in, and you're on your way to

BIG MONEY!

The secretary saw nothing unusual about Fingal coming to the desk a second time, and didn't even blink when the computer decided he was eligible for the accelerated course.

It wasn't easy at first. He really did have little aptitude for electronics, but aptitude is a slippery thing. His personality matrix was as flexible now as it would ever be. A little effort at the right time would go a long way toward self-improvement. What he kept telling himself was that everything that made him what he was etched in that tiny cube wired in to the computer, and if he was careful he could edit it.

Not radically, Joachim told him in a long, helpful letter later in the week. That way led to complete disruption of the FPNA matrix and catatonia, which in this case would be distinguishable from death only to a hairsplitter.

He thought a lot about death as he dug into the books. He was in a strange position. The being known as Fingal would not die in any conceivable outcome of this adventure. For one thing, his body was going toward a sex change and it was hard to imagine what could happen to it that would kill it. Whoever had custody of it now would be taking care of it just as well as the medicos in the slumber room would have. If Joachim was unsuccessful in her attempt to keep him aware and sane in the memory bank, he would merely awake and remember nothing from the time he fell asleep on the table.

If, by some compounded unlikelihood, his body *was* allowed to die, he had an insurance recording safe in the vault of his bank. The recording was three years old. He would awaken in the newly grown clone body knowing nothing of the last three years, and would have a fantastic story to listen to as he was brought up to date.

But none of that mattered to *him*. Humans are a time-binding species, existing in an eternal *now*. The future flows through them and becomes the past, but it is always the present that counts. The Fingal of three years ago was *not* the Fingal in the memory bank. The simple fact about immortality by memory recording was that it was a poor solution. The three-dimensional cross section that was the Fingal of now must always behave as if his life depended on his actions, for he would feel the pain of death if it happened to him. It was small consolation to a dying man to know that he would go on, several years younger and less wise. If Fingal lost out here, he would *die*, because with memory recording he was three people: the one who lived now, the one lost somewhere on Luna, and the one potential person in the bank vault. They were really no more than close relatives.

Everyone knew this, but it was so much better than the alternative that few people rejected it. They tried not to think about it and were generally successful. They had recordings made as often as they could afford them. They heaved a sigh of relief as they got onto the table to have another recording taken, knowing that another chunk of their lives was safe for all time. But they awaited the awakening nervously, dreading being told that it was now twenty years later because they had died sometime after the recording and had to start all over. A lot can happen in twenty years. The person in the new clone body might have to cope with a child he or she had never seen, a new spouse, or the shattering news that his or her employment was now the function of a machine.

So Fingal took Joachim's warnings seriously. Death was death, and though he could cheat it, death still had the last laugh. Instead of taking your whole life from you death now only claimed a percentage, but in many ways it was the most important percentage.

He enrolled in classes. Whenever possible he took the ones that were available over the phone lines so he needn't stir from his room. He ordered his food and supplies by phone and paid his bills by looking at them and willing them out of existence. It could have been intensely boring, or it could have been wildly interesting. After all, it was a dream-world, and who doesn't think of retiring into fantasy from time to time? Fingal certainly did, but firmly suppressed the idea when it came. He intended to get out of his dream.

For one thing, he missed the company of other people. He waited for the weekly letters from Apollonia (she now allowed him to call her by her first name) with a consuming passion and devoured every word. His file of such letters bulged. At lonely moments he would pull one out at random and read it again and again.

On her advice, he left the apartment regularly and stirred around more or less at random. During these outings he had wild adventures. Literally. Apollonia hurled the external stimuli at him during these times and they could be anything from The Mummy's Curse to Custer's Last Stand with the original cast. It beat hell out of the movies. He would just walk down the public corridors and open a door at random. Behind it might be King Solomon's mines or the sultan's harem. He endured them all stoically. He was unable to get any pleasure from sex. He knew it was a one-handed exercise, and it took all the excitement away.

His only pleasure came in his studies. He read everything he could about computer science and came to stand at the head of his class. And as he learned, it began to occur to him to apply his knowledge to his own situation.

He began seeing things around him that had been veiled before. Patterns. The reality was starting to seep through his illusions. Every so often he would look up and see the faintest shadow of the real world of electron flow and fluttering circuits he inhabited. It scared him at first. He asked Apollonia about it on one of his dream journeys, this time to Coney Island in the mid-twentieth century. He liked it there. He could lie on the sand and talk to the surf. Overhead, a skywriter's plane spelled out the answers to his questions. He studiously ignored the brontosaurus rampaging through the roller coaster off to his right.

"What does it mean, O Goddess of Transistoria, when I begin to see circuit diagrams on the walls of my apartment? Overwork?"

"It means the illusion is beginning to wear thin," the plane spelled out over the next half-hour. "You're adapting to the reality you have been denying. It could be trouble, but we're hot on the trail of your body. We should have it soon and get you out of there." This had been too much for the plane. The sun was going down now, the brontosaurus vanished, and the plane ran out of gas. It spiraled into the ocean and the crowds surged closer to the water to watch the rescue. Fingal got up and went back to the boardwalk.

There was a huge billboard. He laced his fingers behind his back and read it.

"Sorry for the delay. As I was saying, we're almost there. Give us another few months. One of our agents thinks he will be at the right medico shop in about one week's time. From there it should go quickly. For now, avoid those places where you see the circuits showing through. They're no good for you, take my word for it."

Fingal avoided the circuits as long as he could. He finished his first courses in computer science and enrolled in the intermediate section. Six months rolled by.

His studies got easier and easier. His reading speed was increasing phenomenally. He found that it was more advantageous for him to see the library as composed of books instead of tapes. He could take a book from the shelf, flip through it rapidly, and know everything that was in it. He knew enough now to realize that he was acquiring a facility to interface directly with the stored knowledge in the computer, bypassing his senses entirely. The books he held in his hands were merely the sensual analogs of the proper terminals to touch. Apollonia was nervous about it, but let him go on. He breezed through the intermediate and graduated into the advanced classes.

But he was surrounded by wires. Everywhere he turned, in the patterns of veins beneath the surface of a man's face, in a plate of french fries he ordered for lunch, in his palmprints, overlying the apparent disorder of a head of blonde hair on the pillow beside him.

The wires were analogs of analogs. There was little in a modern computer that consisted of wiring. Most of it was made of molecular circuits that were either embedded in a crystal lattice or photographically reproduced on a chip of silicon. Visually, they were hard to imagine, so his mind was making up these complex circuit diagrams that served the same purpose but could be experienced directly.

One day he could resist it no longer. He was in the bathroom, on the traditional place for the pondering of the imponderable. His mind wandered, speculating on the necessity of moving his bowels, wondering if he might safely eliminate the need to eliminate. His toe idly traced out the pathways of a circuit board incorporated in the pattern of tiles on the floor.

The toilet began to overflow, not with water, but with coins. Bells were ringing happily. He jumped up and watched in bemusement as his bathroom filled with money.

He became aware of a subtle alteration in the tone of the bells. They changed from the merry clang of jackpot to the tolling of a death knell. He hastily looked around for a manifestation. He knew that Apollonia would be angry.

She was. Her hand appeared and began to write on the wall. This time the writing was in his blood. It dripped menacingly from the words.

"What are you doing?" the hand wrote, and having writ, moved on. "I told you to leave the wires alone. Do you know what you've done? You may have wiped the financial records for Kenya. It could take *months* to straighten them out."

"Well, what do I care?" he exploded. "What have they done for me lately? It's *incredible* that they haven't located my body by now. It's been a full *year*."

The hand was bunched up in a fist. Then it grabbed him around the throat and squeezed hard enough to make his eyes bulge out. It slowly relaxed. When Fingal could see straight, he backed warily away from it.

The hand fidgeted nervously, drummed its fingers on the floor. It went to the wall again.

"Sorry," it wrote, "I guess I'm getting tired. Hold on."

He waited, more shaken than he remembered being since his odyssey began. There's nothing like a dose of pain, he reflected, to make you realize that it *can* happen to you.

The wall with the words of blood slowly dissolved into a heavenly panorama. As he watched, clouds streamed by his vantage point and mixed beautifully with golden rays of sunshine. He heard organ music from pipes the size of sequoias.

He wanted to applaud. It was so overdone, and yet so convincing. In the center of the whirling mass of white mist an angel faded in. She had wings and a halo, but lacked the traditional white robe. She was nude, and hair floated around her as if she were underwater.

She levitated to him, walking on the billowing clouds, and handed him two stone tablets. He tore his eyes away from the apparition and glanced down at the tablets:

> Thou shalt not screw around with
> things you do not understand.

"All right, I promise I won't," he told the angel. "Apollonia, is that you? Really you, I mean?"

"Read the Commandments, Fingal. This is hard on me."

He looked back at the tablets.

Thou shalt not meddle in the hardware systems of the Kenya Corporation, for Kenya shall not hold him indemnifiable who taketh freedoms with its property.

Thou shalt not explore the limits of thy prison. Trust in the Kenya Corporation to extract thee.

Thou shalt not program.

Thou shalt not worry about the location of thy body, for it has been located, help is on the way, the cavalry has arrived, and all is in hand.

Thou shalt meet a tall, handsome stranger who will guide thee from thy current plight.

Thou shalt stay tuned for further developments.

He looked up and was happy to see that the angel was still there.

"I won't, I promise. But where is my body, and why has it taken so long to find it? Can you . . ."

"Know thee that appearing like this is a great taxation upon me,

Mr. Fingal. I am undergoing strains the nature of which I have not time to reveal to thee. Hold thy horses, wait it out, and thou shalt soon see the light at the end of the tunnel."

"Wait, don't go." She was already starting to fade out.

"I cannot tarry."

"But . . . Apollonia, this is charming, but why do you appear to me in these crazy ways? Why all the pomp and circumstance? What's wrong with letters?"

She looked around her at the clouds, the sunbeams, the tablets in his hand, and at her body, as if seeing them for the first time. She threw her head back and laughed like a symphony orchestra. It was almost too beautiful for Fingal to bear.

"Me?" she said, dropping the angelic bearing. "Me? I don't pick 'em, Fingal. I told you, it's *your* head, and I'm just passing through." She arched her eyebrows at him. "And really, sir, I had no idea you felt this way about me. Is it puppy love?" And she was gone, except for the grin.

The grin haunted him for days. He was disgusted with himself about it. He hated to see a metaphor overworked so. He decided his mind was just an inept analogizer.

But everything had its purpose. The grin forced himself to look at his feelings. He was in love; hopelessly, ridiculously, just like a teenager. He got out all his old letters from her and read through them again, searching for the magic words that could have inflicted this on him. Because it was *silly*. He'd never met her except under highly figurative circumstances. The one time he saw her, most of what he saw was the product of his own mind.

There were no clues in the letters. Most of them were as impersonal as a textbook, though they tended to be rather chatty. Friendly, yes; but intimate, poetic, insightful, revealing? No. He failed utterly to put them together in any way that should add up to love, or even a teenage crush.

He attacked his studies with renewed vigor, awaiting the next communication. Weeks dragged by with no word. He called the post office several times, placed personal advertisements in every periodical he could think of, took to scrawling messages on public buildings, sealed notes in bottles and flushed them down the disposal, rented billboards, bought television time. He screamed at the empty walls of his apartment, buttonholed strangers, tapped Morse code on the water pipes, started rumors in skid row taprooms, had leaflets published and distributed all over the solar system. He tried every medium he could think of, and could not contact her. He was alone.

He considered the possibility that he had died. In his present situation, it might be hard to tell for sure. He abandoned it as untestable. That line was hazy enough already without his efforts to determine which side of the life/death dichotomy he inhabited. Besides, the more he thought about existing as nothing more than kinks in a set of macromolecules plugged into a data system, the more it frightened him. He'd survived this long by avoiding such thoughts.

His nightmares moved in on him, set up housekeeping in his apartment. They were a severe disappointment, and confirmed his conclusion that his imagination was not as vivid as it might be. They were infantile bogeymen, the sort that might scare him when glimpsed hazily through the fog of a nightmare, but were almost laughable when exposed to the full light of consciousness. There was a large, talkative snake that was crudely put together, fashioned from the incomplete picture a child might have of a serpent. A toy company could have done a better job. There was a werewolf whose chief claim to dread was a tendency to shed all over Fingal's rugs. There was a woman who consisted mostly of breasts and genitals, left over from his adolescence, he suspected. He groaned in embarrassment every time he looked at her. If he had ever been that infantile he would rather have left the dirty traces of it buried forever.

He kept booting them into the corridor but they drifted in at night like poor relations. They talked incessantly, and always about him. The things they knew! They seemed to have a very low opinion of him. The snake often expressed the opinion that Fingal would never amount to anything because he had so docilely accepted the results of the aptitude tests he took as a child. That hurt, but the best salve for the wound was further study.

Finally a letter came. He winced as soon as he got it open. The salutation was enough to tell him he wasn't going to like it.

Dear Mr. Fingal,
    I won't apologize for the delay this time. It seems that most of my manifestations have included an apology and I feel I deserved a rest this time. I can't be always on call. I have a life of my own.
    I understand that you have behaved in an exemplary manner

since I last talked with you. You have ignored the inner workings of the computer just as I told you to do. I haven't been completely frank with you, and I will explain my reasons.

The hookup between you and the computer is, and always has been, two-way. Our greatest fear at this end had been that you would begin interfering with the workings of the computer, to the great discomfort of everyone. Or that you would go mad and run amuck, perhaps wrecking the entire data system. We installed you in the computer as a humane necessity, because you would have died if we had not done so, though it would have cost you only two days of memories. But Kenya is in the business of selling memories, and holds them to be a sacred trust. It was a mix-up on the part of the Kenya Corporation that got you here in the first place, so we decided we should do everything we could for you.

But it was at great hazard to our operations at this end.

Once, about six months ago, you got tangled in the weather-control sector of the computer and set off a storm over Kilimanjaro that is still not fully under control. Several animals were lost.

I have had to fight the Board of Directors to keep you online, and several times the program was almost terminated. You know what that means.

Now, I've leveled with you. I wanted to from the start, but the people who own things around here were worried that you might start fooling around out of a spirit of vindictiveness if you knew these facts, so they were kept from you. You could still do a great deal of damage before we could shut you off. I'm laying it on the line now, with directors chewing their nails over my shoulder. *Please* stay out of trouble.

On to the other matter.

I was afraid from the outset that what has happened might happen. For over a year I've been your only contact with the world outside. I've been the only other person in your universe. I would have to be an extremely cold, hateful, awful person—which I am not—for you *not* to feel affection for me under those circumstances. You are suffering from intense sensory-deprivation and it's well known that someone in that state becomes pliable, suggestible, and lonely. You've attached your feelings to me as the only thing around worth caring for.

I've tried to avoid intimacy with you for that reason, to keep things firmly on the last-name basis. But I relented during one of your periods of despair. And you read into my letters some things that were not there. Remember, even in the printed medium it is your mind that controls what you see. Your censor has let through what it wanted to see and maybe even added some things of its own. I'm at your mercy. For all I know, you may be reading this letter as a passionate affirmation of love. I've added every reinforcement I know of to make sure the message comes through on a priority channel and is not garbled. I'm sorry to hear that you love me. I do not, repeat not, love you in return. You'll understand why, at least in part, when we get you out of there.

It will never work, Mr. Fingal. Give up.

Apollonia Joachim

Fingal graduated first in his class. He had finished the required courses for his degree during the last long week after his letter from Apollonia. It was a bitter victory for him marching up to the stage to accept the sheepskin, but he clutched it to him fiercely. At least he had made the most of his situation, at least he had not meekly let the wheels of the machine chew him up like a good worker.

He reached out to grasp the hand of the college president and saw it transformed. He looked up and saw the bearded, robed figure flow and writhe and become a tall, uniformed woman. With a surge of joy, he knew who it was. Then the joy became ashes in his mouth, which he hurriedly spit out.

"I always knew you'd choke on a figure of speech," she said, laughing tiredly.

"You're here," he said. He could not quite believe it. He stared dully at her, grasping her hand and the diploma with equal tenacity. She was tall, as the prophecy had said, and handsome. Her hair was cropped short over a capable face, and the body beneath the uniform was muscular. The uniform was open at the throat, and wrinkled. There were circles under her eyes, and the eyes were bloodshot. She swayed slightly on her feet.

"I'm here, all right. Are you ready to go back?" She turned to the assembled students. "How about it, gang? Do you think he deserves to go back?"

The crowd went wild, cheering and tossing mortarboards into the air. Fingal turned dazedly to look at them, with a dawning realization. He looked down at the diploma.

"I don't know," he said. "I don't know. Back to work at the data room?"

She clapped him on the back.

"No. I promise you that."

"But how could it be different? I've come to think of this piece of paper as something . . . real. Real. How could I have deluded myself like that? Why did I accept it?"

"I helped you along," she said. "But it wasn't all a game. You really did learn all the things you learned. It won't go away when you return. That thing in your hand is imaginary, for sure, but who do you think prints the real ones? You're registered where it counts—in the computer—as having passed all the courses. You'll get a real diploma when you return."

Fingal wavered. There was a tempting vision in his head. He'd been here for over a year and had never really exploited the nature of the place. Maybe that business about dying in the memory bank was all a shuck, another lie invented to keep him in his place. In that case, he could remain here and satisfy his wildest desires, become king of the universe with no opposition, wallow in pleasure no emperor ever imagined. Anything he wanted here he could have, anything at all.

And he really felt he might pull it off. He'd noticed many things about this place, and now had the knowledge of computer technology to back him up. He could squirm around and evade their attempts to erase him, even survive if they removed his cube by programming himself into other parts of the computer. He could do it.

With a sudden insight he realized that he had no desires wild enough to keep him here in his navel. He had only one major desire right now, and she was slowly fading out. A lap-dissolve was replacing her with the old college president.

"Coming?" she asked.

"Yes." It was as simple as that. The stage, president, students, and auditorium faded out and the computer room at Kenya faded in. Only Apollonia remained constant. He held onto her hand until everything stabilized.

"Whew," she said, and reached around behind her head. She pulled out a wire from her occipital plug and collapsed into a chair.

Someone pulled a similar wire from Fingal's head, and he was finally free of the computer.

Apollonia reached out for a steaming cup of coffee, on a table littered with empty cups.

"You were a tough nut," she said. "For a minute I thought you'd stay. It happened once. You're not the first to have this happen to you, but you're no more than the twentieth. It's an unexplored area. Dangerous."

"Really?" he said. "You weren't just saying that?"

"No," she laughed. "Now the truth can be told. It *is* dangerous. No one had ever survived more than three hours in that kind of cube, hooked into a computer. You went for six. You *do* have a strong world-picture."

She was watching him to see how he reacted to this. She was not surprised to see him accept it readily.

"I should have known that," he said. "I should have thought of it. It was only six hours out here, and more than a year for me. Computers think faster. Why didn't I see that?"

"I helped you not see it," she admitted. "Like the push I gave you not to question why you were studying so hard. Those two orders worked a lot better than some of the orders I gave you."

She yawned again, and it seemed to go on forever.

"See, it was pretty hard for me to interface with you for six hours straight. No one's ever done it before, it can get to be quite a strain. So we've both got something to be proud of."

She smiled at him but it faded when he did not return it.

"Don't look so hurt, Fingal . . . what *is* your first name? I knew it, but erased it early in the game."

"Does it matter?"

"I don't know. Surely you must see why I haven't fallen in love with you, though you may be a perfectly lovable person. I haven't had *time*. It's been a very long six hours, but it was still only six hours. What can I do?"

Fingal's face was going through awkward changes as he absorbed that. Things were not so bleak after all.

"You could go to dinner with me."

"I'm already emotionally involved with someone else, I should warn you of that."

"You could still go to dinner. You haven't been exposed to my new determination. I'm going to really make a case."

She laughed warmly and got up. She took his hand.

"You know, it's possible that you might succeed. Just don't put wings on me again, all right? You'll never get anywhere like that."

"I promise. I'm through with visions—for the rest of my life."

HORACE, GALAXYCA

Alfred Bester

I'm using the past tense in this remembrance because it all took place a quarter of a century ago. Horace Gold is very much alive and with it today.

As a writer I'm not better than my editor or director or producer inspires me to be. Since I'm a damned good writer I need a damned good editor to form the ideal collaboration, which can create a work that is greater than the sum of its parts. Horace Gold of *Galaxy* was that kind of editor.

He was opinionated (so am I), he had strong ideas about story patterns (so have I), he was psychiatry-oriented (and so are we, all of us, today). His personality and persona were a statement. Twenty-odd years ago he kindled a tremendous amount of hostility in the sf-writing sodality for these reasons. He was a professional, which meant that the job was the boss, and he infuriated lazy and/or incompetent authors by demanding that they write and re-write and re-re-re-write over their heads.

I remember the bitter letters they sent to their sf journal complaining about Horace. There was a sort of informal Hate-Horace Club. Back in those years a novel of mine, *The Demolished Man*, had appeared in *Galaxy* and received what was, at least to me, an astonishing and unexpected *réclame* from these same authors. I was exasperated into writing a defense. Fair play, please.

I told how the novel had come to be written. Horace had phoned me, out of the blue, and asked me to write something for *Galaxy*. I argued that he already had the finest of sf authors contributing, that I was too busy script-writing, and that I wasn't much of an sf author anyway.

Horace kept phoning off and on, trying to persuade me that I was a better sf writer than I thought, and his calls turned into gossipy sessions that both of us enjoyed very much. Writers and editors love to talk shop, and he was trapped in his apartment by agoraphobia resulting from horrendous experiences in World War II.

The upshot of these calls was that I felt so beholden to him for the charming entertainment he gave me—he had a mellifluous baritone voice and witty, perceptive opinions about our colleagues and their work—that I felt obliged to send him a dozen or so suggestions for possible stories.

At this point his professionalism took command and, still via the telephone machine, he discussed the ideas, took them apart, put them together again, and combined and recombined them with me in a wonderful series of editor-author sessions. The crux of those conferences was that we respected each other and could accept or reject each other's suggestions without loss of face or temper. It was an ideal collaboration, and out of it came the novel.

Horace had the tact to leave me alone when the actual writing got under way, but was always available to give advice and comfort when I got stuck and needed help, which happened fairly often. My colleagues understand that writing is damned hard and sometimes discouraging work. Civilians imagine that it's easy. One of them said to me, "Oh, come on! If you've got the knack it just *pours* out."

Horace used to give dos at his apartment near New York's SoHo, and I went occasionally. He was always casually dressed: a biggish man, broad, balding, skin white, almost transparent from his years spent indoors. He would joke, laugh, express his strong opinions and criticisms. Some of the writers there were too much in awe of his personality and powerful buying position to dare disagree with him. Not me, whose middle initial is "H" for "chutzpah." I would disagree with him as often as not, and we had cheerful arguments.

After *Demolished* had appeared, I once gave Horace a story whose ending he didn't like—I'd left it hanging and he wanted me to wrap it up. I insisted that the lack of resolution was the entire point. We couldn't come to a professional agreement on it so I said, "Horace, it's like the joke about the woman trying to give the breast to her baby during a concert. She says to the infant, 'Take, or I'll give to the conductor.' Horace, take or I'll give to Tony and Mick."

He laughed but wouldn't take, so "Hobson's Choice" appeared in *Fantasy and Science Fiction*. Nevertheless we remained firm and cheerful friends. Again, mutual respect. With professionals it's never a case of Love me, love my story. God knows, there were some of

Horace's own stories that I disliked. God knows, there are some of my own that I also dislike.

Later I was fortunate enough to get a movie sale on a TV novel I'd written, so I grabbed the loot and took off for Europe to write *The Stars My Destination* (original title, *Tiger! Tiger!*). I corresponded with Horace, reporting on the progress of the book but not really needing the help I'd required for *Demolished*. After all, this was my third novel and I'd found my own way to cope with the problems of large-scale writing.

When I was forced to return kicking and screaming to the States, I made an astonishing discovery. Science fiction had at long last caught on with the general public and publishers. *Demolished* had been rejected by every agent and publisher in New York and had been virtually impossible to sell as a book. Now there were bids for *Stars*, and I was strongly tempted. Horace, still on the phone, argued that in all conscience the book belonged to *Galaxy*. He had given me my start and I owed it to him. I had to agree. Fair is fair. So the novel was first serialized in *Galaxy*, again to that same amazing *réclame*.

Holiday magazine had been the fiend that had dragged me back from the Continent to become its entertainment feature writer, and so I happily abandoned script-writing and sf to learn the craft of magazines, features, and editing, and so lost touch with Horace. He was suffering his own personal agonies, never with any public complaint, and I heard some outlandish gossip about him. So I wasn't at all surprised to learn that he had abandoned *Galaxy* and the Northeast Corridor to levant to California.

But this remembrance has a happy ending. I attended an sf conference (to prove that I was still alive) and was exploring the rare-book-and-magazine stalls when I came face to face with a biggish, broad, balding, mellow-voiced young man who beamed at me and confessed that he was Horace's son. We embraced and I sent my eternal love and gratitude to Horace, as indeed I do now.

INDEX TO GALAXY MAGAZINE

A comprehensive index (by author) to all issues from October 1950 to May 1979

KEY: R=review, S=story, A=article

Anderson, Poul. *Brain Wave* (R), 9/54. *Broken Sword, The* (R), 5/55. *Corkscrew of Space, The* (S), 2/56. *Day After Doomsday, The (Part I)* (S), 12/61. *Day After Doomsday, The (Conclusion)* (S), 2/62. *Door to Anywhere* (S), 12/66. *Earthman's Burden, The* (R), 5/58. *Ensign Flandry* (R), 6/67. *Even Stars, The* (R), 10/59. *Garden in the Void* (S), 5/52. *High Crusade, The* (R), 8/61. *Horse Trader* (S), 3/53. *Innocent at Large* (S), 7/58. *Inside Earth* (S), 4/51. *Light, The* (S), 3/57. *My Object All Sublime* (S), 6/61. *No World of Their Own* (R), 1/56. *Our Many Roads to the Stars* (A), 9/75. *Outpost of Empire* (S), 12/67. *Poulfinch's Mythology* (S), 10/67. *Satan's World* (R), 3/71. *Sharing of Flesh, The* (S), 12/68. *Three Hearts and Three Lions* (R), 2/62. *Time and Stars* (R), 2/65. *To Build a World* (S), 6/64. *To Outlive Eternity (Part I)* (S), 6/67. *To Outlive Eternity (Conclusion)* (S), 8/67. *Trader to the Stars* (R), 2/65. *Tragedy of Errors, A* (S), 2/68. *Trouble Twisters, The* (R), 2/67. *Vault of the Ages* (R), 3/53. *White King's War, The* (S), 8/69. *World Called Maanerek, A* (S), 7/57. *World Without Stars* (R), 8/67.

Anderson, Rex. *My Friend's Last Show* (S), 11/77.

Anderson, Susan Janice. *Aurora: Beyond Equality* (R), 4/77.

Andrews, Roy Chapman. *Nature's Ways* (R), 11/51.

Anthony, Piers. *Within the Cloud* (S), 4/67.

Antonio, Robles. *Refugee Centaur, The* (R), 3/53.

Anvil, Christopher. *Advance Agent* (S), 2/57. *Behind the Sandrat Hoax* (S), 10/68. *Devise and Conquer* (S), 4/66. *Mind Partner* (S), 8/60. *New Member, The* (S), 4/67. *Trojan Bombardment, The* (S), 2/67.

Apostolides, Alex. *We're Civilized* (S), 8/53.

Arkin, Alan. *People Soup* (S), 11/58. *Whiskaboom* (S), 8/55.

Arr, Stephen. *Chain of Command* (S), 5/54. *Mr. President* (S), 11/53.

Arthur, Robert. *Aggravation of Elmer, The* (S), 5/55.

Ashby, W. Ross. *Design for a Brain* (R), 9/53.

Asimov, Isaac. *1000 Year Plan, The* (R), 1/56. *Asimov's Mysteries* (R), 7/68. *Before the Golden Age* (R), 9/74. *Best of Isaac Asimov, The* (R), 12/74. *Best of Isaac Asimov, The* (R), 9/76. *Buy Jupiter and Other Stories* (R), 3/76. *C-Chute, The* (S), 10/51. *Caves of Steel, The* (R), 7/54. *Caves of Steel, The* (R), 4/56. *Caves of Steel, The (Part 1)* (S), 10/53. *Caves of Steel, The (Part 2)* (S), 11/53. *Caves of Steel, The (Part 3)* (S), 12/53. *Chemicals of Life, The* (R), 6/55. *Clock We Live On, The* (R), 10/60. *Currents of Space* (R), 5/53. *Darwinian Pool Room* (S), 10/50. *Deep, The* (S), 12/52. *Earth Is Room Enough* (R), 6/58. *End of Eternity, The* (R), 2/56. *Fact and Fancy* (R), 12/62. *Foundation* (R), 2/52.

Pheromal Fountain, The (S), 8/77. *Plutonium* (S), 3/76. *Politics of Ratticide, The* (S), 3/75. *Splendid Freedom, The* (S), 9/74. *Through Innocent Eyes* (A), 1/76.

Darwin, Charles Galton. *Next Million Years, The* (R), 5/53.

Davenport, Basil. *To the End of Time: Olaf Stapledon* (R), 11/53.

Davidson, Avram. *Dr. Morris Goldpepper Returns* (S), 12/62. *Enemy of My Enemy, The* (R), 6/67. *Help! I Am Dr. Morris Goldpepper* (S), 7/57. *Island Under the Earth, The* (R), 10/69. *Love Called This Thing* (S), 4/59. *Or All the Seas with Oysters* (S), 5/58. *Paramount Ulf* (S), 10/58. *Tail-Tied Kings, The* (S), 4/62. *Take Wooden Indians* (S), 6/59. *Timeserver* (S), 5/70.

Davies, Hugh S. *Papers of Andrew Melmoth, The* (R), 6/62.

Davis, F. A. *Joey* (S), 1/72.

Davis, Jack. *Mad Reader, The* (R), 5/55.

De Camp, L. Sprague. *Castle of Iron, The* (R), 11/50. *Compleat Enchanter, The* (R), 6/77. *Continent Makers, The* (R), 6/53. *Cosmic Manhunt* (R), 11/54. *Genus Homo* (R), 11/50. *Glory That Was, The* (R), 8/60. *Gun for Dinosaur, A* (S), 3/56. *Lands Beyond* (R), 11/52. *Lands of Yesterday* (A), 11/50. *Life of H. P. Lovecraft, The* (R), 6/75. *Lost Continents* (R), 9/54. *Property of Venus* (S), 7/55. *Rogue Queen* (R), 10/51. *Science Fiction Handbook* (R), 5/54. *Solomon's Stone* (R), 7/58. *Tales of Conan* (R), 7/56. *Undesired Princess, The* (R), 10/51. *Wall of Serpents* (R), 12/61. *Where Were We?* (A), 2/52.

De Cles Jon. *Thinker of Tryllmynrein, The* (S), 7/75.

De La Croix, Robert. *Mysteries of the North Pole* (R), 9/56.

De La Ree, Gerry. *Book of Virgil Finlay* (R), 6/77.

De La Rue, Aubert. *Man and the Winds* (R), 6/56.

De Latil, Pierre. *Man and the Underwater World* (R), 11/56.

De Morgan, Augustus. *Budget of Paradoxes, A* (R), 3/55.

De Vet, Charles V. *Alien's Bequest* (S), 6/67. *Big Stupe* (S), 3/55. *Delayed Action* (S), 9/53. *Growing Up on Big Muddy* (S), 7/57. *Metamorphosis* (S), 12/60. *Monkey on His Back* (S), 6/60. *Wheels Within* (S), 5/52.

De Vries, Leonard. *Book of the Atom, The* (R), 10/61.

De Wohl, Louis. *Second Conquest, The* (R), 9/54.

Dearborn, A. F. *Walden Window, The* (S), 2/75.

Deckert, Kurt. *Creatures of the Deep Sea* (R), 3/57.

Dee, Roger. *Assignment's End* (S), 12/54. *Clean Break* (S), 11/53. *Earth Gone Mad, An* (R), 6/55. *Feeling, The* (S), 4/61. *Pet Farm* (S), 2/54. *Problems on Balak* (S), 9/53. *Today Is Forever* (S), 9/52. *Traders Risk* (S), 2/58. *Wailing Wall* (S), 7/52.

Deford, Miriam Allen. *1980 President, The* (S), 10/64. *Eel, The* (S),

Science Fiction Stories and Novels (R), 11/58. *Best Science Fiction Stories and Novels, 1955* (R), 7/56. *Best Science Fiction Stories and Novels, 1956* (R), 6/57. *Best Science Fiction Stories, 1950* (R), 12/50. *Best Science Fiction Stories, 1952* (R), 1/53. *Best Science Fiction Stories, 1953* (R), 4/54. *Best Science Fiction Stories, The* (R), 2/52. *Every Boy's Book of Outer Space Stories* (R), 8/62. *Great Science Fiction Stories About Mars* (R), 4/67. *Imagination Unlimited* (R), 7/52. *Year's Best Science Fiction Novels* (R), 10/52. *Year's Best Science Fiction Novels, 1953* (R), 10/53. *Year's Best Science Fiction Novels, 1954* (R), 10/54.

Dines, Glen. *Mysterious Machine, The* (R), 5/58.

Disch, Thomas. *Bad Moon Rising* (R), 5/73. *Discovery of the Nullitron, The* (A), 2/67. *Echo of Wrath, The* (S), 2/66. *Genocides, The* (R), 12/66.

Doede, William R. *Birds of Lorrane, The* (S), 8/63. *City near Centaurus, A* (S), 10/62. *God Next Door, The* (S), 8/61. *Jamieson* (S), 12/60.

Donaldy, Ernestine. *Gates of Tomorrow* (R), 3/74.

Dorman, Sonya. *Cool Affection* (S), 5/74. *Journey* (S), 11/72. *When I Was Miss Dow* (S), 6/66.

Dornberger, Walter. *V-2* (R), 2/55.

Doxey, W. S. *End Result, The* (S), 10/75. *Schwarzkind Singularity, The* (S), 1/75.

Doyle, A. Conan. *Lost World, The* (R), 7/54.

Drake, Burgess. *Children of the Wind* (R), 11/54.

Drake, David. *But Loyal to His Own* (S), 10/75. *Butcher's Bill, The* (S), 11/74. *Ranks of Bronze* (S), 8/75. *Under the Hammer* (S), 10/74.

Droke, Maxwell. *You and the World to Come* (R), 6/60.

Dryfoos, Dave. *Bridge Crossing* (S), 5/51. *New Hire* (S), 9/53. *Tree, Spare That Woodman* (S), 10/52.

Dubois, Theodore. *Solution T-25* (R), 6/51.

Dufay, Jean. *Galactic Nebulae and Interstellar Matter* (R), 12/57.

Dugan, James. *Man Under the Sea* (R), 11/56.

Duka, Ira. *Martian and His Friend from Outer Space* (R), 5/56.

Duke, Neville. *Sound Barrier* (R), 3/56.

Duncan, David. *Beyond Eden* (R), 9/55. *Dark Dominion* (R), 8/54. *Immortals, The* (S), 10/60. *Occam's Razor* (R), 5/58.

Dunn, Alan. *Is There Intelligent Life on Earth?* (R), 12/60.

Dunne, Alex. *Better Time, A* (S), 2/76.

Dye, Charles. *Prisoner in the Skull* (R), 4/53. *Syndrome Johnny* (S), 7/51.

Epstein, Samuel. *Rocket Pioneers on the Road to Space, The* (R), 9/55.

Eshback, Lloyd A. *Tyrant of Time* (R), 7/55.

Ettinger, R. C. W. *Man into Superman* (R), 11/74.

Evans, Bill. *Universes of E. E. Smith, The* (R), 4/67.

Evans, Dean. *Furious Rose, The* (S), 1/52. *Moons of Mars, The* (S), 9/52. *Not a Creature Was Stirring* (S), 12/51.

Evans, Everett. *Alien Minds* (R), 4/56.

Evans, I. O. *Discovering the Heavens* (R), 10/60.

Fabian, Stephen. *Best of Stephen Fabian, The* (R), 11/76. *Fantastic Nudes* (R), 12/76. *Starfawn* (R), 12/76.

Fadiman, Clifton. *Fantasia Mathematica* (R), 2/59. *Mathematical Magpie* (R), 2/63.

Fahy, Patrick. *Bad Memory* (S), 12/60.

Fallaw, L. M. *Ugglians, The* (R), 8/57.

Farca, Marie C. *Earth* (R), 7/72.

Farmer, Philip Jose. *Blasphemers, The* (S), 4/64. *Green Odyssey, The* (R), 1/58. *King of the Beasts, The* (S), 6/64. *Lord Tyger* (R), 6/70. *Seventy Years of Decpop* (S), 7/72. *Tarzan Alive* (R), 7/72.

Farrell, Joseph. *Ethical Way, The* (S), 3/58. *Security Plan* (S), 4/59.

Fast, Howard. *General Zapped an Angel, The* (R), 7/72.

Feinberg, J. G. *Atom Story, The* (R), 12/53.

Ferman, Edward L. *Best from* Fantasy and Science Fiction, *The* (R), 2/74. *Best from* Fantasy and Science Fiction, *The* (R), 12/74. *Once and Future Tales* (R), 2/69.

Fermi, Laura. *Atoms in the Family* (R), 5/55.

Fetler, Andrew. *Cool War, The* (S), 6/63. *Cry Snooker* (S), 10/60.

Field, George P. *Pluto—Doorway to the Stars* (A), 12/62.

Filer, Burt. *Bailey's Ark* (S), 7/68. *Time Trawlers, The* (S), 8/68.

Finney, Jack. *Body Snatchers, The* (R), 7/55. *Third Level, The* (R), 5/58.

Firesign Theatre. *Apocalypse Papers, The* (R), 6/77.

Fisher, David E. *East in the Morning* (S), 2/60.

Fisher, Lou. *Outfielder* (S), 4/74. *Triggerman* (S), 9/73.

Fisher, Sandy. *Farewell to the Artifacts* (S), 7/72. *Langley Circuit, The* (S), 5/72.

Fisk, Nicholas. *Trillions* (R), 3/74.

Fitzgerald, Gregory. *Past Present and Future Perfect* (R), 1/74.

Fitzgibbon, Constantine. *When the Kissing Had to Stop* (R), 2/61.

Fitzpatrick, L. D. *Elmo's Box* (S), 4/75.

Flehr, Paul. *Hated, The* (S), 1/58. *Mars by Moonlight* (S), 6/58. *Seven Deadly Virtues* (S), 8/58. *We Never Mention Aunt Nora* (S), 7/58.

Fleming, Roscoe. *Man Who Reached the Moon, The* (R), 5/58.

Flesher, Dann. *Parasite* (S), 3/79.

6/55. *Mea Culpa* (A), 9/57. *No Turban, Please* (A), 4/58. *Notes from an Editor's Pad* (A), 8/61. *Now Look!* (A), 7/56. *Of All Things* (A), 12/59. *Of Two Minds* (A), 5/56. *Old Die Rich and Other Science Fiction* (R), 9/55. *Old Die Rich, The* (S), 3/53. *Open for Business* (A), 4/56. *Other Dark, The* (A), 1/58. *Other People's Mail* (A), 10/59. *Past Performance* (A), 2/55. *Personal Account* (A), 3/57. *Personnel Problem* (S), 9/58. *Postscript* (A), 6/57. *Puzzles for Plotters* (A), 4/61. *Reactions* (A), 12/60. *Readers on Aliens* (A), 8/60. *Repeat Performance* (A), 2/58. *Riches of Embarrassment, The* (S), 4/68. *Richest Planet, The* (A), 10/57. *Roundest Trip, The* (A), 12/57. *Saps Will Rise* (A), 2/56. *Sixth Galaxy Reader, The* (R), 2/63. *So Far* (A), 4/59. *Speaking of Trends* (A), 4/55. *Special Delivery* (A), 6/59. *That's Two Votes* (A), 5/55. *They're Back* (A), 3/58. *Tin Age, The* (A), 11/58. *Transmogrification of Wamba's Revenge, The* (S), 10/67. *Trunk to Tail* (A), 2/61. *Two Upper Lips* (A), 8/55. *Wax and Wane* (A), 12/56. *What Are Aliens Made Of?* (A), 6/60. *What Kind of Fiction?* (A), 2/60. *What'll It Be?* (A), 2/59. *Why, Back Home . . .* (A), 10/56. *World of Tomorrow, The* (A), 4/60. *Worlds to Eat* (A), 6/58. *Yardstick for Science Fiction* (A), 2/51. *You Were Saying?* (A), 7/57.

Gold, H. L. and E. J. *Villains from Vega IV* (S), 10/68.

Goldin, Stephen. *Sweet Dreams, Melissa* (S), 12/68.

Golding, William. *Lord of the Flies* (R), 2/60. *Sometime, Never* (R), 11/57.

Goldman, William. *Princess Bride, The* (R), 8/75.

Gonein, M. Zakaria. *Lost Pyramid, The* (R), 7/57.

Goodale, Earl. *Success Story* (S), 4/60.

Goodstone, Tony. *Pulps, The* (R), 4/71.

Gordon, Isabel S. *Armchair Science Reader, The* (R), 12/60.

Gordon, T. J. *Reflex* (S), 1/73.

Gottlieb, Phyllis. *Dirty Old Men of Maxsec, The* (S), 11/69.

Gotschalk, Felix C. *Growing Up in Tier 3000* (R), 5/76.

Goulart, Ron. *Broke and Hungry, No Place to Go* (S), 11/69. *Subject to Change* (S), 12/60.

Grant, Madeleine. *Louis Pasteur* (R), 10/60.

Graves, J. W. *Sincerest Form, The* (S), 6/64.

Gray, Curme. *Murder in Millennium VI* (R), 8/52.

Green, Joseph. *Decision Makers, The* (S), 4/65. *Jinn* (S), 12/68.

Green, Roland. *Her Fine and Private Planet* (S), 12/73.

Greenberg, Martin. *All About the Future* (R), 6/55. *Coming Attractions* (R), 9/57. *Five Science Fiction Novels* (R), 8/52. *Journey to Infinity* (R), 4/51. *Robot and the Man, The* (R), 9/53. *Travelers of Space* (R), 5/52.

448 Index to Galaxy Magazine

(R), 11/73. *Time for the Stars* (R), 5/57. *Time for the Stars* (R), 3/76. *Unpleasant Profession of Jonathan Hoag, The* (R), 2/61. *Unpleasant Profession of Jonathan Hoag, The* (R), 11/76. *Unpleasant Profession of Jonathan Hoag, The* (R), 5/77. *Where To?* (A), 2/52. *Year of the Jackpot, The* (S), 3/52.

Henderson, Zenna. *People: No Different Flesh, The* (R), 4/77. *Pilgrimage* (R), 4/77. *Pilgrimage: The Book of the People* (S), 12/61. *Something Bright* (S), 2/60.

Hendrickson, Walter B. *Handbook for Space Travellers* (R), 2/61.

Herbert, Don. *Mr. Wizard's Experiments for Young Scientists* (R), 4/60.

Herbert, Frank. *A-W-F Unlimited* (S), 6/61. *Children of Dune* (R), 9/76. *Committee of the Whole* (S), 4/65. *Consentiency, The* (A), 5/77. *Do I Wake or Dream?* (S), 8/65. *Dosadi Experiment, The* (Part 1) (S), 5/77. *Dosadi Experiment, The* (Part 2) (S), 6/77. *Dosadi Experiment, The* (Part 3) (S), 7/77. *Dosadi Experiment, The* (Part 4) (S), 8/77. *Dragon in the Sea, The* (R), 7/56. *Dune* (R), 4/66. *Dune* (R), 9/76. *Dune Messiah* (R), 9/76. *Dune Messiah* (Part I) (S), 7/69. *Dune Messiah* (Part II) (S), 8/69. *Dune Messiah* (Part III) (S), 9/69. *Dune Messiah* (Part IV) (S), 10/69. *Dune Messiah* (Conclusion) (S), 11/69. *Heisenberg's Eyes* (Part I) (S), 6/66. *Heisenberg's Eyes* (Conclusion) (S), 8/66. *Mating Call* (S), 10/61. *Old Rambling House* (S), 4/58. *Primitives, The* (S), 4/66. *Project 40* (Part I) (S), 11/72. *Project 40* (Part II) (S), 1/73. *Project 40* (Part III) (S), 3/73. *Tactful Saboteur, The* (S), 10/64.

Hever, Kenneth. *End of the World, The* (R), 1/54. *Men of Other Planets* (R), 7/51. *Next 50 Billion Years, The* (R), 4/58.

Higgins, Bill. *Created Equal* (S), 2/74.

High, Philip E. *Reality Forbidden* (R), 8/67.

Highe, Jefferson. *What Rough Beast?* (S), 7/54.

Hill, Ernest. *Phylogenetic Factor, The* (S), 6/71. *Tenth Dimension, The* (S), 12/70. *Tip of the Iceberg* (S), 5/71.

Hill, H. Carl. *Easy Rider* (S), 10/74.

Hillegas, Mark R. *Future as Nightmare, The* (R), 9/68.

Hoagland, Dick. *Television: Never-Never Land and . . .* (A), 9/74.

Hoequist, Charles. *Better Rat Trap, A* (S), 12/73.

Hoffman, Peggy. *Wild Rocket, The* (R), 10/61.

Hoglien, Lancelot. *Wonderful World of Energy, The* (R), 9/58.

Hollis, H. H. *Eeeetz Ch* (S), 11/68. *Sword Game* (S), 4/68. *Too Many People* (S), 1/71. *Traveler's Guide to Magahouston* (A), 8/67.

Holly, J. Hunter. *Encounter* (R), 2/60. *Green Planet, The* (R), 4/61.

Holmes, H. H. *Secret of the House* (S), 3/53.

Latham, Philip. *Five Against Venus* (R), 11/52. *Future Forbidden* (S), 5/73.

Laumer, Keith. *And Now They Wake* (Part I) (S), 3/69. *And Now They Wake* (Part II) (S), 4/69. *And Now They Wake* (Part III) (S), 5/69. *Bad Day for Vermin, A* (S), 2/64. *Big Show, The* (S), 2/68. *Body Builders, The* (S), 8/66. *Bolo* (R), 5/77. *Day Before Forever, The* (R), 8/68. *Dinosaur Beach* (R), 2/76. *Doorstep* (S), 2/61. *Dunderbird* (with Harlan Ellison) (S), 1/69. *Earthblood* (S), 6/67. *End as a Hero* (S), 6/63. *Great Time Machine Hoax, The* (R), 2/65. *Kind of the City, The* (S), 8/61. *Limiting Velocity of Orthodoxy, The* (S), 12/70. *Other Side of Time, The* (R), 9/71. *Retief of the CDT* (R), 1/72. *Star Treasure, The* (R), 9/71. *Thunderhead* (S), 4/67. *Thunderhead* (R), 8/68. *War Against the Yukks* (S), 4/65.

Laurance, Alice. *Coloured Element, The* (S), 5/69.

Lawrence, J. A. *Family Program* (S), 9/74. *Opening Problem* (S), 7/74. *Persistence of Memory, The* (S), 11/74.

Lawson, Jack B. *Twenty-Seven Inches of Moonshine* (A), 4/66.

Le Beau, Mary. *Beyond Doubt* (R), 3/57.

Le Guin, Ursula K. *Day Before the Revolution, The* (S), 8/74. *Dispossessed, The* (R), 6/74. *Escape Routes* (A), 12/74. *Field of Vision* (S), 10/73. *Left Hand of Darkness, The* (R), 2/70. *Rocannon's World* (R), 6/77. *Wind's Twelve Quarters, The* (R), 5/77.

Leache, Joy. *Satisfaction Guaranteed* (S), 12/61.

Leahy, John Martin. *Drome* (R), 4/53.

Lee, Stanley R. *Fall of Glass, A* (S), 10/60.

Lee, Walter W. *Reference Guide to Fantastic Films* (Vol. 3) (R), 10/74. *Science Fiction and Fantasy Film Checklist* (R), 2/61.

Leiber, Fritz. *Appointment in Tomorrow* (S), 7/51. *Bad Day for Sales, A* (S), 7/53. *Be of Good Cheer* (S), 10/64. *Beat Cluster, The* (S), 10/61. *Big Engine, The* (S), 2/62. *Big Time, The* (R), 10/67. *Big Time, The* (Part 1) (S), 3/58. *Big Time, The* (Part 2) (S), 4/58. *Black Corridor* (S), 12/67. *Bread Overhead* (S), 2/58. *Bullet with His Name* (S), 7/58. *Coming Attraction* (S), 11/50. *Crazy Annaoj* (S), 2/68. *Creature from Cleveland Depths, The* (S), 12/62. *Crystal Prison, The* (S), 4/66. *Dr. Kometevsky's Day* (S), 2/52. *Gonna Roll the Bones* (Record) (R), 11/76. *Good New Days, The* (S), 10/65. *Green Millennium, The* (R), 5/54. *Last Letter, The* (S), 6/58. *Later Than You Think* (S), 10/50. *Moon Is Green, The* (S), 4/52. *Nice Girl with Five Husbands* (S), 4/51. *Night of the Wolf, The* (R), 2/67. *No Great Magic* (S), 12/63. *Number of the Beast, The* (S), 12/58. *One Station of the Way* (S), 12/68. *Pail of Air, A* (S), 12/51. *Specter Is Haunting Texas, A* (Part I) (S), 7/68. *Spec-*

Worst of All the Comets, The (A), 10/67. *Wreck of La Lutine, The* (A), 2/66. *Written Word, The* (A), 1/69.

Life magazine. *World We Live In, The* (R), 6/56.

Lilley, John C. *Man and Dolphin* (R), 10/62.

Lindsay, David. *Voyage to Arcturus* (R), 12/54.

Locke, William. *Machine Translation of Languages* (R), 11/56.

Lockemann, Georg. *Story of Chemistry, The* (R), 2/61.

Logan, Jeffrey. *Complete Book of Outer Space* (R), 5/54.

Long, Frank B. *Mars Is My Destination* (R), 4/63.

Longsdon, Syd. *To Go Not Gently* (S), 6/78.

Loomis, Noel. *City of Glass* (R), 10/55.

Lovecraft, H. P. *Survivors and Others, The* (R), 12/57.

Lowndes, Robert W. *Believers' World* (R), 2/62. *Mystery of the Third Mine* (R), 8/53.

Luban, Milton. *Spirit Was Willing, The* (R), 10/51.

Ludens, Magnus. *Long, Silvery Day, The* (S), 4/62. *My Lady Selene* (S), 4/63.

Ludwig, Edward W. *Coffin for Jacob, A* (S), 5/56. *Spacemen Die at Home* (S), 10/51.

Lukens, Adam. *Conquest of Life* (R), 6/61. *Sea People, The* (R), 8/60. *Sons of the Wolf* (R), 2/62.

Lunan, Duncan. *Falling Through the World* (S), 5/71. *Galilean Problem* (S), 9/71. *Here Comes the Sun* (S), 3/71. *Liaison Assignment* (S), 4/71. *Moon of Thin Reality, The* (S), 6/70.

Lundwall, Sam J. *Nobody Here but Us Shadows* (S), 8/75. *Science Fiction: What It's All About* (R), 1/72. *Science Fiction: What It's All About* (R), 2/76.

Lupoff, Richard A. *Sandworld* (R), 6/77.

Lutz, John. *Booth 13* (S), 6/68.

Lymington, John. *Froomb!* (R), 2/67.

Lyttleton, Raymond. *Modern Universe, The* (R), 1/58.

Mabarger, John P. *Space Medicine: The Human Factor* (R), 12/51.

Macapp, C. C. *And All the Earth a Grave* (S), 12/63. *Drug, The* (S), 2/61. *Flask of Fine Arcturan, A* (S), 2/65. *Mercurymen, The* (S), 12/65. *Sculptor* (S), 4/65. *Spare That Tree* (S), 6/67.

MacDonald, John D. *Ballroom of the Skies* (R), 6/53. *Common Denominator* (S), 7/51. *Game for Blondes* (S), 10/52. *Wine of the Dreamers* (R), 12/51.

Macewen, Gwendolyn. *Armies of the Moon, The* (R), 6/77.

Macfarlane, W. *220—Advanced Field Exploration* (S), 3/72. *Changing Woman* (S), 9/72. *Dead End* (S), 1/52. *No-Wind Spotted Tiger Planet, The* (S), 5/71. *Quickening* (S), 9/73. *Robbie and David and Little Dahl* (S), 5/72.

Morrison, William. *Addicts, The* (S), 1/52. *Bedside Manner* (S), 5/54. *Dead Man's Planet* (S), 2/55. *Feast of Demons, A* (S), 3/58. *Mel Oliver and Space Rover on Mars* (R), 11/54. *Model of a Judge, The* (S), 10/53. *Picture Bride, The* (S), 6/55. *Runaway* (S), 11/52. *Shipping Clerk* (S), 6/52. *Sly Bungerhop, The* (S), 9/57. *Spoken For* (S), 7/55. *Weather on Mercury, The* (S), 7/53.

Moskowitz, Sam. *Editor's Choice in Science Fiction* (R), 10/54. *Explorers of the Infinite* (R), 12/63. *Immortal Storm, The* (R), 3/57. *Modern Masterpieces of Science Fiction* (R), 10/66. *Science Fiction by Gaslight* (R), 12/68. *Seekers of Tomorrow* (R), 10/66. *Three Stories by Murray Leinster* . . . (R), 8/67.

Mundy, Talbot. *Purple Pirate* (R), 2/60.

Munitz, Milton K. *Theories of the Universe, The* (R), 6/58.

Murphy, Pat. *Eyes of the Wolf* (S), 5/78. *No Mother Near* (S), 10/75.

Murray, Bruce. *Mars and the Mind of Man* (R), 10/73.

Myers, Henry. *O King, Live Forever* (R), 1/54.

Myers, Howard L. *Reluctant Weapons, The* (S), 12/52.

Nayler, J. *High Speed Flight* (R), 2/58.

Nearing, H., Jr. *Sinister Researches of CP Ransom* (R) , 7/54.

Needham, Joseph. *Science and Civilization in China* (V. 1) (R), 3/55.

Neely, Henry M. *Stars by Clock and Fist, The* (R), 1/57.

Neeper, Cary. *Place Beyond Man, A* (R), 3/75.

Negley, Glenn. *Quest for Utopia, The* (R), 1/53.

Nelson, Earl. *There Is Life on Mars* (R), 4/57.

NESFA. *Noreascon Awards Banquet* (Record) (R), 7/77.

Neville, Kris. *Ballenger's People* (S), 4/67. *Fresh Air Fiend* (S), 2/52. *General Max Shorter* (S), 12/62. *Hunt the Hunter* (S), 6/51. *Medical Practices Among the Immortals* (S), 9/72. *Moral Equivalent* (S), 1/57. *Shamar's War* (S), 2/64. *Thyre Planet* (S), 10/68. *Voyage to Far N' Jurd* (S), 4/63.

Newell, Homer E. *Space Book for Young People* (R), 4/59.

Newman, Louis. *License to Steal* (A), 8/59.

Nicholson, R. D. *Far from the Warming Sun* (S), 9/53.

Nicholson, Sam. *Magna Wave* (S), 7/75.

Niven, Larry. *Adults, The* (S), 6/67. *All the Myriad Ways* (S), 10/68. *At the Bottom of a Hole* (S), 12/66. *Building the Mote in God's Eye* (A), 1/76. *Children of the State, The* (Part 1) (S), 9/76. *Children of the State, The* (Part 2) (S), 10/76. *Children of the State, The* (Part 3) (S), 11/76. *Deceivers, The* (S), 4/68. *Down and Out* (S), 2/76. *Eye of an Octopus* (S), 2/66. *Handicap* (S), 12/67. *Hole in Space, A* (R), 6/77. *How the Heroes Die* (S), 10/66. *Inferno* (Part I) (S), 8/75. *Inferno* (Part II) (S), 9/75. *Inferno* (Part III) (S), 10/75. *Long Arm of Gil Hamilton, The*